SHADOWS

uplifted

VOLUME I

Black Women Authors of 19th Century
American Fiction

SHADOWS UPLIFTED ANTHOLOGY

Landmark full-length works published by Black American women writers
in the 19th century.

Volume I: Black Women Authors of 19th Century American Fiction
featuring novels by
Julia C. Collins, Frances Ellen Watkins Harper, and A. E. Johnson

Volume II: Black Women Authors of 19th Century American Personal Narratives &
Autobiographies
featuring novels by
Harriet Jacobs, Elizabeth Keckley, and Harriet E. Wilson

Volume III: Black Women Authors of 19th Century American Poetry
featuring collected verse by
Mary Weston Fordham, Josephine D. Heard, and Frances Ellen Watkins

SHADOWS
uplifted

VOLUME I

Black Women Authors of 19th Century
American Fiction

Published by CSRC Storytelling
Anchorage, AK 99503

ISBN: 978-1-7358967-0-0 (Hardcover)
ISBN: 978-1-7364422-5-8 (Paperback)
ISBN: 978-1-7358967-1-7 (Ebook)

Book jacket design by Hampton Lamoureux
Front cover image by James O. Durgan, from The New York Public Library
https://digitalcollections.nypl.org

First Edition: March 2021

NOTES ON THE VOLUME.

When the history of Black American women are overlooked, the influential roles they have played in both national and international culture are diminished and erased. While compiling novels and stories for the DOUBLE BOOKED™ series, I was struck by the amount of Black female writers who preceded the artistic movement of the Harlem Renaissance that I had never before heard of. My public school education dropped a brief footnote about Phillis Wheatley before jumping a century and a half to the works of Zora Neale Hurston and Lorraine Hansberry, ignoring the women who influenced them and entire generations of writers who were creating works about and from the point of view of Black American women. Giving space to these ancestors and artists, I restored several cornerstone works across multiple volumes. Comparing and contrasting various copies of their original publications, I edited and formatted the writings with the intention to highlight their legacies, which have so often been marginalized.

The books and collections selected for each volume in this anthology were all written by Black women and published in the United States during the 19ᵗʰ century. This first volume contains three fiction novels:

> IOLA LEROY, OR SHADOWS UPLIFTED (1892), an examination of multiracial identity within one family during and after the Civil War, written by suffragist and abolitionist Frances Ellen Watkins Harper.

> THE CURSE OF CASTE, OR THE SLAVE BRIDE (1865), chronicling the lives of a mother and daughter in the antebellum age, originally released as periodical fiction in *The Christian Recorder* by schoolteacher and essayist Julia C. Collins.

> THE HAZELEY FAMILY (1894), the story of Flora Hazeley and her moral standings, written by publisher and editor Amelia E. Johnson.

I want to acknowledge the work done by so many archivists and historians who preserve and restore historical texts, chiefly the Internet Archive and

Project Gutenberg digital libraries and Dr. Henry Louis Gates, Jr., who has been at the forefront of the restoration and preservation of historical texts, buying and publishing texts like *The Bondwoman's Narrative* (2002) which is thought to have been written sometime between 1853 and 1861 by Hannah Crafts, a formerly enslaved Black woman. It was Gates who first reprinted *The Curse of Caste* in 1994 on microfiche in its original serialized form for the Black Periodical Literature Project.

Aside from standardizing and modernizing spelling, paragraphing, capitalization (most notably in the case of the word "Negro" which wasn't commonly capitalized until the early 1900s), italicization, and hyphenation, I have corrected obvious typographical errors, while adding and removing punctuation for increased clarity. In *The Curse of Caste*, the name Hartley has been chosen as the spelling for the proper name that appears as both Hartley and Hartly in the original text.

Taking inspiration from Harper's novel, and struck by the title's overtone boosting the voices of those who are all too frequently left in the dark, discarded, and undervalued, (compared to their white and male historic counterparts), I chose to title the anthology SHADOWS UPLIFTED. This labor of love accompanies my faith that these authors will benefit from having upgraded editions of their work readily available. Let us continue to uplift such shadows in our history, allowing them their corporeal bodies, flesh, blood, and melanated skin. Let us continue to uplift Black women: supporting their stories, their art, and their existence.

C.S.R. CALLOWAY.

CONTENTS OF THE VOLUME.

THE CURSE OF CASTE, OR THE SLAVE BRIDE   197
Julia C. Collins

THE HAZELEY FAMILY
A. E. Johnson

IMAGES IN THE VOLUME.

"Half-portrait of young woman wearing large lace scarf over plaid bodice."
James O. Durgan. 1880-1889 (Approx.). From The New York Public Library.

Half-length drawing of a young man a little larger than life size, in black chalk.
"Kiang O Dongoa, a Pamunkey Chief" (detail). From The New York Public Library.

IOLA LEROY,
or
Shadows Uplifted

FRANCES E. W. HARPER

First edition published in 1892.

TO MY DAUGHTER
MARY E. HARPER,
THIS BOOK IS LOVINGLY DEDICATED.

INTRODUCTION.

I confess when I first learned that Mrs. Harper was about to write "a story" on some features of the Anglo-African race, growing out of what was once popularly known as the "peculiar institution," I had my doubts about the matter. Indeed it was far from being easy for me to think that she was as fortunate as she might have been in selecting a subject which would afford her the best opportunity for bringing out a work of merit and lasting worth to the race—such a work as some of her personal friends have long desired to see from her graphic pen. However, after hearing a good portion of the manuscript read, and a general statement with regard to the object in view, I admit frankly that my partial indifference was soon swept away; at least I was willing to wait for further developments.

Being very desirous that one of the race, so long distinguished in the cause of freedom for her intellectual worth as Mrs. Harper has had the honor of being, should not at this late date in life make a blunder which might detract from her own good name, I naturally proposed to await developments before deciding too quickly in favor of giving encouragement to her contemplated effort.

However, I was perfectly aware of the fact that she had much material in her possession for a most interesting book on the subject of the condition of the colored people in the South. I know of no other woman, white or colored, anywhere, who has come so intimately in contact with the colored people in the South as Mrs. Harper. Since emancipation she has labored in every Southern State in the Union, save two, Arkansas and Texas; in the colleges, schools, churches, and the cabins not excepted, she has found a vast field and open doors to teach and speak on the themes of education, temperance, and good home building, industry, morality, and the like, and never lacked for evidences of hearty appreciation and gratitude.

Everywhere help was needed, and her heart being deeply absorbed in the cause she willingly allowed her sympathies to impel her to perform most heroic services.

With her it was no uncommon occurrence, in visiting cities or towns, to speak at two, three, and four meetings a day; sometimes to promiscuous audiences composed of everybody who would care to come.

But the kind of meetings she took greatest interest in were meetings called exclusively for women. In this attitude she could pour out her sympathies to them as she could not do before a mixed audience; and indeed she felt their needs were far more pressing than any other class.

And now I am prepared to most fully indorse her story. I doubt whether she could, if she had tried ever so much, have hit upon a subject so well adapted to reach a large number of her friends and the public with both entertaining and instructive matter as successfully as she has done in this volume.

The grand and ennobling sentiments which have characterized all her utterances in laboring for the elevation of the oppressed will not be found missing in this book.

The previous books from her pen, which have been so very widely circulated and admired, North and South—*Forest Leaves, Miscellaneous Poems, Moses: a Story of the Nile, Poems*, and *Sketches of Southern Life* (five in number)—these, I predict, will be by far eclipsed by this last effort, which will, in all probability, be the crowning effort of her long and valuable services in the cause of humanity.

While, as indicated, Mrs. Harper has done a large amount of work in the South, she has at the same time done much active service in the temperance cause in the North, as thousands of this class can testify.

Before the war she was engaged as a speaker by anti-slavery associations; since then, by appointment of the Women's Christian Temperance Union, she has held the office of "Superintendent of Colored Work" for years. She has also held the office of one of the Directors of the Women's Congress of the United States.

Under the auspices of these influential, earnest, and intelligent associations, she has been seen often on their platforms with the leading lady orators of the nation.

Hence, being widely known not only amongst her own race but likewise by the reformers, laboring for the salvation of the intemperate and others equally unfortunate, there is little room to doubt that the book will be in great demand and will meet with warm congratulations from a goodly number outside of the author's social connections.

Doubtless the thousands of colored Sunday-schools in the South, in casting about for an interesting, moral story-book, full of practical lessons, will not be content to be without *Iola Leroy, or Shadows Uplifted*.

WILLIAM STILL.

I.
MYSTERY OF MARKET SPEECH AND PRAYER-MEETING.

"Good mornin', Bob; how's butter dis mornin'?"

"Fresh; just as fresh, as fresh can be."

"Oh, glory!" said the questioner, whom we shall call Thomas Anderson, although he was known among his acquaintances as Marster Anderson's Tom.

His informant regarding the condition of the market was Robert Johnson, who had been separated from his mother in his childhood and reared by his mistress as a favorite slave. She had fondled him as a pet animal, and even taught him to read. Notwithstanding their relation as mistress and slave, they had strong personal likings for each other.

Tom Anderson was the servant of a wealthy planter, who lived in the city of C——, North Carolina. This planter was quite advanced in life, but in his earlier days he had spent much of his time in talking politics in his State and National capitals in winter, and in visiting pleasure resorts and watering places in summer. His plantations were left to the care of overseers who, in their turn, employed Negro drivers to aid them in the work of cultivation and discipline. But as the infirmities of age were pressing upon him he had withdrawn from active life, and given the management of his affairs into the hands of his sons. As Robert Johnson and Thomas Anderson passed homeward from the market, having bought provisions for their respective homes, they seemed to be very light-hearted and careless, chatting and joking with each other; but every now and then, after looking furtively around, one would drop into the ears of the other some news of the battle then raging between the North and South which, like two great millstones, were grinding slavery to powder.

As they passed along, they were met by another servant, who said in hurried tones, but with a glad accent in his voice:—

"Did you see de fish in de market dis mornin'? Oh, but dey war splendid, jis' as fresh, as fresh kin be."

"That's the ticket," said Robert, as a broad smile overspread his face.

"I'll see you later."

"Good mornin', boys," said another servant on his way to market. "How's eggs dis mornin'?"

"Fust rate, fust rate," said Tom Anderson. "Bob's got it down fine."

"I thought so; mighty long faces at de pos'-office dis mornin'; but I'd better move 'long," and with a bright smile lighting up his face he passed on with a quickened tread.

There seemed to be an unusual interest manifested by these men in the state of the produce market, and an unanimous report of its good condition. Surely there was nothing in the primeness of the butter or the freshness of the eggs to change careless looking faces into such expressions of gratification, or to light dull eyes with such gladness. What did it mean?

During the dark days of the Rebellion, when the bondman was turning his eyes to the American flag, and learning to hail it as an ensign of deliverance, some of the shrewder slaves, coming in contact with their masters and overhearing their conversations, invented a phraseology to convey in the most unsuspected manner news to each other from the battlefield. Fragile women and helpless children were left on the plantations while their natural protectors were at the front, and yet these bondmen refrained from violence. Freedom was coming in the wake of the Union army, and while numbers deserted to join their forces, others remained at home, slept in their cabins by night and attended to their work by day; but under this apparently careless exterior there was an undercurrent of thought which escaped the cognizance of their masters. In conveying tidings of the war, if they wished to announce a victory of the Union army, they said the butter was fresh, or that the fish and eggs were in good condition. If defeat befell them, then the butter and other produce were rancid or stale.

Entering his home, Robert set his basket down. In one arm he held a bundle of papers which he had obtained from the train to sell to the boarders, who were all anxious to hear from the seat of battle. He slipped one copy out and, looking cautiously around, said to Linda, the cook, in a low voice:—

"Splendid news in the papers. Secesh routed. Yankees whipped 'em out of their boots. Papers full of it. I tell you the eggs and the butter's mighty fresh this morning."

"Oh, sho, chile," said Linda, "I can't read de newspapers, but ole Missus' face is newspaper nuff for me. I looks at her ebery mornin' wen she comes inter dis kitchen. Ef her face is long an' she walks kine o' droopy den I thinks things is gwine wrong for dem. But ef she comes out yere looking mighty pleased, an' larffin all ober her face, an' steppin' so frisky, den I knows de Secesh is gittin' de bes' ob de Yankees. Robby, honey, does you really b'lieve for good and righty dat dem Yankees is got horns?"

"Of course not."

"Well, I yered so."

"Well, you heard a mighty big whopper."

"Anyhow, Bobby, things goes mighty contrary in dis house. Ole Miss is in de parlor prayin' for de Secesh to gain de day, and we's prayin' in de cabins and kitchens for de Yankees to get de bes' ob it. But wasn't Miss Nancy glad wen dem Yankees run'd away at Bull's Run. It was nuffin but Bull's Run an' run away Yankees. How she did larff and skip 'bout de house. An' den me thinks to myself you'd better not holler till you gits out ob de woods. I specs 'fore dem Yankees gits froo you'll be larffin tother side ob your mouf. While you was gone to market ole Miss com'd out yere, her face looking as long as my arm, tellin' us all 'bout de war and saying dem Yankees whipped our folks all to pieces. And she was 'fraid dey'd all be down yere soon. I thought they couldn't come too soon for we. But I didn't tell her so."

"No, I don't expect you did."

"No, I didn't; ef you buys me for a fool you loses your money shore. She said when dey com'd down yere she wanted all de men to hide, for dey'd kill all de men, but dey wouldn't tech de women."

"It's no such thing. She's put it all wrong. Why them Yankees are our best friends."

"Dat's jis' what I thinks. Ole Miss was jis' tryin to skeer a body. An' when she war done she jis' set down and sniffled an' cried, an' I war so glad I didn't know what to do. But I had to hole in. An' I made out I war orful sorry. An' Jinny said, 'O Miss Nancy, I hope dey won't come yere.' An' she said, 'I'se jis' 'fraid dey will come down yere and gobble up eberything dey can lay dere hands on.' An' she jis' looked as ef her heart war mos' broke, an' den she went inter de house. An' when she war gone, we jis' broke loose. Jake turned somersets, and said he warnt 'fraid ob dem Yankees; he know'd which side his brad was buttered on. Dat Jake is a cuter. When he goes down ter git de letters he cuts up all kines ob shines and capers. An' to look at him skylarking dere while de folks is waitin' for dere letters, an' talkin' bout de war, yer wouldn't think dat boy had a thimbleful of sense. But Jake's listenin' all de time wid his eyes and his mouf wide open, an' ketchin' eberything he kin, an' a heap ob news he gits dat way. As to Jinny, she jis' capered and danced all ober de flore. An' I jis' had to put my han' ober her mouf to keep ole Miss from yereing her. Oh, but we did hab a good time. Boy, yer oughter been yere."

"And, Aunt Linda, what did you do?"

"Oh, honey, I war jis' ready to crack my sides larffin, jis' to see what a long face Jinny puts on wen ole Miss is talkin', an' den to see dat face wen missus' back is turned, why it's good as a circus. It's nuff to make a horse larff."

"Why, Aunt Linda, you never saw a circus?"

"No, but I'se hearn tell ob dem, and I thinks dey mus' be mighty funny. An' I know it's orful funny to see how straight Jinny's face looks wen she's almos' ready to bust, while ole Miss is frettin' and fumin' 'bout dem Yankees an' de war. But, somehow, Robby, I rALELY b'lieves dat we cullud folks is mixed up in dis fight. I seed it all in a vision. An' soon as dey fired on dat fort, Uncle Dan'el says to me: 'Linda, we's gwine to git our freedom.' An' I says: 'Wat makes you think so?' An' he says: 'Dey've fired on Fort Sumter, an' de Norf is boun' to whip.'"

"I hope so," said Robert. "I think that we have a heap of friends up there."

"Well, I'm jis' gwine to keep on prayin' an' b'lievin'.'"

Just then the bell rang, and Robert, answering, found Mrs. Johnson suffering from a severe headache, which he thought was occasioned by her worrying over the late defeat of the Confederates. She sent him on an errand, which he executed with his usual dispatch, and returned to some work which he had to do in the kitchen. Robert was quite a favorite with Aunt Linda, and they often had confidential chats together.

"Bobby," she said, when he returned, "I thinks we ort ter hab a prayer-meetin' putty soon."

"I am in for that. Where will you have it?"

"Lem me see. Las' Sunday we had it in Gibson's woods; Sunday 'fore las', in de old cypress swamp; an' nex' Sunday we'el hab one in McCullough's woods. Las' Sunday we had a good time. I war jis' chock full an' runnin' ober. Aunt Milly's daughter's bin monin all summer, an' she's jis' come throo. We had a powerful time. Eberythin' on dat groun' was jis' alive. I tell yer, dere was a shout in de camp."

"Well, you had better look out, and not shout too much, and pray and sing too loud, because, 'fore you know, the patrollers will be on your track and break up your meetin' in a mighty big hurry, before you can say 'Jack Robinson.'"

"Oh, we looks out for dat. We's got a nice big pot, dat got cracked las' winter, but it will hole a lot o' water, an' we puts it whar we can tell it eberything. We has our own good times. An' I want you to come Sunday night an' tell all 'bout the good eggs, fish, and butter. Mark my words, Bobby, we's all gwine to git free. I seed it all in a vision, as plain as de nose on yer face."

"Well, I hope your vision will come out all right, and that the eggs will keep and the butter be fresh till we have our next meetin'.'"

"Now, Bob, you sen' word to Uncle Dan'el, Tom Anderson, an' de rest ob dem, to come to McCullough's woods nex' Sunday night. I want to hab a sin-killin' an' debil-dribin' time. But, boy, you'd better git out er yere. Ole Miss'll be down on yer like a scratch cat."

Although the slaves were denied unrestricted travel, and the holding of meetings without the surveillance of a white man, yet they contrived to meet by stealth and hold gatherings where they could mingle their prayers and tears, and lay plans for escaping to the Union army. Outwitting the vigilance of the patrollers and home guards, they established these meetings miles apart, extending into several States.

Sometimes their hope of deliverance was cruelly blighted by hearing of some adventurous soul who, having escaped to the Union army, had been pursued and returned again to bondage. Yet hope survived all these disasters which gathered around the fate of their unfortunate brethren, who were remanded to slavery through the undiscerning folly of those who were strengthening the hands which were dealing their deadliest blows at the heart of the Nation. But slavery had cast such a glamour over the Nation, and so warped the consciences of men, that they failed to read aright the legible transcript of Divine retribution which was written upon the shuddering earth, where the blood of God's poor children had been as water freely spilled.

2.
CONTRABAND OF WAR.

A few evenings after this conversation between Robert and Linda, a prayer-meeting was held. Under the cover of night a few dusky figures met by stealth in McCullough's woods.

"Howdy," said Robert, approaching Uncle Daniel, the leader of the prayer-meeting, who had preceded him but a few minutes.

"Thanks and praise; I'se all right. How is you, chile?"

"Oh, I'm all right," said Robert, smiling, and grasping Uncle Daniel's hand.

"What's de news?" exclaimed several, as they turned their faces eagerly towards Robert.

"I hear," said Robert, "that they are done sending the runaways back to their masters."

"Is dat so?" said a half dozen earnest voices. "How did you yere it?"

"I read it in the papers. And Tom told me he heard them talking about it last night, at his house. How did you hear it, Tom? Come, tell us all about it."

Tom Anderson hesitated a moment, and then said:—

"Now, boys, I'll tell you all 'bout it. But you's got to be mighty mum 'bout it. It won't do to let de cat outer de bag."

"Dat's so! But tell us wat you yered. We ain't gwine to say nuffin to nobody."

"Well," said Tom, "las' night ole Marster had company. Two big ginerals, and dey was hoppin' mad. One ob dem looked like a turkey gobbler, his face war so red. An' he sed one ob dem Yankee ginerals, I thinks dey called him Beas' Butler, sed dat de slaves dat runned away war some big name—I don't know what he called it. But it meant dat all ob we who com'd to de Yankees should be free."

"Contraband of war," said Robert, who enjoyed the distinction of being a good reader, and was pretty well posted about the war. Mrs. Johnson had taught him to read on the same principle she would have taught a pet animal amusing tricks. She had never imagined the time would come when he would use the machinery she had put in his hands to help overthrow the institution to which she was so ardently attached.

"What does it mean? Is it somethin' good for us?"

15

"I think," said Robert, a little vain of his superior knowledge, "it is the best kind of good. It means if two armies are fighting and the horses of one run away, the other has a right to take them. And it is just the same if a slave runs away from the Secesh to the Union lines. He is called a contraband, just the same as if he were an ox or a horse. They wouldn't send the horses back, and they won't send us back."

"Is dat so?" said Uncle Daniel, a dear old father, with a look of saintly patience on his face. "Well, chillen, what do you mean to do?"

"Go, jis' as soon as we kin git to de army," said Tom Anderson.

"What else did the generals say? And how did you come to hear them, Tom?" asked Robert Johnson.

"Well, yer see, Marster's too ole and feeble to go to de war, but his heart's in it. An' it makes him feel good all ober when dem big ginerals comes an' tells him all 'bout it. Well, I war laying out on de porch fas' asleep an' snorin' dreful hard. Oh, I war so soun' asleep dat wen Marster wanted some ice-water he had to shake me dreful hard to wake me up. An' all de time I war wide 'wake as he war."

"What did they say?" asked Robert, who was always on the lookout for news from the battlefield.

"One ob dem said, dem Yankees war talkin' of puttin' guns in our han's and settin' us all free. An' de oder said, 'Oh, sho! Ef dey puts guns in dere hands dey'll soon be in our'n; and ef dey sets em free dey wouldn't know how to take keer ob demselves.'"

"Only let 'em try it," chorused a half dozen voices, "an' dey'll soon see who'll git de bes' ob de guns; an' as to taking keer ob ourselves, I specs we kin take keer ob ourselves as well as take keer ob dem."

"Yes," said Tom, "who plants de cotton and raises all de crops?"

"'They eat the meat and give us the bones,
　　Eat the cherries and give us the stones,'

"And I'm getting tired of the whole business," said Robert.

"But, Bob," said Uncle Daniel, "you've got a good owner. You don't hab to run away from bad times and wuss a comin'.'"

"It isn't so good, but it might be better. I ain't got nothing 'gainst my ole Miss, except she sold my mother from me. And a boy ain't nothin' without his mother. I forgive her, but I never forget her, and never expect to. But if she were the best woman on earth I would rather have my freedom than belong to her. Well, boys, here's a chance for us just as soon as the Union army gets in sight. What will you do?"

"I'se a goin," said Tom Anderson, "jis' as soon as dem Linkum soldiers gits in sight."

"An' I'se a gwine wid you, Tom," said another. "I specs my ole Marster'll feel right smart lonesome when I'se gone, but I don't keer 'bout stayin' for company's sake."

"My ole Marster's room's a heap better'n his company," said Tom Anderson, "an' I'se a goner too. Dis yer freedom's too good to be lef' behind, wen you's got a chance to git it. I won't stop to bid ole Marse goodbye."

"What do you think," said Robert, turning to Uncle Daniel; "won't you go with us?"

"No, chillen, I don't blame you for gwine; but I'se gwine to stay. Slavery's done got all de marrow out ob dese poor ole bones. Ef freedom comes it won't do me much good; we ole one's will die out, but it will set you youngsters all up."

"But, Uncle Daniel, you're not too old to want your freedom?"

"I knows dat. I lubs de bery name of freedom. I'se been praying and hoping for it dese many years. An' ef I warn't boun', I would go wid you ter-morrer. I won't put a straw in your way. You boys go, and my prayers will go wid you. I can't go, it's no use. I'se gwine to stay on de ole place till Marse Robert comes back, or is brought back."

"But, Uncle Daniel," said Robert, "what's the use of praying for a thing if, when it comes, you won't take it? As much as you have been praying and talking about freedom, I thought that when the chance came you would have been one of the first to take it. Now, do tell us why you won't go with us. Ain't you willing?"

"Why, Robbie, my whole heart is wid you. But when Marse Robert went to de war, he called me into his room and said to me, 'Uncle Dan'el, I'se gwine to de war, an' I want you to look arter my wife an' chillen, an' see dat eberything goes right on de place'. An' I promised him I'd do it, an' I mus' be as good as my word. 'Cept de overseer, dere isn't a white man on de plantation, an' I hear he has to report ter-morrer or be treated as a deserter. An' der's nobody here to look arter Miss Mary an' de chillen, but myself, an' to see dat eberything goes right. I promised Marse Robert I would do it, an' I mus' be as good as my word."

"Well, what should you keer?" said Tom Anderson. "Who looked arter you when you war sole from your farder and mudder, an' neber seed dem any more, and wouldn't know dem today ef you met dem in your dish?"

"Well, dats neither yere nor dere. Marse Robert couldn't help what his father did. He war an orful mean man. But he's dead now, and gone to see 'bout it. But his wife war de nicest, sweetest lady dat eber I did see. She war no more like him dan chalk's like cheese. She used to visit de cabins, an' listen to de pore women when de overseer used to cruelize dem so bad, an' drive dem to work late and early. An' she used to sen' dem nice things when they war sick, and hab der cabins whitewashed an' lookin' like new pins, an' look arter dere chillen. Sometimes she'd try to git ole Marse to take dere part when de oberseer got too mean. But she might as well a sung hymns to a dead horse. All her putty talk war like porin water on a goose's back. He'd jis' bluff her off, an' tell her she didn't run dat plantation, and not for her to bring him any nigger news. I never thought ole Marster war good to her. I often ketched her crying, an' she'd say she had de headache, but I thought it war de heartache. 'Fore ole Marster died, she got so thin an' peaked I war 'fraid she war gwine to die; but she seed him out. He war killed by a tree fallin' on him, an' ef eber de debil got his own he got him. I seed him in a vision arter he war gone. He war hangin' up in a pit, sayin' 'Oh, oh!' wid no close on. He war allers blusterin', cussin', and swearin' at somebody. Marse Robert ain't a bit like him. He takes right arter his mother. Bad as ole Marster war, I think she jis' lob'd de groun' he walked on. Well, women's mighty curious kind of folks anyhow. I sometimes thinks de wuss you treats dem de better dey likes you."

"Well," said Tom, a little impatiently, "what's yer gwine to do? Is yer gwine wid us, ef yer gits a chance?"

"Now, jes' you hole on till I gits a chance to tell yer why I'se gwine to stay."

"Well, Uncle Daniel, let's hear it," said Robert.

"I was jes' gwine to tell yer when Tom put me out. Ole Marster died when Marse Robert war two years ole, and his pore mother when he war four. When he died, Miss Anna used to keep me 'bout her jes' like I war her shadder. I used to nuss Marse Robert jes' de same as ef I were his own fadder. I used to fix his milk, rock him to sleep, ride him on my back, an' nothin' pleased him better'n fer Uncle Dan'el to ride him piggy-back."

"Well, Uncle Daniel," said Robert, "what has that got to do with your going with us and getting your freedom?"

"Now, jes' wait a bit, and don't frustrate my mine. I seed day arter day Miss Anna war gettin' weaker and thinner, an' she looked so sweet and talked so putty, I thinks to myself, 'you ain't long for dis worl''.' And she said to me one day, 'Uncle Dan'el, when I'se gone, I want you to be good to your Marster Robert.' An' she looked so pale and weak I war almost ready to cry. I couldn't help it. She hed allers bin mighty good to me. An' I beliebs in praisin' de bridge dat carries me ober. She said, 'Uncle Dan'el, I wish you war free. Ef I had my way you shouldn't serve any one when I'm gone; but Mr. Thurston had eberything in his power when he made his will. I war tied hand and foot, and I couldn't help it.' In a little while she war gone—jis' faded away like a flower. I belieb ef dere's a saint in glory, Miss Anna's dere."

"Oh, I don't take much stock in white folks' religion," said Robert, laughing carelessly.

"The way," said Tom Anderson, "dat some of dese folks cut their cards yere, I think dey'll be as sceece in hebben as hen's teeth. I think wen some of dem preachers brings de Bible 'round an' tells us 'bout mindin our marsters and not stealin' dere tings, dat dey preach to please de white folks, an' dey frows coleness ober de meetin'."

"An' I," said Aunt Linda, "neber did belieb in dem Bible preachers. I yered one ob dem sayin' wen he war dyin', it war all dark wid him. An' de way he treated his house-girl, pore thing, I don't wonder dat it war dark wid him."

"O, I guess," said Robert, "that the Bible is all right, but some of these church folks don't get the right hang of it."

"May be dat's so," said Aunt Linda. "But I allers wanted to learn how to read. I once had a book, and tried to make out what war in it, but ebery time my mistus caught me wid a book in my hand, she used to whip my fingers.

An' I couldn't see ef it war good for white folks, why it warn't good for cullud folks."

"Well," said Tom Anderson, "I belieb in de good ole-time religion. But arter dese white folks is done fussin' and beatin' de cullud folks, I don't want 'em to come talking religion to me. We used to hab on our place a real Guinea man, an' once he made ole Marse mad, an' he had him whipped. Old Marse war trying to break him in, but dat fellow war spunk to de backbone, an' when he 'gin talkin' to him 'bout savin' his soul an' gittin' to hebbin, he tole him ef he went to hebbin an' foun' he war dare, he wouldn't go in. He wouldn't stay wid any such rascal as he war."

"What became of him?" asked Robert.

"Oh, he died. But he had some quare notions 'bout religion. He thought dat when he died he would go back to his ole country. He allers kep' his ole Guinea name."

"What was it?"

"Potobombra. Do you know what he wanted Marster to do 'fore he died?" continued Anderson.

"No."

"He wanted him to gib him his free papers."

"Did he do it?"

"Ob course he did. As de poor fellow war dying an' he couldn't sell him in de oder world, he jis' wrote him de papers to yumor him. He didn't want to go back to Africa a slave. He thought if he did, his people would look down on him, an' he wanted to go back a free man. He war orful weak when Marster brought him de free papers. He jis' ris up in de bed, clutched dem in his han's, smiled, an' gasped out, 'I'se free at las'; an' fell back on de pillar, an' he war gone. Oh, but he war spunky. De oberseers, arter dey foun' out who he war, gin'rally gabe him a wide birth. I specs his father war some ole Guinea king."

"Well, chillen," said Uncle Daniel, "we's kept up dis meeting long enough. We'd better go home, and not all go one way, cause de patrollers might git us all inter trouble, an' we must try to slip home by hook or crook."

"An' when we meet again, Uncle Daniel can finish his story, an' be ready to go with us," said Robert.

"I wish," said Tom Anderson, "he would go wid us, de wuss kind."

3.
Uncle Daniel's Story.

The Union had snapped asunder because it lacked the cohesion of justice, and the Nation was destined to pass through the crucible of disaster and defeat, till she was ready to clasp hands with the Negro and march abreast with him to freedom and victory.

The Union army was encamping a few miles from C——, in North Carolina. Robert, being well posted on the condition of affairs, had stealthily contrived to call a meeting in Uncle Daniel's cabin. Uncle Daniel's wife had gone to bed as a sick sister, and they held a prayer-meeting by her bedside. It was a little risky, but as Mr. Thurston did not encourage the visits of the patrollers, and heartily detested having them prying into his cabins, there was not much danger of molestation.

"Well, Uncle Daniel, we want to hear your story, and see if you have made up your mind to go with us," said Robert, after he had been seated a few minutes in Uncle Daniel's cabin.

"No, chillen, I've no objection to finishin' my story, but I ain't made up my mind to leave the place till Marse Robert gits back."

"You were telling us about Marse Robert's mother. How did you get along after she died?"

"Arter she war gone, ole Marster's folks come to look arter things. But eberything war lef' to Marse Robert, an' he wouldn't do widout me. Dat chile war allers at my heels. I couldn't stir widout him, an' when he missed me, he'd fret an' cry so I had ter stay wid him; an' wen he went to school, I had ter carry him in de mornin' and bring him home in de ebenin'. An' I learned him to hunt squirrels, an' rabbits, an' ketch fish, an' set traps for birds. I beliebs he lob'd me better dan any ob his kin'. An' he showed me how to read."

"Well," said Tom, "ef he lob'd you so much, why didn't he set you free?"

"Marse Robert tole me, ef he died fust he war gwine ter leave me free—dat I should neber sarve any one else."

"Oh, sho!" said Tom, "Promises, like pie crusts, is made to be broken. I don't trust none ob dem. I'se been yere dese fifteen years, an' I'se neber foun' any troof in dem. An' I'se gwine wid dem North men soon's I gits a chance. An' ef you knowed what's good fer you, you'd go, too."

21

"No, Tom; I can't go. When Marster Robert went to de front, he called me to him an' said: 'Uncle Daniel,' an' he was drefful pale when he said it, 'I are gwine to de war, an' I want yer to take keer of my wife an' chillen, jis' like yer used to take keer of me wen yer called me your little boy.' Well, dat jis' got to me, an' I couldn't help cryin', to save my life."

"I specs," said Tom, "your tear bags must lie mighty close to your eyes. I wouldn't cry ef dem Yankees would make ebery one ob dem go to de front, an' stay dere foreber. Dey'd only be gittin' back what dey's been a doin' to us."

"Marster Robert war nebber bad to me. An' I beliebs in stannin' by dem dat stans by you. Arter Miss Anna died, I had great 'sponsibilities on my shoulders; but I war orful lonesome, an' thought I'd like to git a wife. But dere warn't a gal on de plantation, an' nowhere's roun', dat filled de bill. So I jis' waited, an' 'tended to Marse Robert till he war ole 'nough to go to college. Wen he went, he allers 'membered me in de letters he used to write his grandma. Wen he war gone, I war lonesomer dan eber. But, one day, I jis' seed de gal dat took de rag off de bush. Gundover had jis' brought her from de up-country. She war putty as a picture!" he exclaimed, looking fondly at his wife, who still bore traces of great beauty. "She had putty hair, putty eyes, putty mouth. She war putty all over; an' she know'd how to put on style."

"O, Daniel," said Aunt Katie, half chidingly, "how you do talk."

"Why, it's true. I 'member when you war de puttiest gal in dese diggins; when nobody could top your cotton."

"I don't," said Aunt Katie.

"Well, I do. Now, let me go on wid my story. De fust time I seed her, I sez to myself, 'Dat's de gal for me, an' I means to hab her ef I kin git her.' So I scraped 'quaintance wid her, and axed her ef she would hab me ef our marsters would let us. I warn't 'fraid 'bout Marse Robert, but I warn't quite shore 'bout Gundover. So when Marse Robert com'd home, I axed him, an' he larf'd an' said, 'All right,' an' dat he would speak to ole Gundover 'bout it. He didn't relish it bery much, but he didn't like to 'fuse Marse Robert. He wouldn't sell her, for she tended his dairy, an' war mighty handy 'bout de house. He said, I mought marry her an' come to see her wheneber Marse Robert would gib me a pass. I wanted him to sell her, but he wouldn't hear to it, so I had to put up wid what I could git. Marse Robert war mighty good to me, but ole Gundover's wife war de meanest woman dat I eber did see. She used to go out on de plantation an' boss things like a man. Arter I war married, I had a baby. It war de dearest, cutest little thing you eber did see; but, pore thing, it got sick and died. It died 'bout three o'clock; and in de mornin', Katie, habbin her cows to milk, lef her dead baby in de cabin. When she com'd back from milkin' her thirty cows, an' went to look for her pore little baby, someone had been to her cabin an' took'd de pore chile away an' put it in de groun'. Pore Katie, she didn't eben hab a chance to kiss her baby 'fore it war buried. Ole Gundover's wife has been dead thirty years, an' she didn't die a day too soon. An' my little baby has gone to glory, an' is wingin' wid the angels an' a lookin' out for us. One ob de las' things ole

Gundover's wife did 'fore she died war to order a woman whipped 'cause she com'd to de field a little late when her husband war sick, an' she had stopped to tend him. Dat mornin' she war taken sick wid de fever, an' in a few days she war gone out like de snuff ob a candle. She lef' several sons, an' I specs she would almos' turn ober in her grave ef she know'd she had ten culled granchillen somewhar down in de lower kentry."

"Isn't it funny," said Robert, "how these white folks look down on colored people, an' then mix up with them?"

"Marster war away when Miss 'Liza treated my Katie so mean, an' when I tole him 'bout it, he war tearin' mad, an' went ober an' saw ole Gundover, an' foun' out he war hard up for money, an' he bought Katie and brought her home to lib wid me, and we's been a libin in clover eber sence. Marster Robert has been mighty good to me. He stood by me in my troubles, an' now his trouble's come, I'm a gwine to stan' by him. I used to think Gundover's wife war jealous ob my Katie. She war so much puttier. Gundover's wife couldn't tech my Katie wid a ten foot pole."

"But, Aunt Katie, you have had your trials," said Robert, now that Daniel had finished his story; "don't you feel bitter towards these people who are fighting to keep you in slavery?"

Aunt Katie turned her face towards the speaker. It was a thoughtful, intelligent face, saintly and calm. A face which expressed the idea of a soul which had been fearfully tempest tossed, but had passed through suffering into peace. Very touching was the look of resignation and hope which overspread her features as she replied, with the simple childlike faith which she had learned in the darkest hour, "The Lord says, we must forgive." And with her that thought, as coming from the lips of Divine Love, was enough to settle the whole question of forgiveness of injuries and love to enemies.

"Well," said Thomas Anderson, turning to Uncle Daniel, "we can't count on yer to go wid us?"

"Boys," said Uncle Daniel, and there was grief in his voice, "I'se mighty glad you hab a chance for your freedom; but, ez I tole yer, I promised Marse Robert I would stay, an' I mus' be as good as my word. Don't you youngsters stay for an ole stager like me. I'm ole an' mos' worn out. Freedom wouldn't do much for me, but I want you all to be as free as the birds; so, you chillen, take your freedom when you kin get it."

"But, Uncle Dan'el, you won't say nothin' 'bout our going, will you?" said the youngest of the company.

Uncle Daniel slowly arose. There was a mournful flash in his eye, a tremor of emotion in his voice, as he said, "Look yere, boys, de boy dat axed dat question war a new comer on dis plantation, but some ob you's bin here all ob your lives; did you eber know ob Uncle Dan'el gittin' any ob you inter trouble?"

"No, no," exclaimed a chorus of voices, "but many's de time you've held off de blows wen de oberseer got too mean, an' cruelized us too much, wen Marse Robert war away. An' wen he got back, you made him settle de oberseer's hash."

"Well, boys," said Uncle Daniel, with an air of mournful dignity, "I'se de same Uncle Dan'el I eber war. Ef any ob you wants to go, I habben't a word to say agin it. I specs dem Yankees be all right, but I knows Marse Robert, an' I don't know dem, an' I ain't a gwine ter throw away dirty water 'til I gits clean."

"Well, Uncle Ben," said Robert, addressing a stalwart man whose towering form and darkly flashing eye told that slavery had failed to put the crouch in his shoulders or general abjectness into his demeanor, "you will go with us, for sure, won't you?"

"Yes," spoke up Tom Anderson, "'cause de trader's done took your wife, an' got her for his'n now."

As Ben Tunnel looked at the speaker, a spasm of agony and anger darkened his face and distorted his features, as if the blood of some strong race were stirring with sudden vigor through his veins. He clutched his hands together, as if he were struggling with an invisible foe, and for a moment he remained silent. Then suddenly raising his head, he exclaimed, "Boys, there's not one of you loves freedom more than I do, but—"

"But what?" said Tom. "Do you think white folks is your bes' friends?"

"I'll think so when I lose my senses."

"Well, now, I don't belieb you're 'fraid, not de way I yeard you talkin' to de oberseer wen he war threatnin' to hit your mudder. He saw you meant business, an' he let her alone. But, what's to hinder you from gwine wid us?"

"My mother," he replied, in a low, firm voice. "That is the only thing that keeps me from going. If it had not been for her, I would have gone long ago. She's all I've got, an' I'm all she's got."

It was touching to see the sorrow on the strong face, to detect the pathos and indignation in his voice, as he said, "I used to love Mirandy as I love my life. I thought the sun rose and set in her. I never saw a handsomer woman than she was. But she fooled me all over the face and eyes, and took up with that hellhound of a trader, Lukens; an' he gave her a chance to live easy, to wear fine clothes, an' be waited on like a lady. I thought at first I would go crazy, but my poor mammy did all she could to comfort me. She would tell me there were as good fish in the sea as were ever caught out of it. Many a time I've laid my poor head on her lap, when it seemed as if my brain was on fire and my heart was almost ready to burst. But in course of time I got over the worst of it; an' Mirandy is the first an' last woman that ever fooled me. But that dear old mammy of mine, I mean to stick by her as long as there is a piece of her. I can't go over to the army an' leave her behind, for if I did, an' anything should happen, I would never forgive myself."

"But couldn't you take her with you," said Robert, "the soldiers said we could bring our women."

"It isn't that. The Union army is several miles from here, an' my poor mammy is so skeery that, if I were trying to get her away and any of them Secesh would overtake us, an' begin to question us, she would get skeered almost to death, an' break down an' begin to cry, an' then the fat would be in the fire. So, while I love freedom more than a child loves its mother's milk,

I've made up my mind to stay on the plantation. I wish, from the bottom of my heart, I could go. But I can't take her along with me, an' I don't want to be free and leave her behind in slavery. I was only five years old when my master and, as I believe, father, sold us both here to this lower country, an' we've been here ever since. It's no use talking, I won't leave her to be run over by everybody."

A few evenings after this interview, the Union soldiers entered the town of C——, and established their headquarters near the home of Thomas Anderson.

Out of the little company, almost everyone deserted to the Union army, leaving Uncle Daniel faithful to his trust, and Ben Tunnel hushing his heart's deep aspirations for freedom in a passionate devotion to his timid and affectionate mother.

4·
ARRIVAL OF THE UNION ARMY.

A few evenings before the stampede of Robert and his friends to the army, and as he sat alone in his room reading the latest news from the paper he had secreted, he heard a cautious tread and a low tap at his window. He opened the door quietly and whispered:—

"Anything new, Tom?"

"Yes."

"What is it? Come in."

"Well, I'se done bin seen dem Yankees, an' dere ain't a bit of troof in dem stories I'se bin yerin 'bout 'em."

"Where did you see 'em?"

"Down in de woods whar Marster tole us to hide. Yesterday ole Marse sent for me to come in de settin'-room. An' what do you think? Instead ob makin' me stan' wid my hat in my han' while he went froo a whole rigamarole, he axed me to sit down, an' he tole me he 'spected de Yankees would want us to go inter de army, an' dey would put us in front whar we'd all git killed; an' I tole him I didn't want to go, I didn't want to git all momached up. An' den he said we'd better go down in de woods an' hide. Massa Tom and Frank said we'd better go as quick as eber we could. Dey said dem Yankees would put us in dere wagons and make us haul like we war mules. Marse Tom ain't libin' at de great house jis' now. He's keepin' bachellar's hall."

"Didn't he go to the battle?"

"No; he foun' a pore white man who war hard up for money, an' he got him to go."

"But, Tom, you didn't believe these stories about the Yankees. Tom and Frank can lie as fast as horses can trot. They wanted to scare you, and keep you from going to the Union army."

"I knows dat now, but I didn't 'spect so den."

"Well, when did you see the soldiers? Where are they? And what did they say to you?"

"Dey's right down in Gundover's woods. An' de Gineral's got his headquarters almos' next door to our house."

"That near? Oh, you don't say so!"

27

"Yes, I do. An', oh, golly, ain't I so glad! I jis' stole yere to told you all 'bout it. Yesterday mornin' I war splittin' some wood to git my breakfas', an' I met one ob dem Yankee sogers. Well, I war so skeered, my heart flew right up in my mouf, but I made my manners to him and said, 'Good mornin', Massa.' He said, 'Good mornin'; but don't call me "massa."' Dat war de fust white man I eber seed dat didn't want ter be called 'massa,' eben ef he war as pore as Job's turkey. Den I begin to feel right sheepish, an' he axed me ef my marster war at home, an' ef he war a Reb. I tole him he hadn't gone to de war, but he war Secesh all froo, inside and outside. He war too ole to go to de war, but dat he war all de time gruntin' an' groanin', an' I 'spected he'd grunt hisself to death."

"What did he say?"

"He said he specs he'll grunt worser dan dat fore dey get froo wid him. Den he axed me ef I would hab some breakfas,' an' I said, 'No, t'ank you, sir.' An' I war jis' as hungry as a dorg, but I war 'feared to eat. I war 'feared he war gwine to pizen me."

"Poison you! Don't you know the Yankees are our best friends?"

"Well, ef dat's so, I'se mighty glad, cause de woods is full ob dem."

"Now, Tom, I thought you had cut your eye-teeth long enough not to let them Anderson boys fool you. Tom, you must not think because a white man says a thing, it must be so, and that a colored man's word is no account 'longside of his. Tom, if ever we get our freedom, we've got to learn to trust each other and stick together if we would be a people. Somebody else can read the papers as well as Marse Tom and Frank. My ole Miss knows I can read the papers, an' she never tries to scare me with big whoppers 'bout the Yankees. She knows she can't catch ole birds with chaff, so she is just as sweet as a peach to her Bobby. But as soon as I get a chance I will play her a trick the devil never did."

"What's that?"

"I'll leave her. I ain't forgot how she sold my mother from me. Many a night I have cried myself to sleep, thinking about her, and when I get free I mean to hunt her up."

"Well, I ain't tole you all. De gemman said he war 'cruiting for de army; dat Massa Linkum hab set us all free, an' dat he wanted some more sogers to put down dem Secesh; dat we should all hab our freedom, our wages, an' some kind ob money. I couldn't call it like he did."

"Bounty money," said Robert.

"Yes, dat's jis' what he called it, bounty money. An' I said dat I war in for dat, teeth and toenails."

Robert Johnson's heart gave a great bound. Was that so? Had that army, with freedom emblazoned on its banners, come at last to offer them deliverance if they would accept it? Was it a bright, beautiful dream, or a blessed reality soon to be grasped by his willing hands? His heart grew buoyant with hope; the lightness of his heart gave elasticity to his step and sent the blood rejoicingly through his veins. Freedom was almost in his grasp, and the future was growing rose-tinted and rainbow-hued. All the ties which bound him to his home were as ropes of sand, now that freedom had come so near.

When the army was afar off, he had appeared to be light-hearted and content with his lot. If asked if he desired his freedom, he would have answered, very naively, that he was eating his white bread and believed in letting well enough alone; he had no intention of jumping from the frying-pan into the fire. But in the depths of his soul the love of freedom was an all-absorbing passion; only danger had taught him caution. He had heard of terrible vengeance being heaped upon the heads of some who had sought their freedom and failed in the attempt. Robert knew that he might abandon hope if he incurred the wrath of men whose overthrow was only a question of time. It would have been madness and folly for him to have attempted an insurrection against slavery, with the words of McClellan ringing in his ears: "If you rise I shall put you down with an iron hand," and with the home guards ready to quench his aspirations for freedom with bayonets and blood. What could a set of unarmed and undisciplined men do against the fearful odds which beset their path?

Robert waited eagerly and hopefully his chance to join the Union army; and was ready and willing to do anything required of him by which he could earn his freedom and prove his manhood. He conducted his plans with the greatest secrecy. A few faithful and trusted friends stood ready to desert with him when the Union army came within hailing distance. When it came, there was a stampede to its ranks of men ready to serve in any capacity, to labor in the tents, fight on the fields, or act as scouts. It was a strange sight to see these black men rallying around the Stars and Stripes, when white men were trampling them under foot and riddling them with bullets.

5.
THE RELEASE OF IOLA LEROY.

"Well, boys," said Robert to his trusted friends, as they gathered together at a meeting in Gundover's woods, almost under the shadow of the Union army, "how many of you are ready to join the army and fight for your freedom."

"All ob us."

"The soldiers," continued Robert, "are camped right at the edge of the town. The General has his headquarters in the heart of the town, and one of the officers told me yesterday that the President had set us all free, and that as many as wanted to join the army could come along to the camp. So I thought, boys, that I would come and tell you. Now, you can take your bag and baggage, and get out of here as soon as you choose."

"We'll be ready by daylight," said Tom. "It won't take me long to pack up," looking down at his seedy clothes, with a laugh. "I specs ole Marse'll be real lonesome when I'm gone. An' won't he be hoppin' mad when he finds I'm a goner? I specs he'll hate it like pizen."

"O, well," said Robert, "the best of friends must part. Don't let it grieve you."

"I'se gwine to take my wife an' chillen," said one of the company.

"I'se got nobody but myself," said Tom; "but dere's a mighty putty young gal dere at Marse Tom's. I wish I could git her away. Dey tells me dey's been sellin' her all ober de kentry; but dat she's a reg'lar spitfire; dey can't lead nor dribe her."

"Do you think she would go with us?" said Robert.

"I think she's jis' dying to go. Dey say dey can't do nuffin wid her. Marse Tom's got his match dis time, and I'se glad ob it. I jis' glories in her spunk."

"How did she come there?"

"Oh, Marse bought her ob de trader to keep house for him. But ef you seed dem putty white han's ob hern you'd never tink she kept her own house, let 'lone anybody else's."

"Do you think you can get her away?"

"I don't know; 'cause Marse Tom keeps her mighty close. My, but she's putty! Beautiful long hair comes way down her back; putty blue eyes, an' jis' ez white ez anybody's in dis place. I'd jis' wish you could see her yoresef. I

31

heerd Marse Tom talkin' 'bout her las' night to his brudder; tellin' him she war mighty airish, but he meant to break her in."

An angry curse rose to the lips of Robert, but he repressed it and muttered to himself, "Graceless scamp, he ought to have his neck stretched." Then turning to Tom, said:—

"Get her, if you possibly can, but you must be mighty mum about it."

"Trus' me for dat," said Tom.

Tom was very anxious to get word to the beautiful but intractable girl who was held in durance vile by her reckless and selfish master, who had tried in vain to drag her down to his own low level of sin and shame. But all Tom's efforts were in vain. Finally he applied to the Commander of the post, who immediately gave orders for her release. The next day Tom had the satisfaction of knowing that Iola Leroy had been taken as a trembling dove from the gory vulture's nest and given a place of security. She was taken immediately to the General's headquarters. The General was much impressed by her modest demeanor, and surprised to see the refinement and beauty she possessed. Could it be possible that this young and beautiful girl had been a chattel, with no power to protect herself from the highest insults that lawless brutality could inflict upon innocent and defenseless womanhood? Could he ever again glory in his American citizenship, when any white man, no matter how coarse, cruel, or brutal, could buy or sell her for the basest purposes? Was it not true that the cause of a hapless people had become entangled with the lightnings of heaven, and dragged down retribution upon the land?

The field hospital was needing gentle, womanly ministrations, and Iola Leroy, released from the hands of her tormentors, was given a place as nurse; a position to which she adapted herself with a deep sense of relief. Tom was doubly gratified at the success of his endeavors, which had resulted in the rescue of the beautiful young girl and the discomfiture of his young master who, in the words of Tom, "was mad enough to bite his head off" (a rather difficult physical feat).

Iola, freed from her master's clutches, applied herself readily to her appointed tasks. The beautiful, girlish face was full of tender earnestness. The fresh, young voice was strangely sympathetic, as if some great sorrow had bound her heart in loving compassion to every sufferer who needed her gentle ministrations.

Tom Anderson was a man of herculean strength and remarkable courage. But, on account of physical defects, instead of enlisting as a soldier, he was forced to remain a servant, although he felt as if every nerve in his right arm was tingling to strike a blow for freedom. He was well versed in the lay of the country, having often driven his master's cotton to market when he was a field hand. After he became a coachman, he had become acquainted with the different roads and localities of the country. Besides, he had often accompanied his young masters on their hunting and fishing expeditions. Although he could not fight in the army, he proved an invaluable helper. When tents were to be pitched, none were more ready to help than he.

When burdens were to be borne, none were more willing to bend beneath them than Thomas Anderson. When the battlefield was to be searched for the wounded and dying, no hand was more tender in its ministrations of kindness than his. As a general factotum in the army, he was ever ready and willing to serve anywhere and at any time, and to gather information from every possible source which could be of any service to the Union army. As a Pagan might worship a distant star and wish to call it his own, so he loved Iola. And he never thought he could do too much for the soldiers who had rescued her and were bringing deliverance to his race.

"What do you think of Miss Iola?" Robert asked him one day, as they were talking together.

"I jis' think dat she's splendid. Las' week I had to take some of our pore boys to de hospital, an' she war dere, lookin' sweet an' putty ez an angel, a nussin' dem pore boys, an' ez good to one ez de oder. It looks to me ez ef dey ralely lob'd her shadder. She sits by 'em so patient, an' writes 'em sech nice letters to der frens, an' yit she looks so heart-broke an' pitiful, it jis' gits to me, an' makes me mos' ready to cry. I'm so glad dat Marse Tom had to gib her up. He war too mean to eat good victuals."

"He ought," said Robert, "to be made to live on herrings' heads and cold potatoes. It makes my blood boil just to think that he was going to have that lovely looking young girl whipped for his devilment. He ought to be ashamed to hold up his head among respectable people."

"I tell you, Bob, de debil will neber git his own till he gits him. When I seed how he war treating her I neber rested till I got her away. He bought her, he said, for his housekeeper; as many gals as dere war on de plantation, why didn't he git one ob dem to keep house, an' not dat nice lookin' young lady? Her han's look ez ef she neber did a day's work in her life. One day when he com'd down to breakfas',' he chucked her under de chin, an' tried to put his arm roun' her waist. But she jis' frew it off like a chunk ob fire. She looked like a snake had bit her. Her eyes fairly spit fire. Her face got red ez blood, an' den she turned so pale I thought she war gwine to faint, but she didn't, an' I yered her say, 'I'll die fust.' I war mad 'nough to stan' on my head. I could hab tore'd him all to pieces wen he said he'd hab her whipped."

"Did he do it?"

"I don't know. But he's mean 'nough to do enythin'. Why, dey say she war sole seben times in six weeks, 'cause she's so putty, but dat she war game to de las'."

"Well, Tom," said Robert, "getting that girl away was one of the best things you ever did in your life."

"I think so, too. Not dat I specs enytin' ob it. I don't spose she would think ob an ugly chap like me; but it does me good to know dat Marse Tom ain't got her."

6.
ROBERT JOHNSON'S PROMOTION AND RELIGION.

Robert Johnson, being able to meet the army requirements, was enlisted as a substitute to help fill out the quota of a Northern regiment. With his intelligence, courage, and prompt obedience, he rose from the ranks and became lieutenant of a colored company. He was daring, without being rash; prompt, but not thoughtless; firm, without being harsh. Kind and devoted to the company he drilled, he soon won the respect of his superior officers and the love of his comrades.

"Johnson," said a young officer, Captain Sybil, of Maine, who had become attached to Robert, "what is the use of your saying you're a colored man, when you are as white as I am, and as brave a man as there is among us. Why not quit this company, and take your place in the army just the same as a white man? I know your chances for promotion would be better."

"Captain, you may doubt my word, but today I would rather be a lieutenant in my company than a captain in yours."

"I don't understand you."

"Well, Captain, when a man's been colored all his life it comes a little hard for him to get white all at once. Were I to try it, I would feel like a cat in a strange garret. Captain, I think my place is where I am most needed. You do not need me in your ranks, and my company does. They are excellent fighters, but they need a leader. To silence a battery, to capture a flag, to take a fortification, they will rush into the jaws of death."

"Yes, I have often wondered at their bravery."

"Captain, these battles put them on their mettle. They have been so long taught that they are nothing and nobody, that they seem glad to prove they are something and somebody."

"But, Johnson, you do not look like them, you do not talk like them. It is a burning shame to have held such a man as you in slavery."

"I don't think it was any worse to have held me in slavery than the blackest man in the South."

"You are right, Johnson. The color of a man's skin has nothing to do with the possession of his rights."

"Now, there is Tom Anderson," said Robert, "he is just as black as black can be. He has been bought and sold like a beast, and yet there is not a braver man in all the company. I know him well. He is a noble-hearted fellow. True as steel. I love him like a brother. And I believe Tom would risk his life for me any day. He don't know anything about his father or mother. He was sold from them before he could remember. He can read a little. He used to take lessons from a white gardener in Virginia. He would go between the hours of 9 PM and 4 AM He got a book of his own, tore it up, greased the pages, and hid them in his hat. Then if his master had ever knocked his hat off he would have thought them greasy papers, and not that Tom was carrying his library on his head. I had another friend who lived near us. When he was nineteen years old he did not know how many letters there were in the ABCs. One night, when his work was done, his boss came into his cabin and saw him with a book in his hand. He threatened to give him five hundred lashes if he caught him again with a book, and said he hadn't work enough to do. He was getting out logs, and his task was ten logs a day. His employer threatened to increase it to twelve. He said it just harassed him; it set him on fire. He thought there must be something good in that book if the white man didn't want him to learn. One day he had an errand in the kitchen, and he heard one of the colored girls going over the ABC's. Here was the key to the forbidden knowledge. She had heard the white children saying them, and picked them up by heart, but did not know them by sight. He was not content with that, but sold his cap for a book and wore a cloth on his head instead. He got the sounds of the letters by heart, then cut off the bark of a tree, carved the letters on the smooth inside, and learned them. He wanted to learn how to write. He had charge of a warehouse where he had a chance to see the size and form of letters. He made the beach of the river his copybook, and thus he learned to write. Tom never got very far with his learning, but I used to get the papers and tell him all I knew about the war."

"How did you get the papers?"

"I used to have very good privileges for a slave. All of our owners were not alike. Some of them were quite clever, and others were worse than git out. I used to get the morning papers to sell to the boarders and others, and when I got them I would contrive to hide a paper, and let some of the fellow-servants know how things were going on. And our owners thought we cared nothing about what was going on."

"How was that? I thought you were not allowed to hold meetings unless a white man were present."

"That was so. But we contrived to hold secret meetings in spite of their caution. We knew whom we could trust. My ole Miss wasn't mean like some of them. She never wanted the patrollers around prowling in our cabins, and poking their noses into our business. Her husband was an awful drunkard. He ran through every cent he could lay his hands on, and she was forced to do something to keep the wolf from the door, so she set up a boarding-house. But she didn't take in Tom, Dick, and Harry. Nobody but the big bugs stopped with her. She taught me to read and write, and to cast up accounts. It was so handy for her to have someone who could figure up her accounts, and read or write a note, if she were from home and wanted the like done. She once told her cousin how I could write and figure up. And what do you think her cousin said?"

"'Pleased,' I suppose, 'to hear it.'"

"Not a bit of it. She said, if I belonged to her, she would cut off my thumbs; her husband said, 'Oh, then he couldn't pick cotton.' As to my poor thumbs, it did not seem to be taken into account what it would cost me to lose them. My ole Miss used to have a lot of books. She would let me read any one of them except a novel. She wanted to take care of my soul, but she wasn't taking care of her own."

"Wasn't she religious?"

"She went for it. I suppose she was as good as most of them. She said her prayers and went to church, but I don't know that that made her any better. I never did take much stock in white folks' religion."

"Why, Robert, I'm afraid you are something of an infidel."

"No, Captain, I believe in the real, genuine religion. I ain't got much myself, but I respect them that have. We had on our place a dear, old saint, named Aunt Kizzy. She was a happy soul. She had seen hard times, but was what I call a living epistle. I've heard her tell how her only child had been sold from her, when the man who bought herself did not want to buy her child. Poor little fellow! He was only two years old I asked her one day how she felt when her child was taken away. 'I felt,' she said, 'as if I was going to my grave. But I knew if I couldn't get justice here, I could get it in another world.'"

"That was faith," said Captain Sybil, as if speaking to himself, "a patient waiting for death to redress the wrongs of life."

"Many a time," continued Robert, "have I heard her humming to herself in the kitchen and saying, 'I has my trials, ups and downs, but it won't allers be so. I specs one day to wing and wing wid de angels, Hallelujah! Den I specs to hear a voice sayin', "Poor ole Kizzy, she's done de bes' she kin. Go down, Gabriel, an' tote her in." Den I specs to put on my golden slippers, my long white robe, an' my starry crown, an' walk dem golden streets, Hallelujah!' I've known that dear, old soul to travel going on two miles, after her work was done, to have someone read to her. Her favorite chapter began with, 'Let not your heart be troubled, ye believe in God, believe also in Me.'"

"I have been deeply impressed," said Captain Sybil, "with the childlike faith of some of these people. I do not mean to say that they are consistent Christians, but I do think that this faith has in a measure underlain the life of the race. It has been a golden thread woven amid the sombre tissues of their lives. A ray of light shimmering amid the gloom of their condition. And what would they have been without it?"

"I don't know. But I know what she was with it. And I believe if there are any saints in glory, Aunt Kizzy is one of them."

"She is dead, then?"

"Yes, went all right, singing and rejoicing until the last, 'Troubles over, troubles over, and den my troubles will be over. We'll walk de golden streets all 'roun' in de New Jerusalem.' Now, Captain, that's the kind of religion that I want. Not that kind which could ride to church on Sundays, and talk so solemn with the minister about heaven and good things, then come home and light down on the servants like a thousand of bricks. I have no use for it. I don't believe in it. I never did and I never will. If any man wants to save my soul he ain't got to beat my body. That ain't the kind of religion I'm looking for. I ain't got a bit of use for it. Now, Captain, ain't I right?"

"Well, yes, Robert, I think you are more than half right. You ought to know my dear, old mother who lives in Maine. We have had colored company at our house, and I never saw her show the least difference between her colored and white guests. She is a Quaker preacher, and don't believe in war, but when the rest of the young men went to the front, I wanted to go also. So I thought it all over, and there seemed to be no way out of slavery except through the war. I had been taught to hate war and detest slavery. Now the time had come when I could not help the war, but I could strike a blow for freedom. So I told my mother I was going to the front, that I expected to be killed, but I went to free the slave. It went hard with her. But I thought that I ought to come, and I believe my mother's prayers are following me."

"Captain," said Robert, rising, "I am glad that I have heard your story. I think that some of these Northern soldiers do two things—hate slavery and hate niggers."

"I am afraid that is so with some of them. They would rather be whipped by Rebels than conquer with Negroes. Oh, I heard a soldier," said Captain Sybil, "say, when the colored men were being enlisted, that he would break his sword and resign. But he didn't do either. After Colonel Shaw led his charge at Fort Wagner, and died in the conflict, he got bravely over his prejudices. The conduct of the colored troops there and elsewhere has done much to turn public opinion in their favor. I suppose any white soldier would rather have his black substitute receive the bullets than himself."

7.
TOM ANDERSON'S DEATH.

"Where is Tom?" asked Captain Sybil; "I have not seen him for several hours."

"He's gone down the sound with some of the soldiers," replied Robert.

"They wanted Tom to row them."

"I am afraid those boys will get into trouble, and the Rebs will pick them off," responded Sybil.

"O, I hope not," answered Robert.

"I hope not, too; but those boys are too venturesome."

"Tom knows the lay of the land better than any of us," said Robert. "He is the most wide-awake and gamiest man I know. I reckon when the war is over Tom will be a preacher. Did you ever hear him pray?"

"No; is he good at that?"

"First-rate," continued Robert. "It would do you good to hear him. He don't allow any cursing and swearing when he's around. And what he says is law and gospel with the boys. But he's so good-natured; and they can't get mad at him."

"Yes, Robert, there is not a man in our regiment I would sooner trust than Tom. Last night, when he brought in that wounded scout, he couldn't have been more tender if he had been a woman. How gratefully the poor fellow looked in Tom's face as he laid him down so carefully and staunched the blood which had been spurting out of him. Tom seemed to know it was an artery which had been cut, and he did just the right thing to stop the bleeding. He knew there wasn't a moment to be lost. He wasn't going to wait for the doctor. I have often heard that colored people are ungrateful, but I don't think Tom's worst enemy would say that about him."

"Captain," said Robert, with a tone of bitterness in his voice, "what had we to be grateful for? For ages of poverty, ignorance, and slavery? I think if anybody should be grateful, it is the people who have enslaved us and lived off our labor for generations. Captain, I used to know a poor old woman who couldn't bear to hear any one play on the piano."

"Is that so? Why, I always heard that colored people were a musical race."

39

"So we are; but that poor woman's daughter was sold, and her mistress took the money to buy a piano. Her mother could never bear to hear a sound from it."

"Poor woman!" exclaimed Captain Sybil, sympathetically; "I suppose it seemed as if the wail of her daughter was blending with the tones of the instrument. I think, Robert, there is a great deal more in the colored people than we give them credit for. Did you know Captain Sellers?"

"The officer who escaped from prison and got back to our lines?" asked Robert.

"Yes. Well, he had quite an experience in trying to escape. He came to an aged couple, who hid him in their cabin and shared their humble food with him. They gave him some cornbread, bacon, and coffee which he thought was made of scorched bran. But he said that he never ate a meal that he relished more than the one he took with them. Just before he went they knelt down and prayed with him. It seemed as if his very hair stood on his head, their prayer was so solemn. As he was going away the man took some shingles and nailed them on his shoes to throw the bloodhounds off his track. I don't think he will ever cease to feel kindly towards colored people. I do wonder what has become of the boys? What can keep them so long?"

Just as Captain Sybil and Robert were wondering at the delay of Tom and the soldiers they heard the measured tread of men who were slowly bearing a burden. They were carrying Tom Anderson to the hospital, fearfully wounded, and nigh to death. His face was distorted, and the blood was streaming from his wounds. His respiration was faint, his pulse hurried, as if life were trembling on its frailest cords.

Robert and Captain Sybil hastened at once towards the wounded man. On Robert's face was a look of intense anguish, as he bent pityingly over his friend.

"O, this is dreadful! How did it happen?" cried Robert.

Captain Sybil, pressing anxiously forward, repeated Robert's question.

"Captain," said one of the young soldiers, advancing and saluting his superior officer, "we were all in the boat when it struck against a mud bank, and there was not strength enough among us to shove her back into the water. Just then the Rebels opened fire upon us. For a while we lay down in the boat, but still they kept firing. Tom took in the whole situation, and said: 'Someone must die to get us out of this. I mought's well be him as any. You are soldiers and can fight. If they kill me, it is nuthin'.' So Tom leaped out to shove the boat into the water. Just then the Rebel bullets began to rain around him. He received seven or eight of them, and I'm afraid there is no hope for him."

"O, Tom, I wish you hadn't gone. O, Tom! Tom!" cried Robert, in tones of agony.

A gleam of grateful recognition passed over the drawn features of Tom, as the wail of his friend fell on his ear. He attempted to speak, but the words died upon his lips, and he became unconscious.

"Well," said Captain Sybil, "put him in one of the best wards. Give him into Miss Leroy's care. If good nursing can win him back to life, he shall not want for any care or pains that she can bestow. Send immediately for Dr. Gresham."

Robert followed his friend into the hospital, tenderly and carefully helped to lay him down, and remained awhile, gazing in silent grief upon the sufferer. Then he turned to go, leaving him in the hands of Iola, but hoping against hope that his wounds would not be fatal.

With tender devotion Iola watched her faithful friend. He recognized her when restored to consciousness, and her presence was as balm to his wounds. He smiled faintly, took her hand in his, stroked it tenderly, looked wistfully into her face, and said, "Miss Iola, I ain't long fer dis! I'se 'most home!"

"Oh, no," said Iola, "I hope that you will soon get over this trouble, and live many long and happy days."

"No, Miss Iola, it's all ober wid me. I'se gwine to glory; gwine to glory; gwine to ring dem charmin' bells. Tell all de boys to meet me in heben; dat dey mus' 'list in de hebenly war."

"O, Mr. Tom," said Iola, tenderly, "do not talk of leaving me. You are the best friend I have had since I was torn from my mother. I should be so lonely without you."

"Dere's a frien' dat sticks closer dan a brudder. He will be wid yer in de sixt' trial, an' in de sebbent' he'll not fo'sake yer."

"Yes," answered Iola, "I know that. He is all our dependence. But I can't help grieving when I see you suffering so. But, dear friend, be quiet, and try to go to sleep."

"I'll do enythin' fer yer, Miss Iola."

Tom closed his eyes and lay quiet. Tenderly and anxiously Iola watched over him as the hours waned away. The doctor came, shook his head gravely, and, turning to Iola, said, "There is no hope, but do what you can to alleviate his sufferings."

As Iola gazed upon the kind but homely features of Tom, she saw his eyes open and an unexpressed desire upon his face.

Tenderly and sadly bending over him, with tears in her dark, luminous eyes, she said, "Is there anything I can do for you?"

"Yes," said Tom, with laboring breath; "let me hole yore han', an' sing 'Ober Jordan inter glory' an' 'We'll anchor bye and bye.'"

Iola laid her hand gently in the rough palm of the dying man, and, with a tremulous voice, sang the parting hymns.

Tenderly she wiped the death damps from his dusky brow, and imprinted upon it a farewell kiss. Gratitude and affection lit up the dying eye, which seemed to be gazing into the eternities. Just then Robert entered the room, and, seating himself quietly by Tom's bedside, read the death signs in his face.

"Goodbye, Robert," said Tom, "meet me in de kingdom." Suddenly a look of recognition and rapture lit up his face, and he murmured, "Angels, bright angels, all's well, all's well!"

Slowly his hand released its pressure, a peaceful calm overspread his countenance, and without a sigh or murmur Thomas Anderson, Iola's faithful and devoted friend, passed away, leaving the world so much poorer for her than it was before. Just then Dr. Gresham, the hospital physician, came to the bedside, felt for the pulse which would never throb again, and sat down in silence by the cot.

"What do you think, Doctor," said Iola, "has he fainted?"

"No," said the doctor, "poor fellow! He is dead."

Iola bowed her head in silent sorrow, and then relieved the anguish of her heart by a flood of tears. Robert rose, and sorrowfully left the room.

Iola, with tearful eyes and aching heart, clasped the cold hands over the still breast, closed the waxen lid over the eye which had once beamed with kindness or flashed with courage, and then went back, after the burial, to her daily round of duties, feeling the sad missing of something from her life.

8.
THE MYSTIFIED DOCTOR.

"Colonel," said Dr. Gresham to Col. Robinson, the commander of the post,
"I am perfectly mystified by Miss Leroy."

"What is the matter with her?" asked Col. Robinson. "Is she not faithful to her duties and obedient to your directions?"

"Faithful is not the word to express her tireless energy and devotion to her work," responded Dr. Gresham. "She must have been a born nurse to put such enthusiasm into her work."

"Why, Doctor, what is the matter with you? You talk like a lover."

A faint flush rose to the cheek of Dr. Gresham as he smiled, and said, "Oh, come now, Colonel! Can't a man praise a woman without being in love with her?"

"Of course he can," said Col. Robinson; "but I know where such admiration is apt to lead. I've been there myself. But, Doctor, had you not better defer your lovemaking till you're out of the woods?"

"I assure you, Colonel, I am not thinking of love or courtship. That is the business of the drawing-room, and not of the camp. But she did mystify me last night."

"How so?" asked Col. Robinson.

"When Tom was dying," responded the doctor, "I saw that beautiful and refined young lady bend over and kiss him. When she found that he was dead, she just cried as if her heart was breaking. Well, that was a new thing to me. I can eat with colored people, walk, talk, and fight with them, but kissing them is something I don't hanker after."

"And yet you saw Miss Leroy do it?"

"Yes, and that puzzles me. She is one of the most refined and ladylike women I ever saw. I hear she is a refugee, but she does not look like the other refugees who have come to our camp. Her accent is slightly Southern, but her manner is Northern. She is self-respecting without being supercilious; quiet, without being dull. Her voice is low and sweet, yet at times there are tones of such passionate tenderness in it that you would think some great sorrow has darkened and overshadowed her life. Without being the least gloomy, her face at times is pervaded by an air of inexpressible sadness. I sometimes watch her when she is not aware that I

43

am looking at her, and it seems as if a whole volume was depicted on her countenance. When she smiles, there is a longing in her eyes which is never satisfied. I cannot understand how a Southern lady, whose education and manners stamp her as a woman of fine culture and good breeding, could consent to occupy the position she so faithfully holds. It is a mystery I cannot solve. Can you?"

"I think I can," answered Col. Robinson.

"Will you tell me?" queried the doctor.

"Yes, on one condition."

"What is it?"

"Everlasting silence."

"I promise," said the doctor. "The secret between us shall be as deep as the sea."

"She has not requested secrecy, but at present, for her sake, I do not wish the secret revealed. Miss Leroy was a slave."

"Oh, no," said Dr. Gresham, starting to his feet, "it can't be so! A woman as white as she a slave?"

"Yes, it is so," continued the Colonel. "In these States the child follows the condition of its mother. This beautiful and accomplished girl was held by one of the worst Rebels in town. Tom told me of it and I issued orders for her release."

"Well, well! Is that so?" said Dr. Gresham, thoughtfully stroking his beard. "Wonders will never cease. Why, I was just beginning to think seriously of her."

"What's to hinder your continuing to think?" asked Col. Robinson.

"What you tell me changes the whole complexion of affairs," replied the doctor.

"If that be so I am glad I told you before you got head over heels in love."

"Yes," said Dr. Gresham, absently.

Dr. Gresham was a member of a wealthy and aristocratic family, proud of its lineage, which it could trace through generations of good blood to its ancestral isle. He had become deeply interested in Iola before he had heard her story, but after it had been revealed to him he tried to banish her from his mind; but his constant observation of her only increased his interest and admiration. The deep pathos of her story, the tenderness of her ministrations, bestowed alike on black and white, and the sad loneliness of her condition, awakened within him a desire to defend and protect her all through her future life. The fierce clashing of war had not taken all the romance out of his nature. In Iola he saw realized his ideal of the woman whom he was willing to marry. A woman, tender, strong, and courageous, and rescued only by the strong arm of his Government from a fate worse than death. She was young in years, but old in sorrow; one whom a sad destiny had changed from a lighthearted girl to a heroic woman. As he observed her, he detected an undertone of sorrow in her most cheerful words, and observed a quick flushing and sudden paling of her cheek, as if she were living over scenes that were thrilling her soul with indignation or chilling her heart with horror. As nurse and physician, Iola and Dr. Gresham were constantly thrown together. His friends sent him magazines and books, which he gladly shared with her. The hospital was a sad place. Mangled forms, stricken down in the flush of their prime and energy; pale young corpses, sacrificed on the altar of slavery, constantly drained on her sympathies. Dr. Gresham was glad to have some reading matter which might divert her mind from the memories of her mournful past, and also furnish them both with interesting themes of conversation in their moments of relaxation from the harrowing scenes through which they were constantly passing. Without any effort or consciousness on her part, his friendship ripened into love. To him her presence was a pleasure, her absence a privation; and her loneliness drew deeply upon his sympathy. He would have merited his own self-contempt if, by word or deed, he had done anything to take advantage of her situation. All the manhood and chivalry of his nature rose in her behalf, and, after carefully revolving the matter, he resolved to win her for his bride, bury her secret in his Northern home, and hide from his aristocratic relations all knowledge of her mournful past. One day he said to Iola:—

"This hospital life is telling on you. Your strength is failing, and although you possess a wonderful amount of physical endurance, you must not forget that saints have bodies and dwell in tabernacles of clay, just the same as we common mortals."

"Compliments aside," she said, smiling; "what are you driving at, Doctor?"

"I mean," he replied, "that you are running down, and if you do not quit and take some rest you will be our patient instead of our nurse. You'd better take a furlough, go North, and return after the first frost."

"Doctor, if that is your only remedy," replied Iola, "I am afraid that I am destined to die at my post. I have no special friends in the North, and no home but this in the South. I am homeless and alone."

There was something so sad, almost despairing in her tones, in the drooping of her head, and the quivering of her lip, that they stirred Dr. Gresham's heart with sudden pity, and, drawing nearer to her, he said, "Miss Leroy, you need not be all alone. Let me claim the privilege of making your life bright and happy. Iola, I have loved you ever since I have seen your devotion to our poor, sick boys. How faithfully you, a young and gracious girl, have stood at your post and performed your duties. And now I ask, will you not permit me to clasp hands with you for life? I do not ask for a hasty reply. Give yourself time to think over what I have proposed."

9.
EUGENE LEROY AND ALFRED LORRAINE.

Nearly twenty years before the war, two young men, of French and Spanish descent, sat conversing on a large verandah which surrounded an ancient home on the Mississippi River. It was French in its style of architecture, large and rambling, with no hint of modern improvements.

The owner of the house was the only heir of a Creole planter. He had come into possession of an inheritance consisting of vast baronial estates, bank stock, and a large number of slaves. Eugene Leroy, being deprived of his parents, was left, at an early age, to the care of a distant relative, who had sent him to school and college, and who occasionally invited him to spend his vacations at his home. But Eugene generally declined his invitations, as he preferred spending his vacations at the watering places in the North, with their fashionable and not always innocent gayeties. Young, vivacious, impulsive, and undisciplined, without the restraining influence of a mother's love or the guidance of a father's hand, Leroy found himself, when his college days were over, in the dangerous position of a young man with vast possessions, abundant leisure, unsettled principles, and uncontrolled desires. He had no other object than to extract from life its most seductive draughts of ease and pleasure. His companion, who sat opposite him on the verandah, quietly smoking a cigar, was a remote cousin, a few years older than himself, the warmth of whose Southern temperament had been modified by an infusion of Northern blood.

Eugene was careless, liberal, and impatient of details, while his companion and cousin, Alfred Lorraine, was selfish, eager, keen, and alert; also hard, cold, methodical, and ever ready to grasp the main chance. Yet, notwithstanding the difference between them, they had formed a warm friendship for each other.

"Alfred," said Eugene, "I am going to be married."

Lorraine opened his eyes with sudden wonder, and exclaimed: "Well, that's the latest thing out! Who is the fortunate lady who has bound you with her silken fetters? Is it one of those beautiful Creole girls who were visiting Augustine's plantation last winter? I watched you during our visit there and thought that you could not be proof against their attractions. Which is your choice? It would puzzle me to judge between the two. They had splendid eyes, dark, luminous, and languishing; lovely complexions and magnificent hair. Both were delightful in their manners, refined and cultured, with an air of vivacity mingled with their repose of manner which was perfectly charming. As the law only allows us one, which is your choice? Miss Annette has more force than her sister, and if I could afford the luxury of a wife she would be my choice."

"Ah, Alf," said Eugene, "I see that you are a practical business man. In marrying you want a wife to assist you as an efficient plantation mistress. One who would tolerate no waste in the kitchen and no disorder in the parlor."

"Exactly so," responded Lorraine; "I am too poor to marry a mere parlor ornament. You can afford to do it; I cannot."

"Nonsense, if I were as poor as a church mouse I would marry the woman I love."

"Very fine sentiments," said Lorraine, "and were I as rich as you I would indulge in them also. You know, when my father died I had great expectations. We had always lived in good style, and I never thought for a moment he was not a rich man, but when his estate was settled I found it was greatly involved, and I was forced to face an uncertain future, with scarcely a dollar to call my own. Land, Negroes, cattle, and horses all went under the hammer. The only thing I retained was the education I received at the North; that was my father's best investment, and all my stock in trade. With that only as an outfit, it would be madness for me to think of marrying one of those lovely girls. They remind me of beautiful canary birds, charming and pretty, but not fitted for the wear and tear of plantation life. Well, which is your choice?"

"Neither," replied Eugene.

"Then, is it that magnificent looking widow from New Orleans, whom we met before you had that terrible spell of sickness and to whom you appeared so devoted?"

"Not at all. I have not heard from her since that summer. She was fascinating and handsome, but fearfully high strung."

"Were you afraid of her?"

"No; but I valued my happiness too much to trust it in her hands."

"Sour grapes!" said Lorraine.

"No! But I think that slavery and the lack of outside interests are beginning to tell on the lives of our women. They lean too much on their slaves, have too much irresponsible power in their hands, are narrowed and compressed by the routine of plantation life and the lack of intellectual stimulus."

"Yes, Eugene, when I see what other women are doing in the fields of literature and art, I cannot help thinking an amount of brain power has been held in check among us. Yet I cannot abide those Northern women, with their suffrage views and abolition cant. They just shock me."

"But your mother was a Northern woman," said Eugene.

"Yes; but she got bravely over her Northern ideas. As I remember her, she was just as much a Southerner as if she had been to the manor born. She came here as a schoolteacher, but soon after she came she married my father. He was easy and indulgent with his servants, and held them with a very loose rein. But my mother was firm and energetic. She made the niggers move around. No shirking nor dawdling with her. When my father died, she took matters in hand, but she only outlived him a few months. If she had lived I believe that she would have retrieved our fortune. I know that she had more executive ability than my father. He was very squeamish about selling his servants, but she would have put every one of them in her pocket before permitting them to eat her out of house and home. But whom *are* you going to marry?"

"A young lady who graduates from a Northern seminary next week," responded Eugene.

"I think you are very selfish," said Lorraine. "You might have invited a fellow to go with you to be your best man."

"The wedding is to be strictly private. The lady whom I am to marry has Negro blood in her veins."

"The devil she has!" exclaimed Lorraine, starting to his feet, and looking incredulously on the face of Leroy. "Are you in earnest? Surely you must be jesting."

"I am certainly in earnest," answered Eugene Leroy. "I mean every word I say."

"Oh, it can't be possible! Are you mad?" exclaimed Lorraine.

"Never was saner in my life."

"What under heaven could have possessed you to do such a foolish thing? Where did she come from."

"Right here, on this plantation. But I have educated and manumitted her, and I intend marrying her."

"Why, Eugene, it is impossible that you can have an idea of marrying one of your slaves. Why, man, she is your property, to have and to hold to all intents and purposes. Are you not satisfied with the power and possession the law gives you?"

"No. Although the law makes her helpless in my hands, to me her defenselessness is her best defense."

"Eugene, we have known each other all of our lives, and, although I have always regarded you as eccentric, I never saw you so completely off your balance before. The idea of you, with your proud family name, your vast wealth in land and Negroes, intending to marry one of them, is a mystery I cannot solve. Do explain to me why you are going to take this extremely strange and foolish step."

"You never saw Marie?"

"No; and I don't want to."

"She is very beautiful. In the North no one would suspect that she has one drop of Negro blood in her veins, but here, where I am known, to marry her is to lose caste. I could live with her, and not incur much if any social opprobrium. Society would wink at the transgression, even if after she had become the mother of my children I should cast her off and send her and them to the auction block."

"Men," replied Lorraine, "would merely shrug their shoulders; women would say you had been sowing your wild oats. Your money, like charity, would cover a multitude of faults."

"But if I make her my lawful wife and recognize her children as my legitimate heirs, I subject myself to social ostracism and a senseless persecution. We Americans boast of freedom, and yet here is a woman whom I love as I never loved any other human being, but both law and public opinion debar me from following the inclination of my heart. She is beautiful, faithful, and pure, and yet all that society will tolerate is what I would scorn to do."

"But has not society the right to guard the purity of its blood by the rigid exclusion of an alien race?"

"Excluding it! How?" asked Eugene.

"By debarring it from social intercourse."

"Perhaps it has," continued Eugene, "but should not society have a greater ban for those who, by consorting with an alien race, rob their offspring of a right to their names and to an inheritance in their property, and who fix their social status among an enslaved and outcast race? Don't eye me so curiously; I am not losing my senses."

"I think you have done that already," said Lorraine. "Don't you know that if she is as fair as a lily, beautiful as a houri, and chaste as ice, that still she is a Negro?"

"Oh, come now; she isn't much of a Negro."

"It doesn't matter, however. One drop of Negro blood in her veins curses all the rest."

"I know it," said Eugene, sadly, "but I have weighed the consequences, and am prepared to take them."

"Well, Eugene, your course is *so* singular! I do wish that you would tell me why you take this unprecedented step?"

Eugene laid aside his cigar, looked thoughtfully at Lorraine, and said, "Well, Alfred, as we are kinsmen and lifelong friends, I will not resent your asking my reason for doing that which seems to you the climax of absurdity, and if you will have the patience to listen I will tell you."

"Proceed, I am all attention."

"My father died," said Eugene, "as you know, when I was too young to know his loss or feel his care and, being an only child, I was petted and spoiled. I grew up to be wayward, self-indulgent, proud, and imperious. I went from home and made many friends both at college and in foreign lands. I was well supplied with money and, never having been forced to earn it, was ignorant of its value and careless of its use. My lavish expenditures and liberal benefactions attracted to me a number of parasites, and men older than myself led me into the paths of vice, and taught me how to gather the flowers of sin which blossom around the borders of hell. In a word, I left my home unwarned and unarmed against the seductions of vice. I returned an initiated devotee to debasing pleasures. Years of my life were passed in foreign lands; years in which my soul slumbered and seemed pervaded with a moral paralysis; years, the memory of which fills my soul with sorrow and shame. I went to the capitals of the old world to see life, but in seeing life I became acquainted with death, the death of true manliness and self-respect. You look astonished; but I tell you, Alf, there is many a poor clodhopper, on whom are the dust and grime of unremitting toil, who feels more self-respect and true manliness than many of us with our family prestige, social position, and proud ancestral halls. After I had lived abroad for years, I returned a broken-down young man, prematurely old, my constitution a perfect wreck. A life of folly and dissipation was telling fearfully upon me. My friends shrank from me in dismay. I was sick nigh unto death, and had it not been for Marie's care I am certain that I should have died. She followed me down to the borders of the grave, and won me back to life and health. I was slow in recovering and, during the time, I had ample space for reflection, and the past unrolled itself before me. I resolved, over the wreck and ruin of my past life, to build a better and brighter future. Marie had a voice of remarkable sweetness, although it lacked culture. Often when I was nervous and restless I would have her sing some of those weird and plaintive melodies which she had learned from the plantation Negroes. Sometimes I encouraged her to talk, and I was surprised at the native vigor of her intellect. By degrees I became acquainted with her history. She was all alone in the world. She had no recollection of her father, but remembered being torn from her mother while clinging to her dress. The trader who bought her mother did not wish to buy her. She remembered having a brother, with whom she used to play, but she had been separated from him also, and since then had lost all trace of them. After she was sold from her mother she became the property of an excellent old lady, who seems to have been very careful to imbue her mind with good principles; a woman who loved purity, not only for her own daughters, but also for the defenseless girls in her home. I believe it was the lady's intention to have freed Marie at her death, but she died suddenly, and, the estate being involved, she was sold with it and fell into the hands of my agent. I became deeply interested in her when I heard her story, and began to pity her."

"And I suppose love sprang from pity."

"I not only pitied her, but I learned to respect her. I had met with beautiful women in the halls of wealth and fashion, both at home and abroad, but there was something in her different from all my experience of womanhood."

"I should think so," said Lorraine, with a sneer; "but I should like to know what it was."

"It was something such as I have seen in old cathedrals, lighting up the beauty of a saintly face. A light which the poet tells was never seen on land or sea. I thought of this beautiful and defenseless girl adrift in the power of a reckless man, who, with all the advantages of wealth and education, had trailed his manhood in the dust, and she, with simple, childlike faith in the Unseen, seemed to be so good and pure that she commanded my respect and won my heart. In her presence every base and unholy passion died, subdued by the supremacy of her virtue."

"Why, Eugene, what has come over you? Talking of the virtue of these quadroon girls! You have lived so long in the North and abroad, that you seem to have lost the cue of our Southern life. Don't you know that these beautiful girls have been the curse of our homes? You have no idea of the hearts which are wrung by their presence."

"But, Alfred, suppose it is so. Are they to blame for it? What can any woman do when she is placed in the hands of an irresponsible master; when she knows that resistance is vain? Yes, Alfred, I agree with you, these women are the bane of our Southern civilization; but they are the victims and we are the criminals."

"I think from the airs that some of them put on when they get a chance, that they are very willing victims."

"So much the worse for our institution. If it is cruel to debase a hapless victim, it is an increase of cruelty to make her contented with her degradation. Let me tell you, Alf, you cannot wrong or degrade a woman without wronging or degrading yourself."

"What is the matter with you, Eugene? Are you thinking of taking priest's orders?"

"No, Alf," said Eugene, rising and rapidly pacing the floor, "you may defend the system as much as you please, but you cannot deny that the circumstances it creates, and the temptations it affords, are sapping our strength and undermining our character."

"That may be true," said Lorraine, somewhat irritably, "but you had better be careful how you air your Northern notions in public."

"Why so?"

"Because public opinion is too sensitive to tolerate any such discussions."

"And is not that a proof that we are at fault with respect to our institutions?"

"I don't know. I only know we are living in the midst of a magazine of powder, and it is not safe to enter it with a lighted candle."

"Let me proceed with my story," continued Eugene. "During the long months in which I was convalescing, I was left almost entirely to the companionship of Marie. In my library I found a Bible, which I began to read from curiosity, but my curiosity deepened into interest when I saw the rapt expression on Marie's face. I saw in it a loving response to sentiments to which I was a stranger. In the meantime my conscience was awakened, and I scorned to take advantage of her defenselessness. I felt that I owed my life to her faithful care, and I resolved to take her North, manumit, educate, and marry her. I sent her to a Northern academy, but as soon as some of the pupils found that she was colored, objections were raised, and the principal was compelled to dismiss her. During my search for a school I heard of one where three girls of mixed blood were pursuing their studies, every one of whom would have been ignominiously dismissed had their connection with the Negro race been known. But I determined to run no risks. I found a school where her connection with the Negro race would be no bar to her advancement. She graduates next week, and I intend to marry her before I return home. She was faithful when others were faithless, stood by me when others deserted me to die in loneliness and neglect, and now I am about to reward her care with all the love and devotion it is in my power to bestow. That is why I am about to marry my faithful and devoted nurse, who snatched me from the jaws of death. Now that I have told you my story, what say you?"

"Madness and folly inconceivable!" exclaimed Lorraine.

"What to you is madness and folly is perfect sanity with me. After all, Alf, is there not an amount of unreason in our prejudices?"

"That may be true; but I wasn't reasoned into it, and I do not expect to be reasoned out of it."

"Will you accompany me North?"

"No; except to put you in an insane asylum. You are the greatest crank out," said Lorraine, thoroughly disgusted.

"No, thank you; I'm all right. I expect to start North tomorrow. You had better come and go."

"I would rather follow you to your grave," replied Lorraine, hotly, while an expression of ineffable scorn passed over his cold, proud face.

10.
SHADOWS IN THE HOME.

On the next morning after this conversation Leroy left for the North, to attend the commencement and witness the graduation of his ward. Arriving in Ohio, he immediately repaired to the academy and inquired for the principal. He was shown into the reception-room, and in a few moments the principal entered.

"Good morning," said Leroy, rising and advancing towards him; "how is my ward this morning?"

"She is well, and has been expecting you. I am glad you came in time for the commencement. She stands among the foremost in her class."

"I am glad to hear it. Will you send her this?" said Leroy, handing the principal a card. The principal took the card and immediately left the room.

Very soon Leroy heard a light step, and looking up he saw a radiantly beautiful woman approaching him.

"Good morning, Marie," he said, greeting her cordially, and gazing upon her with unfeigned admiration. "You are looking very handsome this morning."

"Do you think so?" she asked, smiling and blushing. "I am glad you are not disappointed; that you do not feel your money has been spent in vain."

"Oh, no, what I have spent on your education has been the best investment I ever made."

"I hope," said Marie, "you may always find it so. But Mas—"

"Hush!" said Leroy, laying his hand playfully on her lips; "you are free. I don't want the dialect of slavery to linger on your lips. You must not call me that name again."

"Why not?"

"Because I have a nearer and dearer one by which I wish to be called."

Leroy drew her nearer, and whispered in her ear a single word. She started, trembled with emotion, grew pale, and blushed painfully. An awkward silence ensued, when Leroy, pressing her hand, exclaimed: "This is the hand that plucked me from the grave, and I am going to retain it as mine; mine to guard with my care until death us do part."

Leroy looked earnestly into her eyes, which fell beneath his ardent gaze. With admirable self-control, while a great joy was thrilling her heart, she bowed her beautiful head and softly repeated, "Until death us do part."

Leroy knew Southern society too well to expect it to condone his offense against its social customs, or give the least recognition to his wife, however cultured, refined, and charming she might be, if it were known that she had the least infusion of Negro blood in her veins. But he was brave enough to face the consequences of his alliance, and marry the woman who was the choice of his heart, and on whom his affections were centered.

After Leroy had left the room, Marie sat awhile thinking of the wonderful change that had come over her. Instead of being a lonely slave girl, with the fatal dower of beauty, liable to be bought and sold, exchanged, and bartered, she was to be the wife of a wealthy planter; a man in whose honor she could confide, and on whose love she could lean.

Very interesting and pleasant were the commencement exercises in which Marie bore an important part. To enlist sympathy for her enslaved race, and appear to advantage before Leroy, had aroused all of her energies. The stimulus of hope, the manly love which was environing her life, brightened her eye and lit up the wonderful beauty of her countenance. During her stay in the North she had constantly been brought in contact with anti-slavery people. She was not aware that there was so much kindness among the white people of the country until she had tested it in the North. From the anti-slavery people in private life she had learned some of the noblest lessons of freedom and justice, and had become imbued with their sentiments. Her theme was "American Civilization, its Lights and Shadows."

Graphically she portrayed the lights, faithfully she showed the shadows of our American civilization. Earnestly and feelingly she spoke of the blind Sampson in our land, who might yet shake the pillars of our great Commonwealth. Leroy listened attentively. At times a shadow of annoyance would overspread his face, but it was soon lost in the admiration her earnestness and zeal inspired. Like Esther pleading for the lives of her people in the Oriental courts of a despotic king, she stood before the audience, pleading for those whose lips were sealed, but whose condition appealed to the mercy and justice of the Nation. Strong men wiped the moisture from their eyes, and women's hearts throbbed in unison with the strong, brave words that were uttered in behalf of freedom for all and chains for none. Generous applause was freely bestowed, and beautiful bouquets were showered upon her. When it was known that she was to be the wife of her guardian, warm congratulations were given, and earnest hopes expressed for the welfare of the lonely girl, who, nearly all her life, had been deprived of a parent's love and care. On the eve of starting South, Leroy procured a license and united his destiny with the young lady whose devotion in the darkest hour had won his love and gratitude.

In a few days Marie returned as mistress to the plantation from which she had gone as a slave. But as unholy alliances were common in those days between masters and slaves, no one took especial notice that Marie shared

and divided among your relatives. I sometimes lie awake at night thinking of how there might be a screw loose somewhere, and, after all, the children and I might be reduced to slavery."

"Marie, what in the world is the matter with you? Have you had a presentiment of my death, or, as Uncle Jack says, 'hab you seed it in a vision?'"

"No, but I have had such sad forebodings that they almost set me wild. One night I dreamt that you were dead; that the lawyers entered the house, seized our property, and remanded us to slavery. I never can be satisfied in the South with such a possibility hanging over my head."

"Marie, dear, you are growing nervous. Your imagination is too active. You are left too much alone on this plantation. I hope that for your own and the children's sake I will be enabled to arrange our affairs so as to find a home for you where you will not be doomed to the social isolation and ostracism that surround you here."

"I don't mind the isolation for myself, but the children. You have enjoined silence on me with respect to their connection with the Negro race, but I do not think we can conceal it from them very long. It will not be long before Iola will notice the offishness of girls of her own age, and the scornful glances which, even now, I think, are leveled at her. Yesterday Harry came crying to me, and told me that one of the neighbor's boys had called him 'nigger.'"

A shadow flitted over Leroy's face, as he answered, somewhat soberly, "Oh, Marie, do not meet trouble half way. I have manumitted you, and the children will follow your condition. I have made you all legatees of my will. Except my cousin, Alfred Lorraine, I have only distant relatives, whom I scarcely know and who hardly know me."

"Your cousin Lorraine? Are you sure our interests would be safe in his hands?"

"I think so; I don't think Alfred would do anything dishonorable."

"He might not with his equals. But how many men would be bound by a sense of honor where the rights of a colored woman are in question? Your cousin was bitterly opposed to our marriage, and I would not trust any important interests in his hands. I do hope that in providing for our future you will make assurance doubly sure."

"I certainly will, and all that human foresight can do shall be done for you and our children."

"Oh," said Marie, pressing to her heart a beautiful child of six summers, "I think it would almost make me turn over in my grave to know that every grace and charm which this child possesses would only be so much added to her value as an article of merchandise."

As Marie released the child from her arms she looked wonderingly into her mother's face and clung closely to her, as if to find refuge from some unseen evil. Leroy noticed this, and sighed unconsciously, as an expression of pain flitted over his face.

"Now, Marie," he continued, "stop tormenting yourself with useless fears. Although, with all her faults, I still love the South, I will make arrangements either to live North or go to France. There life will be brighter for us all. Now, Marie, seat yourself at the piano and sing:—

> 'Sing me the songs that to me were so dear,
>   Long, long ago.
> Sing me the songs I delighted to hear,
>   Long, long ago.'"

As Marie sang the anxiety faded from her face, a sense of security stole over her, and she sat among her loved ones a happy wife and mother. What if no one recognized her on that lonely plantation! Her world was, nevertheless, there. The love and devotion of her husband brightened every avenue of her life, while her children filled her home with music, mirth, and sunshine.

Marie had undertaken their education, but she could not give them the culture which comes from the attrition of thought, and from contact with the ideas of others. Since her schooldays she had read extensively and thought much, and in solitude her thoughts had ripened. But for her children there were no companions except the young slaves of the plantation, and she dreaded the effect of such intercourse upon their lives and characters.

Leroy had always been especially careful to conceal from his children the knowledge of their connection with the Negro race. To Marie this silence was oppressive.

One day she said to him, "I see no other way of finishing the education of these children than by sending them to some Northern school."

"I have come," said Leroy, "to the same conclusion. We had better take Iola and Harry North and make arrangements for them to spend several years in being educated. Riches take wings to themselves and fly away, but a good education is an investment on which the law can place no attachment. As there is a possibility of their origin being discovered, I will find a teacher to whom I can confide our story, and upon whom I can enjoin secrecy. I want them well-fitted for any emergency in life. When I discover for what they have the most aptitude I will give them especial training in that direction."

A troubled look passed over the face of Marie, as she hesitatingly said: "I am so afraid that you will regret our marriage when you fully realize the complications it brings."

"No, no," said Leroy, tenderly, "it is not that I regret our marriage, or feel the least disdain for our children on account of the blood in their veins; but I do not wish them to grow up under the contracting influence of this race prejudice. I do not wish them to feel that they have been born under a proscription from which no valor can redeem them, nor that any social advancement or individual development can wipe off the ban which clings to them. No, Marie, let them go North, learn all they can, aspire all they may. The painful knowledge will come all too soon. Do not forestall it. I want them simply to grow up as other children; not being patronized by friends nor disdained by foes."

"My dear husband, you may be perfectly right, but are you not preparing our children for a fearful awakening? Are you not acting on the plan, 'After me the deluge?'"

"Not at all, Marie. I want our children to grow up without having their self-respect crushed in the bud. You know that the North is not free from racial prejudice."

"I know it," said Marie, sadly, "and I think one of the great mistakes of our civilization is that which makes color, and not character, a social test."

"I think so, too," said Leroy. "The strongest men and women of a downtrodden race may bare their bosoms to an adverse fate and develop courage in the midst of opposition, but we have no right to subject our children to such crucial tests before their characters are formed. For years, when I lived abroad, I had an opportunity to see and hear of men of African descent who had distinguished themselves and obtained a recognition in European circles, which they never could have gained in this country. I now recall the name of Ira Aldridge, a colored man from New York City, who was covered with princely honors as a successful tragedian. Alexander Dumas was not forced to conceal his origin to succeed as a novelist. When I was in St. Petersburg I was shown the works of Alexander Sergevitch, a Russian poet, who was spoken of as the Byron of Russian literature, and reckoned one of the finest poets that Russia has produced in this century. He was also a prominent figure in fashionable society, and yet he was of African lineage. One of his paternal ancestors was a Negro who had been ennobled by Peter the Great. I can't help contrasting the recognition which these men had received with the treatment which has been given to Frederick Douglass and other intelligent colored men in this country. With me the wonder is not that they have achieved so little, but that they have accomplished so much. No, Marie, we will have our children educated without being subjected to the depressing influences of caste feeling. Perhaps by the time their education is finished I will be ready to wind up my affairs and take them abroad, where merit and ability will give them entrance into the best circles of art, literature, and science."

After this conversation Leroy and his wife went North, and succeeded in finding a good school for their children. In a private interview he confided to the principal the story of the cross in their blood, and, finding him apparently free from racial prejudice, he gladly left the children in his care. Gracie, the youngest child, remained at home, and her mother spared no pains to fit her for the seminary against the time her sister should have finished her education.

II.
THE PLAGUE AND THE LAW.

Years passed, bringing no special change to the life of Leroy and his wife. Shut out from the busy world, its social cares and anxieties, Marie's life flowed peacefully on. Although removed by the protecting care of Leroy from the condition of servitude, she still retained a deep sympathy for the enslaved, and was ever ready to devise plans to ameliorate their condition.

Leroy, although in the midst of slavery, did not believe in the rightfulness of the institution. He was in favor of gradual emancipation, which would prepare both master and slave for a moral adaptation to the new conditions of freedom. While he was willing to have the old rivets taken out of slavery, politicians and planters were devising plans to put in new screws. He was desirous of having it ended in the States; they were clamorous to have it established in the Territories.

But so strong was the force of habit, combined with the feebleness of his moral resistance and the nature of his environment that instead of being an athlete, armed for a glorious strife, he had learned to drift where he should have steered, to float with the current instead of nobly breasting the tide. He conducted his plantation with as much lenity as it was possible to infuse into a system darkened with the shadow of a million crimes.

Leroy had always been especially careful not to allow his children to spend their vacations at home. He and Marie generally spent that time with them at some summer resort.

"I would like," said Marie, one day, "to have our children spend their vacations at home. Those summer resorts are pleasant, yet, after all, there is no place like home. But," and her voice became tremulous, "our children would now notice their social isolation and inquire the cause." A faint sigh arose to the lips of Leroy, as she added: "Man is a social being; I've known it to my sorrow."

There was a tone of sadness in Leroy's voice, as he replied: "Yes, Marie, let them stay North. We seem to be entering on a period fraught with great danger. I cannot help thinking and fearing that we are on the eve of a civil war."

"A civil war!" exclaimed Marie, with an air of astonishment. "A civil war about what?"

63

"Why, Marie, the thing looks to me so wild and foolish I hardly know how to explain. But some of our leading men have come to the conclusion that North and South had better separate, and instead of having one to have two independent governments. The spirit of secession is rampant in the land. I do not know what the result will be, and I fear it will bode no good to the country. Between the fire-eating Southerners and the meddling Abolitionists we are about to be plunged into a great deal of trouble. I fear there are breakers ahead. The South is dissatisfied with the state of public opinion in the North. We are realizing that we are two peoples in the midst of one nation. William H. Seward has proclaimed that the conflict between freedom and slavery is irrepressible, and that the country cannot remain half free and half slave."

"How will *you* go?" asked Marie.

"My heart is with the Union. I don't believe in secession. There has been no cause sufficient to justify a rupture. The North has met us time and again in the spirit of concession and compromise. When we wanted the continuance of the African slave trade the North conceded that we should have twenty years of slave-trading for the benefit of our plantations. When we wanted more territory she conceded to our desires and gave us land enough to carve out four States, and there yet remains enough for four more. When we wanted power to recapture our slaves when they fled North for refuge, Daniel Webster told Northerners to conquer their prejudices, and they gave us the whole Northern States as a hunting ground for our slaves. The Presidential chair has been filled the greater number of years by Southerners, and the majority of offices has been shared by our men. We wanted representation in Congress on a basis which would include our slaves, and the North, whose suffrage represents only men, gave us a three-fifths representation for our slaves, whom we count as property. I think the step will be suicidal. There are extremists in both sections, but I hope, between them both, wise counsels and measures will prevail."

Just then Alfred Lorraine was ushered into the room. Occasionally he visited Leroy, but he always came alone. His wife was the only daughter of an enterprising slave-trader, who had left her a large amount of property.

Her social training was deficient, her education limited, but she was too proud of being a pure white woman to enter the home of Leroy, with Marie as its presiding genius. Lorraine tolerated Marie's presence as a necessary evil, while to her he always seemed like a presentiment of trouble. With his coming a shadow fell upon her home, hushing its music and darkening its sunshine. A sense of dread oppressed her. There came into her soul an intuitive feeling that somehow his coming was fraught with danger. When not peering around she would often catch his eyes bent on her with a baleful expression.

Leroy and his cousin immediately fell into a discussion on the condition of the country. Lorraine was a rank Secessionist, ready to adopt the most extreme measures of the leaders of the movement, even to the reopening of the slave trade. Leroy thought a dissolution of the Union would involve a fearful expenditure of blood and treasure for which, before the eyes of the world, there could be no justification. The debate lasted late into the night, leaving both Lorraine and Leroy just as set in their opinions as they were before they began. Marie listened attentively awhile, then excused herself and withdrew.

After Lorraine had gone Marie said: "There is something about your cousin that fills me with nameless dread. I always feel when he enters the room as if someone were walking over my grave. I do wish he would stay at home."

"I wish so, too, since he disturbs you. But, Marie, you are growing nervous. How cold your hands are. Don't you feel well?"

"Oh, yes; I am only a little faint. I wish he would never come. But, as he does, I must make the best of it."

"Yes, Marie, treat him well for my sake. He is the only relative I have who ever darkens our doors."

"I have no faith in his friendship for either myself or my children. I feel that while he makes himself agreeable to you he hates me from the bottom of his heart, and would do anything to get me out of the way. Oh, I am *so* glad I am your lawful wife, and that you married me before you brought me back to this State! I believe that if you were gone he wouldn't have the least scruple against trying to prove our marriage invalid and remanding us to slavery."

Leroy looked anxiously and soberly at his wife, and said: "Marie, I do not think so. Your life is too lonely here. Write your orders to New Orleans, get what you need for the journey, and let us spend the summer somewhere in the North."

Just then Marie's attention was drawn to some household matters, and it was a short time before she returned.

"Tom," continued Leroy, "has just brought the mail, and here is a letter from Iola."

Marie noticed that he looked quite sober as he read, and that an expression of vexation was lingering on his lips.

"What is the matter?" asked Marie.

"Nothing much; only a tempest in a teapot. The presence of a colored girl in Mr. Galen's school has caused a breeze of excitement. You know Mr. Galen is quite an Abolitionist, and, being true to his principles, he could not consistently refuse when a colored woman applied for her daughter's admission. Of course, when he took her he was compelled to treat her as any other pupil. In so doing he has given mortal offense to the mother of two Southern boys. She has threatened to take them away if the colored girl remains."

"What will he do about it?" asked Marie, thoughtfully.

"Oh, it is a bitter pill, but I think he will have to swallow it. He is between two fires. He cannot dismiss her from the school and be true to his Abolition principles; yet if he retains her he will lose his Southern customers, and I know he cannot afford to do that."

"What does Iola say?"

"He has found another boarding place for her, but she is to remain in the school. He had to throw that sop to the whale."

"Does she take sides against the girl?"

"No, I don't think she does. She says she feels sorry for her, and that she would hate to be colored. 'It is so hard to be looked down on for what one can't help.'"

"Poor child! I wish we could leave the country. I never would consent to her marrying any one without first revealing to him her connection with the Negro race. This is a subject on which I am not willing to run any risks."

"My dear Marie, when you shall have read Iola's letter you will see it is more than a figment of my imagination that has made me so loth to have our children know the paralyzing power of caste."

Leroy, always liberal with his wife and children, spared neither pains nor expense to have them prepared for their summer outing. Iola was to graduate in a few days. Harry was attending a school in the State of Maine, and his father had written to him, apprising him of his intention to come North that season. In a few days Leroy and his wife started North, but before they reached Vicksburg they were met by the intelligence that the yellow fever was spreading in the Delta, and that pestilence was breathing its bane upon the morning air and distilling its poison upon the midnight dews.

"Let us return home," said Marie.

"It is useless," answered Leroy. "It is nearly two days since we left home. The fever is spreading south of us with fearful rapidity. To return home is to walk into the jaws of death. It was my intention to have stopped at Vicksburg, but now I will go on as soon as I can make the connections."

Early next morning Leroy and his wife started again on their journey. The cars were filled with terror-stricken people who were fleeing from death, when death was everywhere. They fled from the city only to meet the dreaded apparition in the country. As they journeyed on Leroy grew restless and feverish. He tried to brace himself against the infection which was creeping slowly but insidiously into his life, dulling his brain, fevering his blood, and prostrating his strength. But vain were all his efforts. He had no armor strong enough to repel the invasion of death. They stopped at a small town on the way and obtained the best medical skill and most careful nursing, but neither skill nor art availed. On the third day death claimed Leroy as a victim, and Marie wept in hopeless agony over the grave of her devoted husband, whose sad lot it was to die from home and be buried among strangers.

But before he died he placed his will in Marie's hands, saying: "I have left you well provided for. Kiss the children for me and bid them goodbye."

He tried to say a parting word to Gracie, but his voice failed, and he fainted into the stillness of death. A mortal paleness overspread his countenance, on which had already gathered the shadows that never deceive. In speechless agony Marie held his hand until it released its pressure in death, and then she stood alone beside her dead, with all the bright sunshine of her life fading into the shadows of the grave. Heartbroken and full of fearful forebodings, Marie left her cherished dead in the quiet village of H—— and returned to her death-darkened home.

It was a lovely day in June, birds were singing their sweetest songs, flowers were breathing their fragrance on the air, when Mam Liza, sitting at her cabin-door, talking with some of the house servants, saw a carriage approaching, and wondered who was coming.

"I wonder," she said, excitedly, "whose comin' to de house when de folks is done gone."

But her surprise was soon changed to painful amazement, when she saw Marie, robed in black, alighting from the carriage, and holding Gracie by the hand. She caught sight of the drooping head and grief-stricken face, and rushed to her, exclaiming:—

"Whar's Marse Eugene?"

"Dead," said Marie, falling into Mammy Liza's arms, sobbing out, "dead! *Died* of yellow fever."

A wild burst of sorrow came from the lips of the servants, who had drawn near.

"Where is he?" said Mam Liza, speaking like one suddenly bewildered.

"He is buried in H——. I could not bring him home," said Marie.

"My pore baby," said Mam Liza, with broken sobs. "I'se drefful sorry. My heart's most broke into two." Then, controlling herself, she dismissed the servants who stood around, weeping, and led Marie to her room.

"Come, honey, lie down an' lem'me git yer a cup ob tea."

"Oh, no; I don't want anything," said Marie, wringing her hands in bitter agony.

"Oh, honey," said Mam Liza, "yer musn't gib up. Yer knows whar to put yer trus'. Yer can't lean on de arm of flesh in dis tryin' time." Kneeling by the side of her mistress she breathed out a prayer full of tenderness, hope, and trust.

Marie grew calmer. It seemed as if that earnest, trustful prayer had breathed into her soul a feeling of resignation.

Gracie stood wonderingly by, vainly trying to comprehend the great sorrow which was overwhelming the life of her mother.

After the first great burst of sorrow was over, Marie sat down to her desk and wrote a letter to Iola, informing her of her father's death. By the time she had finished it she grew dizzy and faint, and fell into a swoon. Mammy Liza tenderly laid her on the bed, and helped restore her to consciousness.

Lorraine, having heard of his cousin's death, came immediately to see Marie. She was too ill to have an interview with him, but he picked up the letter she had written and obtained Iola's address.

Lorraine made a careful investigation of the case, to ascertain whether Marie's marriage was valid. To his delight he found there was a flaw in the marriage and an informality in the manumission. He then determined to invalidate Marie's claim, and divide the inheritance among Leroy's white relations. In a short time strangers, distant relatives of her husband, became frequent visitors at the plantation, and made themselves offensively familiar. At length the dreadful storm burst.

Alfred Lorraine entered suit for his cousin's estate, and for the remanding of his wife and children to slavery. In a short time he came armed with legal authority, and said to Marie:—

"I have come to take possession of these premises."

"By what authority?" she gasped, turning deathly pale. He hesitated a moment, as if his words were arrested by a sense of shame.

"By what authority?" she again demanded.

"By the authority of the law," answered Lorraine, "which has decided that Leroy's legal heirs are his white blood relations, and that your marriage is null and void."

"But," exclaimed Marie, "I have our marriage certificate. I was Leroy's lawful wife."

"Your marriage certificate is not worth the paper it is written on."

"Oh, you must be jesting, cruelly jesting. It can't be so."

"Yes, it is so. Judge Starkins has decided that your manumission is unlawful; your marriage a bad precedent, and inimical to the welfare of society; and that you and your children are remanded to slavery."

Marie stood as one petrified. She seemed a statue of fear and despair. She tried to speak, reached out her hand as if she were groping in the dark, turned pale as death as if all the blood in her veins had receded to her heart, and, with one heart-rending cry of bitter agony, she fell senseless to the floor. Her servants, to whom she had been so kind in her days of prosperity, bent pityingly over her, chafed her cold hands, and did what they could to restore her to consciousness. For a while she was stricken with brain fever, and her life seemed trembling on its frailest cord.

Gracie was like one perfectly dazed. When not watching by her mother's bedside she wandered aimlessly about the house, growing thinner day by day. A slow fever was consuming her life. Faithfully and carefully Mammy Liza watched over her, and did all she could to bring smiles to her lips and light to her fading eyes, but all in vain. Her only interest in life was to sit where she could watch her mother as she tossed to and fro in delirium, and to wonder what had brought the change in her once happy home. Finally she, too, was stricken with brain fever, which intervened as a mercy between her and the great sorrow that was overshadowing her young life. Tears would fill the servants' eyes as they saw the dear child drifting from them like a lovely vision, too bright for earth's dull cares and weary, wasting pain.

12.
SCHOOL-GIRL NOTIONS.

During Iola's stay in the North she found a strong tide of opposition against slavery. Arguments against the institution had entered the Church and made legislative halls the arenas of fierce debate. The subject had become part of the social converse of the fireside, and had enlisted the best brain and heart of the country. Anti-slavery discussions were pervading the strongest literature and claiming, a place on the most popular platforms.

Iola, being a Southern girl and a slave-holder's daughter, always defended slavery when it was under discussion.

"Slavery can't be wrong," she would say, "for my father is a slave-holder, and my mother is as good to our servants as she can be. My father often tells her that she spoils them, and lets them run over her. I never saw my father strike one of them. I love my mammy as much as I do my own mother, and I believe she loves us just as if we were her own children. When we are sick I am sure that she could not do anything more for us than she does."

"But, Iola," responded one of her school friends, "after all, they are not free. Would you be satisfied to have the most beautiful home, the costliest jewels, or the most elegant wardrobe if you were a slave?"

"Oh, the cases are not parallel. Our slaves do not want their freedom. They would not take it if we gave it to them."

"That is not the case with them all. My father has seen men who have encountered almost incredible hardships to get their freedom. Iola, did you ever attend an anti-slavery meeting?"

"No; I don't think these Abolitionists have any right to meddle in our affairs. I believe they are prejudiced against us, and want to get our property. I read about them in the papers when I was at home. I don't want to hear my part of the country run down. My father says the slaves would be very well contented if no one put wrong notions in their heads."

"I don't know," was the response of her friend, "but I do not think that that slave mother who took her four children, crossed the Ohio River on the ice, killed one of the children and attempted the lives of the other two, was a contented slave. And that other one, who, running away and finding herself pursued, threw herself over the Long Bridge into the Potomac, was evidently not satisfied. I do not think the numbers who are coming North on the

Underground Railroad can be very contented. It is not natural for people to run away from happiness, and if they are so happy and contented, why did Congress pass the Fugitive Slave Bill?"

"Well, I don't think," answered Iola, "any of our slaves would run away. I know mamma don't like slavery very much. I have often heard her say that she hoped the time would come when there would not be a slave in the land. My father does not think as she does. He thinks slavery is not wrong if you treat them well and don't sell them from their families. I intend, after I have graduated, to persuade pa to buy a house in New Orleans, and spend the winter there. You know this will be my first season out, and I hope that you will come and spend the winter with me. We will have such gay times, and you will so fall in love with our sunny South that you will never want to come back to shiver amid the snows and cold of the North. I think one winter in the South would cure you of your Abolitionism."

"Have you seen her yet?"

This question was asked by Louis Bastine, an attorney who had come North in the interests of Lorraine. The scene was the New England village where Mr. Galen's academy was located, and which Iola was attending. This question was addressed to Camille Lecroix, Bastine's intimate friend, who had lately come North. He was the son of a planter who lived near Leroy's plantation, and was familiar with Iola's family history. Since his arrival North, Bastine had met him and communicated to him his intentions.

"Yes; just caught a glimpse of her this morning as she was going down the street," was Camille's reply.

"She is a most beautiful creature," said Louis Bastine. "She has the proud poise of Leroy, the most splendid eyes I ever saw in a woman's head, lovely complexion, and a glorious wealth of hair. She would bring $2000 any day in a New Orleans market."

"I always feel sorry," said Camille, "when I see one of those Creole girls brought to the auction block. I have known fathers who were deeply devoted to their daughters, but who through some reverse of fortune were forced to part with them, and I always think the blow has been equally terrible on both sides. I had a friend who had two beautiful daughters whom he had educated in the North. They were cultured, and really belles in society. They were entirely ignorant of their lineage, but when their father died it was discovered that their mother had been a slave. It was a fearful blow. They would have faced poverty, but the knowledge of their tainted blood was more than they could bear."

"What became of them?"

"They both died, poor girls. I believe they were as much killed by the blow as if they had been shot. To tell you the truth, Bastine, I feel sorry for this girl. I don't believe she has the least idea of her Negro blood."

"No, Leroy has been careful to conceal it from her," replied Bastine.

"Is that so?" queried Camille. "Then he has made a great mistake."

"I can't help that," said Bastine; "business is business."

"How can you get her away?" asked Camille. "You will have to be very cautious, because if these pesky Abolitionists get an inkling of what you're doing they will balk your game double quick. And when you come to look at it, isn't it a shame to attempt to reduce that girl to slavery? She is just as white as we are, as good as any girl in the land, and better educated than thousands of white girls. A girl with her apparent refinement and magnificent beauty, were it not for the cross in her blood, I would be proud to introduce to our set. She would be the sensation of the season. I believe today it would be easier for me to go to the slums and take a young girl from there, and have her introduced as my wife, than to have society condone the offense if I married that lovely girl. There is not a social circle in the South that would not take it as a gross insult to have her introduced into it."

"Well," said Bastine, "my plan is settled. Leroy has never allowed her to spend her vacations at home. I understand she is now very anxious to get home, and, as Lorraine's attorney, I have come on his account to take her home."

"How will you do it?"

"I shall tell her her father is dangerously ill, and desires her to come as quickly as possible."

"And what then?"

"Have her inventoried with the rest of the property."

"Don't she know that her father is dead?"

"I think not," said Bastine. "She is not in mourning, but appeared very light-hearted this morning, laughing and talking with two other girls. I was struck with her great beauty, and asked a gentleman who she was. He said, 'Miss Leroy, of Mississippi.' I think Lorraine has managed the affair so as to keep her in perfect ignorance of her father's death. I don't like the job, but I never let sentiment interfere with my work."

Poor Iola! When she said slavery was not a bad thing, little did she think that she was destined to drink to its bitter dregs the cup she was so ready to press to the lips of others.

"How do you think she will take to her situation?" asked Camille.

"O, I guess," said Bastine, "she will sulk and take it pretty hard at first; but if she is managed right she will soon get over it. Give her plenty of jewelry, fine clothes, and an easy time."

"All this business must be conducted with the utmost secrecy and speed. Her mother could not have written to her, for she has been suffering with brain fever and nervous prostration since Leroy's death. Lorraine knows her market value too well, and is too shrewd to let so much property pass out of his hands without making an effort to retain it."

"Has she any brothers or sisters?"

"Yes, a brother," replied Bastine; "but he is at another school, and I have no orders from Lorraine in reference to him. If I can get the girl I am willing to let well enough alone. I dread the interview with the principal more than anything else. I am afraid he will hem and haw, and have his doubts. Perhaps, when he sees my letters and hears my story, I can pull the wool over his eyes."

"But, Louis, this is a pitiful piece of business. I should hate to be engaged in it."

A deep flush of shame overspread for a moment the face of Lorraine's attorney, as he replied: "I don't like the job, but I have undertaken it, and must go through with it."

"I see no '*must*' about it. Were I in your place I would wash my hands of the whole business."

"I can't afford it," was Bastine's hard, businesslike reply. On the next morning after this conversation between these two young men, Louis Bastine presented himself to the principal of the academy, with the request that Iola be permitted to leave immediately to attend the sickbed of her father, who was dangerously ill. The principal hesitated, but while he was deliberating, a telegram, purporting to come from Iola's mother, summoned Iola to her father's bedside without delay. The principal, set at rest in regard to the truthfulness of the dispatch, not only permitted but expedited her departure.

Iola and Bastine took the earliest train, and traveled without pausing until they reached a large hotel in a Southern city. There they were obliged to wait a few hours until they could resume their journey, the train having failed to make connection. Iola sat in a large, lonely parlor, waiting for the servant to show her to a private room. She had never known a great sorrow. Never before had the shadows of death mingled with the sunshine of her life.

Anxious, travel-worn, and heavy-hearted, she sat in an easy chair, with nothing to divert her from the grief and anxiety which rendered every delay a source of painful anxiety.

Oh, I hope that he will be alive and growing better! was the thought which kept constantly revolving in her mind, until she fell asleep. In her dreams she was at home, encircled in the warm clasp of her father's arms, feeling her mother's kisses lingering on her lips, and hearing the joyous greetings of the servants and Mammy Liza's glad welcome as she folded her to her heart. From this dream of bliss she was awakened by a burning kiss pressed on her lips, and a strong arm encircling her. Gazing around and taking in the whole situation, she sprang from her seat, her eyes flashing with rage and scorn, her face flushed to the roots of her hair, her voice shaken with excitement, and every nerve trembling with angry emotion.

"How dare you do such a thing! Don't you know if my father were here he would crush you to the earth?"

"Not so fast, my lovely tigress," said Bastine, "your father knew what he was doing when he placed you in my charge."

"My father made a great mistake, if he thought he had put me in charge of a gentleman."

"I am your guardian for the present," replied Bastine. "I am to see you safe home, and then my commission ends."

"I wish it were ended now," she exclaimed, trembling with anger and mortification. Her voice was choked by emotion, and broken by smothered sobs.

Louis Bastine thought to himself, *She is a real spitfire, but beautiful even in her wrath.*

During the rest of her journey Iola preserved a most freezing reserve towards Bastine. At length the journey was ended. Pale and anxious she rode up the avenue which led to her home.

A strange silence pervaded the place. The servants moved sadly from place to place, and spoke in subdued tones. The windows were heavily draped with crape, and a funeral air pervaded the house.

Mammy Liza met her at the door, and, with streaming eyes and convulsive sobs, folded her to her heart, as Iola exclaimed, in tones of hopeless anguish:

"Oh, papa's dead!"

"Oh, my pore baby!" said mammy. "Ain't you hearn tell 'bout it? Yore par's dead, an' your mar's bin drefful sick. She's better now."

Mam Liza stepped lightly into Mrs. Leroy's room, and gently apprised her of Iola's arrival. In a darkened room lay the stricken mother, almost distracted by her late bereavement.

"Oh, Iola," she exclaimed, as her daughter entered, "is this you? I am so sorry you came."

Then, burying her head in Iola's bosom, she wept convulsively. "Much as I love you," she continued, between her sobs, "and much as I longed to see you, I am sorry you came."

"Why, mother," replied Iola, astonished, "I received your telegram last Wednesday, and I took the earliest train I could get."

"My dear child, I never sent you a telegram. It was a trick to bring you down South and reduce you to slavery."

Iola eyed her mother curiously. What did she mean? Had grief dethroned her reason? Yet her eye was clear, her manner perfectly rational.

Marie saw the astounded look on Iola's face, and nerving herself to the task, said: "Iola, I must tell you what your father always enjoined me to be silent about. I did not think it was the wisest thing, but I yielded to his desires. I have Negro blood in my veins. I was your father's slave before I married him. His relatives have set aside his will. The courts have declared our marriage null and void and my manumission illegal, and we are all to be remanded to slavery."

An expression of horror and anguish swept over Iola's face, and, turning deathly pale, she exclaimed, "Oh, mother, it can't be so! You must be dreaming!"

"No, my child; it is a terrible reality."

Almost wild with agony, Iola paced the floor, as the fearful truth broke in crushing anguish upon her mind. Then bursting into a paroxysm of tears succeeded by peals of hysterical laughter, said:—

"I used to say that slavery is right. I didn't know what I was talking about." Then growing calmer, she said, "Mother, who is at the bottom of this downright robbery?"

"Alfred Lorraine; I have always dreaded that man, and what I feared has come to pass. Your father had faith in him; I never had."

"But, mother, could we not contest his claim. You have your marriage certificate and papa's will."

"Yes, my dear child, but Judge Starkins has decided that we have no standing in the court, and no testimony according to law."

"Oh, mother, what can I do?"

"Nothing, my child, unless you can escape to the North."

"And leave you?"

"Yes."

"Mother, I will never desert you in your hour of trial. But can nothing be done? Had father no friends who would assist us?"

"None that I know of. I do not think he had an acquaintance who approved of our marriage. The neighboring planters have stood so aloof from me that I do not know where to turn for either help or sympathy. I believe it was Lorraine who sent the telegram. I wrote to you as soon as I could after your father's death, but fainted just as I finished directing the letter. I do not think he knows where your brother is, and, if possible, he must not know. If you can by any means, *do* send a letter to Harry and warn him not to attempt to come home. I don't know how you will succeed, for Lorraine has us all under surveillance. But it is according to law."

"What law, mother?"

"The law of the strong against the weak."

"Oh, mother, it seems like a dreadful dream, a fearful nightmare! But I cannot shake it off. Where is Gracie?"

"The dear child has been running down ever since her papa's death. She clung to me night and day while I had the brain fever, and could not be persuaded to leave me. She hardly ate anything for more than a week. She has been dangerously ill for several days, and the doctor says she cannot live. The fever has exhausted all her rallying power, and yet, dear as she is to me, I would rather consign her to the deepest grave than see her forced to be a slave."

"So would I. I wish I could die myself."

"Oh, Iola, do not talk so. Strive to be a Christian, to have faith in the darkest hour. Were it not for my hope of heaven I couldn't stand all this trouble."

"Mother, are these people Christians who made these laws which are robbing us of our inheritance and reducing us to slavery? If this is Christianity I hate and despise it. Would the most cruel heathen do worse?"

"My dear child, I have not learned my Christianity from them. I have learned it at the foot of the cross, and from this book," she said, placing a New Testament in Iola's hands. "Some of the most beautiful lessons of faith and trust I have ever learned were from among our lowly people in their humble cabins."

"Mamma!" called a faint voice from the adjoining room. Marie immediately arose and went to the bedside of her sick child, where Mammy Liza was holding her faithful vigils. The child had just awakened from a fitful sleep.

"I thought," she said, "that I heard Iola's voice. Has she come?"

"Yes, darling; do you want to see her?"

"Oh, yes," she said, as a bright smile broke over her dying features.

Iola passed quickly into the room. Gracie reached out her thin, bloodless hand, clasped Iola's palm in hers, and said: "I am so glad you have come. Dear Iola, stand by mother. You and Harry are all she has. It is not hard to die. You and mother and Harry must meet me in heaven."

Swiftly the tidings went through the house that Gracie was dying. The servants gathered around her with tearful eyes, as she bade them all goodbye. When she had finished, and Mammy had lowered the pillow, an unwonted radiance lit up her eye, and an expression of ineffable gladness overspread her face, as she murmured: "It is beautiful, so beautiful!" Fainter and fainter grew her voice, until, without a struggle or sigh, she passed away beyond the power of oppression and prejudice.

13.
A REJECTED SUITOR.

Very unexpected was Dr. Gresham's proposal to Iola. She had heartily enjoyed his society and highly valued his friendship, but he had never been associated in her mind with either love or marriage. As he held her hand in his a tell-tale flush rose to her cheek, a look of grateful surprise beamed from her eye, but it was almost immediately succeeded by an air of inexpressible sadness, a drooping of her eyelids, and an increasing pallor of her cheek. She withdrew her hand from his, shook her head sadly, and said:—

"No, Doctor; that can never be. I am very grateful to you for your kindness. I value your friendship, but neither gratitude nor friendship is love, and I have nothing more than those to give."

"Not at present," said Dr. Gresham; "but may I not hope your friendship will ripen into love?"

"Doctor, I could not promise. I do not think that I should. There are barriers between us that I cannot pass. Were you to know them I think you would say the same."

Just then the ambulance brought in a wounded scout, and Iola found relief from the wounds of her own heart in attending to his.

Dr. Gresham knew the barrier that lay between them. It was one which his love had surmounted. But he was too noble and generous to take advantage of her loneliness to press his suit. He had lived in a part of the country where he had scarcely ever seen a colored person, and around the race their misfortunes had thrown a halo of romance. To him the Negro was a picturesque being, over whose woes he had wept when a child, and whose wrongs he was ready to redress when a man. But when he saw the lovely girl who had been rescued by the commander of the post from the clutches of slavery, all the manhood and chivalry in his nature arose in her behalf, and he was ready to lay on the altar of her heart his first grand and overmastering love. Not discouraged by her refusal, but determined to overcome her objections, Dr. Gresham resolved that he would abide his time.

Iola was not indifferent to Dr. Gresham. She admired his manliness and respected his character. He was tall and handsome, a fine specimen of the best brain and heart of New England. He had been nurtured under grand and ennobling influences. His father was a devoted Abolitionist. His mother was kindhearted, but somewhat exclusive and aristocratic. She would have looked upon his marriage with Iola as a mistake and feared that such an alliance would hurt the prospects of her daughters.

During Iola's stay in the North, she had learned enough of the racial feeling to influence her decision in reference to Dr. Gresham's offer. Iola, like other girls, had had her beautiful daydreams before she was rudely awakened by the fate which had dragged her into the depths of slavery. In the chambers of her imagery were pictures of noble deeds; of high, heroic men, knightly, tender, true, and brave. In Dr. Gresham she saw the ideal of her soul exemplified. But in her lonely condition, with all its background of terrible sorrow and deep abasement, she had never for a moment thought of giving or receiving love from one of that race who had been so lately associated in her mind with horror, aversion, and disgust. His kindness to her had been a new experience. His companionship was an unexpected pleasure. She had learned to enjoy his presence and to miss him when absent, and when she began to question her heart she found that unconsciously it was entwining around him.

"Yes," she said to herself, "I do like him; but I can never marry him. To the man I marry my heart must be as open as the flowers to the sun. I could not accept his hand and hide from him the secret of my birth; and I could not consent to choose the happiest lot on earth without first finding my poor heart-stricken and desolate mother. Perhaps someday I may have the courage to tell him my sad story, and then make my heart the sepulchre in which to bury all the love which might have gladdened and brightened my whole life."

During the sad and weary months which ensued while the war dragged its slow length along, Dr. Gresham and Iola often met by the bedsides of the wounded and dying, and sometimes he would drop a few words at which her heart would beat quicker and her cheek flush more vividly. But he was so kind, tender, and respectful, that Iola had no idea he knew her race affiliations. She knew from unmistakable signs that Dr. Gresham had learned to love her, and that he had power to call forth the warmest affection of her soul; but she fought with her own heart and repressed its rising love. She felt that it was best for his sake that they should not marry. When she saw the evidences of his increasing love she regretted that she had not informed him at the first of the barrier that lay between them; it might have saved him unnecessary suffering. Thinking thus, Iola resolved, at whatever cost of pain it might be to herself, to explain to Dr. Gresham what she meant by the insurmountable barrier. Iola, after a continuous strain upon her nervous system for months, began to suffer from general debility and nervous depression. Dr. Gresham saw the increasing pallor on Iola's cheek and the loss of buoyancy in her step. One morning, as she turned from the bed of a young soldier for whom she had just written a letter to his mother, there was such a look of pity and sorrow on her face that Dr. Gresham's whole heart went out in sympathy for her, and he resolved to break the silence he had imposed upon himself.

"Iola," he said, and there was a depth of passionate tenderness in his voice, a volume of unexpressed affection in his face, "you are wronging yourself. You are sinking beneath burdens too heavy for you to bear. It seems to me that besides the constant drain upon your sympathies there is some great sorrow preying upon your life; some burden that ought to be shared." He gazed upon her so ardently that each cord of her heart seemed to vibrate, and unbidden tears sprang to her lustrous eyes, as she said, sadly:—

"Doctor, you are right."

"Iola, my heart is longing to lift those burdens from your life. Love, like faith, laughs at impossibilities. I can conceive of no barrier too high for my love to surmount. Consent to be mine, as nothing else on earth is mine."

"Doctor, you know not what you ask," replied Iola. "Instead of coming into this hospital a self-sacrificing woman, laying her every gift and advantage upon the altar of her country, I came as a rescued slave, glad to find a refuge from a fate more cruel than death; a fate from which I was rescued by the intervention of my dear dead friend, Thomas Anderson. I was born on a lonely plantation on the Mississippi River, where the white population was very sparse. We had no neighbors who ever visited us; no young white girls with whom I ever played in my childhood; but, never having enjoyed such companionship, I was unconscious of any sense of privation. Our parents spared no pains to make the lives of their children (we were three) as bright and pleasant as they could. Our home was so happy. We had a large number of servants, who were devoted to us. I never had the faintest suspicion that there was any wrongfulness in slavery, and I never dreamed of the dreadful fate which broke in a storm of fearful anguish over our devoted heads. Papa used to take us to New Orleans to see the Mardi Gras, and while there we visited the theatres and other places of amusement and interest. At home we had books, papers, and magazines to beguile our time. Perfectly ignorant of my racial connection, I was sent to a Northern academy, and soon made many friends among my fellow students. Companionship with girls of my own age was a new experience, which I thoroughly enjoyed. I spent several years in New England, and was busily preparing for my commencement exercises when my father was snatched away—died of yellow fever on his way North to witness my graduation. Through a stratagem, I was brought hurriedly from the North, and found that my father was dead; that his nearest kinsman had taken possession of our property; that my mother's marriage had been declared illegal, because of an imperceptible infusion of Negro blood in her veins; and that she and her children had been remanded to slavery. I was torn from my mother, sold as a slave, and subjected to cruel indignities, from which I was rescued and a place given to me in this hospital. Doctor, I did not choose my lot in life, but I have no other alternative than to accept it. The intense horror and agony I felt when I was first told the story are over. Thoughts and purposes have come to me in the shadow I should never have learned in the sunshine. I am constantly rousing myself up to suffer and be strong. I intend, when this conflict is over, to cast my lot with the freed people as a helper, teacher, and friend. I have passed through a fiery ordeal, but this ministry of suffering will not be in vain. I feel that my mind has matured beyond my years. I am a wonder to myself. It seems as if years had been compressed into a few short months. In telling you this, do you not, can you not, see that there is an insurmountable barrier between us?"

"No, I do not," replied Dr. Gresham. "I love you for your own sake. And with this the disadvantages of birth have nothing to do."

"You say so now, and I believe that you are perfectly sincere. Today your friendship springs from compassion, but, when that subsides, might you not look on me as an inferior?"

"Iola, you do not understand me. You think too meanly of me. You must not judge me by the worst of my race. Surely our country has produced a higher type of manhood than the men by whom you were tried and tempted."

"Tried, but not tempted," said Iola, as a deep flush overspread her face; "I was never tempted. I was sold from State to State as an article of merchandise. I had outrages heaped on me which might well crimson the cheek of honest womanhood with shame, but I never fell into the clutches of an owner for whom I did not feel the utmost loathing and intensest horror. I have heard men talk glibly of the degradation of the Negro, but there is a vast difference between abasement of condition and degradation of character. I was abased, but the men who trampled on me were the degraded ones."

"But, Iola, you must not blame all for what a few have done."

"A few have done? Did not the whole nation consent to our abasement?" asked Iola, bitterly.

"No, Miss Iola, we did not all consent to it. Slavery drew a line of cleavage in this country. Although we were under one government we were farther apart in our sentiments than if we had been divided by lofty mountains and separated by wide seas. And had not Northern sentiment been brought to bear against the institution, slavery would have been intact until today."

"But, Doctor, the Negro is under a social ban both North and South. Our enemies have the ear of the world, and they can depict us just as they please."

"That is true; but the Negro has no other alternative than to make friends of his calamities. Other men have plead his cause, but out of the race must come its own defenders. With them the pen must be mightier than the sword. It is the weapon of civilization, and they must use it in their own defense. We cannot tell what is in them until they express themselves."

"Yes, and I think there is a large amount of latent and undeveloped ability in the race, which they will learn to use for their own benefit. This my hospital experience has taught me."

"But," said Dr. Gresham, "they must learn to struggle, labor, and achieve. By facts, not theories, they will be judged in the future. The Anglo-Saxon race is proud, domineering, aggressive, and impatient of a rival, and, as I think, has more capacity for dragging down a weaker race than uplifting it.

They have been a conquering and achieving people, marvelous in their triumphs of mind over matter. They have manifested the traits of character which are developed by success and victory."

"And yet," said Iola, earnestly, "I believe the time will come when the civilization of the Negro will assume a better phase than you Anglo-Saxons possess. You will prove unworthy of your high vantage ground if you only use your superior ability to victimize feebler races and minister to a selfish greed of gold and a love of domination."

"But, Iola," said Dr. Gresham, a little impatiently, "what has all this to do with our marriage? Your complexion is as fair as mine. What is to hinder you from sharing my Northern home, from having my mother to be your mother?" The tones of his voice grew tender, as he raised his eyes to Iola's face and anxiously awaited her reply.

"Dr. Gresham," said Iola, sadly, "should the story of my life be revealed to your family, would they be willing to ignore all the traditions of my blood, forget all the terrible humiliations through which I have passed? I have too much self-respect to enter your home under a veil of concealment. I have lived in New England. I love the sunshine of her homes and the freedom of her institutions. But New England is not free from racial prejudice, and I would never enter a family where I would be an unwelcome member."

"Iola, dear, you have nothing to fear in that direction."

"Doctor," she said, and a faint flush rose to her cheek, "suppose we should marry, and little children in after years should nestle in our arms, and one of them show unmistakable signs of color, would you be satisfied?"

She looked steadfastly into his eyes, which fell beneath her truth-seeking gaze. His face flushed as if the question had suddenly perplexed him. Iola saw the irresolution on his face, and framed her answer accordingly.

"Ah, I see," she said, "that you are puzzled. You had not taken into account what might result from such a marriage. I will relieve you from all embarrassment by simply saying I cannot be your wife. When the war is over I intend to search the country for my mother. Doctor, were you to give me a palace-like home, with velvet carpets to hush my tread, and magnificence to surround my way, I should miss her voice amid all other tones, her presence amid every scene. Oh, you do not know how hungry my heart is for my mother! Were I to marry you I would carry an aching heart into your home and dim its brightness. I have resolved never to marry until I have found my mother. The hope of finding her has colored all my life since I regained my freedom. It has helped sustain me in the hour of fearful trial. When I see her I want to have the proud consciousness that I bring her back a heart just as loving, faithful, and devoted as the last hour we parted."

"And is this your final answer?"

"It is. I have pledged my life to that resolve, and I believe time and patience will reward me."

There was a deep shadow of sorrow and disappointment on the face of Dr. Gresham as he rose to leave. For a moment he held her hand as it lay limp in his own. If she wavered in her determination it was only for a moment. No quivering of her lip or paling of her cheek betrayed any struggle of her heart. Her resolve was made, and his words were powerless to swerve her from the purpose of her soul.

After Dr. Gresham had gone Iola went to her room and sat buried in thought. It seemed as if the fate of Tantalus was hers, without his crimes. Here she was lonely and heart-stricken, and unto her was presented the offer of love, home, happiness, and social position; the heart and hand of a man too noble and generous to refuse her companionship for life on account of the blood in her veins. Why should she refuse these desirable boons? But, mingling with these beautiful visions of manly love and protecting care she saw the anguish of her heart-stricken mother and the pale, sweet face of her dying sister, as with her latest breath she had said, "Iola, stand by mamma!"

"No, no," she said to herself; "I was right to refuse Dr. Gresham. How dare I dream of happiness when my poor mamma's heart may be slowly breaking? I should be ashamed to live and ashamed to die were I to choose a happy lot for myself and leave poor mamma to struggle alone. I will never be satisfied till I get tidings of her. And when I have found her I will do all I can to cheer and brighten the remnant of her life."

14.
HARRY LEROY.

It was several weeks after Iola had written to her brother that her letter reached him. The trusty servant to whom she delivered it watched his opportunity to mail it. At last he succeeded in slipping it into Lorraine's mail and dropping them all into the post office together. Harry was studying at a boys' academy in Maine. His father had given that State the preference because, while on a visit there, he had been favorably impressed with the kindness and hospitality of the people. He had sent his son a large sum of money, and given him permission to spend a while with some school chums till he was ready to bring the family North, where they could all spend the summer together. Harry had returned from his visit, and was looking for letters and remittances from home, when a letter, all crumpled, was handed him by the principal of the academy. He recognized his sister's handwriting and eagerly opened the letter. As he read, he turned very pale; then a deep flush overspread his face and an angry light flashed from his eyes. As he read on, his face became still paler; he gasped for breath and fell into a swoon. Appalled at the sudden change which had swept over him like a deadly sirocco, the principal rushed to the fallen boy, picked up the missive that lay beside him, and immediately rang for help and dispatched for the doctor. The doctor came at once and was greatly puzzled. Less than an hour before, he had seen him with a crowd of merry, laughter-loving boys, apparently as light-hearted and joyous as any of them; now he lay with features drawn and pinched, his face deadly pale, as if some terrible suffering had sent all the blood in his veins to stagnate around his heart. Harry opened his eyes, shuddered, and relapsed into silence. The doctor, all at sea in regard to the cause of the sudden attack, did all that he could to restore him to consciousness and quiet the perturbation of his spirit. He succeeded, but found he was strangely silent. A terrible shock had sent a tremor through every nerve, and the doctor watched with painful apprehension its effect upon his reason. Giving him an opiate and enjoining that he should be kept perfectly quiet, the doctor left the room, sought the principal, and said:—

"Mr. Bascom, here is a case that baffles my skill. I saw that boy pass by my window not more than half an hour ago, full of animation, and now he lies hovering between life and death. I have great apprehension for his reason. Can you throw any light on the subject?"

Mr. Bascom hesitated.

"I am not asking you as a matter of idle curiosity, but as a physician. I must have all the light I can get in making my diagnosis of the case."

The principal arose, went to his desk, took out the letter which he had picked up from the floor, and laid it in the physician's hand. As the doctor read, a look of indignant horror swept over his face. Then he said: "Can it be possible! I never suspected such a thing. It must be a cruel, senseless hoax."

"Doctor," said Mr. Bascom, "I have been a lifelong Abolitionist and have often read of the cruelties and crimes of American slavery, but never before did I realize the low moral tone of the social life under which such shameless cruelties could be practiced on a defenseless widow and her orphaned children. Let me read the letter again. Just look at it, all tear-blotted and written with a trembling hand:—

> "*DEAR BROTHER:*
>
> *I have dreadful news for you and I hardly know how to tell it. Papa and Gracie are both dead. He died of yellow fever. Mamma is almost distracted. Papa's cousin has taken possession of our property, and instead of heirs we are chattels. Mamma has explained the whole situation to me. She was papa's slave before she married. He loved her, manumitted, educated, and married her. When he died Mr. Lorraine entered suit for his property and Judge Starkins has decided in his favor. The decree of the court has made their marriage invalid, robbed us of our inheritance, and remanded us all to slavery. Mamma is too wretched to attempt to write herself, but told me to entreat you not to attempt to come home. You can do us no good, and that mean, cruel Lorraine may do you much harm. Don't attempt, I beseech you, to come home. Show this letter to Mr. Bascom and let him advise you what to do. But don't, for our sake, attempt to come home.*
>
> *Your heartbroken sister,*
> *IOLA LEROY.*"

"This," said the doctor, "is a very awkward affair. The boy is too ill to be removed. It is doubtful if the nerves which have trembled with such fearful excitement will ever recover their normal condition. It is simply a work of mercy to watch over him with the tenderest care."

Fortunately for Harry he had fallen into good hands, and the most tender care and nursing were bestowed upon him. For a while Harry was strangely silent, never referring to the terrible misfortune which had so suddenly overshadowed his life. It seemed as if the past were suddenly blotted out of his memory. But he was young and of an excellent constitution, and in a few months he was slowly recovering.

"Doctor," said he one day, as the physician sat at his bedside, "I seem to have had a dreadful dream, and to have dreamt that my father was dead, and my mother and sister were in terrible trouble, but I could not help them.

Doctor, was it a dream, or was it a reality? It could not have been a dream, for when I fell asleep the grass was green and the birds were singing, but now the winds are howling and the frost is on the ground. Doctor, tell me how it is? How long have I been here?"

Sitting by his bedside, and taking his emaciated hand in his, the doctor said, in a kind, fatherly tone: "My dear boy, you have been very ill, and everything depends on your keeping quiet, very quiet."

As soon as he was strong enough the principal gave him his letter to read.

"But, Mr. Bascom," Harry said, "I do not understand this. It says my mother and father were legally married. How could her marriage be set aside and her children robbed of their inheritance? This is not a heathen country. I hardly think barbarians would have done any worse; yet this is called a Christian country."

"Christian in name," answered the principal. "When your father left you in my care, knowing that I was an Abolitionist, he confided his secret to me. He said that life was full of vicissitudes, and he wished you to have a good education. He wanted you and your sister to be prepared for any emergency. He did not wish you to know that you had Negro blood in your veins. He knew that the spirit of caste pervaded the nation, North and South, and he was very anxious to have his children freed from its depressing influences. He did not intend to stay South after you had finished your education."

"But," said Harry, "I cannot understand. If my mother was lawfully married, how could they deprive her of her marital rights?"

"When Lorraine," continued Mr. Bascom, "knew your father was dead, all he had to do was to find a flaw in her manumission, and, of course, the marriage became illegal. She could not then inherit property nor maintain her freedom; and her children followed her condition."

Harry listened attentively. Things which had puzzled him once now became perfectly clear. He sighed heavily, and, turning to the principal, said: "I see things in a new light. Now I remember that none of the planters' wives ever visited my mother; and we never went to church except when my father took us to the Cathedral in New Orleans. My father was a Catholic, but I don't think mamma is."

"Now, Harry," said the principal, "life is before you. If you wish to stay North, I will interest friends in your behalf, and try to get you a situation. Going South is out of the question. It is probable that by this time your mother and sister are removed from their home. You are powerless to fight against the law that enslaved them. Should you fall into the clutches of Lorraine, he might give you a great deal of trouble. You would be pressed into the Confederate service to help them throw up barricades, dig trenches, and add to the strength of those who enslaved your mother and sister."

"Never, never!" cried Harry. "I would rather die than do it! I should despise myself forever if I did."

"Numbers of our young men," said Mr. Bascom, "have gone to the war which is now raging between North and South. You have been sick for several months, and much has taken place of which you are unaware. Would you like to enlist?"

"I certainly would; not so much for the sake of fighting for the Government, as with the hope of finding my mother and sister, and avenging their wrongs. I should like to meet Lorraine on the battlefield."

"What kind of a regiment would you prefer, white or colored?"

Harry winced when the question was asked. He felt the reality of his situation as he had not done before. It was as if two paths had suddenly opened before him, and he was forced to choose between them. On one side were strength, courage, enterprise, power of achievement, and memories of a wonderful past. On the other side were weakness, ignorance, poverty, and the proud world's social scorn. He knew nothing of colored people except as slaves, and his whole soul shrank from equalizing himself with them. He was fair enough to pass unchallenged among the fairest in the land, and yet a Christ-less prejudice had decreed that he should be a social pariah. He sat, thoughtful and undecided, as if a great struggle were going on in his mind.

Finally the principal said, "I do not think that you should be assigned to a colored regiment because of the blood in your veins, but you will have, in such a regiment, better facilities for finding your mother and sister."

"You are right, Mr. Bascom. To find my mother and sister I call no task too heavy, no sacrifice too great."

Since Harry had come North he had learned to feel profound pity for the slave. But there is a difference between looking on a man as an object of pity and protecting him as such, and being identified with him and forced to share his lot. To take his place with them on the arena of life was the test of his life, but love was stronger than pride.

His father was dead. His mother and sister were enslaved by a mockery of justice. It was more than a matter of choice where he should stand on the racial question. He felt that he must stand where he could strike the most effective blow for their freedom. With that thought strong in his mind, and as soon as he recovered, he went westward to find a colored regiment. He told the recruiting officer that he wished to be assigned to a colored regiment.

"Why do you wish that," said the officer, looking at Harry with an air of astonishment.

"Because I am a colored man."

The officer look puzzled. It was a new experience. He had seen colored men with fair complexions anxious to lose their identity with the colored race and pose as white men, but here was a man in the flush of his early manhood, to whom could come dreams of promotion from a simple private to a successful general, deliberately turning his back upon every gilded hope and dazzling opportunity, to cast his lot with the despised and hated Negro.

"I do not understand you," said the officer. "Surely you are a white man, and, as such, I will enlist you in a white regiment."

"No," said Harry, firmly, "I am a colored man, and unless I can be assigned to a colored regiment I am not willing to enter the army."

"Well," said the officer, "you are the d——d'st fool I ever saw—a man as white as you are turning his back upon his chances of promotion! But you can take your choice."

So Harry was permitted to enter the army. By his promptness and valor he soon won the hearts of his superior officers, and was made drill sergeant. Having nearly all of his life been used to colored people, and being taught by his mother to be kind and respectful to them, he was soon able to gain their esteem. He continued in the regiment until Grant began the task of opening the Mississippi. After weeks of fruitless effort, Grant marched his army down the west side of the river, while the gunboats undertook the perilous task of running the batteries. Men were found for the hour. The volunteers offered themselves in such numbers that lots were cast to determine who should have the opportunity to enlist in an enterprise so fraught with danger. Harry was one on whom the lot fell.

Grant crossed the river below, coiled his forces around Vicksburg like a boa constrictor, and held it in his grasp. After forty-seven days of endurance the city surrendered to him. Port Hudson, after the surrender of Vicksburg, gave up the unequal contest, and the Mississippi was open to the Gulf.

15.
ROBERT AND HIS COMPANY.

"Good morning, gentlemen," said Robert Johnson, as he approached Colonel Robinson, the commander of the post, who was standing at the door of his tent, talking with Captain Sybil.

"Good morning," responded Colonel Robinson, "I am glad you have come. I was just about to send for you. How is your company getting on?"

"First rate, sir," replied Robert.

"In good health?"

"Excellent. They are all in good health and spirits. Our boys are used to hardship and exposure, and the hope of getting their freedom puts new snap into them."

"I am glad of it," said Colonel Robinson. "They make good fighters and very useful allies. Last night we received very valuable intelligence from some fugitives who had escaped through the Rebel lines. I do not think many of the Northern people realize the service they have been to us in bringing information and helping our boys when escaping from Rebel prisons. I never knew a full-blooded Negro to betray us. A month ago, when we were encamped near the Rebel lines, a colored woman managed admirably to keep us posted as to the intended movements of the enemy. She was engaged in laundry work, and by means of hanging her sheets in different ways gave us the right signals."

"I hope," said Captain Sybil, "that the time will come when some faithful historian will chronicle all the deeds of daring and service these people have performed during this struggle, and give them due credit therefor."

"Our great mistake," said Colonel Robinson, "was our long delay in granting them their freedom, and even what we have done is only partial. The border States still retain their slaves. We ought to have made a clean sweep of the whole affair. Slavery is a serpent which we nourished in its weakness, and now it is stinging us in its strength."

"I think so, too," said Captain Sybil. "But in making his proclamation of freedom, perhaps Mr. Lincoln went as far as he thought public opinion would let him."

"It is remarkable," said Colonel Robinson, "how these Secesh hold out. It surprises me to see how poor white men, who, like the Negroes, are victims of slavery, rally around the Stripes and Bars. These men, I believe, have been looked down on by the aristocratic slaveholders, and despised by the well-fed and comfortable slaves, yet they follow their leaders into the very jaws of death; face hunger, cold, disease, and danger; and all for what? What, under heaven, are they fighting for? Now, the Negro, ignorant as he is, has learned to regard our flag as a banner of freedom, and to look forward to his deliverance as a consequence of the overthrow of the Rebellion."

"I think," said Captain Sybil "that these ignorant white men have been awfully deceived. They have had presented to their imaginations utterly false ideas of the results of Secession, and have been taught that its success would bring them advantages which they had never enjoyed in the Union."

"And I think," said Colonel Robinson, "that the women and ministers have largely fed and fanned the fires of this Rebellion, and have helped to create a public opinion which has swept numbers of benighted men into the conflict. Well, might one of their own men say, 'This is a rich man's war and a poor man's fight.' They were led into it through their ignorance, and held in it by their fears."

"I think," said Captain Sybil, "that if the public school had been common through the South this war would never have occurred. Now things have reached such a pass that able-bodied men must report at headquarters, or be treated as deserters. Their leaders are desperate men, of whom it has been said: 'They have robbed the cradle and the grave.'"

"They are fighting against fearful odds," said Colonel Robinson, "and their defeat is only a question of time."

"As soon," said Robert, "as they fired on Fort Sumter, Uncle Daniel, a dear old father who had been praying and hoping for freedom, said to me: 'Dey's fired on Fort Sumter, an' mark my words, Bob, de Norf's boun' ter whip.'"

"Had we freed the slaves at the outset," said Captain Sybil, "we wouldn't have given the Rebels so much opportunity to strengthen themselves by means of slave labor in raising their crops, throwing up their entrenchments, and building their fortifications. Slavery was a deadly cancer eating into the life of the nation; but, somehow, it had cast such a glamour over us that we have acted somewhat as if our national safety were better preserved by sparing the cancer than by cutting it out."

"Political and racial questions have sadly complicated this matter," said Colonel Robinson. "The North is not wholly made up of anti-slavery people. At the beginning of this war we were not permeated with justice, and so were not ripe for victory. The battle of Bull Run inaugurated the war by a failure. Instead of glory we gathered shame, and defeat in place of victory."

"We have been slow," said Captain Sybil, "to see our danger and to do our duty. Our delay has cost us thousands of lives and millions of dollars. Yet it may be it is all for the best. Our national wound was too deep to be lightly healed. When the President issued his Emancipation Proclamation my heart overflowed with joy, and I said: 'This is the first bright rift in the war cloud.'"

"And did you really think that they would accept the terms of freedom and lay down their arms?" asked Robert.

"I hardly thought they would," continued Captain Sybil. "I did not think that their leaders would permit it. I believe the rank and file of their army are largely composed of a mass of ignorance, led, manipulated, and moulded by educated and ambitious wickedness. In attempting to overthrow the Union, a despotism and reign of terror were created which encompassed them as fetters of iron, and they will not accept the conditions until they have reached the last extremity. I hardly think they are yet willing to confess that such extremity has been reached."

"Captain," said Robert, as they left Colonel Robinson's tent, "I have lived all my life where I have had a chance to hear the 'Secesh' talk, and when they left their papers around I used to read everything I could lay my hands on. It seemed to me that the big white men not only ruled over the poor whites and made laws for them, but over the whole nation."

"That was so," replied Captain Sybil. "The North was strong but forbearing. It was busy in trade and commerce, and permitted them to make the Northern States hunting-grounds for their slaves. When we sent back Simms and Burns from beneath the shadow of Bunker Hill Monument and Faneuil Hall, they mistook us; looked upon us as a lot of money-grabbers, who would be willing to purchase peace at any price. I do not believe when they fired on the 'Star of the West' that they had the least apprehension of the fearful results which were to follow their madness and folly."

"Well, Captain," asked Robert, "if the free North would submit to be called on to help them catch their slaves, what could be expected of us, who all our lives had known no other condition than that of slavery? How much braver would you have been, if your first recollections had been those of seeing your mother maltreated, your father cruelly beaten, or your fellow servants brutally murdered? I wonder why they never enslaved the Indians!"

"You are mistaken, Robert, if you think the Indians were never enslaved. I have read that the Spaniards who visited the coasts of America kidnapped thousands of Indians, whom they sent to Europe and the West Indies as slaves. Columbus himself, we are informed, captured five hundred natives, and sent them to Spain. The Indian had the lesser power of endurance, and Las Cassas suggested the enslavement of the Negro, because he seemed to possess greater breadth of physical organization and stronger power of endurance. Slavery was an old world's crime which, I have heard, the Indians never practiced among themselves. Perhaps it would have been harder to reduce them to slavery and hold them in bondage when they had a vast continent before them, where they could hide in the vastnesses of its mountains or the seclusion of its forests, than it was for white men to visit the coasts of Africa and, with their superior knowledge, obtain cargoes of slaves, bring them across the ocean, hem them in on the plantations, and surround them with a pall of dense ignorance."

"I remember," said Robert, "in reading a history I once came across at our house, that when the Africans first came to this country they did not all speak one language. Some had only met as mutual enemies. They were not all one color, their complexions ranging from tawny yellow to deep black."

"Yes," said Captain Sybil, "and in dealing with the Negro we wanted his labor; in dealing with the Indian we wanted his lands. For one we had weapons of war; for the other we had real and invisible chains, the coercion of force, and the terror of the unseen world."

"That's exactly so, Captain! When I was a boy I used to hear the old folks tell what would happen to bad people in another world; about the devil pouring hot lead down people's throats and stirring them up with a pitchfork; and I used to get so scared that I would be afraid to go to bed at night. I don't suppose the Indians ever heard of such things, or, if they had, I never heard of them being willing to give away all their lands on earth, and quietly wait for a home in heaven."

"But, surely, Robert, you do not think religion has degraded the Negro?"

"Oh, I wouldn't say that. But a man is in a tight fix when he takes his part, like Nat Turner or Denmark Veasy, and is made to fear that he will be hanged in this world and be burned in the next. And, since I come to think of it, we colored folks used to get mightily mixed up about our religion. Mr. Gundover had on his plantation a real smart man. He was religious, but he would steal."

"Oh, Robert," queried Sybil, "how could he be religious and steal?"

"He didn't think," retorted Robert, "it was any harm to steal from his master. I guess he thought it was right to get from his master all he could. He would have thought it wrong to steal from his fellow-servants. He thought that downright mean, but I wouldn't have insured the lives of Gundover's pigs and chickens, if Uncle Jack got them in a tight place. One day there was a minister stopping with Mr. Gundover. As a matter of course, in speaking of his servants, he gave Jack's sins an airing. He would much rather confess Jack's sins than his own. Now Gundover wanted to do two things, save his pigs and poultry, and save Jack's soul. He told the minister that Jack was a liar and a thief, and gave the minister a chance to talk with Uncle Jack about the state of his soul. Uncle Jack listened very quietly, and when taxed with stealing his master's wheat he was ready with an answer. 'Now Massa Parker,' said Jack, 'lem'me tell yer jis' how it war 'bout dat wheat. Wen ole Jack com'd down yere, dis place war all growed up in woods. He go ter work, clared up de groun' an' plowed, an' planted, an' riz a crap, an' den wen it war all done, he hadn't a dollar to buy his ole woman a gown; an' he jis' took a bag ob wheat.'"

"What did Mr. Parker say?" asked Sybil.

"I don't know, though I reckon he didn't think it was a bad steal after all, but I don't suppose he told Jack so. When he came to the next point, about Jack's lying, I suppose he thought he had a clear case; but Jack was equal to the occasion."

"How did he clear up that charge?" interrogated Captain Sybil.

"Finely. I think if he had been educated he would have made a first-rate lawyer. He said, 'Marse Parker, dere's old Joe. His wife don't lib on dis plantation. Old Joe go ober ter see her, but he stayed too long, an' didn't git back in time fer his work. Massa's oberseer kotched him an' cut him all up.

When de oberseer went inter de house, pore old Joe war all tired an' beat up, an' so he lay down by de fence corner and go ter sleep. Bimeby Massa oberseer com'd an' axed, "all bin a workin' libely?" I say "Yes, Massa.'" Then said Mr. Parker, 'You were lying, Joe had been sleeping, not working.' 'I know's dat, but ef I tole on Joe, Massa oberseer cut him all up again, and Massa Jesus says, "Blessed am de Peacemaker.'" I heard, continued Robert, that Mr. Parker said to Gundover, 'You seem to me like a man standing in a stream where the blood of Jesus can reach you, but you are standing between it and your slaves. How will you answer that in the Day of Judgment?'"

"What did Gundover say?" asked Captain Sybil.

"He turned pale, and said, 'For God's sake don't speak of the Day of Judgment in connection with slavery.'"

Just then a messenger brought a communication to Captain Sybil. He read it attentively, and, turning to Robert, said, "Here are orders for an engagement at Five Forks tomorrow. Oh, this wasting of life and scattering of treasure might have been saved had we only been wiser. But the time is passing. Look after your company, and see that everything is in readiness as soon as possible."

Carefully Robert superintended the arrangements for the coming battle of a strife which for years had thrown its crimson shadows over the land. The Rebels fought with a valor worthy of a better cause. The disaster of Bull Run had been retrieved. Sherman had made his famous march to the sea. Fighting Joe Hooker had scaled the stronghold of the storm king and won a victory in the palace chamber of the clouds; the Union soldiers had captured Columbia, replanted the Stars and Stripes in Charleston, and changed that old sepulchre of slavery into the cradle of a newborn freedom. Farragut had been as triumphant on water as the other generals had been victorious on land, and New Orleans had been wrenched from the hands of the Confederacy. The Rebel leaders were obstinate. Misguided hordes had followed them to defeat and death. Grant was firm and determined to fight it out if it took all summer. The closing battles were fought with desperate courage and firm resistance, but at last the South was forced to succumb. On the ninth day of April, 1865, General Lee surrendered to General Grant. The lost cause went down in blood and tears, and on the brows of a ransomed people God poured the chrism of a new era, and they stood a race newly anointed with freedom.

16.
AFTER THE BATTLE.

Very sad and heart-rending were the scenes with which Iola came in constant contact. Well may Christian men and women labor and pray for the time when nations shall learn war no more; when, instead of bloody conflicts, there shall be peaceful arbitration. The battle in which Robert fought, after his last conversation with Captain Sybil, was one of the decisive struggles of the closing conflict. The mills of doom and fate had ground out a fearful grist of agony and death,

> "And lives of men and souls of State
> Were thrown like chaff beyond the gates."

Numbers were taken prisoners. Pale, young corpses strewed the earth; manhood was stricken down in the flush of its energy and prime. The ambulances brought in the wounded and dying. Captain Sybil laid down his life on the altar of freedom. His prediction was fulfilled. Robert was brought into the hospital, wounded, but not dangerously. Iola remembered him as being the friend of Tom Anderson, and her heart was drawn instinctively towards him. For a while he was delirious, but her presence had a soothing effect upon him. He sometimes imagined that she was his mother, and he would tell her how he had missed her; and then at times he would call her sister. Iola, tender and compassionate, humored his fancies, and would sing to him in low, sweet tones some of the hymns she had learned in her old home in Mississippi. One day she sang a few verses of the hymn beginning with the words—

> *"Drooping souls no longer grieve,*
> *Heaven is propitious;*
> *If on Christ you do believe,*
> *You will find Him precious."*

"That," said he, looking earnestly into Iola's face, "was my mother's hymn. I have not heard it for years. Where did you learn it?"

Iola gazed inquiringly upon the face of her patient, and saw, by his clear gaze and the expression of his face, that his reason had returned.

"In my home, in Mississippi, from my own dear mother," was Iola's reply.

"Do you know where she learned it?" asked Robert.

"When she was a little girl she heard her mother sing it. Years after, a Methodist preacher came to our house, sang this hymn, and left the book behind him. My father was a Catholic, but my mother never went to any church. I did not understand it then, but I do now. We used to sing together, and read the Bible when we were alone."

"Do you remember where she came from, and who was her mother?" asked Robert, anxiously.

"My dear friend, you must be quiet. The fever has left you, but I will not answer for the consequences if you get excited."

Robert lay quiet and thoughtful for a while and, seeing he was wakeful, Iola said, "Have you any friends to whom you would like to send a letter?"

A pathetic expression flitted over his face, as he sadly replied, "I haven't, to my knowledge, a single relation in the world. When I was about ten years old my mother and sister were sold from me. It is more than twenty years since I have heard from them. But that hymn which you were singing reminded me so much of my mother! She used to sing it when I was a child. Please sing it again."

Iola's voice rose soft and clear by his bedside, till he fell into a quiet slumber. She remembered that her mother had spoken of her brother before they had parted, and her interest and curiosity were awakened by Robert's story. While he slept, she closely scrutinized Robert's features, and detected a striking resemblance between him and her mother.

"Oh, I *do* wonder if he can be my mother's brother, from whom she has been separated so many years!"

Anxious as she was to ascertain if there was any relationship between Robert and her mother, she forbore to question him on the subject which lay so near her heart. But one day, when he was so far recovered as to be able to walk around, he met Iola on the hospital grounds, and said to her:—

"Miss Iola, you remind me so much of my mother and sister that I cannot help wondering if you are the daughter of my long-lost sister."

"Do you think," asked Iola, "if you saw the likeness of your sister you would recognize her?"

"I am afraid not. But there is one thing I can remember about her: she used to have a mole on her cheek, which mother used to tell her was her beauty spot."

"Look at this," said Iola, handing him a locket which contained her mother's picture.

Robert grasped the locket eagerly, scanned the features attentively, then, handing it back, said: "I have only a faint remembrance of my sister's features; but I never could recognize in that beautiful woman the dear little sister with whom I used to play. Oh, the cruelty of slavery! How it wrenched and tore us apart! Where is *your* mother now?"

"Oh, I cannot tell," answered Iola. "I left her in Mississippi. My father was a wealthy Creole planter, who fell in love with my mother. She was his slave, but he educated her in the North, freed, and married her. My father was very careful to have the fact of our Negro blood concealed from us. I had not the slightest suspicion of it. When he was dead the secret was revealed. His white relations set aside my father's will, had his marriage declared invalid, and my mother and her children were remanded to slavery." Iola shuddered as she pronounced the horrid word, and grew deadly pale; but, regaining her self-possession, continued: "Now, that freedom has come, I intend to search for my mother until I find her."

"I do not wonder," said Robert, "that we had this war. The nation had sinned enough to suffer."

"Yes," said Iola, "if national sins bring down national judgments, then the nation is only reaping what it sowed."

"What are your plans for the future, or have you any?" asked Robert.

"I intend offering myself as a teacher in one of the schools which are being opened in different parts of the country," replied Iola. "As soon as I am able I will begin my search for my dear mother. I will advertise for her in the papers, hunt for her in the churches, and use all the means in my power to get some tidings of her and my brother Harry. What a cruel thing it was to separate us!"

17.
FLAMES IN THE SCHOOL-ROOM.

"Good morning," said Dr. Gresham, approaching Robert and Iola. "How are you both? You have mended rapidly," turning to Robert, "but then it was only a flesh wound. Your general health being good, and your blood in excellent condition, it was not hard for you to rally."

"Where have you been, Doctor? I have a faint recollection of having seen you on the morning I was brought in from the field, but not since."

"I have been on a furlough. I was running down through exhaustion and overwork, and I was compelled to go home for a few weeks' rest. But now, as they are about to close the hospital, I shall be permanently relieved. I am glad that this cruel strife is over. It seemed as if I had lived through ages during these last few years. In the early part of the war I lost my arm by a stray shot, and my armless sleeve is one of the mementos of battle I shall carry with me through life. Miss Leroy," he continued, turning respectfully to Iola, "would you permit me to ask you, as I would have someone ask my sister under the same circumstances, if you have matured any plans for the future, or if I can be of the least service to you? If so, I would be pleased to render you any service in my power."

"My purpose," replied Iola, "is to hunt for my mother, and to find her if she is alive. I am willing to go anywhere and do anything to find her. But I will need a standpoint from whence I can send out lines of inquiry. It must take time, in the disordered state of affairs, even to get a clue by which I may discover her whereabouts."

"How would you like to teach?" asked the Doctor. "Schools are being opened all around us. Numbers of excellent and superior women are coming from the North to engage as teachers of the freed people. Would you be willing to take a school among these people? I think it will be uphill work. I believe it will take generations to get over the duncery of slavery. Some of these poor fellows who came into our camp did not know their right hands from their left, nor their ages, nor even the days of the month. It took me some time, in a number of cases, to understand their language. It saddened my heart to see such ignorance. One day I asked one a question, and he answered, "I no shum'.""

"What did he mean?" asked Iola.

"That he did not see it," replied the doctor. "Of course, this does not apply to all of them. Some of them are wide-awake and sharp as steel traps. I think some of that class may be used in helping others."

"I should be very glad to have an opportunity to teach," said Iola. "I used to be a great favorite among the colored children on my father's plantation."

In a few days after this conversation the hospital was closed. The sick and convalescent were removed, and Iola obtained a position as a teacher. Very soon Iola realized that while she was heartily appreciated by the freedmen, she was an object of suspicion and dislike to their former owners. The North had conquered by the supremacy of the sword, and the South had bowed to the inevitable. But here was a new army that had come with an invasion of ideas, that had come to supplant ignorance with knowledge, and it was natural that its members should be unwelcome to those who had made it a crime to teach their slaves to read the name of the ever blessed Christ. But Iola had found her work, and the freed men their friend.

When Iola opened her school she took pains to get acquainted with the parents of the children, and she gained their confidence and cooperation. Her face was a passport to their hearts. Ignorant of books, human faces were the scrolls from which they had been reading for ages. They had been the sunshine and shadow of their lives.

Iola had found a school-room in the basement of a colored church, where the doors were willingly opened to her. Her pupils came from miles around, ready and anxious to get some "book larnin'." Some of the old folks were eager to learn, and it was touching to see the eyes which had grown dim under the shadows of slavery, donning spectacles and trying to make out the words. As Iola had nearly all of her life been accustomed to colored children she had no physical repulsions to overcome, no prejudices to conquer in dealing with parents and children. In their simple childish fashion they would bring her fruits and flowers, and gladden her lonely heart with little tokens of affection.

One day a gentleman came to the school and wished to address the children. Iola suspended the regular order of the school, and the gentleman essayed to talk to them on the achievements of the white race, such as building steamboats and carrying on business. Finally, he asked how they did it?

"They've got money," chorused the children.

"But how did they get it?"

"They took it from us," chimed the youngsters. Iola smiled, and the gentleman was nonplussed; but he could not deny that one of the powers of knowledge is the power of the strong to oppress the weak.

The school was soon overcrowded with applicants, and Iola was forced to refuse numbers, because their quarters were too cramped. The school was beginning to lift up the home, for Iola was not satisfied to teach her children only the rudiments of knowledge. She had tried to lay the foundation of good character. But the elements of evil burst upon her loved and cherished work. One night the heavens were lighted with lurid flames, and Iola beheld the school, the pride and joy of her pupils and their parents, a smoldering ruin. Iola gazed with sorrowful dismay on what seemed the cruel work of an incendiary's torch. While she sat, mournfully contemplating the work of destruction, her children formed a procession, and, passing by the wreck of their school, sang:—

> *"Oh, do not be discouraged,*
> *For Jesus is your friend."*

As they sang, the tears sprang to Iola's eyes, and she said to herself, "I am not despondent of the future of my people; there is too much elasticity in their spirits, too much hope in their hearts, to be crushed out by unreasoning malice."

18.
SEARCHING FOR LOST ONES.

To bind anew the ties which slavery had broken and gather together the remnants of his scattered family became the earnest purpose of Robert's life. Iola, hopeful that in Robert she had found her mother's brother, was glad to know she was not alone in *her* search. Having sent out lines of inquiry in different directions, she was led to hope, from some of the replies she had received, that her mother was living somewhere in Georgia.

Hearing that a Methodist conference was to convene in that State, and being acquainted with the bishop of that district, she made arrangements to accompany him thither. She hoped to gather some tidings of her mother through the ministers gathered from different parts of that State.

From her brother she had heard nothing since her father's death. On his way to the conference, the bishop had an engagement to dedicate a church, near the city of C——, in North Carolina. Iola was quite willing to stop there a few days, hoping to hear something of Robert Johnson's mother. Soon after she had seated herself in the cars she was approached by a gentleman, who reached out his hand to her, and greeted her with great cordiality. Iola looked up, and recognized him immediately as one of her last patients at the hospital. It was none other than Robert Johnson.

"I am so glad to meet you," he said. "I am on my way to C—— in search of my mother. I want to see the person who sold her last, and, if possible, get some clew to the direction in which she went."

"And I," said Iola, "am in search of *my* mother. I am convinced that when we find those for whom we are searching they will prove to be very nearly related. Mamma said, before we were parted, that her brother had a red spot on his temple. If I could see that spot I should rest assured that my mother is your sister."

"Then," said Robert, "I can give you that assurance," and smilingly he lifted his hair from his temple, on which was a large, red spot.

"I am satisfied," exclaimed Iola, fixing her eyes, beaming with hope and confidence, on Robert. "Oh, I am so glad that I can, without the least hesitation, accept your services to join with me in the further search. What are your plans?"

"To stop for a while in C——," said Robert, "and gather all the information possible from those who sold and bought my mother. I intend to leave no stone unturned in searching for her."

"Oh, I *do* hope that you will succeed. I expect to stop over there a few days, and I shall be so glad if, before I leave, I hear your search has been crowned with success, or, a least, that you have been put on the right track. Although I was born and raised in the midst of slavery, I had not the least idea of its barbarous selfishness till I was forced to pass through it. But we lived so much alone I had no opportunity to study it, except on our own plantation. My father and mother were very kind to their slaves. But it was slavery, all the same, and I hate it, root and branch."

Just then the conductor called out the station.

"We stop here," said Robert. "I am going to see Mrs. Johnson, and hunt up some of my old acquaintances. Where do you stop?"

"I don't know," replied Iola. "I expect that friends will be here to meet us. Bishop B——, permit me to introduce you to Mr. Robert Johnson, whom I have every reason to believe is my mother's brother. Like myself, he is engaged in hunting up his lost relatives."

"And I," said Robert, "am very much pleased to know that we are not without favorable clues."

"Bishop," said Iola, "Mr. Johnson wishes to know where I am to stop. He is going on an exploring expedition, and wishes to let me know the result."

"We stop at Mrs. Allston's, 313 New Street," said the bishop. "If I can be of any use to you, I am at your service."

"Thank you," said Robert, lifting his hat, as he left them to pursue his inquiries about his long-lost mother.

Quickly he trod the old familiar streets which led to his former home. He found Mrs. Johnson, but she had aged very fast since the war. She was no longer the lithe, active woman, with her proud manner and resolute bearing. Her eye had lost its brightness, her step its elasticity, and her whole appearance indicated that she was slowly sinking beneath a weight of sorrow which was heavier far than her weight of years. When she heard that Robert had called to see her she was going to receive him in the hall, as she would have done any of her former slaves, but her mind immediately changed when she saw him. He was not the light-hearted, careless, mischief-loving Robby of former days, but a handsome man, with heavy mustache, dark, earnest eyes, and proud military bearing. He smiled, and reached out his hand to her. She hardly knew how to address him. To her colored people were either boys and girls, or "aunties and uncles." She had never in her life addressed a colored person as "Mr. or Mrs." To do so now was to violate the social customs of the place. It would be like learning a new language in her old age. Robert immediately set her at ease by addressing her under the old familiar name of "Miss Nancy." This immediately relieved her of all embarrassment. She invited him into the sitting-room, and gave him a warm welcome.

"Well, Robby," she said, "I once thought that you would have been the last one to leave me. You know I never ill-treated you, and I gave you everything you needed. People said that I was spoiling you. I thought you were as happy as the days were long. When I heard of other people's servants leaving them I used to say to myself, 'I can trust my Bobby; he will stick to me to the last.' But I fooled myself that time. Soon as the Yankee soldiers got in sight you left me without saying a word. That morning I came down into the kitchen and asked Linda, 'Where's Robert? Why hasn't he set the table?' She said 'she hadn't seen you since the night before.' I thought maybe you were sick, and I went to see, but you were not in your room. I couldn't believe at first that you were gone. Wasn't I always good to you?"

"Oh, Miss Nancy," replied Robert; "you were good, but freedom was better."

"Yes," she said, musingly, "I suppose I would have done the same. But, Robby, it did go hard with me at first. However, I soon found out that my neighbors had been going through the same thing. But it's all over now. Let bygones be bygones. What are you doing now, and where are you living?"

"I am living in the city of P——. I have opened a hardware store there. But just now I am in search of my mother and sister."

"I hope that you may find them."

"How long," asked Robert, "do you think it has been since they left here?"

"Let me see; it must have been nearly thirty years. You got my letter?"

"Yes, ma'am; thank you."

"There have been great changes since you left here," Mrs. Johnson said. "Gundover died, and a number of colored men have banded together, bought his plantation, and divided it among themselves. And I hear they have a very nice settlement out there. I hope, since the Government has set them free, that they will succeed."

After Robert's interview with Mrs. Johnson he thought he would visit the settlement and hunt up his old friends. He easily found the place. It was on a clearing in Gundover's woods, where Robert and Uncle Daniel had held their last prayer-meeting. Now the gloomy silence of those woods was broken by the hum of industry, the murmur of cheerful voices, and the merry laughter of happy children. Where they had trodden with fear and misgiving, freedmen walked with light and bounding hearts. The schoolhouse had taken the place of the slave pen and auction block. "How is yer, ole boy?" asked one laborer of another.

"Everything is lobly," replied the other. The blue sky arching overhead and the beauty of the scenery justified the expression.

Gundover had died soon after the surrender. Frank Anderson had grown reckless and drank himself to death. His brother Tom had been killed in battle. Their mother, who was Gundover's daughter, had died insane. Their father had also passed away. The defeat of the Confederates, the loss of his sons, and the emancipation of his slaves, were blows from which he never recovered. As Robert passed leisurely along, delighted with the evidences of thrift and industry which constantly met his eye, he stopped to admire a garden filled with beautiful flowers, clambering vines, and rustic adornments.

On the porch sat an elderly woman, darning stockings, the very embodiment of content and good humor. Robert looked inquiringly at her. On seeing him, she almost immediately exclaimed, "Shore as I'se born, dat's Robert! Look yere, honey, whar did yer come from? I'll gib my head fer a choppin' block ef dat ain't Miss Nancy's Bob. Ain't yer our Bobby? Shore yer is."

"Of course I am," responded Robert. "It isn't anybody else. How did you know me?"

"How did I know yer? By dem mischeebous eyes, ob course. I'd a knowed yer if I had seed yer in Europe."

"In Europe, Aunt Linda? Where's that?"

"I don't know. I specs its some big city, somewhar. But yer looks jis' splendid. Yer looks good 'nuff ter kiss."

"Oh, Aunt Linda, don't say that. You make me blush."

"Oh you go 'long wid yer. I specs yer's got a nice little wife up dar whar yer comes from, dat kisses yer ebery day, an' Sunday, too."

"Is that the way your old man does you?"

"Oh, no, not a bit. He isn't one ob de kissin' kine. But sit down," she said, handing Robert a chair. "Won't yer hab a glass ob milk? Boy, I'se a libin' in clover. Neber 'spected ter see sich good times in all my born days."

"Well, Aunt Linda," said Robert, seating himself near her, and drinking the glass of milk which she had handed him, "how goes the battle? How have you been getting on since freedom?"

"Oh, fust rate, fust rate! Wen freedom com'd I jist lit out ob Miss Johnson's kitchen soon as I could. I wanted ter re'lize I war free, an' I couldn't, tell I got out er de sight and soun' ob ole Miss. When de war war ober an' de sogers war still stopping' yere, I made pies an' cakes, sole em to de sogers, an' jist made money han' ober fist. An' I kep' on a workin' an' a savin' till my ole man got back from de war wid his wages and his bounty money. I felt right set up an' mighty big wen we counted all dat money. We had neber seen so much money in our lives befo', let alone hab it fer ourselbs. An' I sez, 'John, you take dis money an' git a nice place wid it.' An' he sez, 'Dere's no use tryin', kase dey don't want ter sell us any lan'.' Ole Gundover said, 'fore he died, dat he would let de lan' grow up in trees 'fore he'd sell it to us. An' dere war Mr. Brayton; he buyed some lan' and sole it to some cullud folks, an' his ole frien's got so mad wid him dat dey wouldn't speak ter him, an' he war borned down yere. I tole ole Miss Anderson's daughter dat we wanted ter git some homes ob our ownselbs. She sez, 'Den you won't want ter work for us?' Jis' de same as ef we could eat an' drink our houses. I tell yer, Robby, dese white folks don't know eberything."

"That's a fact, Aunt Linda."

"Den I sez ter John, 'wen one door shuts anoder opens.' An' shore 'nough, ole Gundover died, an' his place war all in debt, an' had to be sole. Some Jews bought it, but dey didn't want to farm it, so dey gib us a chance to buy it. Dem Jews hez been right helpful to cullud people wen dey hab lan' to sell. I reckon dey don't keer who buys it so long as dey gits de money. Well, John didn't gib in at fust; didn't want to let on his wife knowed more dan he did, an' dat he war ruled ober by a woman. Yer know he is an' ole Firginian, an' some ob dem ole Firginians do so lub to rule a woman. But I kep' naggin at him, till I specs he got tired of my tongue, an' he went and buyed dis piece ob lan'. Dis house war on it, an' war all gwine to wrack. It used to belong to John's ole marster. His wife died right in dis house, an' arter dat her husband went right to de dorgs; an' now he's in de pore-house. My, but ain't dem tables turned! When we knowed it war our own, warn't my ole man proud! I seed it in him, but he wouldn't let on. Ain't you men powerful 'ceitful?"

"Oh, Aunt Linda, don't put me in with the rest!"

"I don't know 'bout dat. Put you all in de bag for 'ceitfulness, an' I don't know which would git out fust."

"Well, Aunt Linda, I suppose by this time you know how to read and write?"

"No, chile, sence freedom's com'd I'se bin scratchin' too hard to get a libin' to put my head down to de book."

"But, Aunt Linda, it would be such company when your husband is away, to take a book. Do you never get lonesome?"

"Chile, I ain't got no time ter get lonesome. Ef you had eber so many chickens to feed, an' pigs squealin' fer somethin' ter eat, an' yore ducks an' geese squakin' 'roun' yer, yer wouldn't hab time ter git lonesome."

"But, Aunt Linda, you might be sick for months, and think what a comfort it would be if you could read your Bible."

"Oh, I could hab prayin' and singin'. Dese people is mighty good 'bout prayin' by de sick. Why, Robby, I think it would gib me de hysterics ef I war to try to git book larnin' froo my pore ole head. How long is yer gwine to stay? An' whar is yer stoppin?"

"I got here today," said Robert, "but I expect to stay several days."

"Well, I wants yer to meet my ole man, an' talk 'bout ole times. Couldn't yer come an' stop wid me, or isn't my house sniptious 'nuff?"

"Yes, thank you; but there is a young lady in town whom I think is my niece, my sister's daughter, and I want to be with her all I can."

"Your niece! Whar did you git any niece from?"

"Don't you remember," asked Robert, "that my mother had a little daughter, when Mrs. Johnson sold her? Well, I believe this young lady is that daughter's child."

"Laws a marcy!" exclaimed Aunt Linda, "yer don't tell me so! Whar did yer ketch up wid her?"

"I met her first," said Robert, "at the hospital here, when our poor Tom was dying; and when I was wounded at Five Forks she attended me in the field hospital there. She was just as good as gold."

"Well, did I eber! You jis' fotch dat chile to see me, ef she ain't too fine. I'se pore, but I'se clean, an' I ain't forgot how ter git up good dinners. Now, I wants ter hab a good talk 'bout our feller-sarvants."

"Yes, and I," said Robert, "want to hear all about Uncle Daniel, and Jennie, and Uncle Ben Tunnel."

"Well, I'se got lots an' gobs ter tell yer. I'se kep' track ob dem all. Aunt Katie died an' went ter hebben in a blaze ob glory. Uncle Dan'el stayed on de place till Marse Robert com'd back. When de war war ober he war smashed all ter pieces. I did pity him from de bottom ob my heart. When he went ter de war he looked so brave an' han'some; an' wen he com'd back he looked orful. 'Fore he went he gib Uncle Dan'el a bag full ob money ter take kere ob. An' wen he com'd back Uncle Dan'el gibed him ebery cent ob it. It warn't ebery white pusson he could hab trusted wid it. 'Cause yer know, Bobby, money's a mighty temptin' thing. Dey tells me dat Marster Robert los' a heap ob property by de war; but Marse Robert war always mighty good ter Uncle Dan'el and Aunt Katie. He war wid her wen she war dyin' an' she got holt his han' an' made him promise dat he would meet her in glory. I neber seed anybody so happy in my life. She singed an' prayed ter de last. I tell you dis ole time religion is good 'nuff fer me. Mr. Robert didn't stay yere long arter her, but I beliebs he went all right. But 'fore he went he looked out fer Uncle Dan'el. Did you see dat nice little cabin down dere wid de green shutters an' nice little garden in front? Well, 'fore Marse Robert died he gib Uncle Dan'el dat place, an' Miss Mary and de chillen looks arter him yet; an' he libs jis' as snug as a bug in a rug. I'se gwine ter axe him ter take supper wid you. He'll be powerful glad ter see you."

"Do you ever go to see old Miss?" asked Robert.

"Oh, yes; I goes ebery now and den. But she's jis' fell froo. Ole Johnson jis' drunk hisself to death. He war de biggest guzzler I eber seed in my life. Why, dat man he drunk up ebery thing he could lay his han's on. Sometimes he would go 'roun' tryin' to borrer money from pore cullud folks. 'Twas rale drefful de way dat pore feller did frow hisself away. But drink did it all. I tell you, Bobby, dat drink's a drefful thing wen it gits de upper han' ob you. You'd better steer clar ob it."

"That's so," assented Robert.

"I know'd Miss Nancy's fadder and mudder. Dey war mighty rich. Some ob de real big bugs. Marse Jim used to know dem, an' come ober ter de plantation, an' eat an' drink wen he got ready, an' stay as long as he choose. Ole Cousins used to have wine at dere table ebery day, an' Marse Jim war mighty fon' ob dat wine, an' sometimes he would drink till he got quite boozy. Ole Cousins liked him bery well, till he foun' out he wanted his darter, an' den he didn't want him fer rags nor patches. But Miss Nancy war mighty headstrong, an' allers liked to hab her own way; an' dis time she got it. But didn't she step her foot inter it? Ole Johnson war mighty han'some, but when dat war said all war said. She run'd off an' got married, but wen she got down she war too spunkey to axe her pa for anything. Wen you war wid her, yer know she only took big bugs. But wen de war com'd 'roun' it tore her all ter pieces, an' now she's as pore as Job's turkey. I feel's right sorry fer her. Well, Robby, things is turned 'roun' mighty quare. Ole Mistus war up den, an' I war down; now, she's down, an' I'se up. But I pities her, 'cause she warn't so bad arter all. De wuss thing she eber did war ta sell your mudder, an' she wouldn't hab done dat but she snatched de whip out ob her han' an gib her a lickin'.

Now I belieb in my heart she war 'fraid ob your mudder arter dat. But we women had ter keep 'em from whippin' us, er dey'd all de time been libin' on our bones. She had no man ter whip us 'cept dat ole drunken husband ob hern, an' he war allers too drunk ter whip hisself. He jis' wandered off, an' I reckon he died in somebody's pore-house. He warn't no 'count nohow you fix it. Weneber I goes to town I carries her some garden sass, er a little milk an' butter. An' she's mighty glad ter git it. I ain't got nothin' agin her. She neber struck me a lick in her life, an' I belieb in praising de bridge dat carries me ober. Dem Yankees set me free, an' I thinks a powerful heap ob dem. But it does rile me ter see dese mean white men comin' down yere an' settin' up dere grog-shops, tryin' to fedder dere nests sellin' licker to pore culled people. Deys de bery kine ob men dat used ter keep dorgs to ketch de runaways. I'd be chokin' fer a drink 'fore I'd eber spen' a cent wid dem, a spreadin' dere traps to git de black folks' money. You jis' go down town 'fore sun up to-morrer mornin' an' you see ef dey don't hab dem bars open to sell dere drams to dem hard workin' culled people 'fore dey goes ter work. I thinks some niggers is mighty big fools."

"Oh, Aunt Linda, don't run down your race. Leave that for the white people."

"I ain't runnin' down my people. But a fool's a fool, wether he's white or black. An' I think de nigger who will spen' his hard-earned money in dese yere new grog-shops is de biggest kine ob a fool, an' I sticks ter dat. You know we didn't hab all dese low places in slave times. An' what is dey fer, but to get the people's money. An' its a shame how dey do sling de licker 'bout 'lection times."

"But don't the temperance people want the colored people to vote the temperance ticket?"

"Yes, but some ob de culled people gits mighty skittish ef dey tries to git em to vote dare ticket 'lection time, an' keeps dem at a proper distance wen de 'lection's ober. Some ob dem say dere's a trick behine it, an' don't want to tech it. Dese white folks could do a heap wid de culled folks ef dey'd only treat em right."

"When our people say there is a trick behind it," said Robert, "I only wish they could see the trick before it—the trick of worse than wasting their money, and of keeping themselves and families poorer and more ignorant than there is any need for them to be."

"Well, Bobby, I beliebs we might be a people ef it warn't for dat mizzable drink. An' Robby, I jis' tells yer what I wants; I wants some libe man to come down yere an' splain things ter dese people. I don't mean a politic man, but a man who'll larn dese people how to bring up dere chillen, to keep our gals straight, an' our boys from runnin' in de saloons an' gamblin' dens."

"Don't your preachers do that?" asked Robert.

"Well, some ob dem does, an' some ob dem doesn't. An' wen dey preaches, I want dem to practice wat dey preach. Some ob dem says dey's called, but I jis' thinks laziness called some ob dem. An' I thinks since freedom come deres some mighty pore sticks set up for preachers. Now dere's John Anderson, Tom's brudder; you 'member Tom."

"Yes; as brave a fellow and as honest as ever stepped in shoe leather."

"Well, his brudder war mighty diffrent. He war down in de lower kentry wen de war war ober. He war mighty smart, an' had a good head-piece, an' a orful glib tongue. He set up store an' sole whisky, an' made a lot ob money. Den he wanted ter go to de legislatur. Now what should he do but make out he'd got 'ligion, an' war called to preach. He had no more 'ligion dan my ole dorg. But he had money an' built a meetin' house, whar he could hole meeting, an' hab funerals; an' you know cullud folks is mighty great on funerals. Well dat jis' tuck wid de people, an' he got 'lected to de legislatur. Den he got a fine house, an' his ole wife warn't good 'nuff for him. Den dere war a young schoolteacher, an' he begun cuttin' his eyes at her. But she war as deep in de mud as he war in de mire, an' he jis' gib up his ole wife and married her, a fusty thing. He war a mean ole hypocrit, an' I wouldn't sen' fer him to bury my cat. Robby, I'se down on dese kine ob preachers like a thousand bricks."

"Well, Aunt Linda, all the preachers are not like him."

"No; I knows dat; not by a jug full. We's got some mighty good men down yere, an' we's glad when dey comes, an' orful sorry when dey goes 'way. De las preacher we had war a mighty good man. He didn't like too much hollerin'."

"Perhaps," said Robert, "he thought it were best for only one to speak at a time."

"I specs so. His wife war de nicest and sweetest lady dat eber I did see. None ob yer airish, stuck up folks, like a tarrapin carryin' eberything on its back. She used ter hab meetins fer de mudders, an' larn us how to raise our chillen, an' talk so putty to de chillen. I sartinly did lub dat woman."

"Where is she now?" asked Robert.

"De Conference moved dem 'bout thirty miles from yere. Deys gwine to hab a big meetin' ober dere next Sunday. Don't you 'member dem meetins we used to hab in de woods? We don't hab to hide like we did den. But it don't seem as ef de people had de same good 'ligion we had den. 'Pears like folks is took up wid makin' money an' politics."

"Well, Aunt Linda, don't you wish those good old days would come back?"

"No, chile; neber, neber! Wat fer you take me? I'd ruther lib in a corn-crib. Freedom needn't keep me outer heben; an' ef I'se sich a fool as ter lose my 'ligion cause I'se free, I oughtn' ter git dere."

"But, Aunt Linda, if old Miss were able to take care of you, wouldn't you just as leave be back again?"

There was a faint quiver of indignation in Aunt Linda's voice, as she replied:—

"Don't yer want yer freedom? Well I wants ter pat my free foot. Halleluyah! But, Robby, I wants yer ter go ter dat big meetin' de wuss kine."

"How will I get there?" asked Robert.

"Oh, dat's all right. My ole man's got two ob de nicest mules you eber set yer eyes on. It'll jis' do yer good ter look at dem. I 'spect you'll see some ob yer ole frens dere. Dere's a nice settlemen' of cullud folks ober dere, an' I wants yer to come an' bring dat young lady. I wants dem folks to see wat nice folks I kin bring to de meetin'. I hope's yer didn't lose all your 'ligion in de army."

"Oh, I hope not," replied Robert.

"Oh, chile, yer mus' be shore 'bout dat. I don't want yer to ride hope's hoss down to torment. Now be shore an' come to-morrer an' bring dat young lady, an' take supper wid me. I'se all on nettles to see dat chile."

19.
STRIKING CONTRASTS.

The next day, Robert, accompanied by Iola, went to the settlement to take supper with Aunt Linda, and a very luscious affair it was. Her fingers had not lost their skill since she had tasted the sweets of freedom. Her biscuits were just as light and flaky as ever. Her jelly was as bright as amber, and her preserves were perfectly delicious. After she had set the table she stood looking in silent admiration, chuckling to herself: "Ole Mistus can't set sich a table as dat. She ought'er be yere to see it. Specs 'twould make her mouf water. Well, I mus' let bygones be bygones. But dis yere freedom's mighty good."

Aunt Linda had invited Uncle Daniel, and, wishing to give him a pleasant surprise, she had refrained from telling him that Robert Johnson was the one she wished him to meet.

"Do you know dis gemmen?" said Aunt Linda to Uncle Daniel, when the latter arrived.

"Well, I can't say's I do. My eyes is gittin dim, an I disremembers him."

"Now jis' you look right good at him. Don't yer 'member him?"

Uncle Daniel looked puzzled and, slowly scanning Robert's features, said: "He do look like somebody I used ter know, but I can't make him out ter save my life. I don't know whar to place him. Who is de gemmen, ennyhow?"

"Why, Uncle Dan'el," replied Aunt Linda, "dis is Robby; Miss Nancy's bad, mischeebous Robby, dat war allers playin' tricks on me."

"Well, shore's I'se born, ef dis ain't our ole Bobby!" exclaimed Uncle Daniel, delightedly. "Why, chile, whar did yer come from? Thought you war dead an' buried long 'go."

"Why, Uncle Daniel, did you send anybody to kill me?" asked Robert, laughingly.

"Oh, no'n 'deed, chile! But I yeard dat you war killed in de battle, an' I never 'spected ter see you agin."

"Well, here I am," replied Robert, "large as life, and just as natural. And this young lady, Uncle Daniel, I believe is my niece." As he spoke he turned to Iola. "Do you remember my mother?"

"Oh, yes," said Uncle Daniel, looking intently at Iola as she stepped forward and cordially gave him her hand.

"Well, I firmly believe," continued Robert, "that this is the daughter of the little girl whom Miss Nancy sold away with my mother."

"Well, I'se rale glad ter see her. She puts me mighty much in mine ob dem days wen we war all young togedder; wen Miss Nancy sed, 'Harriet war too high fer her.' It jis' seems like yisterday wen I yeard Miss Nancy say, 'No house could flourish whar dere war two mistresses.' Well, Mr. Robert—"

"Oh, no, no, Uncle Daniel," interrupted Robert, "don't say that! Call me Robby or Bob, just as you used to."

"Well, Bobby, I'se glad klar from de bottom of my heart ter see yer."

"Even if you wouldn't go with us when we left?"

"Oh, Bobby, dem war mighty tryin' times. You boys didn't know it, but Marster Robert hab giben me a bag ob money ter take keer ob, an' I promised him I'd do it an' I had ter be ez good ez my word."

"Oh, Uncle Daniel, why didn't you tell us boys all about it? We could have helped you take care of it."

"Now, wouldn't dat hab bin smart ter let on ter you chaps, an' hab you huntin' fer it from Dan ter Barsheba? I specs some ob you would bin a rootin' fer it yit!"

"Well, Uncle Daniel, we were young then; I can't tell what we would have done if we had found it. But we are older now."

"Yes, yer older, but I wouldn't put it pas' yer eben now, ef yer foun' out whar it war."

"Yes," said Iola, laughing, "they say 'caution is the parent of safety.'"

"Money's a mighty tempting thing," said Robert, smiling.

"But, Robby, dere's nothin' like a klar conscience; a klar conscience, Robby!"

Just then Aunt Linda, who had been completing the preparations for her supper, entered the room with her husband, and said, "Salters, let me interdoos you ter my fren', Mr. Robert Johnson, an' his niece, Miss Leroy."

"Why, is it possible," exclaimed Robert, rising, and shaking hands, "that you are Aunt Linda's husband?"

"Dat's what de parson sed," replied Salters.

"I thought," pursued Robert, "that your name was John Andrews. It was such when you were in my company."

"All de use I'se got fer dat name is ter git my money wid it; an' wen dat's done, all's done. Got 'nuff ob my ole Marster in slave times, widout wearin' his name in freedom. Wen I got done wid him, I got done wid his name. Wen I 'listed, I war John Andrews; and wen I gits my pension, I'se John Andrews; but now Salters is my name, an' I likes it better."

"But how came you to be Aunt Linda's husband? Did you get married since the war?"

"Lindy an' me war married long 'fore de war. But my ole Marster sole me away from her an' our little gal, an' den sole her chile ter somebody else. Arter freedom, I hunted up our little gal, an' foun' her. She war a big woman den. Den I com'd right back ter dis place an' foun' Lindy. She hedn't married agin, nuther hed I; so we jis' let de parson marry us out er de book; an' we war mighty glad ter git togedder agin, an' feel hitched togedder fer life."

"Well, Uncle Daniel," said Robert, turning the conversation toward him, "you and Uncle Ben wouldn't go with us, but you came out all right at last."

"Yes, indeed," said Aunt Linda, "Ben got inter a stream of luck. Arter freedom com'd, de people had a heap of fath in Ben; an' wen dey wanted someone to go ter Congress dey jist voted for Ben ter go. An' he went, too. An' wen Salters went to Washin'ton to git his pension, who should he see dere wid dem big men but our Ben, lookin' jist as big as any ob dem."

"An' it did my ole eyes good jist ter see it," broke in Salters; "if I couldn't go dere myself, I war mighty glad to see someone ob my people dat could. I felt like de boy who, wen somebody said he war gwine to slap off his face, said, 'Yer kin slap off my face, but I'se got a big brudder, an' you can't slap off his face.' I went to see him 'fore I lef, and he war jist de same as he war wen we war boys togedder. He hadn't got de big head a bit."

"I reckon Mirandy war mighty sorry she didn't stay wid him. I know I should be," said Aunt Linda.

"Uncle Daniel," asked Robert, "are you still preaching?"

"Yes, chile, I'se still firing off de Gospel gun."

"I hear some of the Northern folks are down here teaching theology, that is, teaching young men how to preach. Why don't you study theology?"

"Look a yere, boy, I'se been a preachin' dese thirty years, an' you come yere a tellin' me 'bout studying yore ologies. I larn'd my 'ology at de foot ob de cross. You bin dar?"

"Dear Uncle Daniel," said Iola, "the moral aspect of the nation would be changed if it would learn at the same cross to subordinate the spirit of caste to the spirit of Christ."

"Does yer 'member Miss Nancy's Harriet," asked Aunt Linda, "dat she sole away kase she wouldn't let her whip her? Well, we think dis is Harriet's gran'chile. She war sole away from her mar, an' now she's a lookin' fer her."

"Well, I hopes she may fine her," replied Salters. "I war sole 'way from my mammy wen I war eighteen mont's ole, an' I wouldn't know her now from a bunch ob turnips."

"I," said Iola, "am on my way South seeking for my mother, and I shall not give up until I find her."

"Come," said Aunt Linda, "we mustn't stan' yer talkin', or de grub'll git cole. Come, frens, sit down, an' eat some ob my pore supper."

Aunt Linda sat at the table in such a flutter of excitement that she could hardly eat, but she gazed with intense satisfaction on her guests. Robert sat on her right hand, contrasting Aunt Linda's pleasant situation with the old days in Mrs. Johnson's kitchen, where he had played his pranks upon her, and told her the news of the war.

Over Iola there stole a spirit of restfulness. There was something so motherly in Aunt Linda's manner that it seemed to recall the bright, sunshiny days when she used to nestle in Mam Liza's arms, in her own happy home. The conversation was full of army reminiscences and recollections of the days of slavery. Uncle Daniel was much interested, and, as they rose from the table, exclaimed:—

"Robby, seein' yer an' hearin' yer talk, almos' puts new springs inter me. I feel 'mos' like I war gittin' younger."

After the supper, Salters and his guests returned to the front room, which Aunt Linda regarded with so much pride, and on which she bestowed so much care.

"Well, Captin," said Salters, "I neber 'spected ter see you agin. Do you know de las' time I seed yer? Well, you war on a stretcher, an' four ob us war carryin' you ter de hospital. War you much hurt?"

"No," replied Robert, "it was only a flesh wound; and this young lady nursed me so carefully that I soon got over it."

"Is dat de way you foun' her?"

"Yes, Andrews,—"

"Salters, ef you please," interrupted Salters. I'se only Andrews wen I gits my money."

"Well, Salters," continued Robert, "our freedom was a costly thing. Did you know that Captain Sybil was killed in one of the last battles of the war? These young chaps, who are taking it so easy, don't know the hardships through which we older ones passed. But all the battles are not fought, nor all the victories won. The colored man has escaped from one slavery, and I don't want him to fall into another. I want the young folks to keep their brains clear, and their right arms strong, to fight the battles of life manfully, and take their places alongside of every other people in this country. And I cannot see what is to hinder them if they get a chance."

"I don't nuther," said Salters. "I don't see dat dey drinks any more dan anybody else, nor dat dere is any meanness or debilment dat a black man kin do dat a white man can't keep step wid him."

"Yes," assented Robert, "but while a white man is stealing a thousand dollars, a black man is getting into trouble taking a few chickens."

"All that may be true," said Iola, "but there are some things a white man can do that we cannot afford to do."

"I beliebs eberybody, Norf and Souf, is lookin' at us; an' some ob dem ain't got no good blood fer us, nohow you fix it," said Salters.

"I specs cullud folks mus' hab done somethin'," interposed Aunt Linda.

"O, nonsense," said Robert. "I don't think they are any worse than the white people. I don't believe, if we had the power, we would do any more lynching, burning, and murdering than they do."

"Dat's so," said Aunt Linda, "it's ralely orful how our folks hab been murdered sence de war. But I don't think dese young folks is goin' ter take things as we's allers done."

"We war cowed down from the beginnin'," said Uncle Daniel, "but dese young folks ain't comin' up dat way."

"No," said Salters, "fer one night arter some ob our pore people had been killed, an' some ob our women had run'd away 'bout seventeen miles, my gran'son, looking me squar in de face, said: 'Ain't you got five fingers? Can't you pull a trigger as well as a white man?' I tell yer, Cap, dat jis' got to me, an' I made up my mine dat my boy should neber call me a coward."

"It is not to be expected," said Robert, "that these young people are going to put up with things as we did, when we weren't permitted to hold a meeting by ourselves, or to own a club or learn to read."

"I tried," said Salters, "to git a little out'er de book wen I war in de army. On Sundays I sometimes takes a book an' tries to make out words, but my eyes is gittin' dim an' de letters all run togedder, an' I gits sleepy, an' ef yer wants to put me to sleep jis' put a book in my han'. But wen it comes to gittin' out a stan' ob cotton, an' plantin' corn, I'se dere all de time. But dat gran'son ob mine is smart as a steel trap. I specs he'll be a preacher."

Salters looked admiringly at his grandson, who sat grinning in the corner, munching a pear he had brought from the table.

"Yes," said Aunt Linda, "his fadder war killed by the Secesh, one night, comin' home from a politic meetin', an' his pore mudder died a few weeks arter, an' we mean to make a man ob him."

"He's got to larn to work fust," said Salters, "an' den ef he's right smart I'se gwine ter sen' him ter college. An' ef he can't get a libin' one way, he kin de oder."

"Yes," said Iola, "I hope he will turn out an excellent young man, for the greatest need of the race is noble, earnest men, and true women."

"Job," said Salters, turning to his grandson, "tell Jake ter hitch up de mules, an' you stay dere an' help him. We's all gwine ter de big meetin'. Yore grandma hab set her heart on goin', an' it'll be de same as a spell ob sickness ef she don't hab a chance to show her bes' bib an' tucker. That ole gal's as proud as a peacock."

"Now, John Salters," exclaimed Aunt Linda, "ain't you 'shamed ob yourself? Allers tryin' to poke fun at yer pore wife. Never mine; wait till I'se gone, an' you'll miss me."

"Ef I war single," said Salters, "I could git a putty young gal, but it wouldn't be so easy wid you."

"Why not?" said Iola, smiling.

"'Cause young men don't want ole hens, an' ole men want young pullets," was Salter's reply.

"Robby, honey," said Aunt Linda, "when you gits a wife, don't treat her like dat man treats me."

"Oh, his head's level," answered Robert; "at least it was in the army."

"Dat's jis' de way; you see dat, Miss Iola? One man takin' up for de oder. But I'll be eben wid you bof. I must go now an' git ready."

Iola laughed. The homely enjoyment of that evening was very welcome to her after the trying scenes through which she had passed. Further conversation was interrupted by the appearance of the wagon, drawn by two fine mules. John Salters stopped joking his wife to admire his mules.

"Jis' look at dem," he said. "Ain't dey beauties? I bought 'em out ob my bounty-money. Arter de war war ober I had a little money, an' I war gwine ter rent a plantation on sheers an' git out a good stan' ob cotton. Cotton war bringin' orful high prices den, but Lindy said to me, 'Now, John, you'se got a lot ob money, an' you'd better salt it down. I'd ruther lib on a little piece ob lan' ob my own dan a big piece ob somebody else's. Well, I says to Lindy, I dun know nuthin' 'bout buyin' lan', an' I'se 'fraid arter I'se done buyed it an' put all de marrer ob dese bones in it, dat somebody's far-off cousin will come an' say de title ain't good, an' I'll lose it all."

"You're right thar, John," said Uncle Daniel. "White man's so unsartin, black man's nebber safe."

"But somehow," continued Salters, "Lindy warn't satisfied wid rentin', so I buyed a piece ob lan', an' I'se glad now I'se got it. Lindy's got a lot ob gumption; knows most as much as a man. She ain't got dat long head fer nuffin. She's got lots ob sense, but I don't like to tell her so."

"Why not?" asked Iola. "Do you think it would make her feel too happy?"

"Well, it don't do ter tell you women how much we thinks ob you. It sets you up too much. Ole Gundover's overseer war my marster, an' he used ter lib in dis bery house. I'se fixed it up sence I'se got it. Now I'se better off dan he is, 'cause he tuck to drink, an' all his frens is gone, an' he's in de pore-house."

Just then Linda came to the door with her baskets.

"Now, Lindy, ain't you ready yet? Do hurry up."

"Yes, I'se ready, but things wouldn't go right ef you didn't hurry me."

"Well, put your chicken fixins an' cake right in yere. Captin, you'll ride wid me, an' de young lady an' my ole woman'll take de back seat. Uncle Dan'el, dere's room for you ef you'll go."

"No, I thank you. It's time fer ole folks to go to bed. Good night! An', Bobby, I hopes to see you agin'."

20.
A REVELATION.

It was a lovely evening for the journey. The air was soft and balmy. The fields and hedges were redolent with flowers. Not a single cloud obscured the brightness of the moon or the splendor of the stars. The ancient trees were festooned with moss, which hung like graceful draperies. Ever and anon a startled hare glided over the path, and whip-poor-wills and crickets broke the restful silence of the night. Robert rode quietly along, quaffing the beauty of the scene and thinking of his boyish days, when he gathered nuts and wild plums in those woods; he also indulged pleasant reminiscences of later years, when, with Uncle Daniel and Tom Anderson, he attended the secret prayer-meetings. Iola rode along, conversing with Aunt Linda, amused and interested at the quaintness of her speech and the shrewdness of her intellect. To her the ride was delightful.

"Does yer know dis place, Robby," asked Aunt Linda, as they passed an old resort.

"I should think I did," replied Robert. "It is the place where we held our last prayer-meeting."

"An' dere's dat ole broken pot we used, ter tell 'bout de war. But warn't ole Miss hoppin' wen she foun' out you war goin' to de war! I thought she'd go almos' wile. Now, own up, Robby, didn't you feel kine ob mean to go off widout eben biddin' her goodbye? An' I ralely think ole Miss war fon' ob yer. Now, own up, honey, didn't yer feel a little down in de mouf wen yer lef' her."

"Not much," responded Robert. "I only thought she was getting paid back for selling my mother."

"Dat's so, Robby! Yore mudder war a likely gal, wid long black hair, an' kine ob gingerbread color. An' you neber hearn tell ob her sence dey sole her to Georgia?"

"Never," replied Robert, "but I would give everything I have on earth to see her once more. I *do* hope, if she is living, that I may meet her before I die."

"You's right, boy, cause she lub'd you as she lub'd her own life. Many a time hes she set in my ole cabin an' cried 'bout yer wen you war fas' asleep. It's all ober now, but I'se gwine to hole up fer dem Yankees dat gib me my freedom, an' sent dem nice ladies from de Norf to gib us some sense. Some ob dese folks calls em nigger teachers, an' won't hab nuffin to do wid 'em, but I jis' thinks dey's splendid. But dere's some triflin' niggers down yere who'll sell der votes for almost nuffin. Does you 'member Jake Williams an' Gundover's Tom? Well dem two niggers is de las' ob pea-time. Dey's mighty small pertaters an' few in a hill."

"Oh, Aunt Linda," said Robert, "don't call them niggers. They are our own people."

"Dey ain't my kine ob people. I jis' calls em niggers, an' niggers I means; an' de bigges' kine ob niggers. An' if my John war sich a nigger I'd whip him an' leave him."

"An' what would I be a doin'," queried John, suddenly rousing up at the mention of his name.

"Standing still and taking it, I suppose," said Iola, who had been quietly listening to and enjoying the conversation.

"Yes, an' I'd ketch myself stan'in' still an' takin' it," was John's plucky response.

"Well, you oughter, ef you's mean enough to wote dat ticket ter put me back inter slavery," was Aunt Linda's parting shot. "Robby," she continued, "you 'member Miss Nancy's Jinnie?"

"Of course I do," said Robert.

"She married Mr. Gundover's Dick. Well, dere warn't much git up an' go 'bout him. So, wen 'lection time com'd, de man he war workin' fer tole him ef he woted de radical ticket he'd turn him off. Well, Jinnie war so 'fraid he'd do it, dat she jis' follered him fer days."

"Poor fellow!" exclaimed Robert. "How did he come out?"

"He certainly was between two fires," interposed Iola.

"Oh, Jinnie gained de day. She jis' got her back up, and said, 'Now ef yer wote dat ticket ter put me back inter slavery, you take yore rags an' go.' An' Dick jis' woted de radical ticket. Jake Williams went on de Secesh side, woted whar he thought he'd git his taters, but he got fooled es slick es greese."

"How was that?" asked Robert.

"Some ob dem folks, dat I 'spects buyed his wote, sent him some flour an' sugar. So one night his wife hab company ter tea. Dey made a big spread, an' put a lot ob sugar on de table fer supper, an' Tom jis' went fer dat sugar. He put a lot in his tea. But somehow it didn't tase right, an' wen dey come ter fine out what war de matter, dey hab sent him a barrel ob san' wid some sugar on top, an' wen de sugar war all gone de san' war dare. Wen I yeard it, I jis' split my sides a larfin. It war too good to keep; an' wen it got roun', Jake war as mad as a March hare. But it sarved him right."

"Well, Aunt Linda, you musn't be too hard on Uncle Jake; you know he's getting old."

"Well he ain't too ole ter do right. He ain't no older dan Uncle Dan'el. An' I yered dey offered him $500 ef he'd go on dere side. An' Uncle Dan'el wouldn't tech it. An' dere's Uncle Job's wife; why didn't she go dat way? She war down on Job's meanness."

"What did she do?"

"Wen 'lection time 'rived, he com'd home bringing some flour an' meat; an' he says ter Aunt Polly, 'Ole woman, I got dis fer de wote.' She jis' picked up dat meat an' flour an' sent it sailin' outer doors, an' den com'd back an' gib him a good tongue-lashin'. 'Oder people,' she said, 'a wotin' ter lib good, an' you a sellin' yore wote! Ain't you got 'nuff ob ole Marster, an' ole Marster bin cuttin' you up? It shan't stay yere.' An' so she wouldn't let de things stay in de house."

"What did Uncle Job do?"

"He jis' stood dere an' cried."

"And didn't you feel sorry for him?" asked Iola.

"Not a bit! He hedn't no business ter be so shabby."

"But, Aunt Linda," pursued Iola, "if it were shabby for an ignorant colored man to sell his vote, wasn't it shabbier for an intelligent white man to buy it?"

"You see," added Robert, "all the shabbiness is not on our side."

"I knows dat," said Aunt Linda, "but I can't help it. I wants my people to wote right, an' to think somethin' ob demselves."

"Well, Aunt Linda, they say in every flock of sheep there will be one that's scabby," observed Iola.

"Dat's so! But I ain't got no use fer scabby sheep."

"Lindy," cried John, "we's most dar! Don't you yere dat singin'? Dey's begun a'ready."

"Neber mine," said Aunt Linda, "sometimes de las' ob de wine is de bes'."

Thus discoursing they had beguiled the long hours of the night and made their long journey appear short.

Very soon they reached the church, a neat, commodious, frame building, with a blue ceiling, white walls within and without, and large windows with mahogany-colored facings. It was a sight full of pathetic interest to see that group which gathered from miles around. They had come to break bread with each other, relate their experiences, and tell of their hopes of heaven. In that meeting were remnants of broken families—mothers who had been separated from their children before the war, husbands who had not met their wives for years. After the bread had been distributed and the handshaking was nearly over, Robert raised the hymn which Iola had sung for him when he was recovering from his wounds, and Iola, with her clear, sweet tones, caught up the words and joined him in the strain. When the hymn was finished a dear old mother rose from her seat. Her voice was quite strong. With still a lingering light and fire in her eye, she said:—

"I rise, bredren an' sisters, to say I'm on my solemn march to glory."

"Amen!" came from a number of voices. "Glory!"

"I'se had my trials an' temptations, my ups an' downs; but I feels I'll soon be in one ob de many mansions. If it hadn't been for dat hope I 'spects I would have broken down long ago. I'se bin through de deep waters, but dey didn't overflow me; I'se bin in de fire, but de smell ob it isn't on my garments. Bredren an' sisters, it war a drefful time when I war tored away from my pore little chillen."

"Dat's so!" exclaimed a chorus of voices. Some of her hearers moaned, others rocked to and fro, as thoughts of similar scenes in their own lives arose before them.

"When my little girl," continued the speaker, "took hole ob my dress an' begged me ter let her go wid me, an' I couldn't do it, it mos' broke my heart. I had a little boy, an' wen my mistus sole me she kep' him. She carried on a boardin' house. Many's the time I hab stole out at night an' seen dat chile an' sleep'd wid him in my arms tell mos' day. Bimeby de people I libed wid got hard up fer money, an' dey sole me one way an' my pore little gal de oder; an' I neber laid my eyes on my pore chillen sence den. But, honeys, let de wind blow high or low, I 'spects to outwedder de storm an' anchor by'm bye in bright glory. But I'se bin a prayin' fer one thing, an' I beliebs I'll git it; an' dat is dat I may see my chillen 'fore I die. Pray fer me dat I may hole out an' hole on, an' neber make a shipwrack ob faith, an' at las' fine my way from earth to glory."

Having finished her speech, she sat down and wiped away the tears that flowed all the more copiously as she remembered her lost children. When she rose to speak her voice and manner instantly arrested Robert's attention. He found his mind reverting to the scenes of his childhood. As she proceeded his attention became riveted on her. Unbidden tears filled his eyes and great sobs shook his frame. He trembled in every limb. Could it be possible that after years of patient search through churches, papers, and inquiring friends, he had accidentally stumbled on his mother—the mother who, long years ago, had pillowed his head upon her bosom and left her parting kiss upon his lips? How should he reveal himself to her? Might not sudden joy do what years of sorrow had failed to accomplish? Controlling his feelings as best he could, he rose to tell his experience. He referred to the days when they used to hold their meetings in the lonely woods and gloomy swamps. How they had prayed for freedom and plotted to desert to the Union army; and continuing, he said: "Since then, brethren and sisters, I have had my crosses and trials, but I try to look at the mercies. Just think what it was then and what it is now! How many of us, since freedom has come, have been looking up our scattered relatives. I have just been over to visit my old mistress, Nancy Johnson, and to see if I could get some clue to my long-lost mother, who was sold from me nearly thirty years ago."

Again there was a chorus of moans.

On resuming, Robert's voice was still fuller of pathos.

"When," he said, "I heard that dear old mother tell her experience it seemed as if someone had risen from the dead. She made me think of my own dear mother, who used to steal out at night to see me, fold me in her arms, and then steal back again to her work. After she was sold away I never saw her face again by daylight. I have been looking for her ever since the war, and I think at last I have got on the right track. If Mrs. Johnson, who kept the boarding house in C——, is the one who sold that dear old mother from her son, then she is the one I am looking for, and I am the son she has been praying for."

The dear old mother raised her eyes. They were clear and tearless. An expression of wonder, hope, and love flitted over her face. It seemed as if her youth were suddenly renewed and, bounding from her seat, she rushed to the speaker in a paroxysm of joy. "Oh, Robby! Robby, is dis you? Is dat my pore, dear boy I'se been prayin' 'bout all dese years? Oh, glory! Glory!" And overflowing with joyous excitement she threw her arms around him, looking the very impersonation of rapturous content. It was a happy time. Mothers whose children had been torn from them in the days of slavery knew how to rejoice in her joy. The young people caught the infection of the general happiness and rejoiced with them that rejoiced. There were songs of rejoicing and shouts of praise. The undertone of sadness which had so often mingled with their songs gave place to strains of exultation; and tears of tender sympathy flowed from eyes which had often been blurred by anguish. The child of many prayers and tears was restored to his mother.

Iola stood by the mother's side, smiling, and weeping tears of joy. When Robert's mother observed Iola, she said to Robert, "Is dis yore wife?"

"Oh, no," replied Robert, "but I believe she is your grandchild, the daughter of the little girl who was sold away from you so long ago. She is on her way to the farther South in search of her mother."

"Is she? Dear chile! I hope she'll fine her! She puts me in mine ob my pore little Marie. Well, I'se got one chile, an' I means to keep on prayin' tell I fine my daughter. I'm *so* happy! I feel's like a new woman!"

"My dear mother," said Robert, "now that I have found you, I mean to hold you fast just as long as you live. Ever since the war I have been trying to find out if you were living, but all efforts failed. At last, I thought I would come and hunt you myself and, now that I have found you, I am going to take you home to live with me, and to be as happy as the days are long. I am living in the North, and doing a good business there. I want you to see joy according to all the days wherein you have seen sorrow. I do hope this young lady will find *her* ma and that, when found, she will prove to be your daughter!"

"Yes, pore, dear chile! I specs her mudder's heart's mighty hungry fer her. I does hope she's my gran'chile."

Tenderly and caressingly Iola bent over the happy mother, with her heart filled with mournful memories of her own mother.

Aunt Linda was induced to stay until the next morning, and then gladly assisted Robert's mother in arranging for her journey northward. The friends who had given her a shelter in their hospitable home, learned to value her so much that it was with great reluctance they resigned her to the care of her son. Aunt Linda was full of bustling activity, and her spirits overflowed with good humor.

"Now, Harriet," she said, as they rode along on their return journey, "you mus' jis' thank me fer finin' yore chile, 'cause I got him to come to dat big meetin' wid me."

"Oh, Lindy," she cried, "I'se glad from de bottom ob my heart ter see you's all. I com'd out dere ter git a blessin', an' I'se got a double po'tion. De frens I war libin' wid war mighty good ter me. Dey lib'd wid me in de lower kentry, an' arter de war war ober I stopped wid 'em and helped take keer ob de chillen; an' when dey com'd up yere dey brought me wid 'em. I'se com'd a way I didn't know, but I'se mighty glad I'se com'd."

"Does you know dis place?" asked Aunt Linda, as they approached the settlement.

"No'n 'deed I don't. It's all new ter me."

"Well, dis is whar I libs. Ain't you mighty tired? I feels a little stiffish. Dese bones is gittin' ole."

"Dat's so! But I'se mighty glad I'se lib'd to see my boy 'fore I crossed ober de riber. An' now I feel like ole Simeon."

"But, mother," said Robert, "if you are ready to go, I am not willing to let you. I want you to stay ever so long where I can see you."

A bright smile overspread her face. Robert's words reassured and gladdened her heart. She was well satisfied to have a pleasant aftermath from life on this side of the river.

After arriving home Linda's first thought was to prepare dinner for her guests. But, before she began her work of preparation, she went to the cupboard to get a cup of homemade wine.

"Here," she said, filling three glasses, "is some wine I made myself from dat grapevine out dere. Don't it look nice and clar? Jist taste it. It's fus'rate."

"No, thank you," said Robert. "I'm a temperance man, and never take anything which has alcohol in it."

"Oh, dis ain't got a bit ob alcohol in it. I made it myself."

"But, Aunt Linda, you didn't make the law which ferments grape juice and makes it alcohol."

"But, Robby, ef alcohol's so bad, w'at made de Lord put it here?"

"Aunt Lindy," said Iola, "I heard a lady say that there were two things the Lord didn't make. One is sin, and the other alcohol."

"Why, Aunt Linda," said Robert, "there are numbers of things the Lord has made that I wouldn't touch with a pair of tongs."

"What are they?"

"Rattlesnakes, scorpions, and moccasins."

"Oh, sho!"

"Aunt Linda," said Iola, "the Bible says that the wine at last will bite like a serpent and sting like an adder."

"And, Aunt Linda," added Robert, "as I wouldn't wind a serpent around my throat, I don't want to put something inside of it which will bite like a serpent and sting as an adder."

"I reckon Robby's right," said his mother, setting down her glass and leaving the wine unfinished. "You young folks knows a heap more dan we ole folks."

"Well," declared Aunt Linda, "you all is temp'rence to de backbone. But what could I do wid my wine ef we didn't drink it?"

"Let it turn to vinegar, and sign the temperance pledge," replied Robert.

"I don't keer 'bout it myself, but I don't 'spect John would be willin' ter let it go, 'cause he likes it a heap."

"Then you must give it up for his sake and Job's," said Robert. "They may learn to like it too well."

"You know, Aunt Linda," said Iola, "people don't get to be drunkards all at once. And you wouldn't like to feel, if Job should learn to drink, that you helped form his appetite."

"Dat' so! I beliebs I'll let dis turn to winegar, an' not make any more."

"That's right, Aunt Linda. I hope you'll hold to it," said Robert, encouragingly.

Very soon Aunt Linda had an excellent dinner prepared. After it was over Robert went with Iola to C——, where her friend, the bishop, was awaiting her return. She told him the wonderful story of Robert's finding his mother, and of her sweet, childlike faith.

The bishop, a kind, fatherly man, said, "Miss Iola, I hope that such happiness is in store for you. My dear child, still continue to pray and trust. I am old-fashioned enough to believe in prayer. I knew an old lady living in Illinois, who was a slave. Her son got a chance to come North and beg money to buy his mother. The mother was badly treated, and made up her mind to run away. But before she started she thought she would kneel down to pray. And something, she said, reasoned within her, and whispered, 'Stand still and see what I am going to do for you.' So real was it to her that she unpacked her bundle and desisted from her flight. Strange as it may appear to you, her son returned, bringing with him money enough to purchase her freedom, and she was redeemed from bondage. Had she persisted in running away she might have been lost in the woods and have died, exhausted by starvation. But she believed, she trusted, and was delivered. Her son took her North, where she could find a resting place for the soles of her feet."

That night Iola and the bishop left for the South.

21.
A HOME FOR MOTHER.

After Iola had left the settlement, accompanied by Robert as far as the town, it was a pleasant satisfaction for the two old friends to settle themselves down, and talk of times past, departed friends, and long-forgotten scenes.

"What," said Mrs. Johnson, as we shall call Robert's mother, "hab become ob Miss Nancy's husband? Is he still a libin'?"

"Oh, he drunk hisself to death," responded Aunt Linda.

"He used ter be mighty handsome."

"Yes, but drink war his ruination."

"An' how's Miss Nancy?"

"Oh, she's com'd down migh'ly. She's pore as a church mouse. I thought 'twould com'd home ter her wen she sole yer 'way from yore chillen. Dere's nuffin goes ober de debil's back dat don't come under his belly. Do yo 'member Miss Nancy's fardder?"

"Ob course I does!"

"Well," said Aunt Linda, "he war a nice ole gemmen. Wen he died, I said de las' gemmen's dead, an' dere's noboddy ter step in his shoes."

"Pore Miss Nancy!" exclaimed Robert's mother. "I ain't nothin' agin her. But I wouldn't swap places wid her, 'cause I'se got my son; an' I beliebs he'll do a good part by me."

"Mother," said Robert, as he entered the room, "I've brought an old friend to see you. Do you remember Uncle Daniel?"

Uncle Daniel threw back his head, reached out his hand, and manifested his joy with "Well, Har'yet! is dis you? I neber 'spected to see you in dese lower grouns! How does yer do? an' whar hab you bin all dis time?"

"O, I'se been tossin' roun' 'bout; but it's all com'd right at las'. I'se lib'd to see my boy 'fore I died."

"My wife an' boys is in glory," said Uncle Daniel. "But I 'spects to see 'em 'fore long. 'Cause I'se tryin' to dig deep, build sure, an' make my way from earth ter glory."

"Dat's de right kine ob talk, Dan'el. We ole folks ain't got long ter stay yere."

They chatted together until Job and Salters came home for supper. After they had eaten, Uncle Daniel said:—

"We'll hab a word ob prayer."

There, in that peaceful habitation, they knelt down, and mingled their prayers together, as they had done in bygone days, when they had met by stealth in lonely swamps or silent forests.

The next morning Robert and his mother started northward. They were well supplied with a bountiful luncheon by Aunt Linda, who had so thoroughly enjoyed their sojourn with her. On the next day he arrived in the city of P——, and took his mother to his boarding-house, until he could find a suitable home into which to install her. He soon came across one which just suited his taste, but when the agent discovered that Robert's mother was colored, he told him that the house had been previously engaged. In company with his mother he looked at several other houses in desirable neighborhoods, but they were constantly met with the answer, "The house is engaged," or, "We do not rent to colored people."

At length Robert went alone, and, finding a desirable house, engaged it, and moved into it. In a short time it was discovered that he was colored, and, at the behest of the local sentiment of the place, the landlord used his utmost endeavors to oust him, simply because he belonged to an unfashionable and unpopular race. At last he came across a landlord who was broad enough to rent him a good house, and he found a quiet resting place among a set of well-to-do and well-disposed people.

22.
FURTHER LIFTING OF THE VEIL.

In one of those fearful conflicts by which the Mississippi was freed from Rebel intrusion and opened to commerce Harry was severely wounded, and forced to leave his place in the ranks for a bed in the hospital.

One day, as he lay in his bed, thinking of his former home in Mississippi and wondering if the chances of war would ever restore him to his loved ones, he fell into a quiet slumber. When he awoke he found a lady bending over him, holding in her hands some fruit and flowers. As she tenderly bent over Harry's bed their eyes met, and with a thrill of gladness they recognized each other.

"Oh, my son, my son!" cried Marie, trying to repress her emotion, as she took his wasted hand in hers, and kissed the pale cheeks that sickness and suffering had blanched. Harry was very weak, but her presence was a call to life. He returned the pressure of her hand, kissed it, and his eyes grew full of sudden light, as he murmured faintly, but joyfully:—

"Mamma; oh, mamma! Have I found you at last?"

The effort was too much, and he immediately became unconscious.

Anxious, yet hopeful, Marie sat by the bedside of her son till consciousness was restored. Caressingly she bent over his couch, murmuring in her happiness the tenderest, sweetest words of motherly love. In Harry's veins flowed new life and vigor, calming the restlessness of his nerves.

As soon as possible Harry was carried to his mother's home; a home brought into the light of freedom by the victories of General Grant. Nursed by his mother's tender, loving care, he rapidly recovered, but, being too disabled to re-enter the army, he was honorably discharged.

Lorraine had taken Marie to Vicksburg, and there allowed her to engage in confectionery and preserving for the wealthy ladies of the city. He had at first attempted to refugee with her in Texas, but, being foiled in the attempt, he was compelled to enlist in the Confederate Army, and met his fate by being killed just before the surrender of Vicksburg.

"My dear son," Marie would say, as she bent fondly over him, "I am deeply sorry that you are wounded, but I am glad that the fortunes of war have brought us together. Poor Iola! I *do* wonder what has become of her? Just as soon as this war is over I want you to search the country all over. Poor child! How my heart has ached for her!"

Time passed on. Harry and his mother searched and inquired for Iola, but no tidings of her reached them.

Having fully recovered his health, and seeing the great need of education for the colored people, Harry turned his attention toward them, and joined the new army of Northern teachers.

He still continued his inquiries for his sister, not knowing whether or not she had succumbed to the cruel change in her life. He thought she might have passed into the white basis for the sake of bettering her fortunes. Hope deferred, which had sickened his mother's heart, had only roused him to renewed diligence.

A school was offered him in Georgia, and thither he repaired, taking his mother with him. They were soon established in the city of A——. In hope of finding Iola he visited all the conferences of the Methodist Church, but for a long time his search was in vain.

"Mamma," said Harry, one day during his vacation, "there is to be a Methodist Conference in this State in the city of S——, about one hundred and fifty miles from here. I intend to go and renew my search for Iola."

"Poor child!" burst out Marie, as the tears gathered in her eyes. "I wonder if she is living."

"I think so," said Harry, kissing the pale cheek of his mother; "I don't feel that Iola is dead. I believe we will find her before long."

"It seems to me my heart would burst with joy to see my dear child just once more. I am glad that you are going. When will you leave?"

"Tomorrow morning."

"Well, my son, go, and my prayers will go with you," was Marie's tender parting wish.

Early next morning Harry started for the conference, and reached the church before the morning session was over. Near him sat two ladies, one fair, the other considerably darker. There was something in the fairer one that reminded him forcibly of his sister, but she was much older and graver than he imagined his sister to be. Instantly he dismissed the thought that had forced itself into his mind, and began to listen attentively to the proceedings of the conference.

When the regular business of the morning session was over the bishop arose and said:—

"I have an interesting duty to perform. I wish to introduce a young lady to the conference, who was the daughter of a Mississippi planter. She is now in search of her mother and brother, from whom she was sold a few months before the war. Her father married her mother in Ohio, where he had taken her to be educated. After his death they were robbed of their inheritance and enslaved by a distant relative named Lorraine. Miss Iola Leroy is the young lady's name. If any one can give the least information respecting the objects of her search it will be thankfully received."

"I can," exclaimed a young man, rising in the midst of the audience, and pressing eagerly, almost impetuously, forward. "I am her brother, and I came here to look for her."

Iola raised her eyes to his face, so flushed and bright with the glow of recognition, rushed to him, threw her arms around his neck, kissed him again and again, crying: "O, Harry!" Then she fainted from excitement. The women gathered around her with expressions of tender sympathy, and gave her all the care she needed. They called her the "dear child," for without any effort on her part she had slidden into their hearts and found a ready welcome in each sympathizing bosom.

Harry at once telegraphed the glad tidings to his mother, who waited their coming with joyful anticipation. Long before the cars reached the city, Mrs. Leroy was at the depot, restlessly walking the platform or eagerly peering into the darkness to catch the first glimpse of the train which was bearing her treasures.

At length the cars arrived, and, as Harry and Iola alighted, Marie rushed forward, clasped Iola in her arms and sobbed out her joy in broken words.

Very happy was the little family that sat together around the supper-table for the first time for years. They partook of that supper with thankful hearts and with eyes overflowing with tears of joy. Very touching were the prayers the mother uttered, when she knelt with her children that night to return thanks for their happy reunion, and to seek protection through the slumbers of the night.

The next morning, as they sat at the breakfast-table, Marie said:

"My dear child, you are so changed I do not think I would have known you if I had met you in the street!"

"And I," said Harry, "can hardly realize that you are our own Iola, whom I recognized as sister a half dozen years ago."

"Am I so changed?" asked Iola, as a faint sigh escaped her lips.

"Why, Iola," said Harry, "you used to be the most harum-scarum girl I ever knew, laughing, dancing, and singing from morning until night."

"Yes, I remember," said Iola. "It all comes back to me like a dream. Oh, mamma! I have passed through a fiery ordeal of suffering since then. But it is useless," and as she continued her face assumed a brighter look, "to brood over the past. Let us be happy in the present. Let me tell you something which will please you. Do you remember telling me about your mother and brother?"

"Yes," said Marie, in a questioning tone."

"Well," continued Iola, with eyes full of gladness, "I think I have found them."

"Can it be possible!" exclaimed Marie, in astonishment. "It is more than thirty years since we parted. I fear you are mistaken."

"No, mamma; I have drawn my conclusions from good circumstantial evidence. After I was taken from you, I passed through a fearful siege of suffering, which would only harrow up your soul to hear. I often shudder at the remembrance. The last man in whose clutches I found myself was mean, brutal, and cruel. I was in his power when the Union army came into C——, where I was living. A number of colored men stampeded to the Union ranks, with a gentleman as a leader, whom I think is your brother. A friend of his reported my case to the commander of the post, who instantly gave orders for my release. A place was given me as nurse in the hospital. I attended that friend in his last illness. Poor fellow! He was the best friend I had in all the time I have been tossing about. The gentleman whom I think is your brother appeared to be very anxious about his friend's recovery, and was deeply affected by his death. In one of the last terrible battles of the war, that of Five Forks, he was wounded and put into the hospital ward where I was an attendant. For a while he was delirious, and in his delirium he would sometimes think that I was his mother and at other times his sister. I humored his fancies, would often sing to him when he was restless, and my voice almost invariably soothed him to sleep. One day I sang to him that old hymn we used to sing on the plantation:—

> *"Drooping souls no longer grieve,*
> *Heaven is propitious;*
> *If on Christ you do believe,*
> *You will find Him precious."*

"I remember," said Marie, with a sigh, as memories of the past swept over her.

"After I had finished the hymn," continued Iola, "he looked earnestly and inquiringly into my face, and asked, 'Where did you learn that hymn? I have heard my mother sing it when I was a boy, but I have never heard it since.' I think, mamma, the words, 'I was lost but now I'm found; glory! Glory! Glory!' had imprinted themselves on his memory, and that his mind was assuming a higher state of intellectuality. He asked me to sing it again, which I did, until he fell asleep. Then I noticed a marked resemblance between him and Harry, and I thought, 'Suppose he should prove to be your long-lost brother?' During his convalescence we found that we had a common ground of sympathy. We were anxious to be reunited to our severed relations. We had both been separated from our mothers. He told me of his little sister, with whom he used to play. She had a mole on her cheek which he called her beauty spot. He had the red spot on his forehead which you told me of."

23.
DELIGHTFUL REUNIONS.

Very bright and happy was the home where Marie and her children were gathered under one roof. Mrs. Leroy's neighbors said she looked ten years younger. Into that peaceful home came no fearful forebodings of cruel separations. Harry and Iola were passionately devoted to their mother, and did all they could to flood her life with sunshine.

"Iola, dear," said Harry, one morning at the breakfast-table, "I have a new pleasure in store for you."

"What is it, brother mine?" asked Iola, assuming an air of interest.

"There is a young lady living in this city to whom I wish to introduce you. She is one of the most remarkable women I have ever met."

"Do tell me all about her," said Iola. "Is she young and handsome, brilliant and witty?

"She," replied Harry, "is more than handsome, she is lovely; more than witty, she is wise; more than brilliant, she is excellent."

"Well, Harry," said Mrs. Leroy, smiling, "if you keep on that way I shall begin to fear that I shall soon be supplanted by a new daughter."

"Oh, no, mamma," replied Harry, looking slightly confused, "I did not mean that."

"Well, Harry," said Iola, amused, "go on with your description; I am becoming interested. Tax your powers of description to give me her likeness."

"Well, in the first place," continued Harry, "I suppose she is about twenty-five years old."

"Oh, the idea," interrupted Iola, "of a gentleman talking of a lady's age. That is a tabooed subject."

"Why, Iola, that adds to the interest of my picture. It is her combination of earnestness and youthfulness which enhances her in my estimation."

"Pardon the interruption," said Iola; "I am anxious to hear more about her."

"Well, she is of medium height, somewhat slender, and well-formed, with dark, expressive eyes, full of thought and feeling. Neither hair nor complexion show the least hint of blood admixture."

"I am glad of it," said Iola. "Every person of unmixed blood who succeeds in any department of literature, art, or science is a living argument for the capability which is in the race."

"Yes," responded Harry, "for it is not the white blood which is on trial before the world. Well, I will bring her around this evening."

In the evening Harry brought Miss Delany to call on his sister and mother. They were much pleased with their visitor. Her manner was a combination of suavity and dignity. During the course of the evening they learned that she was a graduate of the University of A——. One day she saw in the newspapers that colored women were becoming unfit to be servants for white people. She then thought that if they are not fit to be servants for white people, they are unfit to be mothers to their own children, and she conceived the idea of opening a school to train future wives and mothers. She began on a small scale, in a humble building, and her work was soon crowned with gratifying success. She had enlarged her quarters, increased her teaching force, and had erected a large and commodious schoolhouse through her own exertions and the help of others.

Marie cordially invited her to call again, saying, as she rose to go: "I am very glad to have met you. Young women like you always fill my heart with hope for the future of our race. In you I see reflected some of the blessed possibilities which lie within us."

"Thank you," said Miss Delany, "I want to be classed among those of whom it is said, 'She has done what she could.'"

Very pleasant was the acquaintance which sprang up between Miss Delany and Iola. Although she was older than Iola, their tastes were so congenial, their views of life and duty in such unison, that their acquaintance soon ripened into strong and lasting friendship. There were no foolish rivalries and jealousies between them. Their lives were too full of zeal and earnestness for them to waste in selfishness their power to be moral and spiritual forces among a people who so much needed their helping hands. Miss Delany gave Iola a situation in her school; but before the term was quite over she was force to resign, her health having been so undermined by the fearful strain through which she had passed, that she was quite unequal to the task. She remained at home, and did what her strength would allow in assisting her mother in the work of canning and preserving fruits.

In the meantime, Iola had been corresponding with Robert. She had told him of her success in finding her mother and brother, and had received an answer congratulating her on the glad fruition of her hopes. He also said that his business was flourishing, that his mother was keeping house for him, and, to use her own expression, was as happy as the days are long. She was firmly persuaded that Marie was her daughter, and she wanted to see her before she died.

"There is one thing," continued the letter, "that your mother may remember her by. It was a little handkerchief on which were a number of cats' heads. She gave one to each of us."

"I remember it well," said Marie, "she must, indeed, be my mother. Now, all that is needed to complete my happiness is her presence, and my brother's. And I intend, if I live long enough, to see them both."

Iola wrote Robert that her mother remembered the incident of the handkerchief, and was anxious to see them.

In the early fall Robert started for the South in order to clear up all doubts with respect to their relationship. He found Iola, Harry, and their mother living cosily together. Harry was teaching and was a leader among the rising young men of the State. His Northern education and later experience had done much toward adapting him to the work of the new era which had dawned upon the South.

Marie was very glad to welcome Robert to her home, but it was almost impossible to recognize her brother in that tall, handsome man, with dark-brown eyes and wealth of chestnut-colored hair, which he readily lifted to show the crimson spot which lay beneath it.

But as they sat together, and recalled the long-forgotten scenes of their childhood, they concluded that they were brother and sister.

"Marie," said Robert, "how would you like to leave the South?"

"I should like to go North, but I hate to leave Harry. He's a splendid young fellow, although I say it myself. He is so fearless and outspoken that I am constantly anxious about him, especially at election time."

Harry then entered the room, and, being introduced to Robert, gave him a cordial welcome. He had just returned from school.

"We were talking of you, my son," said Marie.

"What were you saying? Nothing of the absent but good?" asked Harry.

"I was telling your uncle, who wants me to come North, that I would go, but I am afraid that you will get into trouble and be murdered, as many others have been."

"Oh, well, mother, I shall not die till my time comes. And if I die helping the poor and needy, I shall die at my post. Could a man choose a better place to die?"

"Were you aware of the virulence of caste prejudice and the disabilities which surround the colored people when you cast your lot with them?" asked Robert.

"Not fully," replied Harry; "but after I found out that I was colored, I consulted the principal of the school, where I was studying, in reference to the future. He said that if I stayed in the North, he had friends whom he believed would give me any situation I could fill, and I could simply take my place in the rank of workers, the same as any other man. Then he told me of the army, and I made up my mind to enter it, actuated by a desire to find my mother and sister; and at any rate I wanted to avenge their wrongs. I do not feel so now. Since I have seen the fearful ravages of war, I have learned to pity and forgive. The principal said he thought I would be more apt to find my family if I joined a colored regiment in the West than if I joined one of the Maine companies. I confess at first I felt a shrinking from taking the step, but love for my mother overcame all repugnance on my part. Now that

I have linked my fortunes to the race I intend to do all I can for its elevation."

As he spoke Robert gazed admiringly on the young face, lit up by noble purposes and lofty enthusiasm.

"You are right, Harry. I think it would be treason, not only to the race, but to humanity, to have you ignoring your kindred and masquerading as a white man."

"I think so, too," said Marie.

"But, sister, I am anxious for you all to come North. If Harry feels that the place of danger is the post of duty, let him stay, and he can spend his vacations with us. I think both you and Iola need rest and change. Mother longs to see you before she dies. She feels that we have been the children of many prayers and tears, and I want to make her last days as happy as possible. The South has not been a paradise to you all the time, and I should think you would be willing to leave it."

"Yes, that is so. Iola needs rest and change, and she would be such a comfort to mother. I suppose, for her sake, I will consent to have her go back with you, at least for a while."

In a few days, with many prayers and tears, Marie, half reluctantly, permitted Iola to start for the North in company with Robert Johnson, intending to follow as soon as she could settle her business and see Harry in a good boarding place.

Very joyful was the greeting of the dear grandmother. Iola soon nestled in her heart and lent additional sunshine to her once checkered life, and Robert, who had so long been robbed of kith and kin, was delighted with the new accession to his home life.

24.
NORTHERN EXPERIENCE.

"Uncle Robert," said Iola, after she had been North several weeks, "I have a theory that every woman ought to know how to earn her own living. I believe that a great amount of sin and misery springs from the weakness and inefficiency of women."

"Perhaps that's so, but what are you going to do about it?"

"I am going to join the great rank of bread-winners. Mr. Waterman has advertised for a number of saleswomen, and I intend to make application."

"When he advertises for help he means white women," said Robert.

"He said nothing about color," responded Iola.

"I don't suppose he did. He doesn't expect any colored girl to apply."

"Well, I think I could fill the place. At least I should like to try. And I do not think when I apply that I am in duty bound to tell him my great-grandmother was a Negro."

"Well, child, there is no necessity for you to go out to work. You are perfectly welcome here, and I hope that you feel so."

"Oh, I certainly do. But still I would rather earn my own living."

That morning Iola applied for the situation, and, being prepossessing in her appearance, she obtained it.

For a while everything went as pleasantly as a marriage bell. But one day a young colored lady, well-dressed and well-bred in her manner, entered the store. It was an acquaintance which Iola had formed in the colored church which she attended. Iola gave her a few words of cordial greeting, and spent a few moments chatting with her. The attention of the girls who sold at the same counter was attracted, and their suspicion awakened. Iola was a stranger in that city. Who was she, and who were her people? At last it was decided that one of the girls should act as a spy, and bring what information she could concerning Iola.

The spy was successful. She found out that Iola was living in a good neighborhood, but that none of the neighbors knew her. The man of the house was very fair, but there was an old woman whom Iola called "Grandma," and she was unmistakably colored. The story was sufficient. If that were true, Iola must be colored, and she should be treated accordingly.

Without knowing the cause, Iola noticed a chill in the social atmosphere of the store, which communicated itself to the cash-boys, and they treated her so insolently that her situation became very uncomfortable. She saw the proprietor, resigned her position, and asked for and obtained a letter of recommendation to another merchant who had advertised for a saleswoman.

In applying for the place, she took the precaution to inform her employer that she was colored. It made no difference to him; but he said:—

"Don't say anything about it to the girls. They might not be willing to work with you."

Iola smiled, did not promise, and accepted the situation. She entered upon her duties, and proved quite acceptable as a saleswoman.

One day, during an interval in business, the girls began to talk of their respective churches, and the question was put to Iola:—

"Where do you go to church?"

"I go," she replied, "to Rev. River's church, corner of Eighth and L Streets."

"Oh, no; you must be mistaken. There is no church there except a colored one."

"That is where I go."

"Why do you go there?"

"Because I liked it when I came here, and joined it."

"A member of a colored church? What under heaven possessed you to do such a thing?"

"Because I wished to be with my own people."

Here the interrogator stopped, and looked surprised and pained, and almost instinctively moved a little farther from her. After the store was closed, the girls had an animated discussion, which resulted in the information being sent to Mr. Cohen that Iola was a colored girl, and that they protested against her being continued in his employ. Mr. Cohen yielded to the pressure, and informed Iola that her services were no longer needed.

When Robert came home in the evening, he found that Iola had lost her situation, and was looking somewhat discouraged.

"Well, uncle," she said, "I feel out of heart. It seems as if the prejudice pursues us through every avenue of life, and assigns us the lowest places."

"That is so," replied Robert, thoughtfully.

"And yet I am determined," said Iola, "to win for myself a place in the fields of labor. I have heard of a place in New England, and I mean to try for it, even if I only stay a few months."

"Well, if you *will* go, say nothing about your color."

"Uncle Robert, I see no necessity for proclaiming that fact on the house-top. Yet I am resolved that nothing shall tempt me to deny it. The best blood in my veins is African blood, and I am not ashamed of it."

"Hurrah for you!" exclaimed Robert, laughing heartily.

As Iola wished to try the world for herself, and so be prepared for any emergency, her uncle and grandmother were content to have her go to New England. The town to which she journeyed was only a few hours' ride from the city of P——, and Robert, knowing that there is no teacher like experience, was willing that Iola should have the benefit of her teaching.

Iola, on arriving in H——, sought the firm, and was informed that her services were needed. She found it a pleasant and lucrative position. There was only one drawback—her boarding place was too far from her work. There was an institution conducted by professed Christian women, which was for the special use of respectable young working girls. This was in such a desirable location that she called at the house to engage board.

The matron conducted her over the house, and grew so friendly in the interview that she put her arm around her, and seemed to look upon Iola as a desirable accession to the home. But, just as Iola was leaving, she said to the matron: "I must be honest with you; I am a colored woman."

Swift as light a change passed over the face of the matron. She withdrew her arm from Iola, and said: "I must see the board of managers about it."

When the board met, Iola's case was put before them, but they decided not to receive her. And these women, professors of a religion which taught, "If ye have respect to persons ye commit sin," virtually shut the door in her face because of the outcast blood in her veins.

Considerable feeling was aroused by the action of these women, who, to say the least, had not put their religion in the most favorable light.

Iola continued to work for the firm until she received letters from her mother and uncle, which informed her that her mother, having arranged her affairs in the South, was ready to come North. She then resolved to return, to the city of P——, to be ready to welcome her mother on her arrival.

Iola arrived in time to see that everything was in order for her mother's reception. Her room was furnished neatly, but with those touches of beauty that womanly hands are such adepts in giving. A few charming pictures adorned the walls, and an easy chair stood waiting to receive the travel-worn mother. Robert and Iola met her at the depot; and grandma was on her feet at the first sound of the bell, opened the door, clasped Marie to her heart, and nearly fainted for joy.

"Can it be possible dat dis is my little Marie?" she exclaimed.

It did seem almost impossible to realize that this faded woman, with pale cheeks and prematurely whitened hair, was the rosy-cheeked child from whom she had been parted more than thirty years.

"Well," said Robert, after the first joyous greeting was over, "love is a very good thing, but Marie has had a long journey and needs something that will stick by the ribs. How about dinner, mother?"

"It's all ready," said Mrs. Johnson.

After Marie had gone to her room and changed her dress, she came down and partook of the delicious repast which her mother and Iola had prepared for her.

In a few days Marie was settled in the home, and was well pleased with the change. The only drawback to her happiness was the absence of her son, and she expected him to come North after the closing of his school.

"Uncle Robert," said Iola, after her mother had been with them several weeks, "I am tired of being idle."

"What's the matter now?" asked Robert. "You are surely not going East again, and leave your mother?"

"Oh, I hope not," said Marie, anxiously. "I have been so long without you."

"No, mamma, I am not going East. I can get suitable employment here in the city of P——."

"But, Iola," said Robert, "you have tried, and been defeated. Why subject yourself to the same experience again?"

"Uncle Robert, I think that every woman should have some skill or art which would insure her at least a comfortable support. I believe there would be less unhappy marriages if labor were more honored among women."

"Well, Iola," said her mother, "what is your skill?"

"Nursing. I was very young when I went into the hospital, but I succeeded so well that the doctor said I must have been a born nurse. Now, I see by the papers, that a gentleman who has an invalid daughter wants someone who can be a nurse and companion for her, and I mean to apply for the situation. I do not think, if I do my part well in that position, that the blood in my veins will be any bar to my success."

A troubled look stole over Marie's face. She sighed faintly, but made no remonstrance. And so it was decided that Iola should apply for the situation.

Iola made application, and was readily accepted. Her patient was a frail girl of fifteen summers, who was ill with a low fever. Iola nursed her carefully, and soon had the satisfaction of seeing her restored to health. During her stay, Mr. Cloten, the father of the invalid, had learned some of the particulars of Iola's Northern experience as a bread-winner, and he resolved to give her employment in his store when her services were no longer needed in the house. As soon as a vacancy occurred he gave Iola a place in his store.

The morning she entered on her work he called his employés together, and told them that Miss Iola had colored blood in her veins, but that he was going to employ her and give her a desk. If any one objected to working with her, he or she could step to the cashier's desk and receive what was due. Not a man remonstrated, not a woman demurred; and Iola at last found a place in the great army of bread-winners, which the traditions of her blood could not affect.

"How did you succeed?" asked Mrs. Cloten of her husband, when he returned to dinner.

"Admirably! 'Everything is lovely and the goose hangs high.' I gave my employés to understand that they could leave if they did not wish to work with Miss Leroy. Not one of them left, or showed any disposition to rebel."

"I am very glad," said Mrs. Cloten. "I am ashamed of the way she has been treated in our city, when seeking to do her share in the world's work. I am glad that you were brave enough to face this cruel prejudice, and give her a situation."

"Well, my dear, do not make me a hero for a single act. I am grateful for the care Miss Leroy gave our Daisy. Money can buy services, but it cannot purchase tender, loving sympathy. I was also determined to let my employés know that I, not they, commanded my business. So, do not crown me a hero until I have won a niche in the temple of fame. In dealing with Southern prejudice against the Negro, we Northerners could do it with better grace if we divested ourselves of our own. We irritate the South by our criticisms, and, while I confess that there is much that is reprehensible in their treatment of colored people, yet if our Northern civilization is higher than theirs we should 'criticize by creation.' We should stamp ourselves on the South, and not let the South stamp itself on us. When we have learned to treat men according to the complexion of their souls, and not the color of their skins, we will have given our best contribution towards the solution of the Negro problem."

"I feel, my dear," said Mrs. Cloten, "that what you have done is a right step in the right direction, and I hope that other merchants will do the same. We have numbers of business men, rich enough to afford themselves the luxury of a good conscience."

25.
AN OLD FRIEND.

"Good morning, Miss Leroy," said a cheery voice in tones of glad surprise, and, intercepting her path, Dr. Gresham stood before Iola, smiling, and reaching out his hand.

"Why, Dr. Gresham, is this you?" said Iola, lifting her eyes to that well-remembered face. "It has been several years since we met. How have you been all this time, and where?"

"I have been sick, and am just now recovering from malaria and nervous prostration. I am attending a medical convention in this city, and hope that I shall have the pleasure of seeing you again."

Iola hesitated, and then replied: "I should be pleased to have you call."

"It would give me great pleasure. Where shall I call?"

"My home is 1006 South Street, but I am only at home in the evenings."

They walked together a short distance till they reached Mr. Cloten's store; then, bidding the doctor good morning, Iola left him repeating to himself the words of his favorite poet:—

> "Thou art too lovely and precious a gem
> To be bound to their burdens and sullied by them."

No one noticed the deep flush on Iola's face as she entered the store, nor the subdued, quiet manner with which she applied herself to her tasks. She was living over again the past, with its tender, sad, and thrilling reminiscences.

In the evening Dr. Gresham called on Iola. She met him with a pleasant welcome. Dr. Gresham gazed upon her with unfeigned admiration, and thought that the years, instead of detracting from, had only intensified, her loveliness. He had thought her very beautiful in the hospital, in her gray dress and white collar, with her glorious wealth of hair drawn over her ears. But now, when he saw her with that hair artistically arranged, and her finely-proportioned form arrayed in a dark crimson dress, relieved by a shimmer of lace and a bow of white ribbon at her throat, he thought her superbly handsome. The lines which care had written upon her young face had faded away. There was no undertone of sorrow in her voice as she stood up before

143

him in the calm loveliness of her ripened womanhood, radiant in beauty and gifted in intellect. Time and failing health had left their traces upon Dr. Gresham. His step was less bounding, his cheek a trifle paler, his manner somewhat graver than it was when he had parted from Iola in the hospital, but his meeting with her had thrilled his heart with unexpected pleasure. Hopes and sentiments which long had slept awoke at the touch of her hand and the tones of her voice, and Dr. Gresham found himself turning to the past, with its sad memories and disappointed hopes. No other face had displaced her image in his mind; no other love had woven itself around every tendril of his soul. His heart and hand were just as free as they were the hour they had parted.

"To see you again," said Dr. Gresham, "is a great and unexpected pleasure."

"You had not forgotten me, then?" said Iola, smiling.

"Forget you! I would just as soon forget my own existence. I do not think that time will ever efface the impressions of those days in which we met so often. When last we met you were intending to search for your mother. Have you been successful?"

"More than successful," said Iola, with a joyous ring in her voice. "I have found my mother, brother, grandmother, and uncle, and, except my brother, we are all living together, and we are so happy. Excuse me a few minutes," she said, and left the room. Iola soon returned, bringing with her her mother and grandmother.

"These," said Iola, introducing her mother and grandmother, "are the once-severed branches of our family; and this gentleman you have seen before," continued Iola, as Robert entered the room.

Dr. Gresham looked scrutinizingly at him and said: "Your face looks familiar, but I saw so many faces at the hospital that I cannot just now recall your name."

"Doctor," said Robert Johnson, "I was one of your last patients, and I was with Tom Anderson when he died."

"Oh, yes," replied Dr. Gresham; "it all comes back to me. You were wounded at the battle of Five Forks, were you not?"

"Yes," said Robert.

"I saw you when you were recovering. You told me that you thought you had a clue to your lost relatives, from whom you had been so long separated. How have you succeeded?"

"Admirably! I have been fortunate in finding my mother, my sister, and her children."

"Ah, indeed! I am delighted to hear it. Where are they?"

"They are right here. This is my mother," said Robert, bending fondly over her, as she returned his recognition with an expression of intense satisfaction; "and this," he continued, "is my sister, and Miss Leroy is my niece."

"Is it possible? I am very glad to hear it. It has been said that every cloud has its silver lining, and the silver lining of our war cloud is the redemption of a race and the reunion of severed hearts. War is a dreadful thing; but worse than the war was the slavery which preceded it."

"Slavery," said Iola, "was a fearful cancer eating into the nation's heart, sapping its vitality, and undermining its life."

"And war," said Dr. Gresham, "was the dreadful surgery by which the disease was eradicated. The cancer has been removed, but for years to come I fear that we will have to deal with the effects of the disease. But I believe that we have vitality enough to outgrow those effects."

"I think, Doctor," said Iola, "that there is but one remedy by which our nation can recover from the evil entailed upon her by slavery."

"What is that?" asked Robert.

"A fuller comprehension of the claims of the Gospel of Jesus Christ, and their application to our national life."

"Yes," said Robert; "while politicians are stumbling on the barren mountains of fretful controversy and asking what shall we do with the Negro? I hold that Jesus answered that question nearly two thousand years ago when he said, 'Whatsoever ye would that men should do to you, do ye even so to them.'"

"Yes," said Dr. Gresham; "the application of that rule in dealing with the Negro would solve the whole problem."

"Slavery," said Mrs. Leroy, "is dead, but the spirit which animated it still lives; and I think that a reckless disregard for human life is more the outgrowth of slavery than any actual hatred of the Negro."

"The problem of the nation," continued Dr. Gresham, "is not what men will do with the Negro, but what will they do with the reckless, lawless white men who murder, lynch and burn their fellow citizens. To me these lynchings and burnings are perfectly alarming. Both races have reacted on each other—men fettered the slave and cramped their own souls; denied him knowledge, and darkened their spiritual insight; subdued him to the pliancy of submission, and in their turn became the thralls of public opinion. The Negro came here from the heathenism of Africa; but the young colonies could not take into their early civilization a stream of barbaric blood without being affected by its influence and the Negro, poor and despised as he is, has laid his hands on our Southern civilization and helped mould its character."

"Yes," said Mrs. Leroy; "the colored nurse could not nestle her master's child in her arms, hold up his baby footsteps on their floors, and walk with him through the impressible and formative period of his young life without leaving upon him the impress of her hand."

"I am glad," said Robert, "for the whole nation's sake, that slavery has been destroyed."

"And our work," said Dr. Gresham, "is to build over the desolations of the past a better and brighter future. The great distinction between savagery and civilization is the creation and maintenance of law. A people cannot habitually trample on law and justice without retrograding toward barbarism. But I am hopeful that time will bring us changes for the better; that, as we get farther away from the war, we will outgrow the animosities and prejudices engendered by slavery. The short-sightedness of our fathers linked the Negro's destiny to ours. We are feeling the friction of the ligatures which bind us together, but I hope that the time will speedily come when the best members of both races will unite for the maintenance of law and order and the progress and prosperity of the country, and that the intelligence and virtue of the South will be strong to grapple effectually with its ignorance and vice."

"I hope that time will speedily come," said Marie. "My son is in the South, and I am always anxious for his safety. He is not only a teacher, but a leading young man in the community where he lives."

"Yes," said Robert, "and when I see the splendid work he is doing in the South, I am glad that, instead of trying to pass for a white man, he has cast his lot with us."

"But," answered Dr. Gresham, "he would possess advantages as a white man which he could not if he were known to be colored."

"Doctor," said Iola, decidedly, "he has greater advantages as a colored man."

"I do not understand you," said Dr. Gresham, looking somewhat puzzled.

"Doctor," continued Iola, "I do not think life's highest advantages are those that we can see with our eyes or grasp with our hands. To whom today is the world most indebted—to its millionaires or to its martyrs?"

"Taking it from the ideal standpoint," replied the doctor, "I should say its martyrs."

"To be," continued Iola, "the leader of a race to higher planes of thought and action, to teach men clearer views of life and duty, and to inspire their souls with loftier aims, is a far greater privilege than it is to open the gates of material prosperity and fill every home with sensuous enjoyment."

"And I," said Mrs. Leroy, her face aglow with fervid feeling, "would rather —ten thousand times rather—see Harry the friend and helper of the poor and ignorant than the companion of men who, under the cover of night, mask their faces and ride the country on lawless raids."

"Dr. Gresham," said Robert, "we ought to be the leading nation of the earth, whose influence and example should give light to the world."

"Not simply," said Iola, "a nation building up a great material prosperity, founding magnificent cities, grasping the commerce of the world, or excelling in literature, art, and science, but a nation wearing sobriety as a crown and righteousness as the girdle of her loins."

Dr. Gresham gazed admiringly upon Iola. A glow of enthusiasm overspread her beautiful, expressive face. There was a rapt and far-off look in her eye, as if she were looking beyond the present pain to a brighter future for the race with which she was identified, and felt the grandeur of a divine commission to labor for its uplifting.

As Dr. Gresham was parting with Robert, he said: "This meeting has been a very unexpected pleasure. I have spent a delightful evening. I only regret that I had not others to share it with me. A doctor from the South, a regular Bourbon, is stopping at the hotel. I wish he could have been here tonight.

Come down to the Concordia, Mr. Johnson, tomorrow night. If you know any colored man who is a strong champion of equal rights, bring him along. Good night. I shall look for you," said the doctor, as he left the door.

When Robert returned to the parlor he said to Iola: "Dr. Gresham has invited me to come to his hotel tomorrow night, and to bring some wide-awake colored man with me. There is a Southerner whom he wishes me to meet. I suppose he wants to discuss the Negro problem, as they call it. He wants someone who can do justice to the subject. I wonder whom I can take with me?"

"I will tell you who, I think, will be a capital one to take with you, and I believe he would go," said Iola.

"Who?" asked Robert.

"Rev. Carmicle, your pastor."

"He is just the one," said Robert, "courteous in his manner and very scholarly in his attainments. He is a man whom if everybody hated him no one could despise him."

26.
OPEN QUESTIONS.

In the evening Robert and Rev. Carmicle called on Dr. Gresham, and found Dr. Latrobe, the Southerner, and a young doctor by the name of Latimer, already there. Dr. Gresham introduced Dr. Latrobe, but it was a new experience to receive colored men socially. His wits, however, did not forsake him, and he received the introduction and survived it.

"Permit me, now," said Dr. Gresham, "to introduce you to my friend, Dr. Latimer, who is attending our convention. He expects to go South and labor among the colored people. Don't you think that there is a large field of usefulness before him?"

"Yes," replied Dr. Latrobe, "if he will let politics alone."

"And why let politics alone?" asked Dr. Gresham.

"Because," replied Dr. Latrobe, "we Southerners will never submit to Negro supremacy. We will never abandon our Caucasian civilization to an inferior race."

"Have you any reason," inquired Rev. Carmicle, "to dread that a race which has behind it the heathenism of Africa and the slavery of America, with its inheritance of ignorance and poverty, will be able, in less than one generation, to domineer over a race which has behind it ages of dominion, freedom, education, and Christianity?"

A slight shade of vexation and astonishment passed over the face of Dr. Latrobe. He hesitated a moment, then replied:—

"I am not afraid of the Negro as he stands alone, but what I dread is that in some closely-contested election ambitious men will use him to hold the balance of power and make him an element of danger. He is ignorant, poor, and clannish, and they may impact him as their policy would direct."

"Any more," asked Robert, "than the leaders of the Rebellion did the ignorant, poor whites during our late conflict?"

"Ignorance, poverty, and clannishness," said Dr. Gresham, "are more social than racial conditions, which may be outgrown."

"And I think," said Rev. Carmicle, "that we are outgrowing them as fast as any other people would have done under the same conditions."

"The Negro," replied Dr. Latrobe, "always has been and always will be an element of discord in our country."

"What, then, is your remedy?" asked Dr. Gresham.

"I would eliminate him from the politics of the country."

"As disfranchisement is a punishment for crime, is it just to punish a man before he transgresses the law?" asked Dr. Gresham.

"If," said Dr. Latimer, "the Negro is ignorant, poor, and clannish, let us remember that in part of our land it was once a crime to teach him to read. If he is poor, for ages he was forced to bend to unrequited toil. If he is clannish, society has segregated him to himself."

"And even," said Robert, "has given him a Negro pew in your churches and a Negro seat at your communion table."

"Wisely, or unwisely," said Dr. Gresham, "the Government has put the ballot in his hands. It is better to teach him to use that ballot aright than to intimidate him by violence or vitiate his vote by fraud."

"Today," said Dr. Latimer, "the Negro is not plotting in beer-saloons against the peace and order of society. His fingers are not dripping with dynamite, neither is he spitting upon your flag, nor flaunting the red banner of anarchy in your face."

"Power," said Dr. Gresham, "naturally gravitates into the strongest hands. The class who have the best brain and most wealth can strike with the heaviest hand. I have too much faith in the inherent power of the white race to dread the competition of any other people under heaven."

"I think you Northerners fail to do us justice," said Dr. Latrobe. "The men into whose hands you put the ballot were our slaves, and we would rather die than submit to them. Look at the carpet-bag governments the wicked policy of the Government inflicted upon us. It was only done to humiliate us."

"Oh, no!" said Dr. Gresham, flushing, and rising to his feet. "We had no other alternative than putting the ballot in their hands."

"I will not deny," said Rev. Carmicle, "that we have made woeful mistakes, but with our antecedents it would have been miraculous if we had never committed any mistakes or made any blunders."

"They were allies in war," continued Dr. Gresham, "and I am sorry that we have not done more to protect them in peace."

"Protect them in peace!" said Robert, bitterly. "What protection does the colored man receive from the hands of the Government? I know of no civilized country outside of America where men are still burned for real or supposed crimes."

"Johnson," said Dr. Gresham, compassionately, "it is impossible to have a policeman at the back of each colored man's chair, and a squad of soldiers at each crossroad, to detect with certainty, and punish with celerity, each invasion of his rights. We tried provisional governments and found them a failure. It seemed like leaving our former allies to be mocked with the name of freedom and tortured with the essence of slavery. The ballot is our weapon of defense, and we gave it to them for theirs."

"And there," said Dr. Latrobe, emphatically, "is where you signally failed. We are numerically stronger in Congress today than when we went out. You made the law, but the administration of it is in our hands, and we are a unit."

"But, Doctor," said Rev. Carmicle, "you cannot willfully deprive the Negro of a single right as a citizen without sending demoralization through your own ranks."

"I think," said Dr. Latrobe, "that we are right in suppressing the Negro's vote. This is a white man's government, and a white man's country. We own nineteen-twentieths of the land, and have about the same ratio of intelligence. I am a white man, and, right or wrong, I go with my race."

"But, Doctor," said Rev. Carmicle, "there are rights more sacred than the rights of property and superior intelligence."

"What are they?" asked Dr. Latrobe.

"The rights of life and liberty," replied Rev. Carmicle.

"That is true," said Dr. Gresham; "and your Southern civilization will be inferior until you shall have placed protection to those rights at its base, not in theory but in fact."

"But, Dr. Gresham, we have to live with these people, and the North is constantly irritating us by its criticisms."

"The world," said Dr. Gresham, "is fast becoming a vast whispering gallery, and lips once sealed can now state their own grievances and appeal to the conscience of the nation, and, as long as a sense of justice and mercy retains a hold upon the heart of our nation, you cannot practice violence and injustice without rousing a spirit of remonstrance. And if it were not so I would be ashamed of my country and of my race."

"You speak," said Dr. Latrobe, "as if we had wronged the Negro by enslaving him and being unwilling to share citizenship with him. I think that slavery has been of incalculable value to the Negro. It has lifted him out of barbarism and fetich worship, given him a language of civilization, and introduced him to the world's best religion. Think what he was in Africa and what he is in America!"

"The Negro," said Dr. Gresham, thoughtfully, "is not the only branch of the human race which has been low down in the scale of civilization and freedom, and which has outgrown the measure of his chains. Slavery, polygamy, and human sacrifices have been practiced among Europeans in bygone days; and when Tyndall tells us that out of savages unable to count to the number of their fingers and speaking only a language of nouns and verbs, arise at length our Newtons and Shakespeares, I do not see that the Negro could not have learned our language and received our religion without the intervention of ages of slavery."

"If," said Rev. Carmicle, "Mohammedanism, with its imperfect creed, is successful in gathering large numbers of Negroes beneath the Crescent, could not a legitimate commerce and the teachings of a pure Christianity have done as much to plant the standard of the Cross over the ramparts of sin and idolatry in Africa? Surely we cannot concede that the light of the Crescent is greater than the glory of the Cross, that there is less constraining power in the Christ of Calvary than in the Prophet of Arabia? I do not think that I underrate the difficulties in your way when I say that you young men are holding in your hands golden opportunities which it would be madness and folly to throw away. It is your grand opportunity to help build up a new South, not on the shifting sands of policy and expediency, but on the broad basis of equal justice and universal freedom. Do this and you will be blessed, and will make your life a blessing."

After Robert and Rev. Carmicle had left the hotel, Drs. Latimer, Gresham, and Latrobe sat silent and thoughtful awhile, when Dr. Gresham broke the silence by asking Dr. Latrobe how he had enjoyed the evening.

"Very pleasantly," he replied. "I was quite interested in that parson. Where was he educated?"

"In Oxford, I believe. I was pleased to hear him say that he had no white blood in his veins."

"I should think not," replied Dr. Latrobe, "from his looks. But one swallow does not make a summer. It is the exceptions which prove the rule."

"Don't you think," asked Dr. Gresham, "that we have been too hasty in our judgment of the Negro? He has come handicapped into life, and is now on trial before the world. But it is not fair to subject him to the same tests that you would a white man. I believe that there are possibilities of growth in the race which we have never comprehended."

"The Negro," said Dr. Latrobe, "is perfectly comprehensible to me. The only way to get along with him is to let him know his place, and make him keep it."

"I think," replied Dr. Gresham, "every man's place is the one he is best fitted for."

"Why," asked Dr. Latimer, "should any place be assigned to the Negro more than to the French, Irish, or German?"

"Oh," replied Dr. Latrobe, "they are all Caucasians."

"Well," said Dr. Gresham, "is all excellence summed up in that branch of the human race?"

"I think," said Dr. Latrobe, proudly, "that we belong to the highest race on earth and the Negro to the lowest."

"And yet," said Dr. Latimer, "you have consorted with them till you have bleached their faces to the whiteness of your own. Your children nestle in their bosoms; they are around you as body servants, and yet if one of them should attempt to associate with you your bitterest scorn and indignation would be visited upon them."

"I think," said Dr. Latrobe, "that feeling grows out of our Anglo-Saxon regard for the marriage relation. These white Negroes are of illegitimate origin, and we would scorn to share our social life with them. Their blood is tainted."

"Who tainted it?" asked Dr. Latimer, bitterly. "You give absolution to the fathers, and visit the misfortunes of the mothers upon the children."

"But, Doctor, what kind of society would we have if we put down the bars and admitted everybody to social equality?"

"This idea of social equality," said Dr. Latimer, "is only a bugbear which frightens well-meaning people from dealing justly with the Negro. I know of no place on earth where there is perfect social equality, and I doubt if there is such a thing in heaven. The sinner who repents on his deathbed cannot be the equal of St. Paul or the Beloved Disciple."

"Doctor," said Dr. Gresham, "I sometimes think that the final solution of this question will be the absorption of the Negro into our race."

"Never, never!" exclaimed Dr. Latrobe, vehemently. "It would be a death blow to American civilization."

"Why, Doctor," said Dr. Latimer, "you Southerners began this absorption before the war. I understand that in one decade the mixed bloods rose from one-ninth to one-eighth of the population, and that as early as 1663 a law was passed in Maryland to prevent English women from intermarrying with slaves; and, even now, your laws against miscegenation presuppose that you apprehend danger from that source."

"Doctor, it is no use talking," replied Dr. Latrobe, wearily. "There are niggers who are as white as I am, but the taint of blood is there and we always exclude it."

"How do you know it is there?" asked Dr. Gresham.

"Oh, there are tricks of blood which always betray them. My eyes are more practiced than yours. I can always tell them. Now, that Johnson is as white as any man; but I knew he was a nigger the moment I saw him. I saw it in his eye."

Dr. Latimer smiled at Dr. Latrobe's assertion, but did not attempt to refute it; and bade him good night.

"I think," said Dr. Latrobe, "that our war was the great mistake of the nineteenth century. It has left us very serious complications. We cannot amalgamate with the Negroes. We cannot expatriate them. Now, what are we to do with them?"

"Deal justly with them," said Dr. Gresham, "and let them alone. Try to create a moral sentiment in the nation, which will consider a wrong done to the weakest of them as a wrong done to the whole community. Whenever you find ministers too righteous to be faithless, cowardly, and time serving; women too Christly to be scornful; and public men too noble to be tricky and too honest to pander to the prejudices of the people, stand by them and give them your moral support."

"Doctor," said Latrobe, "with your views you ought to be a preacher striving to usher in the millennium."

"It can't come too soon," replied Dr. Gresham.

27.
DIVERGING PATHS.

On the eve of his departure from the city of P——, Dr. Gresham called on Iola, and found her alone. They talked awhile of reminiscences of the war and hospital life, when Dr. Gresham, approaching Iola, said:—

"Miss Leroy, I am glad the great object of your life is accomplished, and that you have found all your relatives. Years have passed since we parted, years in which I have vainly tried to get a trace of you and have been baffled, but I have found you at last!" Clasping her hand in his, he continued, "I would it were so that I should never lose you again! Iola, will you not grant me the privilege of holding this hand as mine all through the future of our lives? Your search for your mother is ended. She is well cared for. Are you not free at last to share with me my Northern home, free to be mine as nothing else on earth is mine." Dr. Gresham looked eagerly on Iola's face, and tried to read its varying expression. "Iola, I learned to love you in the hospital. I have tried to forget you, but it has been all in vain. Your image is just as deeply engraven on my heart as it was the day we parted."

"Doctor," she replied, sadly, but firmly, as she withdrew her hand from his, "I feel now as I felt then, that there is an insurmountable barrier between us."

"What is it, Iola?" asked Dr. Gresham, anxiously.

"It is the public opinion which assigns me a place with the colored people."

"But what right has public opinion to interfere with our marriage relations? Why should we yield to its behests?"

"Because it is stronger than we are, and we cannot run counter to it without suffering its penalties."

"And what are they, Iola? Shadows that you merely dread?"

"No! No! The penalties of social ostracism North and South, except here and there some grand and noble exceptions. I do not think that you fully realize how much prejudice against colored people permeates society, lowers the tone of our religion, and reacts upon the life of the nation. After freedom came, mamma was living in the city of A——, and wanted to unite with a Christian church there. She made application for membership. She passed her examination as a candidate, and was received as a church member. When she was about to make her first communion, she unintentionally took her seat at the head of the column. The elder who was administering the communion gave her the bread in the order in which she sat, but before he gave her the wine someone touched him on the shoulder and whispered a word in his ear. He then passed mamma by, gave the cup to others, and then returned to her. From that rite connected with the holiest memories of earth, my poor mother returned humiliated and depressed."

"What a shame!" exclaimed Dr. Gresham, indignantly.

"I have seen," continued Iola, "the same spirit manifested in the North. Mamma once attempted to do missionary work in this city. One day she found an outcast colored girl, whom she wished to rescue. She took her to an asylum for fallen women and made an application for her, but was refused. Colored girls were not received there. Soon after mamma found among the colored people an outcast white girl. Mamma's sympathies, unfettered by class distinction, were aroused in her behalf, and, in company with two white ladies, she went with the girl to that same refuge. For her the door was freely opened and admittance readily granted. It was as if two women were sinking in the quicksands, and on the solid land stood other women with life-lines in their hands, seeing the deadly sands slowly creeping up around the hapless victims. To one they readily threw the lines of deliverance, but for the other there was not one strand of salvation. Sometime since, to the same asylum, came a poor fallen girl who had escaped from the clutches of a wicked woman. For her the door would have been opened, had not the vile woman from whom she was escaping followed her to that place of refuge and revealed the fact that she belonged to the colored race. That fact was enough to close the door upon her, and to send her back to sin and to suffer, and perhaps to die as a wretched outcast. And yet in this city where a number of charities are advertised, I do not think there is one of them which, in appealing to the public, talks more religion than the managers of this asylum. This prejudice against the colored race environs our lives and mocks our aspirations."

"Iola, I see no use in your persisting that you are colored when your eyes are as blue and complexion as white as mine."

"Doctor, were I your wife, are there not people who would caress me as a white woman who would shrink from me in scorn if they knew I had one drop of Negro blood in my veins? When mistaken for a white woman, I should hear things alleged against the race at which my blood would boil. No, Doctor, I am not willing to live under a shadow of concealment which I thoroughly hate as if the blood in my veins were an undetected crime of my soul."

"Iola, dear, surely you paint the picture too darkly."

"Doctor, I have painted it with my heart's blood. It is easier to outgrow the dishonor of crime than the disabilities of color. You have created in this country an aristocracy of color wide enough to include the South with its treason and Utah with its abominations, but too narrow to include the best and bravest colored man who bared his breast to the bullets of the enemy during your fratricidal strife. Is not the most arrant Rebel today more acceptable to you than the most faithful colored man?"

"No! No!" exclaimed Dr. Gresham, vehemently. "You are wrong. I belong to the Grand Army of the Republic. We have no separate State Posts for the colored people, and, were such a thing proposed, the majority of our members, I believe, would be against it. In Congress colored men have the same seats as white men, and the color line is slowly fading out in our public institutions."

"But how is it in the Church?" asked Iola.

"The Church is naturally conservative. It preserves old truths, even if it is somewhat slow in embracing new ideas. It has its social as well as its spiritual side. Society is woman's realm. The majority of church members are women, who are said to be the aristocratic element of our country. I fear that one of the last strongholds of this racial prejudice will be found beneath the shadow of some of our churches. I think, on account of this social question, that large bodies of Christian temperance women and other reformers, in trying to reach the colored people even for their own good, will be quicker to form separate associations than our National Grand Army, whose ranks are open to black and white, liberals and conservatives, saints and agnostics. But, Iola, we have drifted far away from the question. No one has a right to interfere with our marriage if we do not infringe on the rights of others."

"Doctor," she replied, gently, "I feel that our paths must diverge. My life-work is planned. I intend spending my future among the colored people of the South."

"My dear friend," he replied, anxiously, "I am afraid that you are destined to sad disappointment. When the novelty wears off you will be disillusioned, and, I fear, when the time comes that you can no longer serve them they will forget your services and remember only your failings."

"But, Doctor, they need me; and I am sure when I taught among them they were very grateful for my services."

"I think," he replied, "these people are more thankful than grateful."

"I do not think so; and if I did it would not hinder me from doing all in my power to help them. I do not expect all the finest traits of character to spring from the hot-beds of slavery and caste. What matters it if they do forget the singer, so they don't forget the song? No, Doctor, I don't think that I could best serve my race by forsaking them and marrying you."

"Iola," he exclaimed, passionately, "if you love your race, as you call it, work for it, live for it, suffer for it, and, if need be, die for it; but don't marry for it. Your education has unfitted you for social life among them."

"It was," replied Iola, "through their unrequited toil that I was educated, while they were compelled to live in ignorance. I am indebted to them for the power I have to serve them. I wish other Southern women felt as I do. I think they could do so much to help the colored people at their doors if they would look at their opportunities in the light of the face of Jesus Christ. Nor am I wholly unselfish in allying myself with the colored people. All the rest of my family have done so. My dear grandmother is one of the excellent of the earth, and we all love her too much to ignore our relationship with her. I did not choose my lot in life, and the simplest thing I can do is to accept the situation and do the best I can."

"And is this your settled purpose?" he asked, sadly.

"It is, Doctor," she replied, tenderly but firmly. "I see no other. I must serve the race which needs me most."

"Perhaps you are right," he replied; "but I cannot help feeling sad that our paths, which met so pleasantly, should diverge so painfully. And yet, not only the freedmen, but the whole country, need such helpful, self-sacrificing teachers as you will prove; and if earnest prayers and holy wishes can brighten your path, your lines will fall in the pleasantest places."

As he rose to go, sympathy, love, and admiration were blended in the parting look he gave her; but he felt it was useless to attempt to divert her from her purpose. He knew that for the true reconstruction of the country something more was needed than bayonets and bullets, or the schemes of selfish politicians or plotting demagogues. He knew that the South needed the surrender of the best brain and heart of the country to build, above the wastes of war, more stately temples of thought and action.

28.
DR. LATROBE'S MISTAKE.

On the morning previous to their departure for their respective homes, Dr. Gresham met Dr. Latrobe in the parlor of the Concordia.

"How," asked Dr. Gresham, "did you like Dr. Latimer's paper?"

"Very much, indeed. It was excellent. He is a very talented young man. He sits next to me at lunch and I have conversed with him several times. He is very genial and attractive, only he seems to be rather cranky on the Negro question. I hope if he comes South that he will not make the mistake of mixing up with the Negroes. It would be throwing away his influence and ruining his prospects. He seems to be well versed in science and literature and would make a very delightful accession to our social life."

"I think," replied Dr. Gresham, "that he is an honor to our profession. He is one of the finest specimens of our young manhood."

Just then Dr. Latimer entered the room. Dr. Latrobe arose and, greeting him cordially, said: "I was delighted with your paper; it was full of thought and suggestion."

"Thank you," answered Dr. Latimer, "it was my aim to make it so."

"And you succeeded admirably," replied Dr. Latrobe. "I could not help thinking how much we owe to heredity and environment."

"Yes," said Dr. Gresham. "Continental Europe yearly sends to our shores subjects to be developed into citizens. Emancipation has given us millions of new citizens, and to them our influence and example should be a blessing and not a curse."

"Well," said Dr. Latimer, "I intend to go South, and help those who so much need helpers from their own ranks."

"I hope," answered Dr. Latrobe, "that if you go South you will only sustain business relations with the Negroes, and not commit the folly of equalizing yourself with them."

"Why not?" asked Dr. Latimer, steadily looking him in the eye.

"Because in equalizing yourself with them you drag us down; and our social customs must be kept intact."

"You have been associating with me at the convention for several days; I do not see that the contact has dragged you down, has it?"

"You! What has that got to do with associating with niggers?" asked Dr. Latrobe, curtly.

"The blood of that race is coursing through my veins. I am one of them," replied Dr. Latimer, proudly raising his head.

"You!" exclaimed Dr. Latrobe, with an air of profound astonishment and crimsoning face.

"Yes," interposed Dr. Gresham, laughing heartily at Dr. Latrobe's discomfiture. "He belongs to that Negro race both by blood and choice. His father's mother made overtures to receive him as her grandson and heir, but he has nobly refused to forsake his mother's people and has cast his lot with them."

"And I," said Dr. Latimer, "would have despised myself if I had done otherwise."

"Well, well," said Dr. Latrobe, rising, "I was never so deceived before. Good morning!"

Dr. Latrobe had thought he was clear-sighted enough to detect the presence of Negro blood when all physical traces had disappeared. But he had associated with Dr. Latimer for several days, and admired his talent, without suspecting for one moment his racial connection. He could not help feeling a sense of vexation at the signal mistake he had made.

Dr. Frank Latimer was the natural grandson of a Southern lady, in whose family his mother had been a slave. The blood of a proud aristocratic ancestry was flowing through his veins, and generations of blood admixture had effaced all trace of his Negro lineage. His complexion was blonde, his eye bright and piercing, his lips firm and well moulded; his manner very affable; his intellect active and well stored with information. He was a man capable of winning in life through his rich gifts of inheritance and acquirements. When freedom came, his mother, like Hagar of old, went out into the wide world to seek a living for herself and child. Through years of poverty she labored to educate her child, and saw the glad fruition of her hopes when her son graduated as an M.D. from the University of P——.

After his graduation he met his father's mother, who recognized him by his resemblance to her dear, departed son. All the mother love in her lonely heart awoke, and she was willing to overlook "the missing link of matrimony," and adopt him as her heir, if he would ignore his identity with the colored race.

Before him loomed all the possibilities which only birth and blood can give a white man in our Democratic country. But he was a man of too much sterling worth of character to be willing to forsake his mother's race for the richest advantages his grandmother could bestow.

Dr. Gresham had met Dr. Latimer at the beginning of the convention, and had been attracted to him by his frank and genial manner. One morning, when conversing with him, Dr. Gresham had learned some of the salient points of his history, which, instead of repelling him, had only deepened his admiration for the young doctor. He was much amused when he saw the pleasant acquaintanceship between him and Dr. Latrobe, but they agreed to be silent about his racial connection until the time came when they were ready to divulge it; and they were hugely delighted at his signal blunder.

29.
VISITORS FROM THE SOUTH.

"Mamma is not well," said Iola to Robert. "I spoke to her about sending for a doctor, but she objected and I did not insist."

"I will ask Dr. Latimer, whom I met at the Concordia, to step in. He is a splendid young fellow. I wish we had thousands like him."

In the evening the doctor called. Without appearing to make a professional visit he engaged Marie in conversation, watched her carefully, and came to the conclusion that her failing health proceeded more from mental than physical causes.

"I am so uneasy about Harry," said Mrs. Leroy. "He is so fearless and outspoken. I do wish the attention of the whole nation could be turned to the cruel barbarisms which are a national disgrace. I think the term 'bloody shirt' is one of the most heartless phrases ever invented to divert attention from cruel wrongs and dreadful outrages."

Just then Iola came in and was introduced by her uncle to Dr. Latimer, to whom the introduction was a sudden and unexpected pleasure.

After an interchange of courtesies, Marie resumed the conversation, saying: "Harry wrote me only last week that a young friend of his had lost his situation because he refused to have his pupils strew flowers on the streets through which Jefferson Davis was to pass."

"I think," said Dr. Latimer, indignantly, "that the Israelites had just as much right to scatter flowers over the bodies of the Egyptians, when the waves threw back their corpses on the shores of the Red Sea, as these children had to strew the path of Jefferson Davis with flowers. We want our boys to grow up manly citizens, and not cringing sycophants. When do you expect your son, Mrs. Leroy?"

"Some time next week," answered Marie.

"And his presence will do you more good than all the medicine in my chest."

"I hope, Doctor," said Mrs. Leroy, "that we will not lose sight of you, now that your professional visit is ended; for I believe your visit was the result of a conspiracy between Iola and her uncle."

Dr. Latimer laughed, as he answered, "Ah, Mrs. Leroy, I see you have found us all out."

"Oh, Doctor," exclaimed Iola, with pleasing excitement, "there is a young lady coming here to visit me next week. Her name is Miss Lucille Delany, and she is my ideal woman. She is grand, brave, intellectual, and religious."

"Is that so? She would make some man an excellent wife," replied Dr. Latimer.

"Now isn't that perfectly manlike," answered Iola, smiling. "Mamma, what do you think of that? Did any of you gentlemen ever see a young woman of much ability that you did not look upon as a flotsam all adrift until some man had appropriated her?"

"I think, Miss Leroy, that the world's work, if shared, is better done than when it is performed alone. Don't you think your life-work will be better done if someone shares it with you?" asked Dr. Latimer, slowly, and with a smile in his eyes.

"That would depend on the person who shared it," said Iola, faintly blushing.

"Here," said Robert, a few evenings after this conversation, as he handed Iola a couple of letters, "is something which will please you."

Iola took the letters, and, after reading one of them, said: "Miss Delany and Harry will be here on Wednesday; and this one is an invitation which also adds to my enjoyment."

"What is it?" asked Marie; "an invitation to a hop or a german?"

"No; but something which I value far more. We are all invited to Mr. Stillman's to a *conversazione*."

"What is the object?"

"His object is to gather some of the thinkers and leaders of the race to consult on subjects of vital interest to our welfare. He has invited Dr. Latimer, Professor Gradnor, of North Carolina, Mr. Forest, of New York, Hon. Dugdale, Revs. Carmicle, Cantnor, Tunster, Professor Langhorne, of Georgia, and a few ladies, Mrs. Watson, Miss Brown, and others."

"I am glad that it is neither a hop nor a german," said Iola, "but something for which I have been longing."

"Why, Iola," asked Robert, "don't you believe in young people having a good time?"

"Oh, yes," answered Iola, seriously, "I believe in young people having amusements and recreations; but the times are too serious for us to attempt to make our lives a long holiday."

"Well, Iola," answered Robert, "this is the first holiday we have had in two hundred and fifty years, and you shouldn't be too exacting."

"Yes," replied Marie, "human beings naturally crave enjoyment, and if not furnished with good amusements they are apt to gravitate to low pleasures."

"Someone," said Robert, "has said that the Indian belongs to an old race and looks gloomily back to the past, and that the Negro belongs to a young race and looks hopefully towards the future."

"If that be so," replied Marie, "our race-life corresponds more to the follies of youth than the faults of maturer years."

On Dr. Latimer's next visit he was much pleased to see a great change in Marie's appearance. Her eye had grown brighter, her step more elastic, and the anxiety had faded from her face. Harry had arrived, and with him came Miss Delany.

"Good evening, Dr. Latimer," said Iola, cheerily, as she entered the room with Miss Lucille Delany. "This is my friend, Miss Delany, from Georgia. Were she not present, I would say she is one of the grandest women in America."

"I am very much pleased to meet you," said Dr. Latimer, cordially; "I have heard Miss Leroy speak of you. We were expecting you," he added, with a smile.

Just then Harry entered the room, and Iola presented him to Dr. Latimer, saying, "This is my brother, about whom mamma was so anxious."

"Had you a pleasant journey?" asked Dr. Latimer, after the first greetings were over.

"Not especially," answered Miss Delany. "Southern roads are not always very pleasant to travel. When Mr. Leroy entered the cars at A——, where he was known, had he taken his seat among the white people he would have been remanded to the colored."

"But after a while," said Harry, "as Miss Delany and myself were sitting together, laughing and chatting, a colored man entered the car, and, mistaking me for a white man, asked the conductor to have me removed, and I had to insist that I was colored in order to be permitted to remain. It would be ludicrous, if it were not vexatious, to be too white to be black, and too black to be white."

"Caste plays such fantastic tricks in this country," said Dr. Latimer.

"I tell Mr. Leroy," said Miss Delany, "that when he returns he must put a label on himself, saying, 'I am a colored man,' to prevent annoyance."

30.
FRIENDS IN COUNCIL.

On the following Friday evening, Mr. Stillman's pleasant, spacious parlors were filled to overflowing with a select company of earnest men and women deeply interested in the welfare of the race.

Bishop Tunster had prepared a paper on "Negro Emigration." Dr. Latimer opened the discussion by speaking favorably of some of the salient points, but said:—

"I do not believe self-exilement is the true remedy for the wrongs of the Negro. Where should he go if he left this country?"

"Go to Africa," replied Bishop Tunster, in his bluff, hearty tones. "I believe that Africa is to be redeemed to civilization, and that the Negro is to be gathered into the family of nations and recognized as a man and a brother."

"Go to Africa?" repeated Professor Langhorne, of Georgia. "Does the United States own one foot of African soil? And have we not been investing our blood in the country for ages?"

"I am in favor of missionary efforts," said Professor Gradnor, of North Carolina, "for the redemption of Africa, but I see no reason for expatriating ourselves because some persons do not admire the color of our skins."

"I do not believe," said Mr. Stillman, "in emptying on the shores of Africa a horde of ignorant, poverty-stricken people, as missionaries of civilization or Christianity. And while I am in favor of missionary efforts, there is need here for the best heart and brain to work in unison for justice and righteousness."

"America," said Miss Delany, "is the best field for human development. God has not heaped up our mountains with such grandeur, flooded our rivers with such majesty, crowned our valleys with such fertility, enriched our mines with such wealth, that they should only minister to grasping greed and sensuous enjoyment."

"Climate, soil, and physical environments," said Professor Gradnor, "have much to do with shaping national characteristics. If in Africa, under a tropical sun, the Negro has lagged behind other races in the march of civilization, at least for once in his history he has, in this country, the privilege of using climatic advantages and developing under new conditions."

"Yes," replied Dr. Latimer, "and I do not wish our people to become restless and unsettled before they have tried one generation of freedom."

"I am always glad," said Mr. Forest, a tall, distinguished-looking gentleman from New York, "when I hear of people who are ill treated in one section of the country emigrating to another. Men who are deaf to the claims of mercy, and oblivious to the demands of justice, can feel when money is slipping from their pockets."

"The Negro," said Hon. Dugdale, "does not present to my mind the picture of an effete and exhausted people, destined to die out before a stronger race. Gilbert Haven once saw a statue which suggested this thought, 'I am black, but comely; the sun has looked down upon me, but I will teach you who despise me to feel that I am your superior.' The men who are acquiring property and building up homes in the South show us what energy and determination may do even in that part of the country. I believe such men can do more to conquer prejudice than if they spent all their lives in shouting for their rights and ignoring their duties. No! As there are millions of us in this country, I think it best to settle down and work out our own salvation here."

"How many of us today," asked Professor Langhorne, "would be teaching in the South, if every field of labor in the North was as accessible to us as to the whites? It has been estimated that a million young white men have left the South since the war, and, had our chances been equal to theirs, would we have been any more willing to stay in the South with those who need us than they? But this prejudice, by impacting us together, gives us a common cause and brings our intellect in contact with the less favored of our race."

"I do not believe," said Miss Delany, "that the Southern white people themselves desire any wholesale exodus of the colored from their labor fields. It would be suicidal to attempt their expatriation."

"History," said Professor Langhorne, "tells that Spain was once the place where barbarian Europe came to light her lamp. Seven hundred years before there was a public lamp in London you might have gone through the streets of Cordova amid ten miles of lighted lamps, and stood there on solidly paved land, when hundreds of years afterwards, in Paris, on a rainy day you would have sunk to your ankles in the mud. But she who bore the name of the 'Terror of Nations,' and the 'Queen of the Ocean,' was not strong enough to dash herself against God's law of retribution and escape unscathed. She inaugurated a crusade of horror against a million of her best laborers and artisans. Vainly she expected the blessing of God to crown her work of violence. Instead of seeing the fruition of her hopes in the increased prosperity of her land, depression and paralysis settled on her trade and business. A fearful blow was struck at her agriculture; decay settled on her manufactories; money became too scarce to pay the necessary expenses of the king's exchequer; and that once mighty empire became a fallen kingdom, pierced by her crimes and dragged down by her transgressions."

"We did not," said Iola, "place the bounds of our habitation. And I believe we are to be fixtures in this country. But beyond the shadows I see the coruscation of a brighter day; and we can help usher it in, not by answering hate with hate, or giving scorn for scorn, but by striving to be more generous, noble, and just. It seems as if all creation travels to respond to the song of the Herald angels, 'Peace on earth, goodwill toward men.'"

The next paper was on "Patriotism," by Rev. Cantnor. It was a paper in which the white man was extolled as the master race, and spoke as if it were a privilege for the colored man to be linked to his destiny and to live beneath the shadow of his power. He asserted that the white race of this country is the broadest, most Christian, and humane of that branch of the human family.

Dr. Latimer took exception to his position. "Law," he said, "is the pivot on which the whole universe turns; and obedience to law is the gauge by which a nation's strength or weakness is tried. We have had two evils by which our obedience to law has been tested—slavery and the liquor traffic. How have we dealt with them both? We have been weighed in the balance and found wanting. Millions of slaves and serfs have been liberated during this century, but not even in semi-barbaric Russia, heathen Japan, or Catholic Spain has slavery been abolished through such a fearful conflict as it was in the United States. The liquor traffic still sends its floods of ruin and shame to the habitations of men, and no political party has been found with enough moral power and numerical strength to stay the tide of death."

"I think," said Professor Gradnor, "that what our country needs is truth more than flattery. I do not think that our moral life keeps pace with our mental development and material progress. I know of no civilized country on the globe, Catholic, Protestant, or Mohammedan, where life is less secure than it is in the South. Nearly eighteen hundred years ago the life of a Roman citizen in Palestine was in danger from mob violence. That pagan government threw around him a wall of living clay, consisting of four hundred and seventy men, when more than forty Jews had bound themselves with an oath that they would neither eat nor drink until they had taken the life of the Apostle Paul. Does not true patriotism demand that citizenship should be as much protected in Christian America as it was in heathen Rome?"

"I would have our people," said Miss Delany, "more interested in politics. Instead of forgetting the past, I would have them hold in everlasting remembrance our great deliverance. Hitherto we have never had a country with tender, precious memories to fill our eyes with tears, or glad reminiscences to thrill our hearts with pride and joy. We have been aliens and outcasts in the land of our birth. But I want my pupils to do all in their power to make this country worthy of their deepest devotion and loftiest patriotism. I want them to feel that its glory is their glory, its dishonor their shame."

"Our esteemed friend, Mrs. Watson," said Iola, "sends regrets that she cannot come, but has kindly favored us with a poem, called the "Rallying Cry." In her letter she says that, although she is no longer young, she feels that in the conflict for the right there's room for young as well as old. She hopes that we will here unite the enthusiasm of youth with the experience of age, and that we will have a pleasant and profitable conference. Is it your pleasure that the poem be read at this stage of our proceedings, or later on?"

"Let us have it now," answered Harry, "and I move that Miss Delany be chosen to lend to the poem the charm of her voice."

"I second the motion," said Iola, smiling, and handing the poem to Miss Delany.

Miss Delany took the poem and read it with fine effect. The spirit of the poem had entered her soul.

A RALLYING CRY.

Oh, children of the tropics,
    Amid our pain and wrong
Have you no other mission
    Than music, dance, and song?

When through the weary ages
    Our dripping tears still fall,
Is this a time to dally
    With pleasure's silken thrall?

Go, muffle all your viols;
    As heroes learn to stand,
With faith in God's great justice
    Nerve every heart and hand.

Dream not of ease nor pleasure,
    Nor honor, wealth, nor fame,
Till from the dust you've lifted
    Our long-dishonored name;

And crowned that name with glory
    By deeds of holy worth,
To shine with light emblazoned,
    The noblest name on earth.

Count life a dismal failure,
    Unblessing and unblest,
That seeks 'mid ease inglorious
    For pleasure or for rest.

With courage, strength, and valor
    Your lives and actions brace;
Shrink not from toil or hardship,
    And dangers bravely face.

Engrave upon your banners,
    In words of golden light,
That honor, truth, and justice
    Are more than godless might.

Above earth's pain and sorrow
    Christ's dying face I see;
I hear the cry of anguish:—
    "Why hast thou forsaken me?"

In the pallor of that anguish
    I see the only light,
To flood with peace and gladness
    Earth's sorrow, pain, and night.

Arrayed in Christly armor
    'Gainst error, crime, and sin,
The victory can't be doubtful,
    For God is sure to win.

The next paper was by Miss Iola Leroy, on the "Education of Mothers."

"I agree," said Rev. Eustace, of St. Mary's parish, "with the paper. The great need of the race is enlightened mothers."

"And enlightened fathers, too," added Miss Delany, quickly. "If there is anything I chafe to see it is a strong, hearty man shirking his burdens, putting them on the shoulders of his wife, and taking life easy for himself."

"I always pity such mothers," interposed Iola, tenderly.

"I think," said Miss Delany, with a flash in her eye and a ring of decision in her voice, "that such men ought to be drummed out of town!" As she spoke, there was an expression which seemed to say, "And I would like to help do it!"

Harry smiled, and gave her a quick glance of admiration.

"I do not think," said Mrs. Stillman, "that we can begin too early to teach our boys to be manly and self-respecting, and our girls to be useful and self-reliant."

"You know," said Mrs. Leroy, "that after the war we were thrown upon the nation a homeless race to be gathered into homes, and a legally unmarried race to be taught the sacredness of the marriage relation. We must instill into our young people that the true strength of a race means purity in women and uprightness in men; who can say, with Sir Galahad:—

'My strength is the strength of ten,
Because my heart is pure.'

And where this is wanting neither wealth nor culture can make up the deficiency."

"There is a field of Christian endeavor which lies between the schoolhouse and the pulpit, which needs the hand of a woman more in private than in public," said Miss Delany.

"Yes, I have often felt the need of such work in my own parish. We need a union of women with the warmest hearts and clearest brains to help in the moral education of the race," said Rev. Eustace.

"Yes," said Iola, "if we would have the prisons empty we must make the homes more attractive."

"In civilized society," replied Dr. Latimer, "there must be restraint either within or without. If parents fail to teach restraint within, society has her checkreins without in the form of chain gangs, prisons, and the gallows."

The closing paper was on the "Moral Progress of the Race," by Hon. Dugdale. He said: "The moral progress of the race was not all he could desire, yet he could not help feeling that, compared with other races, the outlook was not hopeless. I am so sorry to see, however, that in some States there is an undue proportion of colored people in prisons."

"I think," answered Professor Langhorne, of Georgia, "that this is owing to a partial administration of law in meting out punishment to colored offenders. I know red-handed murderers who walk in this Republic unwhipped of justice, and I have seen a colored woman sentenced to prison for weeks for stealing twenty-five cents. I knew a colored girl who was executed for murder when only a child in years. And it was through the intervention of a friend of mine, one of the bravest young men of the South, that a boy of fifteen was saved from the gallows."

"When I look," said Mr. Forest, "at the slow growth of modern civilization —the ages which have been consumed in reaching our present altitude, and see how we have outgrown slavery, feudalism, and religious persecutions, I cannot despair of the future of the race."

"Just now," said Dr. Latimer, "we have the fearful grinding and friction which comes in the course of an adjustment of the new machinery of freedom in the old ruts of slavery. But I am optimistic enough to believe that there will yet be a far higher and better Christian civilization than our country has ever known."

"And in that civilization I believe the Negro is to be an important factor," said Rev. Cantnor.

"I believe it also," said Miss Delany, hopefully, "and this thought has been a blessed inspiration to my life. When I come in contact with Christ-less prejudices, I feel that my life is too much a part of the Divine plan, and invested with too much intrinsic worth, for me to be the least humiliated by indignities that beggarly souls can inflict. I feel more pitiful than resentful to those who do not know how much they miss by living mean, ignoble lives."

"My heart," said Iola, "is full of hope for the future. Pain and suffering are the crucibles out of which come gold more fine than the pavements of heaven, and gems more precious than the foundations of the Holy City."

"If," said Mrs. Leroy, "pain and suffering are factors in human development, surely we have not been counted too worthless to suffer."

"And is there," continued Iola, "a path which we have trodden in this country, unless it be the path of sin, into which Jesus Christ has not put His feet and left it luminous with the light of His steps? Has the Negro been poor and homeless? The birds of the air had nests and the foxes had holes, but the Son of man had not where to lay His head. Has our name been a synonym for contempt? 'He shall be called a Nazarene.' Have we been despised and trodden under foot? Christ was despised and rejected of men. Have we been ignorant and unlearned? It was said of Jesus Christ, 'How knoweth this man letters, never having learned?' Have we been beaten and bruised in the prison-house of bondage? 'They took Jesus and scourged Him.' Have we been slaughtered, our bones scattered at the graves' mouth? He was spit upon by the mob, smitten and mocked by the rabble, and died as died Rome's meanest criminal slave. Today that cross of shame is a throne of power. Those robes of scorn have changed to habiliments of light, and that crown of mockery to a diadem of glory. And never, while the agony of Gethsemane and the sufferings of Calvary have their hold upon my heart, will I recognize any religion as His which despises the least of His brethren."

As Iola finished, there was a ring of triumph in her voice, as if she were reviewing a path she had trodden with bleeding feet, and seen it change to lines of living light. Her soul seemed to be flashing through the rare loveliness of her face and etherealizing its beauty.

Everyone was spellbound. Dr. Latimer was entranced, and, turning to Hon. Dugdale, said, in a low voice and with deep-drawn breath, "She is angelic!"

Hon. Dugdale turned, gave a questioning look, then replied, "She is strangely beautiful! Do you know her?"

"Yes; I have met her several times. I accompanied her here tonight. The tones of her voice are like benedictions of peace; her words a call to higher service and nobler life."

Just then Rev. Carmicle was announced. He had been on a Southern tour, and had just returned.

"Oh, Doctor," exclaimed Mrs. Stillman, "I am delighted to see you. We were about to adjourn, but we will postpone action to hear from you."

"Thank you," replied Rev. Carmicle. "I have not the cue to the meeting, and will listen while I take breath."

"Pardon me," answered Mrs. Stillman. "I should have been more thoughtful than to press so welcome a guest into service before I had given him time for rest and refreshment; but if the courtesy failed on my lips it did not fail in my heart. I wanted our young folks to see one of our thinkers who had won distinction before the war."

"My dear friend," said Rev. Carmicle, smiling, "some of these young folks will look on me as a back number. You know the cry has already gone forth, 'Young men to the front.'"

"But we need old men for counsel," interposed Mr. Forest, of New York.

"Of course," said Rev. Carmicle, "we older men would rather retire gracefully than be relegated or hustled to a back seat. But I am pleased to see doors open to you which were closed to us, and opportunities which were denied us embraced by you."

"How," asked Hon. Dugdale, "do you feel in reference to our people's condition in the South?"

"Very hopeful, although at times I cannot help feeling anxious about their future. I was delighted with my visits to various institutions of learning, and surprised at the desire manifested among the young people to obtain an education. Where toil-worn mothers bent beneath their heavy burdens their more favored daughters are enjoying the privileges of education. Young people are making recitations in Greek and Latin where it was once a crime to teach their parents to read. I also became acquainted with colored professors and presidents of colleges. Saw young ladies who had graduated as doctors. Comfortable homes have succeeded old cabins of slavery. Vast crops have been raised by free labor. I read with interest and pleasure a number of papers edited by colored men. I saw it estimated that two millions of our people had learned to read, and I feel deeply grateful to the people who have supplied us with teachers who have stood their ground so nobly among our people."

"But," asked Mr. Forest, "you expressed fears about the future of our race. From whence do your fears arise?"

"From the unfortunate conditions which slavery has entailed upon that section of our country. I dread the results of that racial feeling which ever and anon breaks out into restlessness and crime. Also, I am concerned about the lack of home training for those for whom the discipline of the plantation has been exchanged for the penalties of prisons and chain gangs. I am sorry to see numbers of our young men growing away from the influence of the church and drifting into prisons. I also fear that in some sections, as colored men increase in wealth and intelligence, there will be an increase of race rivalry and jealousy. It is said that savages, by putting their ears to the ground, can hear a far-off tread. So, today, I fear that there are savage elements in our civilization which hear the advancing tread of the Negro and would retard his coming. It is the incarnation of these elements that I dread. It is their elimination I do so earnestly desire. Whether it be outgrown or not is our unsolved problem. Time alone will tell whether or not the virus of slavery and injustice has too fully permeated our Southern civilization for a complete recovery. Nations, honey-combed by vice, have fallen beneath the weight of their iniquities. Justice is always uncompromising in its claims and inexorable in its demands. The laws of the universe are never repealed to accommodate our follies."

"Surely," said Bishop Tunster, "the Negro has a higher mission than that of aimlessly drifting through life and patiently waiting for death."

"We may not," answered Rev. Carmicle, "have the same dash, courage, and aggressiveness of other races, accustomed to struggle, achievement, and dominion, but surely the world needs something better than the results of arrogance, aggressiveness, and indomitable power. For the evils of society there are no solvents as potent as love and justice, and our greatest need is not more wealth and learning, but a religion replete with life and glowing with love. Let this be the impelling force in the race and it cannot fail to rise in the scale of character and condition."

"And," said Dr. Latimer, "instead of narrowing our sympathies to mere racial questions, let us broaden them to humanity's wider issues."

"Let us," replied Rev. Carmicle, "pass it along the lines, that to be willfully ignorant is to be shamefully criminal. Let us teach our people not to love pleasure or to fear death, but to learn the true value of life, and to do their part to eliminate the paganism of caste from our holy religion and the lawlessness of savagery from our civilization."

"How did you enjoy the evening, Marie?" asked Robert, as they walked homeward.

"I was interested and deeply pleased," answered Marie.

"I," said Robert, "was thinking of the wonderful changes that have come to us since the war. When I sat in those well-lighted, beautifully-furnished rooms, I was thinking of the meetings we used to have in bygone days. How we used to go by stealth into lonely woods and gloomy swamps, to tell of our hopes and fears, sorrows and trials. I hope that we will have many more of these gatherings. Let us have the next one here."

"I am sure," said Marie, "I would gladly welcome such a conference at any time. I think such meetings would be so helpful to our young people."

31.
DAWNING AFFECTIONS.

"Doctor," said Iola, as they walked home from the *conversazione*, "I wish I could do something more for our people than I am doing. I taught in the South till failing health compelled me to change my employment. But, now that I am well and strong, I would like to do something of lasting service for the race."

"Why not," asked Dr. Latimer, "write a good, strong book which would be helpful to them? I think there is an amount of dormant talent among us, and a large field from which to gather materials for such a book."

"I would do it, willingly, if I could; but one needs both leisure and money to make a successful book. There is material among us for the broadest comedies and the deepest tragedies, but, besides money and leisure, it needs patience, perseverance, courage, and the hand of an artist to weave it into the literature of the country."

"Miss Leroy, you have a large and rich experience; you possess a vivid imagination and glowing fancy. Write, out of the fullness of your heart, a book to inspire men and women with a deeper sense of justice and humanity."

"Doctor," replied Iola, "I would do it if I could, not for the money it might bring, but for the good it might do. But who believes any good can come out of the black Nazareth?"

"Miss Leroy, out of the race must come its own thinkers and writers. Authors belonging to the white race have written good racial books, for which I am deeply grateful, but it seems to be almost impossible for a white man to put himself completely in our place. No man can feel the iron which enters another man's soul."

"Well, Doctor, when I write a book I shall take you for the hero of my story."

"Why, what have I done," asked Dr. Latimer, in a surprised tone, "that you should impale me on your pen?"

"You have done nobly," answered Iola, "in refusing your grandmother's offer."

"I only did my duty," he modestly replied.

"But," said Iola, "when others are trying to slip out from the race and pass into the white basis, I cannot help admiring one who acts as if he felt that the weaker the race is the closer he would cling to it."

"My mother," replied Dr. Latimer, "faithful and true, belongs to that race. Where else should I be? But I know a young lady who could have cast her lot with the favored race, yet chose to take her place with the freed people, as their teacher, friend, and adviser. This young lady was alone in the world. She had been fearfully wronged, and to her stricken heart came a brilliant offer of love, home, and social position. But she bound her heart to the mast of duty, closed her ears to the siren song, and could not be lured from her purpose."

A startled look stole over Iola's face, and, lifting her eyes to his, she faltered:—

"Do you know her?"

"Yes, I know her and admire her; and she ought to be made the subject of a soul-inspiring story. Do you know of whom I speak?"

"How should I, Doctor? I am sure you have not made me your confidante," she responded, demurely; then she quickly turned and tripped up the steps of her home, which she had just reached.

After this conversation Dr. Latimer became a frequent visitor at Iola's home, and a firm friend of her brother. Harry was at that age when, for the young and inexperienced, vice puts on her fairest guise and most seductive smiles. Dr. Latimer's wider knowledge and larger experience made his friendship for Harry very valuable, and the service he rendered him made him a favorite and ever-welcome guest in the family.

"Are you all alone," asked Robert, one night, as he entered the cosy little parlor where Iola sat reading. "Where are the rest of the folks?"

"Mamma and grandma have gone to bed," answered Iola. "Harry and Lucille are at the concert. They are passionately fond of music, and find facilities here that they do not have in the South. They wouldn't go to hear a seraph where they must take a Negro seat. I was too tired to go. Besides, 'two's company and three's a crowd,'" she added, significantly.

"I reckon you struck the nail on the head that time," said Robert, laughing. "But you have not been alone all the time. Just as I reached the corner I saw Dr. Latimer leaving the door. I see he still continues his visits. Who is his patient now?"

"Oh, Uncle Robert," said Iola, smiling and flushing, "he is out with Harry and Lucille part of the time, and drops in now and then to see us all."

"Well," said Robert, "I suppose the case is now an affair of the heart. But I cannot blame him for it," he added, looking fondly on the beautiful face of his niece, which sorrow had touched only to chisel into more loveliness. "How do you like him?"

"I must have within me," answered Iola, with unaffected truthfulness, "a large amount of hero worship. The characters of the Old Testament I most admire are Moses and Nehemiah. They were willing to put aside their own advantages for their race and country. Dr. Latimer comes up to my ideal of a high, heroic manhood."

"I think," answered Robert, smiling archly, "he would be delighted to hear your opinion of him."

"I tell him," continued Iola, "that he belongs to the days of chivalry. But he smiles and says, 'he only belongs to the days of hard-pan service.'"

"Someone," said Robert, "was saying today that he stood in his own light when he refused his grandmother's offer to receive him as her son."

"I think," said Iola, "it was the grandest hour of his life when he made that decision. I have admired him ever since I heard his story."

"But, Iola, think of the advantages he set aside. It was no sacrifice for me to remain colored, with my lack of education and race sympathies, but Dr. Latimer had doors open to him as a white man which are forever closed to a colored man. To be born white in this country is to be born to an inheritance of privileges, to hold in your hands the keys that open before you the doors of every occupation, advantage, opportunity, and achievement."

"I know that, uncle," answered Iola; "but even these advantages are too dearly bought if they mean loss of honor, true manliness, and self respect. He could not have retained these had he ignored his mother and lived under a veil of concealment, constantly haunted by a dread of detection. The gain would not have been worth the cost. It were better that he should walk the ruggedest paths of life a true man than tread the softest carpets a moral cripple."

"I am afraid," said Robert, laying his hand caressingly upon her head, "that we are destined to lose the light of our home."

"Oh, uncle, how you talk! I never dreamed of what you are thinking," answered Iola, half reproachfully.

"And how," asked Robert, "do you know what I am thinking about?"

"My dear uncle, I'm not blind."

"Neither am I," replied Robert, significantly, as he left the room.

Iola's admiration for Dr. Latimer was not a one-sided affair. Day after day she was filling a larger place in his heart. The touch of her hand thrilled him with emotion. Her lightest words were an entrancing melody to his ear. Her noblest sentiments found a response in his heart. In their desire to help the race their hearts beat in loving unison. One grand and noble purpose was giving tone and color to their lives and strengthening the bonds of affection between them.

32.
WOOING AND WEDDING.

Harry's vacation had been very pleasant. Miss Delany, with her fine conversational powers and ready wit, had added much to his enjoyment. Robert had given his mother the pleasantest room in the house, and in the evening the family would gather around her, tell her the news of the day, read to her from the Bible, join with her in thanksgiving for mercies received and in prayer for protection through the night. Harry was very grateful to Dr. Latimer for the kindly interest he had shown in accompanying Miss Delany and himself to places of interest and amusement. He was grateful, too, that in the city of P—— doors were open to them which were barred against them in the South.

The bright, beautiful days of summer were gliding into autumn, with its glorious wealth of foliage, and the time was approaching for the departure of Harry and Miss Delany to their respective schools, when Dr. Latimer received several letters from North Carolina, urging him to come South, as physicians were greatly needed there. Although his practice was lucrative in the city of P——, he resolved he would go where his services were most needed.

A few evenings before he started he called at the house, and made an engagement to drive Iola to the park.

At the time appointed he drove up to the door in his fine equipage. Iola stepped gracefully in and sat quietly by his side to enjoy the loveliness of the scenery and the gorgeous grandeur of the setting sun.

"I expect to go South," said Dr. Latimer, as he drove slowly along.

"Ah, indeed," said Iola, assuming an air of interest, while a shadow flitted over her face. "Where do you expect to pitch your tent?"

"In the city of C——, North Carolina," he answered.

"Oh, I wish," she exclaimed, "that you were going to Georgia, where you could take care of that high-spirited brother of mine."

"I suppose if he were to hear you he would laugh, and say that he could take care of himself. But I know a better plan than that."

"What is it?" asked Iola, innocently.

"That you will commit yourself, instead of your brother, to my care."

"Oh, dear," replied Iola, drawing a long breath. "What would mamma say?"

"That she would willingly resign you, I hope."

"And what would grandma and Uncle Robert say?" again asked Iola.

"That they would cheerfully acquiesce. Now, what would I say if they all consent?"

"I don't know," modestly responded Iola.

"Well," replied Dr. Latimer, "I would say:—

> "Could deeds my love discover,
>   Could valor gain thy charms,
> To prove myself thy lover
>   I'd face a world in arms."

"And prove a good soldier," added Iola, smiling, "when there is no battle to fight."

"Iola, I am in earnest," said Dr. Latimer, passionately. "In the work to which I am devoted every burden will be lighter, every path smoother, if brightened and blessed with your companionship."

A sober expression swept over Iola's face, and, dropping her eyes, she said: "I must have time to think."

Quietly they rode along the river bank until Dr. Latimer broke the silence by saying:—

"Miss Iola, I think that you brood too much over the condition of our people."

"Perhaps I do," she replied, "but they never burn a man in the South that they do not kindle a fire around my soul."

"I am afraid," replied Dr. Latimer, "that you will grow morbid and nervous. Most of our people take life easily—why shouldn't you?"

"Because," she answered, "I can see breakers ahead which they do not."

"Oh, give yourself no uneasiness. They will catch the fret and fever of the nineteenth century soon enough. I have heard several of our ministers say that it is chiefly men of disreputable characters who are made the subjects of violence and lynch-law."

"Suppose it is so," responded Iola, feelingly. "If these men believe in eternal punishment they ought to feel a greater concern for the wretched sinner who is hurried out of time with all his sins upon his head, than for the godly man who passes through violence to endless rest."

"That is true; and I am not counseling you to be selfish; but, Miss Iola, had you not better look out for yourself?"

"Thank you, Doctor, I am feeling quite well."

"I know it, but your devotion to study and work is too intense," he replied.

"I am preparing to teach, and must spend my leisure time in study. Mr. Cloten is an excellent employer, and treats his employés as if they had hearts as well as hands. But to be an expert accountant is not the best use to which I can put my life."

"As a teacher you will need strong health and calm nerves. You had better let me prescribe for you. You need," he added, with a merry twinkle in his eyes, "change of air, change of scene, and change of name."

"Well, Doctor," said Iola, laughing, "that is the newest nostrum out. Had you not better apply for a patent?"

"Oh," replied Dr. Latimer, with affected gravity, "you know you must have unlimited faith in your physician."

"So you wish me to try the faith cure?" asked Iola, laughing.

"Yes, faith in me," responded Dr. Latimer, seriously.

"Oh, here we are at home!" exclaimed Iola. "This has been a glorious evening, Doctor. I am indebted to you for a great pleasure. I am extremely grateful."

"You are perfectly welcome," replied Dr. Latimer. "The pleasure has been mutual, I assure you."

"Will you not come in?" asked Iola.

Tying his horse, he accompanied Iola into the parlor. Seating himself near her, he poured into her ears words eloquent with love and tenderness.

"Iola," he said, "I am not an adept in courtly phrases. I am a plain man, who believes in love and truth. In asking you to share my lot, I am not inviting you to a life of ease and luxury, for year after year I may have to struggle to keep the wolf from the door, but your presence would make my home one of the brightest spots on earth, and one of the fairest types of heaven. Am I presumptuous in hoping that your love will become the crowning joy of my life?"

His words were more than a tender strain wooing her to love and happiness, they were a clarion call to a life of high and holy worth, a call which found a response in her heart. Her hand lay limp in his. She did not withdraw it, but, raising her lustrous eyes to his, she softly answered: "Frank, I love you."

After he had gone, Iola sat by the window, gazing at the splendid stars, her heart quietly throbbing with a delicious sense of joy and love. She had admired Dr. Gresham and, had there been no barrier in her way, she might have learned to love him; but Dr. Latimer had grown irresistibly upon her heart. There were depths in her nature that Dr. Gresham had never fathomed; aspirations in her soul with which he had never mingled. But as the waves leap up to the strand, so her soul went out to Dr. Latimer. Between their lives were no impeding barriers, no inclination impelling one way and duty compelling another. Kindred hopes and tastes had knit their hearts; grand and noble purposes were lighting up their lives; and they esteemed it a blessed privilege to stand on the threshold of a new era and labor for those who had passed from the old oligarchy of slavery into the new commonwealth of freedom.

On the next evening, Dr. Latimer rang the bell and was answered by Harry, who ushered him into the parlor, and then came back to the sitting-room, saying, "Iola, Dr. Latimer has called to see you."

"Has he?" answered Iola, a glad light coming into her eyes. "Come, Lucille, let us go into the parlor."

"Oh, no," interposed Harry, shrugging his shoulders and catching Lucille's hand. "He didn't ask for you. When we went to the concert we were told three's a crowd. And I say one good turn deserves another."

"Oh, Harry, you are so full of nonsense. Let Lucille go!" said Iola.

"Indeed I will not. I want to have a good time as well as you," said Harry.

"Oh, you're the most nonsensical man I know," interposed Miss Delany. Yet she stayed with Harry.

"You're looking very bright and happy," said Dr. Latimer to Iola, as she entered.

"My ride in the park was so refreshing! I enjoyed it so much! The day was so lovely, the air delicious, the birds sang so sweetly, and the sunset was so magnificent."

"I am glad of it. Why, Iola, your home is so happy your heart should be as light as a schoolgirl's."

"Doctor," she replied, "I must be prematurely old. I have scarcely known what it is to be light-hearted since my father's death."

"I know it, darling," he answered, seating himself beside her, and drawing her to him. "You have been tried in the fire, but are you not better for the crucial test?"

"Doctor," she replied, "as we rode along yesterday, mingling with the sunshine of the present came the shadows of the past. I was thinking of the bright, joyous days of my girlhood, when I defended slavery, and of how the cup that I would have pressed to the lips of others was forced to my own. Yet, in looking over the mournful past, I would not change the Iola of then for the Iola of now."

"Yes," responded Dr. Latimer, musingly,

> "'Darkness shows us worlds of light
> We never saw by day.'"

"Oh, Doctor, you cannot conceive what it must have been to be hurled from a home of love and light into the dark abyss of slavery; to be compelled to take your place among a people you have learned to look upon as inferiors and social outcasts; to be in the power of men whose presence would fill you with horror and loathing, and to know that there is no earthly power to protect you from the highest insults which brutal cowardice could shower upon you. I am so glad that no other woman of my race will suffer as I have done."

The flush deepened on her face, a mournful splendor beamed from her beautiful eyes, into which the tears had slowly gathered.

"Darling," he said, his voice vibrating with mingled feelings of tenderness and resentment, "you must forget the sad past. You are like a tender lamb snatched from the jaws of a hungry wolf, but who still needs protecting, loving care. But it must have been terrible," he added, in a painful tone.

"It was indeed! For a while I was like one dazed. I tried to pray, but the heavens seemed brass over my head. I was wild with agony, and had I not been placed under conditions which roused all the resistance of my soul, I would have lost my reason."

"Was it not a mistake to have kept you ignorant of your colored blood?"

"It was the great mistake of my father's life, but dear papa knew something of the cruel, crushing power of caste; and he tried to shield us from it."

"Yes, yes," replied Dr. Latimer, thoughtfully, "in trying to shield you from pain he plunged you into deeper suffering."

"I never blame him, because I know he did it for the best. Had he lived he would have taken us to France, where I should have had a life of careless ease and pleasure. But now my life has a much grander significance than it would have had under such conditions. Fearful as the awakening was, it was better than to have slept through life."

"Best for you and best for me," said Dr. Latimer. "There are souls that never awaken; but if they miss the deepest pain they also lose the highest joy."

Dr. Latimer went South, after his engagement, and through his medical skill and agreeable manners became very successful in his practice. In the following summer, he built a cosy home for the reception of his bride, and came North, where, with Harry and Miss Delany as attendants, he was married to Iola, amid a pleasant gathering of friends, by Rev. Carmicle.

33.
CONCLUSION.

It was late in the summer when Dr. Latimer and his bride reached their home in North Carolina. Over the cottage porch were morning-glories to greet the first flushes of the rising day, and roses and jasmines to distill their fragrance on the evening air. Aunt Linda, who had been apprised of their coming, was patiently awaiting their arrival, and Uncle Daniel was pleased to know that "dat sweet young lady who had sich putty manners war comin' to lib wid dem."

As soon as they arrived, Aunt Linda rushed up to Iola, folded her in her arms, and joyfully exclaimed: "How'dy, honey! I'se so glad you's come. I seed it in a vision dat somebody fair war comin' to help us. An' wen I yered it war you, I larffed and jist rolled ober, and larffed and jist gib up."

"But, Aunt Linda, I am not very fair," replied Mrs. Latimer.

"Well, chile, you's fair to me. How's all yore folks in de up kentry?"

"All well. I expect them down soon to live here."

"What, Har'yet, and Robby, an' yer ma? Oh, dat is too good. I allers said Robby had san' in his craw, and war born for good luck. He war a mighty nice boy. Har'yet's in clover now. Well, ebery dorg has its day, and de cat has Sunday. I allers tole Har'yet ter keep a stiff upper lip; dat it war a long road dat had no turn."

Dr. Latimer was much gratified by the tender care Aunt Linda bestowed on Iola.

"I ain't goin' to let her do nuffin till she gits seasoned. She looks as sweet as a peach. I allers wanted some nice lady to come down yere and larn our gals some sense. I can't read myself, but I likes ter yere dem dat can."

"Well, Aunt Linda, I am going to teach in the Sunday school, help in the church, hold mothers' meetings to help these boys and girls to grow up to be good men and women. Won't you get a pair of spectacles and learn to read?"

"Oh, yer can't git dat book froo my head, no way you fix it. I knows nuff to git to hebben, and dat's all I wants to know." Aunt Linda was kind and obliging, but there was one place where she drew the line, and that was at learning to read.

Harry and Miss Delany accompanied Iola as far as her new home, and remained several days. The evening before their departure, Harry took Miss Delany a drive of several miles through the pine barrens.

"This thing is getting very monotonous," Harry broke out, when they had gone some distance.

"Oh, I enjoy it!" replied Miss Delany. "These stately pines look so grand and solemn, they remind me of a procession of hooded monks."

"What in the world are you talking about, Lucille?" asked Harry, looking puzzled.

"About those pine trees," replied Miss Delany, in a tone of surprise.

"Pshaw, I wasn't thinking about them. I'm thinking about Iola and Frank."

"What about them?" asked Lucille.

"Why, when I was in P——, Dr. Latimer used to be first-rate company, but now it is nothing but what Iola wants, and what Iola says, and what Iola likes. I don't believe that there is a subject I could name to him, from spinning a top to circumnavigating the globe, that he wouldn't somehow contrive to bring Iola in. And I don't believe you could talk ten minutes to Iola on any subject, from dressing a doll to the latest discovery in science, that she wouldn't manage to lug in Frank."

"Oh, you absurd creature!" responded Lucille, "this is their honeymoon, and they are deeply in love with each other. Wait till you get in love with someone."

"I am in love now," replied Harry, with a serious air.

"With whom?" asked Lucille, archly.

"With you," answered Harry, trying to take her hand.

"Oh, Harry!" she exclaimed, playfully resisting. "Don't be so nonsensical! Don't you think the bride looked lovely, with that dress of spotless white and with those orange blossoms in her hair?"

"Yes, she did; that's a fact," responded Harry. "But, Lucille, I think there is a great deal of misplaced sentiment at weddings," he added, more seriously.

"How so?"

"Oh, here are a couple just married, and who are as happy as happy can be; and people will crowd around them wishing much joy; but who thinks of wishing joy to the forlorn old bachelors and restless old maids?"

"Well, Harry, if you want people to wish you much happiness, why don't you do as the doctor has done, get yourself a wife?"

"I will," he replied, soberly, "when you say so."

"Oh, Harry, don't be so absurd."

"Indeed there isn't a bit of absurdity about what I say. I am in earnest." There was something in the expression of Harry's face and the tone of his voice which arrested the banter on Lucille's lips.

"I think it was Charles Lamb," replied Lucille, "who once said that schoolteachers are uncomfortable people, and, Harry, I would not like to make you uncomfortable by marrying you."

"You will make me uncomfortable by not marrying me."

"But," replied Lucille, "your mother may not prefer me for a daughter. You know, Harry, complexional prejudices are not confined to white people."

"My mother," replied Harry, with an air of confidence, "is too noble to indulge in such sentiments."

"And Iola, would she be satisfied?"

"Why, it would add to her satisfaction. She is not one who can't be white and won't be black."

"Well, then," replied Lucille, "I will take the question of your comfort into consideration."

The above promise was thoughtfully remembered by Lucille till a bridal ring and happy marriage were the result.

Soon after Iola had settled in C—— she quietly took her place in the Sunday school as a teacher, and in the church as a helper. She was welcomed by the young pastor, who found in her a strong and faithful ally. Together they planned meetings for the especial benefit of mothers and children. When the dens of vice are spreading their snares for the feet of the tempted and inexperienced her doors are freely opened for the instruction of the children before their feet have wandered and gone far astray. She has no carpets too fine for the tread of their little feet. She thinks it is better to have stains on her carpet than stains on their souls through any neglect of hers. In lowly homes and windowless cabins her visits are always welcome. Little children love her. Old age turns to her for comfort, young girls for guidance, and mothers for counsel. Her life is full of blessedness.

Doctor Latimer by his kindness and skill has won the name of the "Good Doctor." But he is more than a successful doctor; he is a true patriot and a good citizen. Honest, just, and discriminating, he endeavors by precept and example to instill into the minds of others sentiments of good citizenship. He is a leader in every reform movement for the benefit of the community; but his patriotism is not confined to race lines. "The world is his country, and mankind his countrymen." While he abhors their deeds of violence, he pities the short-sighted and besotted men who seem madly intent upon laying magazines of powder under the cradles of unborn generations. He has great faith in the possibilities of the Negro, and believes that, enlightened and Christianized, he will sink the old animosities of slavery into the new community of interests arising from freedom; and that his influence upon the South will be as the influence of the sun upon the earth. As when the sun passes from Capricorn to Cancer, beauty, greenness, and harmony spring up in his path, so he hopes that the future career of the Negro will be a greater influence for freedom and social advancement than it was in the days of yore for slavery and its inferior civilization.

Harry and Lucille are at the head of a large and flourishing school. Lucille gives her ripening experience to her chosen work, to which she was too devoted to resign. And through the school they are lifting up the homes of the people. Some have pitied, others blamed, Harry for casting his lot with the colored people, but he knows that life's highest and best advantages do not depend on the color of the skin or texture of the hair. He has his reward in the improved condition of his pupils and the superb manhood and noble life which he has developed in his much needed work.

Uncle Daniel still lingers on the shores of time, a cheery, lovable old man, loved and respected by all; a welcome guest in every home. Soon after Iola's marriage, Robert sold out his business and moved with his mother and sister to North Carolina. He bought a large plantation near C——, which he divided into small homesteads, and sold to poor but thrifty laborers, and his heart has been gladdened by their increased prosperity and progress. He has seen the one-roomed cabins change to comfortable cottages, in which cleanliness and order have supplanted the prolific causes of disease and death. Kind and generous, he often remembers Mrs. Johnson and sends her timely aid.

Marie's pale, spiritual face still bears traces of the beauty which was her youthful dower, but its bloom has been succeeded by an air of sweetness and dignity. Though frail in health, she is always ready to lend a helping hand wherever and whenever she can.

Grandmother Johnson was glad to return South and spend the remnant of her days with the remaining friends of her early life. Although feeble, she is in full sympathy with her children for the uplifting of the race. Marie and her mother are enjoying their aftermath of life, one by rendering to others all the service in her power, while the other, with her face turned toward the celestial city, is

> "Only waiting till the angels
> Open wide the mystic gate."

The shadows have been lifted from all their lives; and peace, like bright dew, has descended upon their paths. Blessed themselves, their lives are a blessing to others.

NOTE.

From threads of fact and fiction I have woven a story whose mission will not be in vain if it awaken in the hearts of our countrymen a stronger sense of justice and a more Christlike humanity in behalf of those whom the fortunes of war threw, homeless, ignorant and poor, upon the threshold of a new era. Nor will it be in vain if it inspire the children of those upon whose brows God has poured the chrism of that new era to determine that they will embrace every opportunity, develop every faculty, and use every power God has given them to rise in the scale of character and condition, and to add their quota of good citizenship to the best welfare of the nation. There are scattered among us materials for mournful tragedies and mirth-provoking comedies, which some hand may yet bring into the literature of the country, glowing with the fervor of the tropics and enriched by the luxuriance of the Orient, and thus add to the solution of our unsolved American problem.

The race has not had very long to straighten its hands from the hoe, to grasp the pen and wield it as a power for good, and to erect above the ruined auction block and slave pen institutions of learning, but

> There is light beyond the darkness,
> Joy beyond the present pain;
> There is hope in God's great justice
> And the Negro's rising brain.
> Though the morning seems to linger
> O'er the hill-tops far away,
> Yet the shadows bear the promise
> Of a brighter coming day.

ABOUT THE AUTHOR.

FRANCES ELLEN WATKINS HARPER (1825–1911) was born free in Baltimore, Maryland and raised by her aunt and uncle after being orphaned at the age of three. Following in the activist footsteps of her uncle Reverend William J. Watkins, Sr., Harper became an abolitionist, a suffragist, a public speaker, and a teacher. She supported refugees from slavery on their journey along the Underground Railroad in 1851. Later that decade, and almost a century before the Montgomery Bus Boycott, she refused to give up her seat and move to the colored section on a segregated Philadelphia trolley car.

Campaigning for equality of the sexes and races, Harper also served as superintendent of the Colored Section of the Philadelphia and Pennsylvania Women's Christian Temperance Union and as Vice President of the National Association of Colored Women, which she cofounded.

Hawkins's first volume of poetry, *Forest Leaves*, was published in 1845 under her maiden name Frances Ellen Watkins. Nine years later, *Poems on Miscellaneous Subjects* became her biggest commercial success and was reprinted twenty recorded times within Harper's lifetime. *Iola Leroy, or Shadows Uplifted*, her third novel, was first published in 1892 when the author was sixty-seven.

"Studio portrait of young woman wearing chain necklace." 1880 - 1889 *(Approx.).*
From The New York Public Library.

THE CURSE OF CASTE,

or The Slave Bride

JULIA C. COLLINS

First edition published in 1865.

NOTES ON THE NOVEL.

The Curse of Caste, or The Slave Bride was originally released in periodical form within the pages of *The Christian Recorder*, from February 25th to September 23rd of 1865. Author Julia C. Collins passed away from tuberculosis, known commonly then as consumption, in November of that year, leaving the story without an official conclusion. There has been no attempt within this volume to provide any type of alternate or formulated ending, and all modifications are limited to minor edits with spelling, punctuation, and other grammatical adjustments.

The original issues of *The Christian Recorder* that contain chapters 3, 12, 17, and 30 have yet to be located. The numerical headings are included here as visual markers for the story's missing segments.

CHAPTER I.

February 25, 1865

"My schooldays are over, and now farewell to books and quiet happiness," said Claire Neville, with a sigh, on the morning following the closing exercises of L—Seminary, as she was gathering books, papers, pens, and drawing materials with sundry other articles pertaining to boarding school life, into an indiscriminate mass, preparatory to packing them away. "I am weak and foolish, I know," said Claire aloud, "to feel so badly about leaving old friends and associations, to go forth into a cold and uncharitable world, but I cannot help it. As my very soul shrinks from coming in contact with strangers, who will not understand my nature, and, therefore, cannot sympathize with me." And the proud head was bowed upon her clasped hands, and bright, pearly tears were falling thick and fast. "Just one moment of weakness," murmured she, "and I shall be strong again, strong to do and dare." Claire Neville formed a beautiful and striking picture as she sat, with bowed head and drooping figure, the seeming embodiment of grief; for Claire was strangely, wildly, and darkly beautiful. Hers was that rich tropical loveliness, consisting of a tall, well-developed form, with rare, creamy complexion, cheeks like full-blown damask roses, eyes of midnight blackness, overshadowed by slightly arching brows of the same jetty hue, a broad, pure forehead, bound by a wealth of purple black hair, which in its natural loveliness enveloped her like a cloud, and a perfect mouth, disclosing rows of even, pearl-white teeth, formed, in all, a picture so strikingly beautiful, that once beheld, you voluntarily turn to gaze again. Claire was so absorbed in grief that she noted not the opening of the door, nor the bright sunbeam that entered with the person of a lovely young girl, until a gentle hand rested caressingly on the drooping head, and a sweet voice murmured, in slightly surprised accents:

"Dear Claire in tears, can it be possible that you have a grief unshared by me? But tell me darling, what is it that disturbs you so?" said Ella Summers, pausing. But failing to elicit a reply, said this time, with pained expression of countenance and quivering lip, "Cannot you trust me, who have always endeavored to be a true friend?"

"Forgive me, Ella dear, if by my silence I have wounded your gentle heart, for believe me, you are the dearest friend I have on earth, and there is none to whom I would reveal my inmost heart, as I have to you. But I cannot help feeling the bitter isolation of my life."

"Let us speak of something else," said Ella, "You are despondent, I see."

Claire smiled faintly, while Ella resumed: "I have just received a long letter from mamma, in which she desires me to bring my friend Claire home with me, to make a long visit; and you will go, of course," she added, coaxingly, "and we will have a splendid time; for brother Charles is coming home to spend vacation, and cousins Harry and Fanny Leeburn are coming to spend the summer months with us, down by the lake. Such rides, such picnics, and sails by moonlight on the silvery lake, as will astound the simple natives of Ashton. Why, it is exhilarating, even to think of, after a season of such unremitting study as we have had."

Claire was deeply moved by her friend's disinterested kindness, and replied, in a voice tremulous with emotion, "Dear Ella, I hope you will not deem me ungrateful if I decline your much tempting invitation, as it pains me to refuse that which would afford me so much real pleasure."

"Then, why do you decline?" said Ella, her blue eyes extended a trifle beyond their usual width with astonishment, "when you acknowledge it gives you pain to refuse, and would impart pleasure to accept."

"Ella," responded Claire, with great frankness, all traces of former weakness effectually banished, "you are inexpressibly dear to me, and your past friendship will shed a gentle halo over the gloom of many hours to come in the dark, untried future, but you don't understand my position in life—how wide the differences between your lot and mine. While you are the child of wealth and position, I am the child of poverty and misfortune!"

Claire was rapidly pacing the floor now, her queenly form drawn to the proudest height. Ella had never, during their long acquaintance, seen her uniformly quiet and reserved friend in such an excited state of mind, so she wisely forbore interrupting her, and was content to look the astonishment she dared not express. Claire continued:

"You have a host of kind and loving friends to cherish and protect you, who make your pleasure a constant study, and seek to anticipate your every wish, while I am homeless and almost friendless—have never known a mother's kind, protecting care, and I don't know that I even have a right to the name I bear. I know nothing of my mother, not even her name. I know not if a shadow rested on her fair fame. The only link between my past and present life, is an old beloved nurse, named Juno, whom, I am confident, knows all, but I can prevail upon her to impart nothing. I am even indebted to a person unknown for my education, except that I saw him several times during my earlier years. It is six years now since I saw him. So you can not fail to see the disparity of our social positions, and, therefore, must acknowledge how utterly impossible it is for us to retain our old relation, now that our school days are over; nor would your mother desire it, if she knew all, and I should sacrifice my self respect; if I intruded myself upon her friendship and hospitality in any other than my true position."

Ella now ventured to remonstrate, "O Claire, you mustn't think what you have just told can make the least difference in my feelings toward you, for I love you now better than ever, and I know my dear mamma too well to think that she would love you less, because you fail to know who your parents were. It is one phase of life we fail to read, and to know you, Claire, is only to know that your parents, whatever obscurity rests on them, were persons of purity and refinement."

Claire looked up gratefully, and said, "I feel, too, my parents were pure and good; it is only when I think of the vague mystery that surrounds my birth and parentage, that the doubt comes."

"Claire dear, believe my words prophetic when I say the time will come when all will be made clear, and you will find in your parents all your loving heart could wish. Cannot you trust me?"

"Yes, Ella, I can and do trust you, but with the trust comes the presentiment of sorrow connected with the revelation. But I will cease to repine, and will school myself to hope that all will yet be well."

After conversing some time longer, Ella found that Claire was firm in declining to make the proposed visit. She asked Claire what she intended doing, now that their schooldays were over.

CHAPTER II.

March 4, 1865

"I shall try the life of a governess," said Claire, quietly smiling at the dissatisfaction mirrored in her friend's expressive countenance. "But," said Ella, "you will necessarily have to wait some time ere you can obtain a position that would be desirable."

"Not so," said Claire. "I have a situation already, and have only to make preparations to take my respective position in life.'

"Now, Claire!" exclaimed Ella, with lively interest, "tell me all about it."

"There is but little to tell," said Claire, "but that little you shall know. Our dear preceptress, Miss Ellwood, received a letter from an old school friend, who married, years ago, Col. Tracy, a rich Southern gentleman, and went to reside in New Orleans. But some trouble in their family, relative to the marriage of a son, has rendered Mrs. Tracy, for years, a confirmed invalid. Seeing one of the circulars of L— Seminary, she observed the name of Miss Maria Ellwood as preceptress; and, knowing it could be none other than the Maria of schoolday remembrances, she wrote her a long and interesting letter, which proved the correctness of her supposition. She also requested Miss Ellwood to get a young lady of suitable qualifications, to be a companion for her, and act as governess to two little girls, aged respectively ten and twelve years, offering an excellent salary; and Miss Ellwood, knowing my intention of becoming a governess, offered me the situation, saying, 'She knew of no one she would so cheerfully recommend.' So I have accepted the situation, and shall start South with a Mr and Mrs. Harrington, friends of Mrs. Tracy who have been North, and have kindly consented to take me under their charge. So you see my path is marked out, and I have only time to follow it."

"Well, Claire Neville, I think you have taken sudden leave of your senses, going South to be a governess and companion to an invalid and two little girls. 'Hypochondrian' and 'hoydens,' which words, I suppose, would be well substituted for invalid and little girls. I can well imagine what your life would be," exclaimed Ella, vehemently. "And should there be a young man in the question,—"

"There is one in the family," interrupted Claire, merrily.

"As there has been trouble about one son's marriage," replied Ella, "they will be in perpetual fear of the beautiful Yankee governess, and you will be kept back on all and every occasion."

"I think," said Claire, a little haughtily, "I shall know my place so well, that the snubbing, as you term it, will be quite unnecessary."

"And," continued Ella, "if there is a grown daughter, and should she, by chance, be handsome, she will be jealous of you. I can tell you, Claire, I would never be governess in a Southern family."

Claire replied, by saying: "Miss Belle Tracy is very beautiful, and is considered the belle of New Orleans."

"It matters not," said Ella, "if you will go, I sincerely hope you may be happy in your new position."

"I leave at one o'clock," said Claire, looking at her watch, "so I must go and make my adieus."

"But, Claire," said Ella, "in your new life do not forget your Ella."

A few more parting words, a few tears, a loving embrace, and the friends parted.

Claire, indeed, knew nothing of her past life. She never knew a mother's care. Juno, an old colored nurse, had taken care of her as long as she could remember. No friends had ever visited them, with the exception of a tall, dark man, who came at long intervals, and always had long talks with Juno concerning Claire. He often tried to win the confidence of the dark beautiful child, but to no purpose; for Claire shrank from him with instinctive dislike. They lived thus together, Juno and the lovely little girl, until Claire had reached her twelfth year, when, closely following the last visit of the handsome but repulsive stranger, Claire was placed at the L— Seminary, where she remained for six years, happy in the love of her schoolmates and kind preceptress, Miss Ellwood.

At the last mentioned visit of the stranger, Claire remembered to have heard him frequently repeat the name of Richard. Who was Richard she wondered? And she instinctively felt that he was, in some way or other, connected with her past life. On entering the room after the stranger had gone, she observed a handkerchief lying on the floor. She picked it up to examine it, and found in one corner the name of George Manville. Claire said nothing to Juno, but resolved to retain the handkerchief, asking herself many times—"Who is George Manville?"

Claire was not long in preparing her simple wardrobe, and went to pay Juno a visit, who was delighted to see her dear child, but loud in her remonstrances against Claire's going South; but when Claire mentioned the name of Colonel Tracy, her excitement was without bounds, as she exclaimed: "Miss Claire, for the love of heaven, don't go to be governess in the old Colonel's family. What would Master Richard say to your going to be governess in the Tracy family?"

"Who and what is Richard? And what is he to me?" interrupted Claire, in an eager tone.

Juno felt that she had committed herself, and, therefore, could not be induced to say another word about Richard, whoever he might be, but continued to entreat Claire to forego going South. But Claire was firm in her resolution to go. Juno, finding it quite useless to remonstrate, resigned herself to listen to Claire's plans, which, when ended, she said, with clouded brow and sad voice, "Dear child, I fear you will see great sorrow, and will often wish you had taken poor old Juno's advice, and never gone to be a governess in that proud family. Yes, poor child," she continued, "I know your poor heart will feel many a hard pang, but I will never cease to pray for you, darling, and," she added, doubtfully, "I hope you may be happy."

Claire felt Juno's words to be an echo of her own feelings.

"I have something to give you," said Juno, leaving the room. She quickly returned, however, bringing with her a little rosewood box, from which she lifted a beautiful ring of strange and exquisite workmanship. She handed it to Claire, simply saying, "It was your mother's."

Claire gazed on the glittering circlet with tearful eyes. On an inner plate were the initials R.T. to L. Claire examined it a long while, then placed it on her own slender finger. The parting, between the faithful old nurse and the child she had watched over so long, was touching in the extreme.

Now that we have introduced Juno to our readers, she will appear, from time to time, with the other characters who play an important part in the following narrative.

CHAPTER III.

March 11, 1865

MISSING—This chapter appeared in an issue of the *Christian Recorder* that has yet to be located.

CHAPTER IV.

March 18, 1865

This was not a difficult matter, as the Count was pleased at first sight with Isabelle, who was, indeed, the most fascinating woman he had ever met. Thus things were progressing in the Tracy family when Claire entered it as governess. Count Sayvord was unremitting in attention to Isabelle, and she inordinately jealous if he deviated in the slightest. But, thus far, the Count had failed in reading her true character.

But, to do the young man justice, we will add that he had thought but little of marriage—but little as connected with Isabelle Tracy. There was a nameless something which always deterred him from broaching the subject, when frequent opportunities occurred; and Isabelle secretly wondered why he did not propose.

Col. Tracy was proud of Isabelle's great beauty, and he secretly hoped she might win young Sayvord, whom he had reason to consider a desirable match for his favorite child.

After tea, Claire retired with Laura and Nellie while the others adjourned to the parlors. Claire spent another hour with Mrs. Tracy, and then retired to the room assigned her, which was light, airy and pleasant; and, when she was at liberty to indulge in her own reflections, she felt pleased with her situation, and thought she should like it; but, when she thought of Isabelle Tracy's searching black eyes, a cold chill ran through her, for there was something so repelling in that cold, haughty glance, which seemed to scintillate hatred. She tried to forget it, but turn which way she would those great black eyes were before her! Did it augur evil, or what? Her dreams were an odd mixture of "black eyes and blue."

The morning dawned beautifully, and Claire walked out on the verandah to inhale the morning air. As she came forth, she was met by Laura and Nellie, who were anxiously awaiting her appearance, and, each taking a hand, led her forth chatting the while in a lively strain. Roses, cape-jessamines, and crape myrtle were in profusion, and Claire being a passionate lover of flowers, was delighted with the beauty and luxuriance of the floral shrubbery. At almost every step she encountered the curious gaze of the Negroes, who looked wonderingly at her.

After following various paths and windings, they came suddenly upon a beautiful arbor almost embowered in orange trees. Claire was about to express her delight when she observed, extended at full length, reading, the young Count Sayvord, who arose at their entrance, bowed politely, and would have withdrawn, but that they passed on without stopping and continued their rambles until the bell summoned them to breakfast. As they came up to the house, Isabelle was standing on the verandah and bowed coldly, and again Claire shuddered as she encountered the piercing glance which seemed to read her very soul. They passed on to the breakfast room, and were soon followed by the Count and Isabelle, who was covered with smiles and blushes. Claire noticed and wondered at the change.

After breakfast, Claire repaired to Mrs. Tracy's room, ready to begin her new duties. Mrs. Tracy thought, as it was now Thursday, they would not commence any lessons until the following Monday, and that Claire was at liberty to use her time as she pleased, much of which she spent in the company of the invalid, who was mild and affectionate, quite unlike her proud daughter.

On Friday evening, after tea, as they were leaving the tea-room, Laura said, "Oh, Miss Neville, you have not sung for us, yet."

"Yes," chimed in little Nellie, "you promised you would."

"I hope Miss Neville will not refuse," said Lloyd Tracy, with an encouraging smile, while Sayvord's look expressed the interest he felt in her answer.

Col. Tracy, at this moment, came forward, and placing Claire's little hand within his arm, led the way to the parlor, saying, "They would not take a refusal." So Claire consented, notwithstanding the haughty displeasure expressed in Isabelle's countenance.

Claire took her seat at the piano with quiet dignity and the utmost composure, which only seemed to annoy Miss Tracy, who hoped at least to detect some frustration of manner, but in vain, for Claire, after playing a short prelude, glided into a beautiful song, and, as her rich clear voice swelled on the air, every voice save the singer's was hushed.

Lloyd arose, as if impelled by some unseen power, and came to Claire's side; Col. Tracy was strangely affected, and was walking the floor with perturbed mien; and Sayvord never once withdrew his gaze from the face of the songstress. Isabelle, alone, seemed unmoved.

After the song was ended, Sayvord requested another, and the little girls and Lloyd warmly seconded the request. Claire, with Lloyd's assistance, sang several songs of great beauty and pathos.

Claire possessed a voice of unusual depth and sweetness, and Miss Ellwood early noticing her great talent for music, both vocal and instrumental, had afforded her every possible advantage for improvement, and the result was her musical powers were highly cultivated.

After the songs were ended, Claire bade them a courteous "good evening," and retired in company with Laura and Nellie.

A long silence ensued, broken only by Col. Tracy's steady tread when he abruptly turned to Lloyd, saying in a husky tone, "Is there any one of whom Miss Neville reminds you?"

Lloyd started perceptibly, and briefly answered, "Richard."

Sayvord and Isabelle had walked to the window opening on the verandah, and were just passing out when the name of Miss Neville arrested the attention of Sayvord, whose thoughts were still with the singer. He noticed the question asked with an anxiety of manner and eagerness of tone, as though he hoped, yet feared the reply, and Lloyd's brief answer, "Richard," caused the Count to give a low whistle of surprise, quite forgetting the lady at his side, who was thoughtfully tearing to pieces a beautiful rose and scattering the leaves at her feet. She had heard neither the question nor the answer.

Sayvord now knew why it was that Claire's face always seemed familiar, and why her voice always arrested his attention by its very sadness; it was the striking resemblance she bore to an American gentleman he had met at his uncle Clayburch Sayvord's country seat, in France, whose sad voice and melancholy face had haunted him for a long time. What could it all mean? Was Claire indeed a relative of that strange, dark man, over whom a shadow seemed to have fallen, and, if so, why should she occupy the position she did in Col. Tracy's house? Sayvord was sorely at his wit's end; but he determined to fathom the mystery that enveloped the young governess. He dismissed the subject from his thoughts, for the present, and began a lively conversation with Isabelle.

Col. Tracy sat in his arm chair buried in thought, and, seemingly, not of the most pleasant nature. Lloyd was extended at full length on one of the garden sofas, quietly enjoying a segar and looking at the moon, but it was quite evident that his thoughts were otherwise engaged, for, ever and anon, he murmured, "Poor Dick, I cannot but pity, while I blame him. It was a sad blow for one so young and gifted as he. And the beautiful but ill-fated Lina! How he must have loved her to encounter the rage of my proud, passionate father who would rather have slain him with his own hand than have had the disgrace of that marriage. Poor Dick!" he concluded with a deep sigh.

A spirit of disquietude seemed to have taken possession of all. Claire, when she bade the children good night and paid a last visit to the invalid, sought her own room; the moon shone brightly on the floor, and flooded the room with a soft light. Claire, drawing her chair to the open window, fell into a deep reverie. Her thoughts naturally reverted to her Northern home. She thought of Miss Ellwood, of all her kindness through her lonely childhood, of Juno's last words, and her own presentiment of evil; a feeling of sadness pervaded her soul as memory lingered over the scenes of the past. She looked at Juno's parting gift through tear-dimmed eyes; the little circlet glittered in the moonlight as the bright teardrops fell on its shining surface. Why could not Juno have told her just a little of the mother she had never known? What dark mystery surrounded her father? She would rather know the worst than always live in suspense, dreading something she knew not what. Why was she not born happy and careless, like Rosa, the nimble-fingered, light-footed creature, who was always smiling, and never seemed to have a thought beyond pleasing her mistress and the children, whom she fairly worshipped?

Claire was thoroughly unhappy, and she at last retired to rest. But, it seemed, sleep had fled her pillow; for a long while she tossed restlessly about, sometimes thinking of Isabelle's cold manner and fierce black eyes; then of Sayvord's earnest gaze, and Lloyd's respectful attention; then she wondered at the likeness she bore to the Tracy's. It was singular, to say the least, and she felt herself an object of curiosity even to the Negroes, who regarded her wonderingly, and talked mysteriously of somebody and something Claire knew not what. At last sleep came to her relief, and happiness dawned on her troubled mind.

CHAPTER V.

March 25, 1865

A Heart's History.

Col. Tracy's father, or old John Tracy, as he was familiarly designated, was a Connecticut man, but had emigrated to Louisiana, bought himself a plantation well stocked with slaves (that indispensable appendage of Southern life) worked it, multiplied the Negroes, and at last died immensely rich, leaving his vast property to be equally divided between Col. Tracy, who was then a young man of twenty-one years of age, and his sister Laura, a young lady of seventeen years, who were the only living heirs of John Tracy, whose young wife had died in giving birth to the infant Laura years ago, in their New England home.

Laura had always resided in the North with an old maiden aunt, who, unlike most old maids we read of, was as gentle, cheerful, and dark-eyed a little woman as you could wish to see. She was greatly attached to her young niece, and Laura had never felt the loss of the mother her infant eyes had never beheld.

The winter previous to John Tracy's death, his fast failing health caused him often to think of the home of his youth, and at last, to write a letter to his only sister, inviting her to come and make his house her home, because he longed for the faces of his own kindred and was wearied of the dusky countenances of the Negroes, who were flitting in and out of their humble efforts to aid the lonely, and, not infrequently, irritable master.

Miss Tracy, on being apprised of her brother's illness, accompanied by Laura, went South, and, by their united efforts, succeeded in cheering the lone invalid and rendering his last moments happy, by kind attention and loving care.

One lovely afternoon, just as the sun was sinking behind a bank of crimson clouds, John Tracy had all the slaves brought, one by one, to his bedside, and took an affectionate leave of all; and, when the daylight was fast fading into darkness, surrounded by a group of weeping Negroes, his head supported on the bosom of his loving sister, Frank and Laura kneeling, grief-stricken, at his bedside, the soul of John Tracy passed from earth away—passed from death unto life.

After the remains of John Tracy were consigned to their last resting place, and all other matters relating to the effects of the deceased parent properly adjusted, the old house, which was always lonely, but now more desolate than ever, was locked up, the plantation and Negroes left to the care of a trusty overseer, Miss Tracy, with Laura and Frank, started for her Northern home.

Laura was delighted to see her old home again, and hovered like a bird over each familiar object, while Frank only shrugged his shoulders, saying that the North was too bleak and cold for him, and that he should soon seek his sunny, Southern home, where roses bloomed the year round.

"But man proposes, and God disposes." Frank was destined to fall hopelessly and irretrievably in love with brown-eyed, brown-haired Nellie Thornton, a sweet and winsome little maiden who was Laura's dearest friend.

Thus, the winter wore away. Spring came with its burden of flowers, sunshine and showers. Summer waned into autumn. Still Frank lingered in the little New England village; and, when he did start for his home, it was but to return again to bear to his Southern home a beautiful Northern bride.

Thus, Nellie Thornton became the wife of him we shall know hereafter as Col. Tracy, and went to preside over the heart and home of him to whom she had given herself and trusted with her heart's first love. A year was wafted by on the wings of time, when a beautiful boy came to bless their happy union; and for years little Richard's was the only voice that rung in childish glee, and his the only little feet that pattered through the great halls. Then came little Lillie, who lived but one short year, and then a little, short grave in the old cemetery marked the last resting place of the flower that was too fair and fragile for earth. Then came a pair of twins, beautiful, cherubic boys, who smiled on earth but a few short months when the fell destroyer came again, and little Frank and Willie were laid, side by side, in their white-robed beauty, in their cold, silent tombs.

Gentle Nellie Tracy grieved long and deeply over her lost treasures, and little Richard became again their only and idolized child. For some years none other came to bless.

At the age of sixteen, Richard was sent to college. A year later, an event occurred which shed joy over the silent household. Little Lloyd Tracy came to brighten the gloom of the old homestead; and, in the course of years other children were added, whom we will have occasion to introduce hereafter; but, for a while we leave them to their quiet happiness, while we follow the fortune of young Richard.

Richard, after passing a successful collegiate course and graduating with honor, was on his return home, down the noble Mississippi on board the beautiful steamer Alhambra, when he formed the acquaintance of a party of fellow-travelers, one of whom deeply interested him. The party consisted of two young ladies and a gentleman, who registered their names as Hartley. The gentleman was the brother of one of the ladies, while the other lady seemed only a distant relative.

The brother and sister, whom we shall call Ralph and Mary, appeared to be much absorbed with some topic, the nature of which apparently greatly annoyed them. There was something distant and repelling in their treatment of the second young lady, whom we will call Lina. Richard was interested in the young stranger from his first acquaintance, and her apparent loneliness enlisted his warmest sympathies. Thus he came to spend much of his time, which would otherwise have passed drearily enough, in her society.

Lina was as beautiful as the fancied image of a poet's dream: a form of medium size, with dark flashing eyes and a profusion of curling black hair, which defied all efforts on her part to keep in bands or braids, but would, naturally, fall in graceful ringlets about her neck and shoulders. One singular feature in Lina's beauty was her dark, rich-looking complexion; she was not a brunette, but hers was that dark brownish skin which we observe in the Spaniard and half-breed Indians, which, combined with features of striking regularity, rendered Lina, as she indeed was, a singularly attractive young lady.

Lina possessed a voice of sweet and thrilling power, and Richard never wearied of hearing her sing those old ballads, which she sang with such deep pathos and exquisite feeling. She soon learned to watch for his coming, and blushed beautifully when he bent to whisper some impassioned strain, or allowed his dark eloquent eyes to rest earnestly on her downcast face. They sought not to analyze their feelings; they were happy, and that was enough.

But the trip down the Mississippi, like all earthly things, must have an end. On the last night of their voyage, the moon shone clear and bright as Richard and Lina were walking the deck of the Alhambra, her hand resting on his arm. It seemed, indeed, a fitting time to disclose their tale of love; and, from Lina's blushing, downcast face and Richard's proud and happy bearing, it was quite evident that his had been a successful wooing. Lina was the first to speak:

"Richard," she said, while something like sadness vibrated through her voice, "I fear my happiness is too great to last. A presentiment of evil hovers over me. It is foolish, no doubt," she added, as Richard began smiling, "but I cannot divine why Ralph and Mary treat me so strangely. I always believed we were sisters, notwithstanding the difference in our appearance and dispositions. Mary is my senior by two years. Our father placed us in the convent as sisters to be educated, and we have there remained, being frequently visited by our father, who was always good and kind. But since Ralph Hartley came for us, there has been a marked change in the deportment of Mary, while Ralph, I verily believe, hates me; for I often look up and find him gazing at me with an expression that is almost fiendish. I may be penniless or even worse. I know not what this conduct presages. And Richard," the little hand pressing his arm more firmly, "perhaps you would cease to love me, and, if so, I should die." This was said in a low, firm voice, entirely free from passion.

Richard needed but one glance in the dark, truthful eyes of Lina to be assured of her earnestness, when he replied with deep emotion: "Lina, whatever be your fate or fortune, I will never desert you, so help me God! I will make you my own dear wife; my arm shall protect you, and all the love of my warm, true heart shall be yours. Lina, do I look like one who would speak lightly or break a vow once made? No power on earth shall take you from me!"

Lina silently placed her hand in Richard's, saying, "I trust you; I cannot doubt you now."

So absorbed was each in the conversation of the other, that they had not noticed the change in the heavens. Piles of black clouds were rising in the West, and had almost obscured the fair face of the moon, when a loud peel of thunder startled them, and, for the first time, they noticed that all the other passengers had retired to the cabins and state-rooms, and they were about following their example, when a vivid flash of lightning and a few large drops of rain hurried their exit from the deck. At the door of the ladies' cabin, Richard bade Lina good night.

The storm raged for an hour, and then cleared away, the moon shining brightly as ever. Many of the gentlemen returned on deck, among whom were Richard and Ralph Hartley. Richard had often conversed with Ralph and always found him courteous and gentlemanly in deportment; but there was a nameless something about him which alternately attracted and repelled him. On this occasion, the gentlemen merely exchanged a few common place remarks, as each appeared to be buried in his own reflections.

On the following morning, as the Alhambra neared the beautiful Crescent City, Richard sought Lina aside to exchange a few last words. Lina told him they were going to Hartley Hall, on her father's plantation, about fifty miles above New Orleans. So Richard parted with Lina, promising to visit her father soon, which recalled one of Lina's blushes, and a bright crystal drop fell on the hand that clasped her own; a moment more, and they were lost to view in the hurrying crowd. Theirs was indeed a bright dream! Would it ever be realized?

CHAPTER VI.

April 1, 1865

Richard was warmly greeted by his parents, and the Negroes were jubilant over massa's return. Mrs. Tracy felt proud of the great, tall, noble-looking youth, who stooped to kiss her still blooming cheek. And well might she feel proud, for never was a nobler, better son given to gladden a mother's heart.

Col. Tracy took especial pride in introducing his son to all his acquaintances, but was horrified and dismayed to hear Richard give expression to many anti-slavery principles, which he had imbibed while at the North. He tried to reason with him about the absurdity of entertaining such notions as social equality between races so widely divergent, in every respect, as the white and black. But Richard stoutly adhered to his belief that it was wrong for one man to enslave another, and keep in bondage a human being, having a mind and soul susceptible of improvement and cultivation.

Col. Tracy found too much of his own spirit infused into his son's character to think of eradicating these sentiments by argument, but trusted to time and the influence of Southern principles and society to effect the desired change. Thus the subject was dropped, and both father and son avoided alluding to it again.

Richard, while at a party made in honor of his return, formed the acquaintance of a young man by the name of George Manville. Young Manville was a gay, good-looking fellow, good-natured and perfectly well acquainted with the city and the circle in which Richard moved. They soon became fast friends. Manville was rich and handsome, and much sought after by those who failed in reading his true character, as did Richard Tracy. But Manville was a villain—the beautiful casket enshrined a heart black as the shadows of Hades, and dead to all the finer feelings, those minor chords which render the life of man replete with living beauty.

Richard sometimes felt the subtle influence that this Manville exerted over him without understanding it; however, for candid and honorable himself, he did not readily doubt others. These two men were fated to be connected in a degree through life.

One morning, at breakfast, Col. Tracy declared his intention of going up to the plantation for a few days on business. We will here state that Col.

Tracy had moved to the city of New Orleans, the old homestead being occupied by his overseer's family.

During his father's absence, Richard usually spent the mornings with his mother and little Lloyd. He told her of his love for the beautiful Lina, of their betrothal, and her singular presentiment of evil. Mrs. Tracy was interested in the unknown girl, whose cause her son pleaded so eloquently.

"You would only need see her, to love her," he said, persuasively.

Mrs. Tracy did not doubt that Lina was all Richard's fond imagination painted, but she asked:

"Do you know any thing of this family of Hartleys? You know your father's prejudice against persons marrying with those beneath them in rank and fortune, no matter what their qualities may be."

"I know, mother," said the young man, "but should Lina become poor by any untoward circumstance, that is no reason why I should seek to absolve the vows registered in the sight of Heaven. Of Lina's family I know nothing. I only know she is good and pure. I hope, for my father's sake, she may be rich and her family such as he would desire my alliance with. But, my gentle mother, whatever misfortune may befall Lina, I will marry her just the same."

"God bless you, my noble son," said Nellie Tracy, with deep feeling. "I trust all may be well."

That same morning Richard's portrait was sent home. It had been painted by a celebrated artist, who had succeeded admirably in giving the picture a true and lifelike expression. Before they had finished hanging the picture, Manville was announced, and with the freedom of a privileged friend, came into the room. When at last the picture was hung in a proper position, with just enough light to give a good effect, all stood back to take a full view of it. Mrs. Tracy remembered, years after, the feelings she experienced when that picture was hung. All were pleased and expressed their satisfaction.

When Col. Tracy returned from his visit to the plantation, he told Richard, in the presence of Manville and Mrs. Tracy, that he had made a very foolish investment. All looked inquiringly at him.

"I attended a sale of slaves, the property of old Hartley, who resides about fifty miles up the river, and was formerly a man of considerable wealth, but being of a wild, reckless disposition, has, in a few years, squandered his fortune, and degenerated into a confirmed drunkard and gambler. I purchased several plantation and house servants among whom is a beautiful quadroon, who is the daughter of old Hartley, I understand, and has been educated at a Catholic school, in Canada, and believed herself his lawful child. The young girl is beautiful, and I think, well educated. Her distress was really affecting, and, out of pity for the young thing, I bought her with the lot, but what I am to do with the baggage, I cannot conceive, for slaves educated at the North are not just the thing to be introduced into a Southern household. So, I guess I will sell this bit of humanity at the first offer. Why she had the audacity to faint, when, by accident, she learned the name of her future master was Col. Tracy. I must say, although I claim to be a kind and indulgent master, I have no use for this sensitive class of Negroes."

Col. Tracy, at this juncture, noticed the effect of his language upon his wife and son, which seemed to him as singular as it was inexplicable. Mrs. Tracy looked pale and horrified, while Richard's pale and almost defiant expression betokened a fixed resolution, although he uttered not a word, and soon left the house, accompanied by Manville. Mrs. Tracy soon left the room also, and Col. Tracy was the sole occupant, and was at liberty to digest his astonishment as best he might.

A few hours later, Manville returned, and after a long conference with Col. Tracy, departed with the document in his pocket, which pronounced him lawful owner of the young quadroon.

Richard returned at tea time with seeming composure, but his mother's eye penetrated the veil. She alone read his feelings, and felt the resolution he had taken. Her heart was too full for utterance, when, after tea, Richard motioned her to follow him. He led the way to the library. A long time elapsed ere they appeared again. Mrs. Tracy was deeply agitated, while Richard's face still wore the same determined expression. What passed during that strange conference, none ever knew. Richard followed his mother to the parlor, when he kissed her gently, saying fervently:

"Mother, pray for me. I hope all may yet be well. Pray for Lina, too. Poor child! God knows she needs your prayers."

A moment more, and Mrs. Tracy was alone. Richard had gone. Where this would all end, she could not tell.

One beautiful morning, in a quiet New England village, far from their own home, Richard Tracy and the beautiful quadroon, Lina, were united for life. It was a quiet bridal, witnessed only by Manville and Richard's aunt, whom we have known as Col. Tracy's sister Laura, while Laura's husband performed the rite, which united this ill-fated couple.

We will here state that all correspondence had ceased, long years ago, between Laura Tracy and her brother. Her marriage with a poor minister, Alfred Hays, had incurred his lasting displeasure. Laura had several times sought to conciliate her brother, but without success. Alfred Hays was good and noble, and with his lovely wife, joined his efforts to make the young bride happy.

Richard was happy, and soon the shadows left Lina's fair brow. They were happy, but it was as the calm that precedes the raging storm. Did Richard— did Lina—feel its dread coming? Had they no warning of the shadow, that would soon fall, crushing the life from their young hearts?

CHAPTER VII.

April 8, 1865

Lina's Home.

Richard and Lina were indeed truly happy. Little they thought of the future that loomed so darkly before them. They were happy in each other's love, and therefore content. Alfred Hays and his gentle wife smiled serenely upon the young pair, but wondered how this strange affair would end.

Manville remained until he could not help but feel that he was de trop, when he reluctantly took his departure for the South. Richard entrusted him with an important letter to his father, which letter Manville promised faithfully to deliver into the hands of Col. Tracy immediately upon his arrival in New Orleans.

Soon after Richard's marriage, Alfred Hays received an appointment in a thriving Western village, to which he cheerfully assented, and their beautiful home was soon to become the abode of strangers. Laura's heart clung fondly to the home in which she had passed the first years of her married life. The sale of "Rose Cottage," as Laura had fancifully named it, was often the interesting subject of discussion in the family circle. At last a happy thought dawned on Richard's mind. He proposed to purchase the little homestead.

"I think it would just answer our purpose," he said, looking inquiringly at Lina, whose eloquent eyes fully expressed her delight and satisfaction.

So Rose Cottage became the property of Richard and the home of Lina. Then followed a short season of busy preparation, and the Hays were en route for the far West. Rose Cottage was well named, for it was really embowered in roses and trailing vines. Roses bloomed 'neath the windows, and climbing roses blossomed o'er the door. The air was ever laden with their fragrance. Other beautiful shrubs and flowers there were, but the "sweet brier" predominated. The cottage was repainted and furnished anew, and the services of Juno, a competent colored woman who had lived with the Hays many years, were secured, and the house-keeping began. Juno was an efficient hand, and under her supervision every thing underwent an entire change, while every where Lina's exquisite taste was visible, in the arrangement of the light and elegant furniture. Curtains of a light, airy fabric were gracefully looped back from the windows, while choice paintings and exquisite engravings adorned the walls, and last, but not least in order, was a cottage piano, which was a prominent feature in the arrangement of the little parlor. And oft when the twilight was falling, and Juno was quietly knitting 'neath the shade of the lofty tamarack trees, could the mingled voices of Richard and Lina be heard, freighting the fragrant air with melody. And it often happened that they prolonged their singing far into the evening, and passers would linger at the little white gate, as song after song thrilled and trembled on the night air, and long for a glimpse of the beautiful songstress, whom those more fortunate had reported as wondrously fair.

Would that this dream of happiness could last. Would that it were in my power to paint a picture with naught but scenes of beauty, but alas, no. Richard had put off the evil hour as long as possible, but now it could be averted no longer. He must return home to meet an angry father, perhaps to be disfranchised forever from that father's love.

Sad as was that too probable result, yet he did not regret the choice he had made. The half year of married life had only seemed to render Lina more dear than ever. No, he did not regret the sacrifice he had made for her sake. His father would disinherit him without doubt. But he still possessed quite a fortune in his own right, left him by a will of his great aunt, John Tracy's sister. But a father's curse is an awful thing, and that thought embittered many hours of his daily life. Yet he breathed not his fears in his young wife's ears, but always spoke hopefully of the future, though his own heart sadly misgave him, as week after week passed, and yet no answer came to the letter sent with Manville. The thought of that troubled him. He could not but fear the worst, yet he sought to keep all from Lina.

But the watchful eyes of love soon detected the change. His voice was less cheerful, his step less buoyant, and his smile less frequent. And when he did smile it was sometimes so sadly, as to bring tears to Lina's eyes. From that time she ceased to be perfectly happy. Her spirits varied with her husband's. If Richard was lively and gay, Lina was happy too, but if Richard's brow was thoughtful, or wore a look of care, the smiles faded from her lips and the rose from her cheek. Hers was a nature that could bloom while surrounded by the sunshine of love and happiness. But let them be withdrawn, let the chill breath of sorrow and adversity fall on her young heart, and the beautiful flower would droop and die.

At last Richard summoned up courage to broach the subject to his young and sensitive wife. He dreaded the effect it might have upon her excitable nature. He spoke hopefully of the result of his intended visit, for he had already noted her pale cheek and languid step. She looked frightened when he told her he was going, but she uttered not one word of remonstrance, for she felt it was his duty to go. And yet she felt that she would almost rather die than have him do so. She felt as if a cloud had suddenly enveloped his spirit. Why she dreaded to have her husband go to New Orleans, she could not tell. She would as soon have doubted the veracity of a Heavenly messenger, as to have doubted Richard's truth and fidelity.

But it was finally settled that he would start South on the following Monday, and all necessary preparations were made for his journey. He would write from every point on the route. Juno must regularly attend the village post office, every day after the stage came in, to bring the letters, which would be anxiously waited for by the lonely little wife.

On the eventful Monday morning, when Richard was to take his departure, he gave Lina a thousand loving injunctions, as to being cheerful, taking care of her health, and so on, and playfully importuned Juno to bring the rose to his lady love's cheek ere his return. He kissed Lina goodbye, and went smiling down the walk to meet the Ruthford stage as it passed. He left her smiling and waving his handkerchief as a last adieu. Lina sought to console herself, and wait with patience for the promised letters.

CHAPTER VIII.

April 15, 1865

The Flower Fadeth.

Time passed slowly with the inmates of Rose Cottage, until the first letter would be received from Richard. Lina wandered about the cottage and garden with a listless air, and Juno seemed more quiet and thoughtful. She knew more of the real state of affairs than the young wife supposed. Juno had lived so long with Laura Hays that she was well acquainted with the history of the Tracys. She also knew much of the character and disposition of Colonel Frank Tracy; she was about twelve years old when Frank was married to pretty Nellie Thornton. She was then living with Laura's aunt. Juno saw Frank Tracy once after that; it was when he came to forbid Laura's marriage with the young minister, Alfred Hays. She knew well his overweening family pride and love of wealth and position. Alfred Hays was one of nature's noblemen, but wealth and position he had not. Juno was not likely to forget the terrible family quarrel that ensued when Laura, who possessed much of her brother's spirit and resolution, persisted in marrying the poor minister, declaring that she had the right and was capable of choosing her own husband, and was prepared to follow the dictates of her own heart. Frank, finding that Laura would not be persuaded to give Alfred up, said, angrily:

"Laura, if you persist in marrying that beggar, that mere fortune hunter, you are no longer a sister of mine, so reflect well ere you decide. I will never receive him as a brother."

He was about leaving the room when his sister's voice arrested him. She said, in a low firm tone, "I need not time for reflection, my decision is already made; I will marry Alfred. If he is poor, he is good and noble, while your interference is unnatural and cruelly unjust, and—"

"Enough," cried Frank, impatiently interrupting and pushing her from him. "I will say no more; you have taken your own course, and must abide by the consequences." And he strode from the room, leaving his sister heart-stricken and aghast.

Poor Laura had not quite expected this unhappy turn affairs had taken, yet she was not prepared to sacrifice her life's happiness to her brother's selfish demands.

Frank sought his aunt, and told her the result of his interview with his sister. Laura need not indulge the hope that he would relent his cruel decision; it was unalterable. He departed without seeing Laura again, and from that time all communication between them ceased.

Not until after their marriage did Alfred Hays learn the bitter sacrifice his gentle wife had made when she fulfilled her plighted troth with him. Miss Tracy then went to reside with her niece, taking Juno with her. A few years later she died, leaving her entire fortune, with the exception of a legacy of ten thousand dollars, to her niece, Laura. The above legacy was willed to Frank Tracy's little son, Richard, to be placed in the care of Alfred Hays, until the young heir should become of age, the interest of which was payable on or after his nineteenth birthday. What had induced Miss Tracy to leave this legacy to little Richard, whom she had never seen, would be impossible to say, but future events proved the wisdom of her last act of kindness.

Juno knew all this; she also knew that all was not satisfactory in relation to Richard's marriage. She knew that some trouble was expected, though the exact nature of it she did not know, but her suspicions were very nearly correct.

Juno always had her "suspicions," and the remarkable part of it is, they were nearly always right. At last a letter came from Richard—a kind and hopeful letter—which did much towards reviving Lina's spirits. It was soon followed by others, all written in the same hopeful, happy style, from various points on the route, and, finally, one written immediately upon his arrival in New Orleans. "Manville," he said, "was at present out of the city. I shall go home this evening. You need not look for a letter again for some time, as I shall not write until I know the final result of my visit."

Several weeks elapsed and yet no other letter came. In vain it was that Juno went to the village post office every day, after the Ruthford stage came in; she failed to bring the white-winged messenger that would have won back the lost smile to Lina's sad face. Truly "hope deferred maketh the heart sick," for Lina's face grew more pale and sad and her step more languid, as week after week sped by, and she received no tidings from the absent one.

Every day, when it drew near the time for Juno's return from the village, she would walk down to the little gate, and wait anxiously for her coming, with eager and expectant face, but when Juno reported her ill success, she would turn away with such a look of keen disappointment, such hopeless despair as to make Juno shed tears of sympathy with the fragile creature that leaned heavily upon her arm.

At last Lina ceased to look for a letter. She never complained, but that quiet despairing look was pitiful to behold. It was in vain Juno taxed her brain in the manufacture of choice delicacies to tempt the palate of the gentle invalid, who invariably thanked her faithful friend with a sweet smile, but failed to do justice to the dainties she prepared. The golden autumn days had passed, and dreary November, with its leaden sky, made all without seem cheerless. The wind moaned dismally through the branches of the tamaracks at the door, and played at "hide and seek" among the leafless rose bushes. One day, after Lina had been more despondent than ever, and Juno, having finished her household duties, was sitting with folded hands, seemingly intent upon the gambols of a playful kitten; but in reality thinking of Lina and considering what she had best do, her mistress said:

"Juno, I wish to have a long talk with you."

This was just what Juno had long been wishing for, and she arose with alacrity and followed Lina into the little parlor, where a cheerful fire was burning on the hearth, which, with the heavy red curtains, served to give the room a cheerful appearance. The piano stood open, but no light fingers called forth its lively notes. Juno would open it every morning, saying, apologetically, "that it made the room look more pleasant-like, and more as if master Richard was home."

Lina seated herself in a large easy chair, while Juno took a seat on a low ottoman at her feet.

"Juno, I have never confided to you my early history. I have been thinking much of late, and have concluded to tell you all about myself." Whereupon she told Juno all the reader already knows, together with other facts which it is not our purpose at present to disclose.

"Juno," she continued, after a long silence, during which she had been toying with a beautiful ring on her third finger—it was Richard's gift, "I sometimes think I shall not live long, and, indeed, I should not wish to, if Richard never returns, for I could not live without him."

"Oh, my dear mistress Lina, don't talk that way! Master will come back! You must not talk of dying!" cried Juno, striving to keep back the tears that would fall in spite of all effort to restrain them.

"No, Juno, you cannot deceive me. I know that I cannot get well. You know my situation, and it is not best that you should be with me any longer alone. I wish you to engage the services of some competent old lady immediately. My marriage certificate and letters you will find in a little rose-wood box in my work-stand drawer. When I am gone, Juno, put this ring with the other things, and keep them carefully for my sake. If Richard ever comes home, you may give them to him. Tell him that though my heart was breaking, I loved him to the last. That is all now; I am tired and wish to sleep. You may stop at the post office as you come through the village."

Juno was successful in finding an old lady of suitable qualifications. Old Mrs. Butterworth had just arrived by the Ruthford stage, and was one of those fat, motherly, smiling, rosy-cheeked old ladies that straightway win one's confidence. So home she went with Juno, who, though delighted with her success, did not forget to stop at the post office.

The postmaster, from Juno's frequent visits and disappointed face, had learned to know her, and on this occasion hastened to produce and hand to the astonished woman a letter bearing the New Orleans postmark, and address to Mrs. Lina H. Tracy. Juno gave an exclamation of delight, as she thought of the joyful tidings she hoped to convey to the anxious, weary wife.

Lina was standing by the window when Juno and Mrs. Butterworth came up the walk, the former holding the letter triumphantly aloft. Lina sank nervous and trembling into a seat, as Juno rushed tumultuously into the room, exclaiming, "a letter from master Richard!" and could only articulate faintly, "Give it to me, Juno."

She glanced at the well-known superscription, and, with trembling hand, opened the fatal letter, to read the cruel words which would freeze the life from her young heart, and extinguish the life of the rapidly fading flower. Once, twice she read, with staring eyes, the words that closed her brief dream of happiness, when she fell heavily to the floor in a death-like swoon.

CHAPTER IX.

April 22, 1865

"Rest for the weary."

Mrs. Butterworth and Juno hastened to raise the insensible Lina, and lay her upon the sofa. The mischievous letter had fluttered from Lina's nerveless hand, and now lay quietly on the bright red carpet. Juno, with wise forethought, secured it, and then started in quest of the village physician, while Mrs. Butterworth used every effort to try and restore the pale creature who had already enlisted her warmest sympathy. Juno soon returned with the venerable Dr. Murdoch, who gravely shook his head, as he gazed on the sharp outlines of the deathlike face before him.

After a while Lina opened her eyes wearily, looked from one to the other with a sadly bewildered air, and then, shudderingly, closed them again, ever and anon murmuring, wildly, incoherent sentences, but seemed not to notice any one.

The daylight was fast waning. A gray November evening was ushered in. The tea kettle was steaming over a cheerful fire in the bright little kitchen, and Juno was quietly preparing supper for the Doctor and Mrs. Butterworth. The lamps were lighted; the curtains drawn; the pet kitten quietly dozed on the stool near the fire; all seemed cheerful and home-like.

After tea, all were seated around the couch of the sufferer; hour after hour sped by, and naught was heard save the heavy breathing of the invalid and the ticking of the little French clock upon the mantel, until after the little time-piece had chimed, in silvery tones, the hour of midnight; then, there were troubled faces, anxious whispers, and hurried steps, through the remaining hours of the night; and, when the cloudless morning dawned, a fair form was wrapped in the calm repose of death. Sweet Lina slept the dreamless sleep, the sleep that knows no waking here on earth. One of earth's weary ones—surely in heaven there is rest for such as thee. In the large easy chair, nestled amid its crimson depths, a beautiful babe was sleeping, a tender waif, cast motherless upon the sea of life. Poor little one, it would seem thou wert too fair and fragile to dwell in this cold world of ours! How striking the contrast between mother and child! The one had drooped and faded beneath the burden of life's trials until death released her weary spirit and she found rest; the other, sweet innocent, slept all unconscious of the great future. What trials were in store for that little one were wisely withheld.

Lina had lived long enough to kiss and bless her babe, and to whisper in the ear of Juno, to "call her Claire Neville Tracy. Be faithful to my child, Juno; never forsake her, and, as you may be faithful to her, my Father in heaven will reward you."

Poor Juno, with tearful eyes, promised all that Lina had required, and then, with choking voice, asked, "Have you not one word for Master Richard?" A beautiful smile lighted up her pale face, and she faintly whispered, "I love and—" but the sentence died on her lips; and, ere Juno relinquished the little hand, the lids had closed over eyes into which the misty shadows of death were fast stealing. "Such is life!"

Strange hands robed the form of the departed for the grave; strange but kind hands smoothed the shining curls, and placed the lovely snow-flowers on her meek bosom. Dr. Murdoch kindly superintended all arrangements for the funeral, which many of the warmhearted villagers attended, and Lina was laid to rest on the bleak hillside, where soon the pure, white snow would lie heavy on the lonely grave, and fierce northern winds would moan through the tall pines; but, when the Spring comes, fragrant roses and wild wood flowers would bloom until the chill Autumn blasts would rob them of their fleeting beauty.

Mrs. Butterworth remained to assist Juno in taking care of the baby, Claire, upon whom every care was bestowed. The little one grew, fair and rosy, and would open its great black eyes and try to look about, and soon learn to chirrup its delight when Juno's good-humored face crossed its infant vision, much to the satisfaction and encouragement of its kind nurses.

Thus the long dreary winter passed away, and a fitful New England March was on hand. Near the close of a pleasant afternoon Mrs. Butterworth and Juno were taking an early tea. Little Claire was sleeping in the cradle, her round cheeks rosy with the hue of health. A knock at the door arrested the flow of pleasant tea-table chat; Juno answered the summons, and was surprised at the unexpected vision of George Manville, who greeted her warmly and with smiling face.

"Where is Master Richard?" was Juno's first inquiry.

"In Europe, I suppose," was the immediate reply. "Did you not know it?"

"No!" said Juno, with astonishment. "What could have taken him to Europe without coming to see Miss Lina?" continued Juno, indignantly. "And that's just what killed her, poor thing!"

"Killed her!" ejaculated Manville, with pale face and aghast manner. "Did I understand you to say Mrs. Tracy was dead?" he asked with quivering lips.

"Yes, she is dead!" replied Juno. "And this is her child," said she, taking up little Claire, who had just awaked from her long afternoon nap.

Manville gazed long on the beautiful child which was a miniature likeness of his handsome and noble friend. What thoughts were passing through his brain it would be difficult to devise.

Mrs. Butterworth prepared supper for Manville, and, while discussing the merits of the same, he asked Juno what she intended doing. She could not tell, as she had still thought Richard would come back; but, now that he was not coming, she concluded to ask his advice.

Manville advised the sale of the cottage and furniture, the proceeds of which would enable her to live comfortably with little Claire, and then to remove to some other village. Juno acquiesced in this arrangement. So Manville took up his abode at the cottage, and undertook the management of affairs.

In a few days, Rose Cottage was advertised for sale; a gentleman and his daughter, seeing the advertisement, called to look at the cottage, and were so pleased with it, that, finding the furniture also was for sale, proposed to buy the cottage already furnished, which proposal just suited Manville, and pretty Rose Cottage became the home of Mr. Villars, who was a native of Vermont.

Addie Villars was delighted with every thing in and about the cottage; "O, papa!" she exclaimed, with animation, "such exquisite taste, such harmony of color in the arrangement of every thing; I know I should have loved Mrs. Tracy."

Mr. Villars smiled at his daughter's enthusiasm, saying, "that he did not doubt Mrs. Tracy was a very worthy person."

Addie decided that no change should be made in the disposition of the furniture, but that every thing should remain as it was. After her mistress' death, Juno had taken scrupulous care to have every thing placed just as Lina used to arrange and loved to see them. And the result was that months later, when a pale, emaciated stranger stopped at the cottage, it wore the same appearance as when Richard and Lina were its happy occupants, and his apparent agitation drew tears of sympathy from the gentle Addie Villars, who, with the sad stranger, visited the lone grave on the hill side.

Mrs. Butterworth went home. A few weeks after, Juno, with the infant Claire, was snugly installed in a cozy little house many miles from her old home. Manville had taken particular care to have every thing arranged for her comfort and convenience. Juno was satisfied and grateful, and thought Manville very kind. But had she known the villainous heart masked by that faultless exterior, she could have formed a better estimate of his real character. And Richard, so deeply wronged, so basely deceived, should have known that "a man may smile and be a villain still."

CHAPTER X.

April 29, 1865

Richard in New Orleans.

Soon after Richard's arrival in New Orleans he wended his way home. It was late in the afternoon. Colonel Tracy was seated on the verandah, reading, when Richard came up. "Good afternoon, father," he said, cheerfully extending his hand at the same time.

Colonel Tracy took no notice of the proffered hand, but exclaimed, angrily, "So sir, you have come to insult me with your presence! But follow me to the library, I wish not to quarrel with you here!"

Richard followed the choleric old gentleman, as requested, into the library. Colonel Tracy closed and locked the door, to secure them from intrusion, then confronting his son, with threatening mien, said: "Now, sir, give an account of your proceedings; I want no evasion whatever, but a clear and concise statement of facts."

Richard related all that had transpired, from his first acquaintance with Lina to the present time: his betrothal on the Alhambra; the scene at the dinner table after Colonel Tracy's return from the plantation; Manville's purchase of the slave girl Lina, which was only a ruse, as Manville merely acted for his friend; the departure of the trio for the North; the quiet bridal at the little New England parsonage; Alfred Hays' departure; the purchase of Rose Cottage; and subsequent experiences for the Colonel's benefit, in his usual characteristic manner.

The Colonel's rage was without bounds, and he wrathfully exclaimed, "Oh, that a son of mine should thus disgrace himself and family, as to marry a negress—a slave—the illegitimate offspring of a spendthrift, a drunkard, and a libertine, a being sunk so low in the scale of humanity as to be unworthy the name of a man. It's awful! 'Tis abominable! Fool that you are, to allow yourself to be thus entrapped by a pretty face; and, no doubt, by this time you have wearied of your toy. If you have, it will be well, for as you are under age, your marriage is illegal, and, with the assistance of a trusty lawyer, its validity may be annulled. You can visit Europe a year or two, until the memory of this disgraceful affair has died out. I will settle an annuity on your—" he could not add the word wife. It would have choked him, so he corrected himself by saying, "—on the girl, which will be sufficient to support her decently, and that is much better than she deserves, the artful wench, to palm herself off for a lady. Our society is getting into a pretty state, when the sons of the best families stoop to marry their fathers' slaves. You have imbibed the pernicious sentiments of Northern demagogues until they have encompassed your ruin. What is to become of our institution, if we take our slaves upon an equality with ourselves? What slave on the plantation would properly respect you as their master, while they knew your wife was a Negro slave—yes, worse than a slave? But to return to the point in question, will you renounce that girl? The way is perfectly clear, and the desired result may be arrived at with little difficulty. Of course it will cause some commotion in the 'upper circles,' and give your name an unpleasant notoriety for a season, but in the course of time that will wear away. As I said before, visit Europe a year or two, and when you return, there is not a young lady in New Orleans that would not accept your hand and fortune."

Colonel Tracy stopped abruptly and turned to his son, who sat erect, with livid face and flashing eyes, and with an air of such resolute determination that he felt very uncertain as to the impression produced by his reasoning, and he imperatively asked: "Well, sir, what is your decision?"

Richard possessed extraordinary power of self-control, and replied, in those calm, measured tones which always give such an advantage in an exciting discussion and voluntarily win the respect of an opponent, "Father, as much as I love and respect you, I cannot accede to a proposal that would so deeply involve my honor and integrity. I cannot forsake my wife. I did not win Lina's affections to basely deceive her, nor did I marry her to cruelly desert her. I would submit to any fate rather than become a party to such a degrading proceeding. I see no honorable avenue of escape, if I desired one, and I earnestly assure you I do not. Those pernicious sentiments, as you are pleased to term them, which I have imbibed at the North, only teach me to respect the rights of my fellow citizens. Lina is not responsible for her unfortunate birth and surroundings. She is pure, refined, and good, has been educated far from the contaminating influence which Southern society exerts over its followers. All else I can well overlook. I would not own a slave if I possessed the wealth of a Croesus. The institution of slavery is of itself accursed, and will yet prove the fatal Nemesis of the South, for do not think that a just God will allow any people so deeply wronged to go unavenged."

Colonel Tracy sat speechless with rage and astonishment, while Richard was speaking, and when he had finished he rose from his chair and confronting his son said: "Richard, if you persist in carrying out this unexampled piece of folly, I shall disinherit you. Not a penny of mine shall go to you or yours, and my doors shall ever be closed against you. Your mother and brother shall never acknowledge you as son and brother, and your name shall be as that of one who has slept a century in his tomb, uncared for and forgotten; so you can make your choice; you know the conditions."

"I cannot forsake my wife," was the firm, unfaltering reply. "Your judgment is severe, and—perhaps, it is just, but I will abide by it without murmuring."

"You dare to defy me!" yelled the Colonel, his face black with rage. "But I will conquer you yet! For I will see you die at my feet before you shall return to the arms of that accursed wife! Yes, I will kill you, and suffer hanging for it!" and drawing a pistol from his pocket took deliberate aim and fired.

Richard, having risen from his chair, exclaimed:

"Father, would you murder your own son!" and fell heavily to the floor, writhing in his own blood, the ball having entered his right side.

Hurrying feet were heard traversing the wide halls—the door was burst open, and Mrs. Tracy rushed into the library, closely followed by Manville, who had just returned, and hearing of Richard's arrival, had come direct to Colonel Tracy's, while groups of frightened Negroes crowded the door and thronged the hall, presenting a weird scene, as the twilight shadows were now gathering.

Nellie Tracy gazed from the insensible form of her son to her husband, exclaiming, "Frank, O! Frank! May God forgive you! You have killed my child!" and then sunk fainting to the floor.

Colonel Tracy stood gazing upon the forms of his wife and son, with wild, glaring eyes. Manville alone possessed some presence of mind. He directed the Negroes to take charge of their mistress, while he turned his attention to Colonel Tracy. "Come, my friend," he said, attempting to lead him from the library.

"Manville, I am perfectly sane; I know what I have done. Take that boy away, any where, out of my sight and hearing, for I care not whether he lives or dies."

Manville knew that the Colonel was in earnest, so he hailed a passing hack, and, with the assistance of the driver and several of the slaves, the wounded man was carefully placed in it, and driven slowly to a quiet private boarding house, in a retired part of the city, while others were dispatched in quest of medical aid.

It would be impossible to attempt a description of Colonel Tracy's feelings. Indignation against Richard, and apprehension for his delicate wife, were the predominant workings of his soul. Mrs. Tracy was indeed in a critical state, and well might her passionate husband tremble for her safety. Through the long watches of the night great was the anxiety of that wretched man, for the life of his loved one hung, as it were, by a thread.

CHAPTER XI.

May 6, 1865

An equivocal friend.

Mrs. Lisle, the landlady of the private boarding house to which the insensible Richard was taken, was a widow of prepossessing appearance, and had evidently been in much better circumstances than at the present. She was kindhearted, sensitive and refined. She was shocked, when Manville and his assistant brought the wounded man into the hall, and, in the glare of light, she saw the face of Richard so frightfully pale. But, knowing the necessity of immediate assistance, with the aid of Lettie, a little colored girl, she soon prepared a room and couch for the reception of Richard, at which time Dr. Singleton arrived, who, after a careful examination, pronounced Richard in a very critical state, his wound being a severe one; and, in falling, his head had grazed some heavy article of furniture, inflicting a severe bruise on the temple. With some difficulty, the hateful ball was extracted and the wound dressed; after which, Dr. Singleton prepared a solution, sleep-provoking in its nature, and Richard was comparatively comfortable for the night.

He slept quietly for several hours, when he became restless, moaning and murmuring sadly incoherent sentences; and, ere the morning dawned, Dr. Singleton, who had made an early visit, found his patient much worse; the scarlet cheeks, parched lips, heated breath, and wildly beating pulse, betokening the presence of the fever he so much dreaded.

"This is bad, Mrs. Lisle, very bad," he remarked: "I feared this. He has been quite delirious through the night, you say?" he asked, while preparing the necessary medicines.

"Yes!" replied Mrs. Lisle, "he has talked alternately of his mother, of Lina, and an enraged father. I think it is a family quarrel; but, from the confused and disconnected nature of his raving, I could not, of course, determine the exact nature of the trouble."

At this moment, Richard moved uneasily, and murmured quite audibly, "Lina, he will not forgive me! But we will live for each other now, darling! It was so cruelly unjust to attempt to take you from me!" A pause, and then in a pitifully pleading voice, "Lina, don't leave me; it is all dark and lonely here."

Dr. Singleton leaned over his patient, and placing his cool hand upon Richard's heated brow, spoke to him in calm soothing tones. The pleading glance of those bright, dark eyes, went straight to the doctor's heart: for he too had been a father, and his only child, a young man of Richard's age, had been suddenly stricken down in a foreign land—had died among strangers, and was buried upon the banks of the beautiful Rhine.

The Doctor was thinking of all this, as he gazed with compassion upon the unconscious youth, when Richard exclaimed in ringing tones, "You will not take my beautiful Lina from me! What matters it, if her skin is dark, if the blood of the despised race tinges her veins? Oh, believe me, she is good and pure! Oh! you must save her! You will not, must not let them take her!"

The Doctor stood somewhat aghast! What was the solution of this strange language? To what did the unconscious sufferer allude? Could it be, that he was given to one of the popular vices of Southern society? One glance at his patient, and he was reassured. Dissipation had not placed its foul mark upon that fresh beardless face, surrounded by clustering, black curls. No, the stigma of vice had not attached itself to that noble youth! The Doctor felt this, and determined to befriend the young man whose acquaintance he was forming under such peculiar circumstances, and who, he believed, was worthy of his deepest sympathy.

Thus, Richard unconsciously won for himself a warm friend—one who was destined greatly to influence his after life; and thus it is, in life, we sometimes unconsciously win friendship, while we fail, signally, when earnestly striving to gain and retain it.

Soon after Dr. Singleton took his leave, Manville appeared, refreshed and smiling, from a fresh toilette and an excellent breakfast. Mrs. Lisle was prepossessed in the young man's favor. He seemed so thoughtful of his friend's comfort—so anxious to alleviate his sufferings, that she willingly resigned her position as nurse, for the present, in favor of Manville, while she went to look after her various household duties.

As the days passed, Richard continued to grow worse, and Dr. Singleton's visits more frequent and prolonged. Mrs. Lisle spent many hours by the couch of the sufferer, while Manville devoted his entire time to nursing his friend. As the weeks passed slowly by, Richard's spirit fluctuated between life and death, while his voice might be heard sometimes in ringing tones, and at other times, in almost sobbing wail, imploring the imaginary Lina not to forsake him.

At last the crisis was passed, and Richard was convalescent. Dr. Singleton was fairly jubilant when able to pronounce his patient out of danger. As soon as Richard was permitted to converse with any one, he asked Manville, in the absence of Dr. Singleton and Mrs. Lisle, if he had written to Lina concerning his illness. Manville was unprepared for this question. He had not thought of it, and inwardly blamed himself for his stupidity, in not being prepared for this emergency; as it was, he could only admit the truth, he had not; and his eyes fell beneath Richard's glance, so full of reproach and indignation.

"Oh, George, how could you be so careless, not to use a harsher term? Such forgetfulness is really criminal. It will kill my wife, not to hear from me through all these long weeks, and not understanding the cause of this strange silence. It was cruelly unkind to forget her. Poor Lina, I know your little heart is breaking." He was growing restless and excited. "George, you must write for me immediately; bring ink and paper to my bedside, and write, while I dictate." Manville did as requested, and the blank sheet was soon filled with kind and loving words from Richard. He spoke guardedly of his illness, and every allusion that would have had the slightest tendency to alarm his wife, was anxiously suppressed. "I shall be home soon," he kindly remarked, "when, I hope, we shall part no more!" How thoughtful of her, his only care! Kind and encouraging messages were also sent to Juno.

After the letter was finished, Richard said, excitedly, "Now read it for me, George Manville! Read it to the end! That will do," he said with a sigh of satisfaction and sunk back upon his pillow, wearily closing his eyes; while Manville, who promised to mail the letter immediately, passed out, and, proceeding direct to his sleeping apartment, lighted a small silver lamp, drew the letter, around which cling so many hopes and fears, from an inner pocket, gazed upon it a few seconds, scornfully curling his lips, and, a sinister light flashing from his eyes, held it over the ruthless blaze until the curled, crisp embers fell at his feet, exclaimed exultingly, "So perish all your dreams of happiness!"

CHAPTER XII.

May 13, 1865

MISSING—This chapter appeared in an issue of the *Christian Recorder* that has yet to be located.

CHAPTER XIII.

May 20, 1865

The Tracys.

On the morning following the tragic event before narrated, Colonel Tracy was pacing his room like a caged lion. His wife, his idolized Nellie, was ill, perhaps dying, while he was rigidly excluded from her presence. And if she died, he was her murderer. Oh, the agony of thought! What of Richard? He resolutely tried to banish all thoughts of his son, but despite every effort, the vision of that pale, noble face, passed before him. And these last words in ringing tones, "Father, would you murder your own son?" haunted his memory. He seemed to hear them still. Was he, indeed, the murderer of his son? This question presented itself many times. His reflections were sad, and bitter. He half-expected a visit or message from Manville, but received neither. His anxiety for his wife increased as hours passed, and the invariable reply of the attendants as they passed to and from his wife's chamber, "No better, Massa" grated harshly upon his ear. This suspense was unendurable, he would bear it no longer. At this moment Mattie, the nurse, entered the room. Colonel Tracy scarcely vouchsafed a single glance upon the pink-faced, black-eyed baby she respectfully presented, but asked almost fiercely, "How is my wife?"

"Very bad, Massa," replied the woman, sadly.

For days Mrs. Tracy's life was despaired of, and through those days of awful uncertainty, Colonel Tracy was constant in his care of baby Belle. Next to his wife, his every thought was of her. He almost idolized the little black-eyed stranger, and much of that idolatry clung to him through life. Belle was always her father's favorite, and right royally did the little beauty queen it over her father's heart.

But Nellie Tracy did not die. Slowly she struggled back to partial health, but so changed, so faded, a mere semblance of her former self. Her husband followed her like a shadow, anticipating her every wish, doing every thing in the most kind and gentle manner, evincing by a thousand little acts of thoughtful kindness how dear she was to him. Nellie was pleased and grateful to her husband, but this was not what she needed to bring perfect health to the dropping figure, roses to the pale cheek, and the light of happiness to the brown eyes which revealed such a world of sadness in their liquid depths. Richard, her first born pride, her noble son: it was of him she longed to know, yet dared not ask. And her husband never alluded to his son. Colonel Tracy, perhaps, with a view of remedying the true evil, proposed a visit to Italy. Nellie faintly acquiesced, but ere their departure, she gained through Mattie the intelligence that Richard was living. That was all, but she felt better and improved perceptibly, and with a slight semblance of cheerfulness watched the busy preparation for departure. Mattie, the nurse, went with them to take charge of baby Belle and Little Lloyd. Mattie was shrewd and intelligent, and Nellie, in poor health as she was, could not trust her children to the care of a stranger, and Mattie had nursed and loved little Richard even as she now loved little Lloyd and Isabelle. Nellie always found a ready and sympathetic listener in her faithful attendant, when talking of her son.

Long years the Tracys were absent from New Orleans. And many times they were near, very near a sad, thoughtful-browed man, who was rarely known to smile, and would stand up as if spellbound, in the mammoth hotels, gazing upon the register where one line claimed his attention, (Colonel Tracy and wife, nurse and two children). Were they indeed so near him? His heart bounded when he thought of his gentle mother. He would see her and talk to her. But then came the bitter memory of his father's curse. No, he would not seek her, but all unknown to them, he would at least look upon her fair face. One evening little Lloyd was seated with half-closed eyes upon the sofa in the nurse's room waiting for Mattie to return and put him to bed. He was suddenly clasped by a pair of stout arms. Warm kisses fell on cheek, brow and lips. The wondering child opened his eyes wide and looked up into the sad face above him with a confiding smile. A few moments more he was soundly sleeping, upon the stranger's bosom. Richard strained the little fellow convulsively to his heart. His thoughts were busy with the past,—time passed unheeded. Mattie entered the room, unconscious of the surprise that awaited her. An exclamation more vehement than elegant escaped the astonished woman as her eyes fell upon Richard.

"Oh! Massa Richard, dear Massa, I'm so glad to see you," and poor Mattie fairly broke down from her excess of joy, threw her apron over her head and wept like a child. Richard was deeply affected by Mattie's expression of feeling, and, waiting till she became calmer, asked for his father and mother. Mattie related all that had transpired. Richard was visibly affected when Mattie spoke of his mother's ill health, and her anxiety concerning him. He hastily traced a few lines upon a leaf from his diary, handed them to Mattie, and said, "Give them to mother," and he hesitated a moment. "If I could look upon my mother, if for only one moment, I would be so thankful." He looked wistfully in Mattie's face; she divined his wish. "Follow me," she said, leading the way to Mrs. Tracy's room. They entered with noiseless step. Nellie was calmly sleeping, her brown hair swept back from the pale forehead: perhaps in her dreams she felt his loved presence, for the sweet lips wreathed in a beautiful smile. Richard, with tearful eyes kneeled by her couch and prayed such a prayer as the angels love to listen to, and the effect of that fervent humble prayer was felt by Nellie Tracy. Even in her sleep a holy smile rested upon her features. Richard arose, pressed one long, loving kiss upon his mother's lips, and passed from the room with Mattie.

"Oh! Mattie, be kind and faithful to mother." He pressed a piece of gold into her hand and was gone, just in time to avoid a meeting with Colonel Tracy, who was returning from a dinner party. The next morning Mrs. Tracy said to Mattie, "I dreamed such a beautiful dream! I thought Richard was here, I seem to feel his kiss upon my lips yet." Mattie made no reply but gave her Richard's note, which read as follows:

> DEAR MOTHER:
> *With the deepest sorrow I learned from Mattie of your failing health. —*
> *Have no anxiety about me; I have suffered much. Perhaps we will meet no*
> *more on earth, but I am looking forward to a happy reunion in heaven.*
> *Your loving son,*
> RICHARD.

Mr. Villars and Addie were interested in their guest and rendered him every attention. After he had paid a visit to the lone grave on the hillside where sweet wild flowers were blooming, it was late ere he returned and Addie heard, until the morning light dawned, the unbroken steps of Richard as he walked his room with steady and unceasing tread. At breakfast he looked pale and care worn. "Miss Addie, will you accompany me this morning to visit my wife's grave?" Addie kindly assented, and together they visited the grave.

"Would you, Miss Addie, grant me one favor if I ask it?"

"Certainly," replied his companion.

"Thank you! It is this—will you sometimes visit Lina's grave when I am gone, it will be so lonely on this hillside. I cannot bear the thought that none should visit her last resting place."

Addie promised and nobly did she fulfill her promise. Richard left them with many thanks for their kindness. And, as years passed, Mr. Villars and Addie spoke often of Richard, and Addie wondered if he would ever return to Rose Cottage.

CHAPTER XIV.

May 27, 1865

Claire and Isabelle.

Isabelle Tracy was alone in her luxuriously furnished boudoir; curtains of light and elegant material shaded the windows, so that a soft voluptuous light pervaded the silent apartment. A carpet, adorned with large roses, upon a delicate white ground, covered the floor. Chairs and divans, elegant and expensive, were disposed about the room in charming negligence; rare old paintings and exquisite engravings adorned the walls, bespeaking rare artistic taste in the beautiful owner. Between the windows a perfect cataract of lace fell on either side of an elegant toilet table, prettily hiding a collection of beautiful cups, flagons, boxes and vases, containing rare perfumes and pomades, as curious as costly. Of what was Isabelle thinking, as she sat with contracted brow, flashing eyes, and compressed lips, while a crimson spot burned on each cheek, and her white hands were clasped and unclasped in a sort of mechanical, absent-minded manner?

At last, giving expression to her thoughts, she said: "Who and what is this Claire Neville, whose striking resemblance to myself is already the theme of conversation with every body? O, I hate her, with her queenly air and stately walk! Her beauty, they say, is almost marvelous. Can it be possible that she surpasses me in loveliness?"

And Isabelle stood before the faithful mirror, which reflected a fair face, striking in its singular beauty. Eagerly she scrutinized every feature: the brilliant, almond-shaped black eyes, with curving, black brows and sweeping silken lashes; the small mouth, which rivaled a half-blown rose in its dewy loveliness, displaying rows of even, pearl-white teeth; the soft, oval cheeks, now flushed with excitement, and the crowning attraction, a wealth of beautiful black hair, which rippled in curling waves to her slender waist.

As she continued to gaze a smile of satisfaction wreathed her lovely lips. What had she to fear from the self-possessed governess? She pulled the bell-cord, and in a few moments her summons was answered by a trim-looking mulatto girl.

"Mira, you may dress me now," she said.

While Mira was selecting the proper articles of dress, Isabelle resumed, "I wish you to dress my hair with great care this afternoon. You have not forgotten the new style you learned from the French hairdresser?"

"Oh no, Miss," was Mira's quick reply, as she separated her mistress' long, shining hair, and with nimble fingers plaited beautiful braids to take the place of the straggling tresses.

The task being completed, Isabelle, with a gratified smile, said, "Mira, you have indeed succeeded well, and you shall be suitably rewarded."

When Isabelle was pleased she was exceedingly gracious. Before descending to the parlor, she turned to take another look in the mirror, and surveyed with ill-concealed pride her beautiful face and magnificent figure.

Count Sayvord, who was lounging about the parlor, advanced to greet her. "You are looking fair, my belle," he said, with a courtly bow. Isabelle rewarded him with a most fascinating smile.

Count Sayvord possessed rare conversational powers. He had read much and travelled a great deal, and was also a close observer of human nature, and the manners and customs of the different people he had been among.

An hour passed, and the handsome ormula clock upon the mantel chimed four. A shadow rested upon Isabelle's brow. This was the hour for the children to take their music lesson.

Claire was a perfect model of punctuality and precision. Isabelle knew this, and thought, *Now for an infliction of that everlasting governess. If she was only safe in the land of 'steady habits,' I would willingly be responsible for the education of a dozen little sisters.* As a realization of her fears, the musical voice of Claire was heard in the distance, in company with Laura and Nellie.

A peculiar expression passed over the Count's face, as he noticed the too visible vexation of his companion. Perhaps he understood, and perhaps he did not.

The trio entered the parlor. Claire acknowledged the presence of the Count and Isabelle by a graceful inclination of the head, and passed on. Sayvord continued his conversation with Isabelle, but his eyes continually wandered to where Claire sat, instructing her young charge. He was mystified in a chaos of doubt and perplexities. Who was this unassuming and stately Claire? Whenever he thought of Claire, she was strangely associated with the tall, dark stranger he had met years before at his uncle Clayburn Sayvord's residence. He also observed that Claire was an object of deep interest to Lloyd and Colonel Tracy, and it was quite evident, whatever the mystery was, that they were also puzzled to account for the resemblance between Claire Neville and Isabelle Tracy. Those two, so very like in appearance, yet so unlike in disposition.

Sayvord answered Isabelle's questions with the air of one whose thoughts are far otherwise engaged. She noticed this, and was almost ready to openly resent it. To crown all, the Count excused himself, and wended his way to the arbor, to enjoy a quiet siesta, and, perhaps, to dream of the beautiful governess. Ah, Count Sayvord, unraveling the mystery that envelopes a beautiful woman is dangerous business.

Isabelle was angry. Was the Count becoming infatuated with that detested governess? What subtle charm did she cast about her? Lloyd had eyes, but he could see no one but Claire. And now Sayvord was about to follow his example. Her father, too, was unaccountably drawn towards the young stranger, while the Negroes gazed after her with wonder, and talked mysteriously of somebody and something, with extra variations in the way of (not very pretty) grimaces and significant glances, and all the elite of New Orleans became suddenly interested in the health and welfare of their charming friend, Miss Tracy.

Carriages could be seen at all hours before the aristocratic mansion of the Tracys. Isabelle understood perfectly the curiosity, and, in not a few cases, the animosity which prompted these solicitous visits. "This is becoming unendurable," she murmured. "I must speak to papa," and she darted a haughty glance at the unconscious Claire, who was the innocent cause of all this commotion.

Claire was warmly attached to her young pupils, and they improved rapidly under her gentle tuition. Mrs. Tracy loved her with almost maternal affection, and Claire, poor, motherless Claire, repaid her by every kind and loving attention affection could devise. Lloyd regarded her as he would a favorite sister. He noticed his sister's antipathy towards her and sought to render every thing pleasant. Claire felt his natural goodness of heart, and was less reserved with him than with others. She would, while in his presence, cast aside her dignity and become for a little while her own charming self. He never wearied gazing upon her fair face, which shadowed forth the innocent heart beneath, and always felt more happy while in her company. Sayvord envied his friend the pleasure of the governess' society.

CHAPTER XV.

June 3, 1865

The Veiled Picture.

In the soft, early twilight, Mrs. Tracy and Claire sat hand in hand. For a long while neither spoke, but a subdued expression rested upon the face of each. Mrs. Tracy passed her hand caressingly over Claire's glossy braids, and murmured softly,

"Sweet Claire, you know not half how dear you are to me. I have learned to think I could not live, bereft of your presence. There is something in your voice and manner that draws me irresistibly towards you, and I hope you will never think of leaving me."

"Dear Mrs. Tracy," replied Claire, her sweet voice tremulous with emotion, "it would be unkind, as well as ungrateful, for me to leave you. I have no mother to care for me, no home where kind and loving friends impatiently endure my absence, and anxiously await my return. You have been kind, very kind, to me, and I already love you as a dear mother, and you have taught me how great was my loss in never knowing one whom I possessed a right to call by the blessed name of mother. You have been kind in allowing me to love you," and the proud Claire, who was cold and indifferent to all others, was weeping bitterly, her proud head pillowed upon Nellie Tracy's gentle breast, who talked in low, soft tones, tender and endearing words, until Claire was soothed, and lay like a weary child, her large, tender eyes resting with a dreamy expression upon Mrs. Tracy's pale, placid face.

"Claire, I will tell you of my married life. I have suffered, God alone knows how deeply. I could not confide my history to an indifferent person, but with your kind, sensitive heart, I know you will sympathize with me."

Claire's eyes were full of interest, and, as Mrs. Tracy proceeded, she drew instinctively nearer, her crimson lips apart, and the color deepening and fading from her cheeks. She was strangely interested in the fate of Richard and his slave bride. What was there in that history, sad though it was, to make the blood thrill through her veins and her heart to throb almost painfully? When Mrs. Tracy finished speaking, Claire pressed her hand fondly, and imprinted a warm kiss upon her white brow, which delicate manifestation fully expressed her beautiful sympathy.

"Claire, dear, you remind me, in a thousand ways, of my poor absent son. Your face, voice, and manner, are so like his, that I almost fancy he is speaking to me through you. It is a foolish fancy, perhaps, but I have dreamed that a nearer and stronger tie than mere friendship, bound us together. This strange resemblance first enlisted my affection for you, but I love you for yourself alone, since I have learned to know your gentle heart."

The two, so strangely yet strongly attached, conversed long. Claire repaid her friend's confidence by giving a history of her lonely and almost friendless childhood. Mrs. Tracy listened with breathless interest, and it was quite evident her thoughts were busy with the past.

"Stay with me always, Claire, and you shall never again sigh for a mother's love."

Gratefully the great, sad eyes were lifted to her face, and Claire murmured her thanks in a low tone. After a pause, she said:

"You spoke of Richard's picture. If you would only let me see it," and her voice was singularly pleading.

"I am pleased that I can gratify you," replied Mrs. Tracy. "The old library has been unopened for years, except when visited by myself. The picture is veiled. I have one of the keys; the other was unaccountably lost. But you can take mine. You must be careful not to be seen visiting the library by Col. Tracy, or any one of the servants. He has forbidden any one to visit the library, and should any of the Negroes observe your visit, they would not fail to report the same to him, and he would be greatly displeased." Gentle Nellie Tracy stood somewhat in awe of her lordly husband. "If you are not timid, tonight, after all have retired, would be the best time. I always go about midnight, and if you desire it, I will go with you."

Claire was pleased, and thanked her. Together they sat, sometimes silent, sometimes conversing in low tones, until the great bell in an adjoining yard tolled the hour of twelve. Mrs. Tracy arose, handed Claire a small lamp, took a large key from a private drawer, and prepared to lead the way to the old library.

Lightly they sped along the dark halls, streaked here and there by the pale yellow moonbeams. Arriving at the door, they listened breathlessly, until assured they were unobserved, and then inserted the key. The door was with difficulty unlocked, and swung back upon its hinges with a dull, grating sound. Claire looked around with blanched face and frightened air. Mrs. Tracy reassured her with a smile that fell athwart the gloomy apartment like a ray of bright sunlight. Mrs. Tracy closed and locked the door after them, and withdrawing the key, laid it on the heavy oaken desk. The key once withdrawn, the little guard fell over the keyhole with a sharp click, totally excluding every ray of light from penetrating the great, rambling hall without.

Mrs. Tracy drew aside the veil, and together they stood before the picture that seemed lifelike and breathing in the flickering, uncertain light of the small lamp. The handsome face seemed to smile down serenely upon those two women, who gazed upon it with such deep emotion. Claire's eyes were riveted upon that striking face. Eagerly she drank in its dark, noble beauty, with quivering lips and flushed cheeks. What awful mystery was it, at which she vainly clutched, and as vainly sought to unravel? Mrs. Tracy gazed attentively upon the two faces, which seemed an exact counterpart of each other. Her eyes rested first upon her son and then upon the beautiful, trembling girl at her side. Claire turned, their eyes met. One earnest, searching glance, and they read each other's thoughts. Claire exclaimed, excitedly:

"Mrs. Tracy, who am I? Oh, that face has haunted me in my dreams since my earliest recollection! Can it be that—?"

The sentence died upon her pale lips. A cautious step was heard traversing the hall. Nearer, nearer, it came, and slowly approached the library door, and stopped. A key turned in the lock, the door swung heavily back, and the affrighted women stood face to face with Col. Tracy, whose pale, haggard face bespoke great mental suffering. The trio gazed upon each other with equal consternation.

CHAPTER XVI.

June 10, 1865

Remorse.

Our readers, no doubt, are asking, what has become of Col. Tracy? With your permission we will invade the colonel's sanctuary, or, as Lloyd called the new library, "Pa's Retreat." Col. Tracy sits in the huge armchair, and bright, joyous sunbeams streaming in at the west windows fall warmly on the once raven locks, now closely threaded with silver. The little sunbeam all unnoticed, slides slowly down, and at last rests, quivering, deepening and fading upon the bright carpets. The colonel is thinner and paler than when we first knew him. His proud form is slightly bowed, and his searching, black eyes have an eager, restless glance that but too truly betokens a mind ill at ease.

The colonel is living under a shadow, and has lived under it for years. But the iron will, the overweening pride, which gave him strength to do and dare all things, was fast giving way, and the proud man felt as we all must feel some time: he was growing old.

How vain were all his vast possessions, as long as they failed to bring him happiness. Yes, there was the great secret. He had lived in vain. He had buoyed himself up with the belief that he was happy, while all the time the knowledge of ruin was nestled like a canker worm at his heart. But he had resolutely banished all thought of that one dark epoch in his life's history.

The colonel had become strangely unlike himself of late. He was unusually taciturn when in the presence of his family, and spent hours alone in his retreat, communing with his own sad thoughts. He would allow his mind to wander far back through the dim shadowy vista of the past, which was thronged with accusing spirits. Remorseless memory dragged to light those scenes he had been for years striving to forget. Long silenced conscience was doing her work, and remorse, if not penitence, was fast tugging at the heartstrings of the stubborn old man. He groaned aloud, and perspiration bathed the pale brow, and saturated the heavy masses of hair.

"Why is it," he exclaimed excitedly, "the pale face of Claire Neville haunts my sleeping and waking hours, follows me like an avenging spirit? Her voice and smile madden me. Fool that I am to allow myself to be thus

257

imprisoned." And the colonel made a desperate but vain attempt to rally his spirits.

"This is more than useless," he exclaimed. "Oh, Richard, my son! my son! my punishment is indeed greater than I can bear! A thousand times have I bitterly execrated that deed. My curse has recoiled upon my own head. Oblivion would be a heaven, but even that is denied me." He bowed his head upon his hands, as if to shut out the horrid picture that would present itself to his perturbed imagination. What was it to the guilty, wretched man, if the beautiful sunbeams deepened and faded, if the birds sang cheerily, and the flowers diffused their rich fragrance throughout the apartment? What was it to him if the wealth of mind, of poet, sage and statesman, loomed above him? He heeded not the setting sun, as the rays of his glory departed, and were hid behind a bank of gold and purple clouds. He heeded not the rosy twilight, freighted with the chirpings of myriads of insects. And all unheeded, the little stars came trooping forth, and pale Phoebus shed her mellow rays upon all God's creatures. The high and lowly, the happy and miserable, the good and wicked, alike shared her beneficence. Truly the hour of retribution comes to all.

Hours passed unheeded, the conscience stricken man sat motionless, absorbed in grief. Years had passed since he had looked upon his son. Strange, that he had never thought to visit the picture in the old library. Years had passed since he had crossed the bloodstained threshold. An irresistible inclination to visit that picture seemed to take possession of him. Yes, he would go. But it seemed very like weakness. He did not wish to be observed visiting the old library, which the Negroes regarded with superstitious dread and conversed in suppressed whispers as they passed it. No, it would not do to allow any one to know of this visit, and as a safeguard against unpleasant comments, he concluded to wait until the inmates of the household were buried in slumber, then, unobserved, wend his way to the library.

Music, mirth, and laughter were wafted to his ears on the night air, from the parlors. Evidently there was no sorrow there. At length the songs and laughter were hushed. He heard the "Good night," spoken in many tones, as the group in the parlor separated for the night. He waited an hour longer, and taking a small lamp, with cautious steps, threaded his way through the shadowy halls. It was rather humiliating to be stealing through his own house like a thief, at midnight. He cautiously approached the door, paused, and listened; he thought—was almost certain that he heard voices within. Listening a moment longer, and hearing nothing, he thought it only a freak of his perturbed imagination. Inserting his key in the lock, with one effort the heavy oaken door swung back, disclosing to his astonished gaze, his wife and Claire Neville standing before the veiled picture, their faces white with terror. What had brought these two women to the bloodstained library, at that hour? Again, the likeness of Claire Neville to his son, arrested his attention. He gazed alternately, with staring eyes upon the portrait of

Richard, and the pale, trembling girl. It must be; it must be, he muttered, half audibly; but the proof, the proof.

Mrs. Tracy, from weakness and excessive fright, had fainted, and now rested like a broken lily upon Claire's bosom, who turned her imploring gaze upon Colonel Tracy, and said: "For the love of heaven take your wife; I fear this fright will kill her."

CHAPTER XVII.

June 17, 1865

MISSING—This chapter appeared in an issue of the *Christian Recorder* that has yet to be located.

CHAPTER XVIII.

June 24, 1865

Dr. Singleton at Work.

After a lapse of eighteen years we renew our acquaintance with the somewhat eccentric, but worthy son of Aesculapius, Dr. Singleton. The doctor is slightly changed during these long years, and presents a pleasing picture of healthy old age. His white hair is swept back from a brow somewhat furrowed by arduous labors, constant study, and the passage of years, which have all left a greater or less impression. But his eagle eye retains its wonted fire, and his powerful mind the vigor of his youthful days. The doctor is as genial as in the olden time. He has no skeleton which he seeks to hide from the gaze of all others, and which he himself looks upon with a strange fascination and horrid dread. The doctor is very popular, and his professional services are in great demand.

During many visits to various patients, he heard the all-absorbing topic of the day fully discussed and commented upon. Col. Tracy's Yankee governess had created a great sensation throughout the upper circles. Once, too, he caught a slight glimpse of the sweet, fair face, as he was hurriedly whirled past Col. Tracy's carriage, in which were seated Col. Tracy's children and their governess. That pale, sad face brought in its wake the memory of another face, patient and suffering. He turned and looked eagerly after the carriage, which, with its burden of youth and beauty, was fast retreating in the distance.

I must know more of that young lady, he mentally decided. He discovered that the governess was the prevailing subject under discussion. Dame Rumor and Madam Gossip vied with each other in furnishing a proper solution to the inexplicable problem. The old doctor said nothing, but carefully noting the opinion of the masses, was able to form an idea of his own, and, with his usual acuteness, was very nearly correct.

"Now," said he, "if I could get trace of Manville, I think I could solve this mystery. If not by direct inquiry, perhaps by strategy I could gain the necessary information. I must make inquiry concerning his whereabouts."

The doctor was one of those with whom to think is to act. He immediately ordered dinner, after which, donning his hat and gloves, he sallied forth upon his tour of observation, and hoped for discovery. He knew that Manville had gradually degenerated from a gentlemanly coxcomb into a confirmed roue. He had often noticed the flushed and dim eyes of Manville, who passed him with unsteady step and shrinking eye. But it had been a long while now, since he had seen or heard any thing of Manville. The doctor, with a zeal worthy of him, made inquiry in various directions without eliciting the desired information. The old gentleman was not to be discouraged, but pertinaciously questioned everyone whom he thought knew aught of Manville. He visited the haunts of vice and dissipation, with the hope of being able to hear something, but in vain.

Weeks passed, and he had failed as yet in gaining the desired knowledge. But tardy fortune at last smiled upon him. He learned, from a low, hired trader, that Manville had been seriously wounded, while intoxicated, at one of the fashionable restaurants and gambling saloons that infest the Crescent City, and was now slowly dragging out the remainder of his life, a miserable cripple, with the attending horrors of an accusing conscience.

The doctor lost no time in searching out his former acquaintance. In a dilapidated old building, far out of the city, Dr. Singleton found George Manville, the once handsome, gay, reckless, and iniquitous young man, now prematurely old, and trembling upon the verge of the grave, his mind assailed by a myriad of torturing thoughts, and the great wrong he had done Richard Tracy was not the least.

He was attended by an indifferent mulatto girl, who promptly answered all the doctor's queries, and conducted him without ceremony to Manville's apartment, which was sadly in need of a regenerating spirit.

Manville looked annoyed, as the bustling old gentleman proceeded to throw open the small windows and doors that a current of fresh air might penetrate the squalid room.

"You are dying, man, for the want of pure air! You must have air, and plenty of it, too, or you will not live a week! This is murder, nothing short of murder! Who is your medical advisor?"

This question was followed by a dozen others, all asked in one breath, and before Manville had time to answer the first. The doctor then turned his attention to Manville, and found indeed, that there was no hope of his recovery. The sick man was conscious of his state, and was at times perfectly indifferent to his fate. Again he seemed terrified by the visions his perturbed imagination conjured up. On the day of the doctor's visit, he was comparatively quiet. The old gentleman restrained his curiosity, and did not ask any questions during his first visit, but tried to render the sick man comfortable, and to put him at his ease in his presence, which it was quite evident he was far from feeling.

Every day Dr. Singleton wended his way out of the city, and might be seen entering the dilapidated old building. The sick room soon appeared to far greater advantage, for under the doctor's direction, Elynthia had effected a most wonderful change.

Manville had learned to like the eccentric old gentleman, whose quaint speeches and genial smile dispelled a portion of the gloom that surrounded him, and he watched eagerly for the hour that would bring the promised visit. He grew weaker and weaker as the sultry days passed, and the doctor thought it was not best to delay the subject any longer, and one afternoon, when Manville seemed somewhat lively, after a few introductory remarks, he said:

"Manville, do you ever hear of Richard Tracy? I have found his child, and wish to find means of communicating with him."

CHAPTER XIX.

July 1, 1865

A Summons.

With a wildly beating heart, Claire wended her way to the library, where Col. Tracy impatiently awaited her. When she entered he greeted her with a strange blending of tenderness and formality. Claire sunk trembling into one of the huge chairs which was extending its kindly arms towards her. She glanced at the Colonel. He looked pale, and the hard lines about the proud mouth had strangely softened, and an inquiring light beamed from his dark eyes, as he bent them searchingly upon the face of the young girl. After taking several rapid turns across the library, he seated himself where he could obtain a full view of Claire's face, and said:

"Miss Neville, the striking resemblance which you bear to members of my family has deeply interested me, and created the desire to know something of your parents and early life. Do not hesitate to tell me," he said, encouragingly, "it is from purely disinterested motives that I seek this information. Sad events have transpired in my family in years passed, and a clear, concise statement of facts in relation to your parentage and childhood may serve to throw light upon several little circumstances which have always proved inexplicable to me."

Claire colored painfully as she felt that she must confess the humiliating truth. She knew nothing of her parents, not even their names. It was a comparatively easy matter to speak of this to Mrs. Tracy, but to talk with the stern old colonel was quite another thing. She, however, summoned sufficient courage to reply.

"What I know of my friendless, lonely childhood, I will willingly tell you, but of my parents I know nothing. I was raised by a colored nurse, who lives a few miles from the village of L—. I lived a wild, joyous life until my twelfth year, when I was placed at L— Seminary to be educated, at the expense of a stranger. True, the gentleman had been in the habit of visiting Juno at long intervals, and talking mysteriously of me, and sometimes talking of someone whom they called Richard. (Col. Tracy moved a little nearer to Claire.) The gentleman was handsome, tall, and dark. He often tried to win my confidence, but I shrank instinctively from him. His handsome face was

267

repulsive in the extreme. For a long time I did not even know his name. At the last visit he paid Juno before I was placed at the Seminary, he dropped a handkerchief, which bore on one corner the name of—"

"Who?" interrupted the colonel, totally unable to be silent longer.

"George Manville!" continued Claire, "I kept the handkerchief and have always thought he was in some way connected with my parents."

"I thought so, I thought so!" said the colonel excitedly. Then turning to Claire, he asked: "How long is it since you saw George Manville?"

"Six years ago, this spring."

"Would you know him again?"

"His face seems stamped upon my memory."

"I am glad of that, for George Manville lives in New Orleans, and you shall see him, and perhaps learn something of your parents. By the way, have you no little memento or keepsake that belonged to your father or mother?"

"Only this," sliding a beautiful little ring, Juno's parting gift, from her finger, and handing it to Col. Tracy.

The initials "R.T. to L." seemed to be engraved in letters of fire.

"This was your mother's?" he said, inquiringly.

"It was," replied Claire, "Juno gave it to me just before I started South."

"Juno must know all about your parents," said the colonel, as he finished examining, and returned the glittering ring.

"She does," replied Claire, "but she would never tell me any thing in regard to them. I remember she was greatly excited when she learned that I was to be governess in your family, and said, 'What would Master Richard say of your going to be governess in that proud family?' I asked who Richard was, and importuned her, as I had many times before, to tell me who my parents were. But, as on all similar occasions, she remained obstinately silent. My resemblance to your daughter first excited Mr. and Mrs. Harrington's astonishment, who, as many others here, thought that I must be a relative of the family."

"Your appearance certainly verifies the supposition, and it may be proved that those suppositions are correct. One thing is certain, we must find George Manville, and obtain the knowledge we wish from him. It will be necessary to see Juno in the course of our investigation. I am somewhat apprehensive of finding Manville right away, as I think he is out of the city. However, I will find out where he is."

An hour passed in conversation without eliciting any thing new. Col. Tracy prepared to go out in search of George Manville. Claire was leaving the library when Col. Tracy requested that she should come to the library again at nine o'clock that evening, and he would report what success he had met with. Claire was strangely distracted all the afternoon, and little Nellie opened her brown eyes with astonishment, to find her poorly learned French lesson passed over without a reprimand, or even a gentle rebuke, from her teacher. While taking their music lesson, the same abstraction was visible. Her mind was in a chaos of hope and fear, doubt and perplexity.

Count Sayvord was lounging through the parlors with the air of man who is at a loss to know what disposal to make of time. He carelessly turned the leaves of elegantly bound volumes. Paintings and rare gems of art were looked at or handled with the same careless indifference. He tried to interest himself by looking at the beautiful grounds beyond the verandah, but some how his eyes would wander to where a graceful figure presided at the piano. When the lesson ended, the children pleaded for their accustomed song. Claire would gladly have excused herself, but Sayvord, who had joined the group, pleaded for just one song. Without further importuning, Claire sang an old ballad, which accorded well with her perturbed state of mind. Doubtless it touched an answering chord in the Count's heart, for he joined her in singing, and together their rich voices penetrated the hall, through which Isabelle was passing. She clenched her white hands until the pink, shell-like nails penetrated the tender flesh. The glittering black eyes spoke volumes of hate for the unconscious songstress. When the song ended, Claire sought her own room to think over the exciting events of the last twenty-four hours. In a little while Rose entered, holding a neat little volume of Tennyson's poems very gingerly.

"Massa Count Sayvord say to present dis book, and hopes you will 'ruse it well."

A little exclamation of surprise escaped Claire as she took the book from the young girl. Rose left the room. As Claire mechanically opened the little volume, a white note fluttered to the floor. She picked it up. It ran as follows:

> *MISS NEVILLE:*
> *I hope you will pardon my seeming boldness. I have something of importance to communicate. This must be my excuse. Say that I can see you and when.*
> *Respectfully,*
> *SAYVORD.*

Scarcely had the astonished girl finished the perusal of Sayvord's strange note, when Rose reappeared, and placed the following note in her hand:

> *CLAIRE NEVILLE:*
> *George Manville is dying. He wishes to see you. Come immediately in my carriage. Lose not a moment, or you may be too late.*
> *DR. SINGLETON*

CHAPTER XX.

July 8, 1865

Death.

Dr. Singleton knew well how cautious Manville was, and how jealously he guarded his secret, and determined to use no false delicacy, but abruptly to ask the question around which clustered such great interests. The question was certainly abrupt, and some might feel inclined to censure the doctor a little harshly for his injudicious haste but the doctor knew well the character he had to deal with.

Manville was startled by the question, so unlooked for, and which seemed indeed an echo of his own sad and troubled thoughts. And the emphatic avowal of the old gentleman, "I have found his daughter and wish to find means of communicating with him," startled him. He looked slightly disconcerted an instant, but resting his emaciated, trembling hand on Dr. Singleton's arm, said, in earnest and impressive tones, "I would give the slight hold I have upon life this instant, if I could see Richard Tracy, and just talk with him one hour. I have wronged him, how deeply God alone knows, and the thought is terrifying that I must die with this accursed memory of crime clinging to my mind. I have not the least idea where Richard is."

"I heard from a party of travelers a few years ago," said the doctor, "that he had been traveling restlessly about for years, and at last settled in the southern part of France, and was living the life of a recluse, seeking the society of none and visited by few."

"It seems hard," said Manville, "to die without being allowed to make even the slight restitution of which I am capable. I know that I cannot live much longer, for I am growing weaker with each passing breath, but I cannot die until I have atoned as far as lies in my power for the wrong done Richard Tracy. I could not live to see Richard touch our American shores again. Tell me, doctor, what shall I do?"

Dr. Singleton mused a moment, and said, "Write your confession, and I will promise to find Tracy, if he is living, and deliver it safely to him."

A spasm of pain distorted the pale face of Manville, as he expressively raised his mutilated right hand.

"I see," said the old man, "I was thoughtless, stupid, if you will, to forget that you had lost the use of that hand." The old gentleman looked thoughtful a moment, and then said, "Perhaps I could act as your amanuensis. If you wish, I will do so."

"I have been thinking of asking you to do so for some time," replied Manville, "but hesitated to request such a sacrifice of your time, which, I know, is so valuable."

"Oh, never mind the time!" said the doctor, good-naturedly. "Only tell me just what you want to say. Do not let false delicacy, nor any other motive, cause you to hesitate in making the last slight amendment for a lifetime of wrong."

"Have no fear of that," said Manville. "Doctor, if you have writing materials at hand, we will begin now, for I feel that should we delay another day, it will be too late."

Dr. Singleton glanced at his patient, and felt his words to be true. Another day and it would be too late. Drawing a light stand to the side of the couch, and placing upon it the necessary articles, Dr. Singleton pronounced himself ready. Many times during the afternoon the old doctor was obliged to stop writing, to assist Elynthia in preparing stimulants and fanning Manville, who was sinking rapidly, while a mortal paleness overspread his countenance, and he spoke with difficulty. And at last the doctor had to bend his ear, to catch the faintly whispered words, but the dread confession once made, he seemed to breathe easier, and when he saw the manuscript made into a neat little package, and safely lodged in the doctor's capacious pocket, his dim eyes seemed to brighten for a moment, as he faintly whispered his thanks.

"Is there any thing more I can do for you?" asked Dr. Singleton.

"Nothing, Doctor."

"Is there any one whom you would like to see?"

"No one but Claire Tracy; were it possible for me to see her, and receive her forgiveness for the great wrong I have done her, I think I could die in peace."

"You shall see her," said the doctor, and he hurriedly penned a short note to Claire Neville, and dispatched his colored boy with his carriage to Col. Tracy's mansion.

In the mean time Manville was kept perfectly quiet, but his dim eyes were ever turned toward the door, and it was evident that he was intently listening for the arrival of the carriage. It came at last. There were footsteps in the narrow hall; the boy was not alone. A moment more and Claire Neville was ushered into the presence of the dying man. Dr. Singleton led her to the side of the couch, when Manville imploringly reached forth his left hand, and said, with difficulty:

"I am dying. I have wronged you deeply, but can you forgive me? Say that you can, and I die in peace."

"I forgive you," said the sweet voice of Claire, "as I hope my Father in heaven will forgive me."

"Tell Richard, when he returns, that my last breath was spent trying, and I hope not vainly, to undo some of the great wrong I have done him."

"I will do all you ask," said Claire. "But have you sought the forgiveness of One before whom you must stand to pass a solemn test. I can and do freely forgive you the wrong you have done me: only assure me that you are prepared to die, prepared to meet your God," and the pale, lovely creature, in her earnestness, had taken the hand of the dying man in both hers, and tears, large and pearly, fell upon Manville's face. He looked startled, and whispered, with thrilling earnestness:

"Pray for me, for I am not prepared. I cannot meet my God."

Claire knelt by the couch and fervently commended the soul which was fast approaching the gates of death to the mercy of the all wise Father. The last effort of Manville had been too much for his enfeebled state. A few crimson spots upon the white counterpane told the startling truth.

"A hemorrhage," said the doctor softly, as he gently placed Manville in a more comfortable position. It was pitiful to witness the appealing look, in the glazing eyes, as they rested upon Dr. Singleton's face. Thus he died without one hope expressed in the great hereafter—died with the last rays of the setting sun, which fell lovingly upon the head of the kneeling girl. Dr. Singleton was deeply moved, and after regaining his composure, gently faced Claire and led her from the chamber of death. While placing her in the carriage, he said, taking her small hand in his, "Take courage, child, all will yet be well. The darkest hour precedes the dawn."

CHAPTER XXI.

July 15, 1865

Little Nellie's First Sorrow.

Heartsick and weary, Claire sank back in the carriage, and was only roused from a painful reverie by their arrival at Col. Tracy's. Sayvord was sitting on the verandah, and regarded her earnestly as she walked slowly up the path with a sad, pale face, upon which remained the traces of recent tears. His presence reminded her of his requested interview.

As she was passing in the door little Nellie came bounding to her side, and said, while the beautiful brown eyes filled with tears,

"Mamma has been so sick, and she wanted to see you and you were gone, and papa was not here. Sister Belle and the servants did not know how to relieve her as you do, dear Miss Neville."

While Nellie was talking Claire was rapidly ascending the stairs. Divesting herself of bonnet and shawl, she hastened to Mrs. Tracy's room. Isabelle was sitting by the bed side, and several of the servants were in attendance. Isabelle's were the only eyes that did not smile a welcome to Claire as she entered the apartment.

Mrs. Tracy wearily opened her eyes, and, as her glance fell upon her young friend, an exclamation of glad surprise escaped her lips. But at last, noticing Claire's pale, careworn face, she said, reproachfully,

"It is very selfish in me to wish for your attendance when you are ill yourself, but I have missed you sadly today. I have been suffering with a nervous headache, but I am better now, and you must retire early; for I see you are suffering as well as myself, and need rest. Isabelle can remain with me if I need any one."

Claire hastened to assure her she was not ill, and preferred to remain with her. And Isabelle, thinking of Sayvord, who was the sole occupant of the parlor, said,

"Yes, mamma, I think Miss Neville had better stay with you," and without waiting to hear her mother's remonstrance, swept from the room, and descended to the parlor, while Claire remained to soothe the weary invalid.

Sayvord had been anxiously waiting for a note or message from Claire, and now, as he heard light footsteps approaching, and the faint rustle of female garments, he hoped it might be her. His expressive face plainly betrayed his disappointment as the vision, not of the stately Claire, but the haughty Isabelle, dawned upon him. He rose with more haste than politeness, and coldly bowing to the discomfited young lady, left the room. Slowly the color faded from the beautiful face, and the black eyes were dilated with rage as she murmured the one expressive word, infatuated, and with that detested Yankee governess. A few moments she sat looking the very embodiment of anger and disappointment, then taking a seat at the piano, made it fairly tremble beneath her fingers, as she rattled through polkas, waltzes, quadrilles, and quicksteps, in a manner that would have astonished our Claire; but it served somewhat in calming her excited feelings.

Claire possessed a sort of mesmeric influence over Mrs. Tracy. The soft touch of her velvet-like hands, the soothing tones of her sweet, musical voice, her swift, quiet movements as she flitted here and there through the apartment, were sleep-provoking in the extreme.

Nellie Tracy was soon calmly sleeping, and Claire sat by the window so quietly, that Lloyd, looking in his mother's room as he passed down to supper, did not notice the still figure sitting half-concealed by the light curtains, and wondered why her chair was vacant? Why, was it not enough to be absent from dinner? Where could she be? Sayvord and Col. Tracy, too, asked themselves the question: Where could she be? Little Nellie could scarcely eat for looking at the vacant chair by her side, and wondering what kept Miss Neville so long, thinking she must be very hungry. She did not eat any dinner either, thought the little one; she is almost starved I know. I'll go and ask mamma to let her come down to supper; and, intent upon her purpose, her kind, little heart filled with concern for the dear governess, whom her vivid imagination pictured as bordering on the state of starvation. Suddenly dropping her knife and fork, she slid from her chair, and ran hastily up stairs, never stopping until she reached her mother's room. Standing on tip-toe by the bed she could see that her mother was sleeping. Coming close to Claire's side, she peered earnestly into the sad, pale face, while the large eyes filled with tears, and a nervous twitching was visible about the corners of her rosy mouth.

"What is it, darling?" asked Claire, seeing the child was deeply agitated.

"You didn't eat any dinner, and now you are not coming down to supper," said she, and one after another, great tears rolled over her round cheeks and fell upon Claire's hand.

"Who thought there is one, at least, who thinks and cares for me," thought Claire, and she kissed the sweet one who pleaded so hard for her to only go to supper.

Claire would gladly have gone with the little girl, but she felt how utterly impossible it would be for her to eat one mouthful in her present state of mind, so she said:

"You are very thoughtful, Nellie, and I thank you very much for thinking of me. I do not wish any supper, and could not eat if I should go down, so you must excuse me tonight."

Nellie resolutely kept back her tears as she thought whatever ailed Miss Neville must be very bad. A person that hadn't eaten any dinner and yet didn't want any supper was a case beyond her childish comprehension. Without another word she turned, and went slowly back to the tea-room.

Sayvord had guessed her object in leaving the table, and looked disappointed when she returned alone. One glance at the vacant chair, and the little girl's fortitude gave way, and she sobbed aloud.

Col. Tracy looked surprised. "What is the matter with my little Nellie?" he asked.

"Why, she won't come," sobbed Nellie, unable to proceed for the moment.

"Who won't come?" asked her father, somewhat mystified as to her meaning.

"Why, Miss Neville won't come down to supper, and she had no dinner. I know she is awful tired and hungry, for she is just as pale. Oh dear, oh dear," she said, pushing back her plate, "I don't want any supper either."

"I would not act so foolishly if a dozen Miss Nevilles would not come to their supper," said Belle, petulantly.

While Lloyd's sense of the ludicrous was so strong, that, utterly unable to suppress his risibles, his merry laugh echoed through the room, much to the distress of Nellie, who, fearing she had no sympathizers, utterly refused to be comforted, and, leaving the room, went out on the verandah, where she now sat looking very disconsolate.

Jim had been a quiet, though not an uninterested, spectator of the scene at the table, and the result was that he soon appeared by Nellie's side bearing a small tray, on which was a slice of delicately browned toast, a cup of fragrant tea, and several choice delicacies, very neatly arranged.

"Miss Nellie," said he, "let us take Miss Neville her supper."

Nellie had not thought of this, and the idea struck her as a good one and together they ascended the stairs followed by the earnest eyes of Count Sayvord.

Chapter XXII.

July 22, 1865

Across the Atlantic.

The scene changes. From the troubled household of the Tracy's, in the old Crescent City, we find ourselves transferred across the wide Atlantic, to the elegant country seat of Clayburn Sayvord, in the southern part of France, a few miles north of the beautiful city of Marseilles.

In a richly furnished apartment sit two gentlemen, quietly discussing the merits of a late breakfast. Let us closely observe them. The elder of the two, a little bright-eyed, sharp-nosed, old gentleman of nearly sixty, very diminutive in size, and faultless in style of dress, is Clayburn Sayvord. A pair of gold spectacles bestrode the sharp nose, through which the little gray eyes seemed to twinkle, as it were, with very kindness. His general appearance, from the hair of his carefully adjusted wig, to the tips of his elegant French boots, of the most delicate proportions, bespoke a good-natured, but very particular man—very precise in all his dealings with the world, shrewd and far-seeing. He was wont, when pleased, to rub his small, claw-like hands together much after the fashion of a pleased child. The character of the old gentleman will portray itself through the following chapters of our narrative.

The sad, thoughtful browed man who sat opposite, with large, melancholy black eyes, which mirrored forth a world of sadness from their quiet depths, is none other than our old friend Richard Tracy. But sorrow, not the flight of years, has furrowed the noble brow, and bowed the tall, lithe form; but it is our Richard still, with the old, sweet, winning smile. He comes to us again, after the lapse of many years, with heart and principles unchanged—the uncompromising advocate of equity and justice—the friend of the oppressed, and a bitter enemy of the accursed system of slavery, and its twin evil, Caste. Bitterly had he realized, and to its greatest extent, the misery, the horror, the degradation, and even crime, embodied in the sentence "The curse of caste." Would that the word could be blotted out at once and forever, from the memory of man.

Clayburn Sayvord was well acquainted with Richard's early history, and it was the topic of conversation this morning. Their conversation was brought to a close by the appearance of Pierre Dupont, *the valet de chambre*, laden with dispatches, letters and papers, which he heaped upon a small silver tray, and placed by M. Sayvord's side, who, rubbing his hands gleefully said:

"Really, this looks like business."

He passed the papers to Richard who had received no letters by this mail, settled himself more comfortably in his chair, and prepared to read the letters from his numerous correspondents. The dispatches were read and carefully laid aside. Letter after letter was perused, when he took up rather a bulky letter, bearing the New Orleans postmark.

"A letter from your old home," he said, looking at Richard. "From the Count," he continued, as he carefully polished the glass, and readjusted the gold spectacles. Then, carefully re-settling himself in his chair, (by the way, M. Sayvord did every thing carefully) the better to digest the contents of the letter, which certainly was long, and promised to be interesting. After reading a little while, Monsieur became very red in the face, and altogether quite fidgety, casting frequent and expressive glances at Richard, who was deeply absorbed in a speech of Lord Brougham's, but was finally attracted by Monsieur's frequent exclamations, such as, "O!" "Wonderful!" and so on, to the end of the chapter of interjections. He could not suppress a smile as M. Clayburn Sayvord, laying down the letter, polished his glasses again, and this time most carefully adjusted them to prepare to read it the second time, after which he turned to Richard abruptly, and said, with startling distinctness:

"Tracy, did it never occur to you that there may have been some mistake in the reported death of your child? Have you proof that the child died? Do you know where it was buried? What do you know, or do you know any thing about the matter?" asked the excited little man (while the glasses were in imminent danger of another removal).

Richard's heart throbbed painfully, as he thought what these strange questions might presage. He hardly dared allow himself to think. Had he not trusted too implicitly in the honor of others?

"I have no proof but Manville's word. He wrote that my infant daughter died immediately after birth, and was entombed with its mother. I visited Lina's grave before leaving the United States."

"But where was Juno, the black nurse?" asked Monsieur. "Could she not have told better than any one else?"

"Juno was devoted to my frail young wife, and I never could quite understand why she went away without waiting to see me. She must have known that I would come. I gave Manville permission to do with every thing as he deemed best. The cottage and furniture became the home and property of Mr. Villars. Juno had moved away, but where, they (the Villars) could not tell. But why this strange questioning? What does it portend?"

"Read the Count's letter," was Monsieur's only reply, as he passed the letter to Richard.

Count Sayvord, in his letter, had given a most minute description of Claire Neville, her advent in the Tracy family, her striking resemblance to the family, the mystified air of Colonel Tracy and Lloyd, the astonishment of the

Negroes, the hatred of the haughty Isabelle toward the beautiful Yankee governess, were all faithfully drawn. One paragraph read as follows:

There is a sad story connected with this family. Uncle, you remember Richard Tracy, the sad browed man who was visiting you at the country seat, some years ago? Well, that same Richard is Col. Tracy's oldest son. His marriage displeased his father, though for what reason I have yet to learn, but it is believed by everyone that Claire is the offspring of that marriage, and the granddaughter of Col. Tracy. Of course, there is no proof of such being the true state of affairs, but I with all others, believe it to be the true version of the case. I have determined to unravel the mystery, let it be what it will. If Richard Tracy is with you, or you know where he is, tell him of Claire Neville, and all I have written to you of the family. Learn what you can of his life history, and transmit the same to me without delay. I will keep you well informed as to my success.

Your nephew,

SAYVORD.

CHAPTER XXIII.

July 29, 1865

This Side of the Atlantic.

Monsieur Sayvord finished the reading of his letters, and glanced anxiously at Richard, who was sitting motionless, absorbed in thought, with the open letter before him. Monsieur wondered what he could be thinking of, that he did not speak.

Yes, Richard was thinking. Far back through the hazy vistas of the past, came sweet and bitter memories, hand in hand. Again he stood with his lovely betrothed upon the deck of the noble Alhambra,—again he pressed to his heart the trembling form of his blushing bride, and imprinted the first husband's kiss upon her pure brow. Again he and his gentle Lina were the happy inmates of Rose Cottage, while Juno, sitting 'neath the shade of the lofty tamaracks, forced a pleasing picture in the background. Again he was parting with—was looking for the last time upon the sweet, pale face shadowed by undefined sorrow. The journey South; the interview with his angry father; the long, weary days when his spirits feebly fluctuated between life and death; his partial recovery; the weary, weary, waiting for the letter which would never come again; Manville's visit to Rose Cottage; the letter; the death of his wife and child; the darker days which followed, when his unceasing prayer had been that he too, might die,—might sleep the long, dreamless sleep, which knows no waking here on earth; that last visit to his young wife's grave; his departure from the United States, and the long years of lonely wandering, of aimless existence, that followed. All passed, in rapid review before his mind's eye.

Now came this letter from Count Sayvord, so strange as to appear impossible, that this young girl, whom the Count speaks of as being strangely beautiful and accomplished, could be his child. No. It could not be.

Had not Manville written that the child had died, and was buried with its young mother? Had he not visited their lone grave on the hillside, where the twinkling stars kept nightly vigil, and the night winds sighed a requiem for the loved and early lost. No, it could not be. But all the while his heart thrilled strangely. And the name of Claire Neville, where had he heard it before? It sounded strangely familiar. A moment of intense thought, and he had solved the mystery surrounding the name of Claire Neville. He had often heard Lina speak of a dear school friend, bearing that name. This knowledge suggested another thought, and a tiny spark of hope burned in his heart. A hope that this Claire, so far away, between himself and whom rolled the waters of the wide Atlantic, might prove to be his own dear child.

So he thought on, unconscious of Monsieur, who sat opposite, nearly convulsed with excitement and curiosity suppressed, trying to school his patience until Richard should speak. But time sped on; an hour had passed, yet Richard moved not, spoke not,—only hoped and dreamed on, with the open letter before him. Monsieur looked uneasily at Richard, fidgeted about in his chair, and finally got up and put his letters and papers away, hoping thus to attract the attention of his friend, but in vain. What should he do to arouse him? The expediency of the letter being answered immediately presented itself. Hastily crossing the room, he laid his hand upon Richard's shoulder, and said, very emphatically:

"Tracy, this letter must be answered this hour, in order to catch the first mail, which leaves at 4 PM It is now half past twelve. So you see, man, it behooves us to be moving."

This had the desired effect. Richard was awake, and ready to begin the work before him. Monsieur rang the bell, ordered the breakfast dishes removed, and writing materials placed in their stead. For a long while no sound was heard save that caused by rapidly moving pens, over vast sheets of snowy paper, and at precisely five minutes of four o'clock, two bulky letters were sealed and directed, and Pierre Dupont summoned to mail them.

Richard had faithfully narrated every incident connected with his married life, that could serve in any way to throw light upon the real parentage of the young girl, with the urgent request that Count Sayvord would learn all facts relating to the childhood of Claire Neville, and compare them with his letters, and, knowing his anxiety, to write to him at length.

Upon the reception of these letters, Count Sayvord felt more confident than ever that Claire was Richard Tracy's daughter, and upon the strength of these letters he resolved to ask her confidence, and then tell her all he had learned.

With this object in view, he penned a hasty note requesting an interview, and dispatched it by Rose in a small volume of Tennyson's poems, and waited impatiently for a reply. He saw Claire depart a few minutes afterwards, attended only by a young Negro boy. He noted the exceeding paleness of her face, and wondered what was the meaning of so strange a proceeding. He seated himself upon the verandah to await her return.

The Count was beginning to grow restless, and glanced frequently up and down the long street, when the carriage rolled into view. He watched her with a tender light in his large blue eyes, as she stepped slowly and wearily up the long walk. Her pale face was worn and weary. He expected, at least, to see her at tea time, but she did not appear. He sympathized heartily in little Nellie's sorrow. He knew Claire was suffering, and he determined to reward Jim handsomely for his thoughtfulness of the governess' welfare.

Jim and Nellie entered the room very quietly, so as not to wake Mrs. Tracy. Nellie hastily transferred the books and ornaments from a small stand to a chair, placed the stand by Claire's side, upon which Jim placed the silver tray with a well-pleased air.

"Now, Miss Neville, you must drink some of this tea. 'Tis the very best, and Aunt Hopsy says it will do you as much good as the 'tents of a hull potecary shop.'"

Claire smiled faintly, and Nellie said, coaxingly:

"Please, Miss Neville, eat just a little supper. If you don't, I'll tell papa to send for Doctor Thorne, and then you will wish you had taken my advice, if I am a little girl."

Nellie, with an assumption of great dignity, motioned Jim to follow her, and softly closing the door, they went down stairs.

Claire did not offer to taste the contents of the little tray, but pressing her fingers to her aching brow, longed for the hour of nine, when she was to meet Col. Tracy. Then she would be at liberty to retire. She turned to look at the little clock on the mantle, but she could not distinguish the figures. The little timepiece usually so staid and orderly, was actually executing a pirouette, after the most approved fashion. Vases and perfumery bottles, and various little mantle and table ornaments, seemed to be infected with the same spirit, and were merrily

"Tripping the light fantastic-toe"

The chairs were very neighborly, and were rapidly changing position. The pictures on the wall expressed their approbation of the proceedings by swinging lazily back and forth.

"I must be going crazy," murmured Claire, tightly pressing her burning brow. Then bursting into a wild, hysterical laugh, she fell heavily to the floor.

That laugh, so wild and ringing, followed by the heavy fall, awoke Mrs. Tracy, who, in her extreme fright, alternately screamed and pulled the bell-cord.

CHAPTER XXIV.

August 5, 1865

Poor Claire.

The frantic cries of Mrs. Tracy, together with the violent ringing of the bell in the servant's hall, brought the entire household to her assistance. Lloyd was first to enter the apartment. He advanced towards his mother, while surprise and alarm were plainly portrayed upon his fine face. Mrs. Tracy motioned him back, and pointed to the prostrate form of Claire. An exclamation of mingled astonishment and regret escaped his lips, and he gently raised the inanimate form to the sofa, as Col. Tracy, Sayvord, and Isabelle entered, followed by a troop of frightened Negroes, whose dusky faces thronged every available door and window. A hurried consultation was held, and Jim was sent in haste to summon Dr. Thorne, the family physician.

Jim made all possible speed and soon arrived at the residence of Dr. Thorne, which worthy gentleman he found busily discussing the chemical qualities of a new medicine, with none other than our friend, Dr. Singleton.

Jim entered the doctor's study without ceremony. He was quite a favorite with the gentleman, and proceeded, while the doctor was getting ready, to give a short version of the case: how Miss Neville had gone away in a strange carriage, and returned, looking so pale, and just as if she had been crying; how she had refused to come down to supper, and he and Miss Nellie had taken up her tea on the little tray, and left her sitting by the window, looking awful pale; how they had just got down stairs when the bell rang violently, and terrible screams were heard coming from Mrs. Tracy's room; how Col. Tracy and every body ran up stairs, and found Massa Lloyd lifting the governess to the sofa.

"Then I was sent for you," said Jim, ending with a bow, and stood, hat in hand, waiting Dr. Thorne's orders.

The doctor turned to his friend with the intention of apologizing for his hurried departure, when Dr. Singleton precluded the necessity of so doing, by saying,

"Thorne, I am greatly interested in this young lady; besides, I have an object in wishing to be introduced to the Tracy family, and if you have no objection, I will accompany you."

"Very well, you are quite welcome to go, if it be your desire," replied Thorne, wondering much, on their way to the carriage, what could be Singleton's object in wishing so particularly, to become acquainted with the Tracy's, but that he had an object, he did not doubt, for Dr. Singleton was never guilty of jesting.

Arriving at Col. Tracy's, the doctors were shown to Mrs. Tracy's room, and after applying the proper restoratives, it was long ere Claire exhibited signs of returning life. At last, after moving slightly, she slowly opened her large black eyes, and gazed from one to the other of the anxious faces above her, with a bright but meaningless glance. Alas! The light of reason had fled those beautiful orbs. Searchingly the bright eyes seemed to rest upon each face. Isabelle, who had been standing somewhat in the shadow, now stepped directly under the blazing chandelier. When Claire's gaze fell upon her, she uttered a piercing shriek, clasping her hands convulsively over her eyes, as if to shut out some hateful vision.

"Mercy, oh, have mercy!" she shrieked. "Those eyes are burning through my brain. Save me, oh, save me! She will kill me!"

The doctors exchanged glances of surprise, while Isabelle, secretly determining to annoy her as much as possible, turned away with a mocking smile.

Dr. Singleton placed his hand on Claire's brow, much after the fashion he used to do with Richard, and was surprised at the likeness existing between the two. Claire's illness was pronounced brain fever.

"Brought on," added Dr. Singleton, "by unusual excitement, and excessive strain on the mental faculties."

Little Nellie was almost heartbroken, and utterly refused to be comforted. Col. Tracy sought to lead the child from the room, but she utterly refused to go unless first allowed to kiss Miss Neville. Her father lifted her up to kiss the pale, sweet face. Nellie pressed her little, chubby hands to both Claire's cheeks, and kissed her crimson lips repeatedly, while burning tears rolled over her cheeks.

"I will go now, Papa," she said, with a choking voice, and was carried, sobbing, from the room. Laura, less demonstrative than Nellie, passed quietly from the sick room, and sought the deserted parlor, where, unobserved, she could quietly indulge her grief. Claire was a favorite with all the Negroes, and the house that night looked gloomy with their sad, dusky faces.

Claire was delirious all night. Sometimes she raved of great, burning, black eyes. Sometimes of Juno, and her Northern home. Sometimes she called plaintively for Miss Elwood; then she would hold long talks with her dear friend, Ella Summers. Again she would ask, in ringing tones:

"Who am I? Oh, someone tell me! This suspense will kill me. If Richard is my father, why don't he come? Oh, George Manville, why did you rob me of a father's love? It was cruel."

Thus it was for days. No dawning of returned reason for the suffering girl. No dawn of hope for the anxious physicians. It seemed almost in vain that the queenly little head was shorn of its wealth of purple black hair, but Dr. Singleton said that was their last hope. So the barber was called in, and the sharp, glittering, ruthless shears soon severed the heavy mass, which lay, bright and shining, upon the snowy counterpane. Almost in vain it seemed, that every care was bestowed, that every remedy was applied. Vain it seemed, were the prayers of Mrs. Tracy, always joined by dear little Nellie, whose solemn and fervently uttered prayer, "Please God, do make dear Miss Neville well," was affecting to hear. Mrs. Tracy loved and wept over her darling child.

Poor Claire had a warm place in many hearts. And now the old house, void of her sweet smiles and songs, was too lonely. Isabelle wondered if Claire would get well, and every time her glance fell upon that well-shaped head, shorn of its crowning glory, a triumphant smile curled her scornful lips. Isabelle was compelled to visit the room when Claire was sleeping, for during her wakeful hours, Isabelle's presence in the room rendered her almost unmanageable. She imagined Isabelle some destroying spirit from whose baleful influence there was no escape. Thus we leave our Claire for the present, to look after old Juno, the faithful friend and nurse.

CHAPTER XXV.

August 12, 1865

Juno.

Just after you turn the bend in the long, dusty road leading many miles from the thriving town of L—, you can espy through a wilderness of shrubbery, a neat little cottage, almost embowered in green trees and trailing vines. The cottage presents such a pleasing exterior, that we will extend our ramble, and learn something of its inmates. As we pass through the gate and up the neatly arranged walk, our eyes are almost blinded by coming in contact with a pyramid of shining milk pans, which reflect the rays of the sun. Passing the moss-grown well, whose waters look cool and sparkling, we are constrained to quaff a draught from the gourd, hanging at its side. Entering the cozy kitchen, whose snowy chairs, table and floor, with rows of shining tins, and polished cooking stove are forcibly suggestive of neatness and comfort. Baskets filled with newly washed muslins, looking very much like great drifts of snow, were standing waiting the deft hands of the mistress of the cottage, who, standing before one of the snowy tables, is deep in the mysteries of sprinkling.

The countenance, pleasing and familiar, is that of Juno, slightly changed by the lapse of years, only a little more corpulent. We will here state for the satisfaction of the reader, that soon after Claire had entered L— Seminary, Juno, in consideration of her extreme loneliness, had taken to herself a husband. Martin Ray was a worthy, industrious man, with an unlimited confidence in his wife's opinion. They lived quietly and happily together.

On this afternoon, as Juno carefully dampens and rolls the clothes into compact rolls, she thoughtfully soliloquizes:

"No use trying to deceive Juno! I know Claire is in trouble. Something's happened, or what is the meaning of all these strange dreams. Martin said that when I dreamed that Squire Farley's barn burned, it signified hasty news. Martin's going to L— tomorrow. He must go and see Miss Ellwood and ask about the child. It seems an awful while since I heard from Claire, an' this poor old heart is longing for the precious lamb. After all, perhaps I was wrong not to tell Claire who her father was. If I had, she never would have gone to be governess in old Col. Tracy's family. But I always thought it best that Claire should never know she was tainted with black blood. But I must say, this child don't see the difference,—don't see why black blood ain't just as good as white any day! (Unsophisticated Juno, others have asked the same question, without receiving a satisfactory answer). But I always thought Claire would hate me if I told her about it. So I put it off again and again. But it's got to come out some time, and might as well have been first as last. But it is too late now. I didn't tell her before, and somehow I feel that Master Richard *will come*, and tell it all himself. And I believe he will," she said, as she finished laying the white shirts, compactly rolled, into the basket, just as Martin entered, with two brimming pails of milk.

"We must have a good, long talk this evening," she said, as she proceeded to strain the milk into four shining milk pans.

After putting it carefully away in the cool spring-house, she prepared their evening meal, and all the evening chores completed, Martin and Juno repaired to the pleasant, vine-wreathed porch, to have the promised talk. It was late ere they retired, and after Martin had interpreted Juno's dreams for the fiftieth time, perhaps, it was decided that when Martin went to L— on the following day, he should go and see Miss Ellwood and ask her all about Claire.

It was late in the afternoon, and piles of spotless shirts, with bosoms glossy and stiff, displayed the housewife's industry. Juno walked frequently to the door, and shading her eyes from the rays of the setting sun, gazed wistfully down the long, dusty road, and failing to see Martin, returned to her ironing table.

At last she recognized Bobby, Martin's horse, in the distance. She waited their nearer approach, and finding that Martin was not alone, hastened to throw open the pretty little parlor.

"Miss Ellwood, as I live!" exclaimed Juno, delightedly, as she ushered the good lady into the cool and inviting room, and placed the rocking chair for her greater comfort, and impatiently waited to hear what she was indebted for the honor of the visit. Miss Ellwood looked very grave, as she gently said:

"Juno, I am very sorry to be the bearer of bad news."

Juno looked a little frightened, as the lady proceeded to tell how she had received a letter from Col. Tracy, written in great haste, stating that Claire was very ill, perhaps would never recover, and requesting that Miss Ellwood would find Claire's old nurse, and find out who Claire's parents really were, and also obtain any little keepsake or memento that had belonged to either of the parents.

"It is of the utmost importance that we have this proof, and hope you will lose no time in seeking out the black nurse, and transmitting to me the knowledge obtained," wrote Col. Tracy, in conclusion.

"Now, Juno," said Miss Ellwood, addressing the weeping woman, "you must not cry, but sit down here, by my side, and tell me all you know of Claire's father and mother."

Taking out her writing materials, which she had brought with her, she proceeded to narrate the facts as Juno stated them. After finishing the letter, Miss Ellwood asked if there were any letters that had passed between Richard and Lina, or any thing that would assist in unraveling the mystery surrounding her dear young friend.

Juno produced the rosewood box. Miss Ellwood looked over the letters and little ornaments, and finding the certificate of the marriage of Richard and Lina, she proceeded to make them into a package to forward by the next mail to Col. Tracy. After thanking Juno, and bidding her be of good cheer, Miss Ellwood departed.

But we must leave Juno in her quiet cottage home, and hie again to bonny France, and learn what has transpired in our absence.

Chapter XXVI.

August 19, 1865

Richard counted the days and hours it would take his letter to reach the United States, then how long it would take it to reach New Orleans. But, count as he would, it seemed almost an age until he could receive an answer, even if the Count replied immediately. Hours were spent in dreaming over the Claire so far away. Many times he sketched her face, as he imagined it must be beautiful and pale, with hair and eyes intensely black. He would gaze long and lovingly upon the beautiful shadows he created, and hoped the original of the sweet vision might prove to be his child and Lina's. It would be a happiness that language would prove inadequate to express; it would compensate him in a degree for long years of suffering. But then—and the thought came sadly and bitterly—the curse would be upon her, too. That thought was enough to drive all pleasing anticipations far from him, and introduce perplexing and harrowing meditations. So he allowed himself to brood over the matter, and grow more unhappy and very taciturn in consequence thereof.

Mons. Sayvord was wild with excitement and as impatient as his friend to hear from the Western world. He passed the most of his leisure time in trying to conjecture how the affair would end, and if Claire would really prove to be Richard's daughter. Twenty times a day he would startle his friend in the midst of a painful reverie by asking some strange question, which had presented itself to his fertile brain, and as many times declaring his intention of taking a journey to New Orleans himself. "I am an old man, I know," he would add, "but I know I could stand it. Will you go, Richard?" But the latter shrank from the thought of visiting his old home. He had suffered so much, so bitterly, that he deemed the ordeal more than he could bear.

"Pshaw, Tracy, be a man! Such thoughts are unworthy of you! Make up your mind to go and investigate this matter for yourself. Say that you will go, and I will accompany you to the 'land of the free and the home of the brave.'"

They finally concluded to await another letter from the Count. Then, if it should seem necessary, they would start immediately. So they waited impatiently through the long weeks that followed ere the letter came. It came at last—but not so full of hope as they could have desired. Its burden was:

Claire Neville, we fear, is dying; but I feel more convinced than ever that she **is** *Richard Tracy's child. We have quite an eccentric character here, a Dr. Singleton, who seems singularly interested in the young governess. I sometimes think he knows something of her parents, and I have determined to ask him on the first opportunity that presents itself. He is an intimate friend of Dr. Thorne, the family physician—and if Claire Neville ever recovers, it will be owing to the skill and untiring zeal of Dr. Singleton, who says he hopes, through God, to bring her back to health. You will hear from me again soon. I will address my next to Richard. I expect to have something of importance to write him.*

After concluding the letter, Sayvord said, "Well, Richard, what do you say now—will you go to America nor not?"

Richard hesitated awhile, but finally reluctantly consented to go; but many times during their preparation for departure, he repented of his weakness in promising Mons. Sayvord to take this voyage, and would fain have given it up. But Monsieur, full of life and spirits, was quite captivated with the idea of going to America. "Oh, I know I shall stand the journey," he would say to his friend; "may be a little seasick crossing the Atlantic, but I cannot expect any thing else!"

Whenever Richard expressed his unwillingness to go, Monsieur rallied him unmercifully upon his lack of fortitude and strength of resolution; but at last all preparations were completed, and the journey to Havre accomplished, without any thing occurring to mar Monsieur's felicity and good spirits. His unfailing good humor was contagious, and Richard, becoming infected with it, grew cheerful and hopeful, and it was decided that before they proceeded to New Orleans, they should visit Richard's old home, Rose Cottage. Monsieur was terribly seasick while crossing the Atlantic, but the little old gentleman bore it bravely, never once giving up the belief that he could and would stand it. Arriving in Boston, they remained a few days to get rested and enable Monsieur to see the lions. Then they entered Connecticut, and upon reaching the thriving manufacturing town of Danbury, found no longer the old Ruthford stage, which was now classed among the things that were, and of which, only the memory remained. The cars now passed through the little village, towards which Richard was wending his way. While standing upon the platform at the neat little depot waiting for the train, which was somewhat late, Richard was accosted by an old lady, whose corpulency of proportion amused him somewhat, but whose gentle becoming smile prepossessed him in her behalf.

"Will you please see that I get safely on board the cars—for I never was on them, and I feel a little timid."

Richard would do this, of course; and, upon asking her destination, was surprised to find it the same as his own. And when at last they were comfortably rested in the cars, Richard began conversing with the old lady, who was none other than Mrs. Butterworth, the nurse, looking scarcely a day older than when we saw her last at Rose Cottage.

Mrs. Butterworth was very communicative, and talked of the inhabitants of Ruthford and surrounding villages for twenty-five years back.

Who knows, thought Richard, *but this very pleasant old lady may know something of Rose Cottage and its inmates!* He resolved to ask her. In reply to his question, the old lady said:

"I don't know the family that lives in the Cottage now; for it is many years since I was there. Let me see," she added, thoughtfully, "I guess it is about eighteen years this very fall since I went to nurse Mrs. Tracy, a young, delicate creature, who died in that Cottage, leaving a beautiful infant daughter to the care of an old colored nurse. If I should live to be a much older woman than I am, I never could forget that young, dying wife's prayer for her absent husband."

CHAPTER XXVII.

August 26, 1865

Mrs. Butterworth's Revelation.

"Her last words were, when asked if she had no word to leave for her husband, for she avoided speaking of him, 'Tell him I loved and—,' but the sentence was never finished. Poor, young thing! It was well she died as soon as she did," continued the matter-of-fact Mrs. Butterworth, who had thus far failed to notice the extreme agitation of her questioners, "for her husband was a villain, and she escaped a great many trials, by passing from the earth thus early."

Richard was deeply agitated, and motioning Monsieur Sayvord to proceed with questioning their fellow traveler, he prepared to await further developments. Monsieur Sayvord proceeded to question the old lady with his usual abruptness.

"So the child did not die, you say?"

"No, sir; it lived, and was as fine and healthy a child as you could wish to see."

"What was the colored nurse's name?"

"Juno Hays."

"And what induced you to think that Mrs. Tracy's husband was a villain?"

"Why," replied the old lady, her round honest eyes flashing with indignation, "if he had been a good and honorable man, he would have written to his poor little heartbroken wife, as a husband ought. He would never have gone to Europe without her knowledge, leaving her among strangers to die alone. May God forgive the wicked man, wherever he may be!"

"How do you know he went to Europe? And what became of the child and nurse?"

Mrs. Butterworth then related the particulars of Manville's visit, the sale of Rose Cottage, and subsequent removal of Juno and baby Claire to the eastern part of the State. That was all she knew, and since that time she had lost all trace of them.

"But," suggested Mrs. Butterworth, seeing how deeply interested the gentlemen were, "I think Dr. Murdoch could tell you more concerning them. Maybe you're a relation?" she said inquiringly.

Without answering her question directly, Monsieur Sayvord replied:

"We are very much interested in any thing that relates to Mrs. Tracy, and thank you for the information you have given. And I wish to disabuse your mind of false opinions concerning Richard Tracy. I know him well. He is a true and noble man, and mourns yet the early death of his young and gentle wife, who, with himself, was the victim of that designing villain, Manville. Through his representations, Richard has believed, until very recently, that the child had died immediately after birth, and was buried with its mother."

Mrs. Butterworth was very much astonished at this view of the case, but readily transferred her indignation from Richard to Manville. And our friend possessed her sympathy as he has always had ours.

Arriving at the end of their journey, they parted company with the old nurse, and repaired to the best hotel the village afforded. After Richard had partially regained his composure, and they had partaken of a genuine New England dinner, they started in quest of Dr. Murdoch, the old village physician, whose professional business was now carried on by Dr. Murdoch, Jr. The old gentleman was pleased with their visit, and cheerfully related what he knew of the inmates of Rose Cottage. It wrung Richard's heart to hear him talk so touchingly about Lina.

"Mr. Villars owns the cottage now. He bought it, furniture and all, when that dashing young Southerner came and took away Juno and the little baby, who was fast becoming a great favorite with me. I suppose she is a young lady now," said the old doctor, thoughtfully. "Ah, me! how time flies. Why, it is eighteen years ago, and I was an old man then."

"Do you know to what town or village they moved?"

"Somewhere in the vicinity of the town of L—, but that you know, was so long ago, they may have moved again."

Thus learning all they could, they took leave of Dr. Murdoch, and returned to the hotel, when they determined, much to the discomfiture of the landlord, who did not like the idea of losing two such distinguished guests, to take the night express for Danbury, and so be enabled to take the first eastern train the following day. It was their intention to seek out Juno before starting for New Orleans. They knew Claire was ill,—perhaps dying, but Richard felt that he must see Juno first. And impatient as was Monsieur Sayvord, he thought it best to go to L— and make inquiry concerning the old nurse.

Taking the night express they arrived at Danbury at 4 AM, and taking the train for the East at 11 AM, they reached L— at seven o'clock on the morning of the following day. After a fresh toilet, and a hasty breakfast, they started out upon their tour of inquiry. For a long time they could learn nothing. It was very evident Juno did not live in L—.

"She may be living in the country, some where," suggested Monsieur, as he noticed his friend's despairing look. "Here comes a nice looking colored man, let us ask him."

This colored man proved to be none other than Thomas, Miss Ellwood's hired man, who built fires, and did chores about the Seminary. In answer to their inquiry, Thomas replied:

"Yes, sir; there is such a woman living a few miles from this place. I do not know much about her myself, but the lady I live with can tell you, for she often comes to the Seminary, to see Miss Ellwood, and before Miss Claire left school, Juno used to visit her sometimes."

"Well, my man, I think we have been very fortunate in meeting you, and you will further oblige us by leading the way to the Seminary."

Miss Ellwood was quite astonished when she learned that one of her unexpected guests was the son of Col. Tracy, and more astonished when he declared himself to be the father of her favorite pupil, Claire Neville. She told him how Manville had placed Claire in the Seminary, six years before with the understanding that she (Miss Ellwood) was to spare neither pains nor expense upon the child's education. The bills were always regularly paid, one year in advance. She told Richard much of Claire's disposition and habits, and related many little incidents of her school life.

Thomas had returned from the post office in the mean time, bringing various letters for Miss Ellwood, one of which was from Col. Tracy, acknowledging the receipt of her package. Richard waited with ill-concealed impatience, until she had finished reading the somewhat lengthy epistle. Miss Ellwood turned to him with a smile when she had finished the letter and said, gently—

CHAPTER XXVIII.

September 2, 1865

Further Developments.

"'Claire is better,' Col. Tracy writes. 'We dare to indulge the hope that she will again be restored to perfect health. The certificate and letters prove beyond the least semblance of a doubt that Claire Neville is our granddaughter—the offspring of my son's unfortunate union. We can, of course, say nothing of this to Claire for a long time to come. But I frequently ask myself, 'Where is my son, whom I have made an exile from his native land?' You, of course, know nothing of him. But if, by any strange or unexpected combination of circumstances, you should learn any thing concerning him, lose no time in transmitting the knowledge to me.'"

A sigh of relief escaped Richard, as Miss Elwood ceased speaking. He would yet press his darling child to his heart, which was already overflowing with paternal love. And his father, it was evident, had not quite forgotten.

It was decided that Mons. Sayvord and Richard should remain the guests of Miss Elwood until the following day, when, in company with their kind hostess, they would pay a visit to old Juno.

"Martin, I had a strange dream, last night, and shall hear good news ere the day closes," said Juno, cheerfully.

Martin looked up, with a gratified smile. He was gladdened by any thing that betokened a return of Juno's wonted spirits; for ever since she learned of Claire's illness, she had been sad and silent, frequently indulging in long crying spells.

Martin had often reasoned with her, and persuaded her to be more hopeful, but all to no purpose, for Juno persistently refused to be comforted. But on this glorious morning Juno seemed more like her former self. And at noon, when Martin returned to dinner, he found Juno singing, and seemingly somewhat excited. Every window was hoisted, every door was at its widest extension, while carpets and furniture underwent a thorough sweeping and dusting. Martin looked on in perfect astonishment, as his wife hurriedly put the various articles in their proper places. "Why, Juno, what do you mean?" he found time and breath to ask, as Juno peremptorily ordered him to kill two of the spring pullets.

"Well," said she, in reply, "the truth is, I expect company."

"Who?" queried Martin, eagerly.

"Oh, I don't know who—but the rooster crowed before the door three times this morning; so I know somebody's coming; and I want to be prepared, that's all."

After they were seated at the table, Juno sat for some minutes looking thoughtfully into her teacup, and then said, in low and impressive tones:

"Martin, I tell you, Master Richard is coming. I know it. I feel it. He may not come today, nor yet tomorrow, but he is coming, and that very soon, too."

Martin thought it was very likely that Richard would come. If his wife had said, "Martin, the moon will fall tomorrow night," he would have believed it quite possible. However, the meal dispatched and the two spring pullets killed, Martin returned to his work in the south meadow, while Juno, upon the strength of her dreams and the crowing chanticleer, continued her busy preparation. She frequently sought the door, and strained her eyes far down the dusty road, but failing to discern any one in the distance, returned to her work. But ere long her attentive ear caught the sound of wheels. She ran to the door just in time to see Miss Elwood coming up the neatly bordered walks, accompanied by two gentlemen. Juno bent one piercing glance upon the taller of the two gentlemen, and sank in a chair, exclaiming in an excited voice, "God be praised! It is Master Richard!"

And when the two entered the little parlor, and Richard shook her warmly by the hand, saying, "My dear old friend, I am rejoiced to see you!" Juno could only sob aloud and fervently ejaculate:

"Thank the Lord! Thank the Lord!"

It was some time before she was composed enough to relate to Richard the closing scenes in his young wife's life. The entire party was more or less affected as Juno, in simple but eloquent words, repeated Lina's trials—how the young wife's cheek grew pale and her step feeble as she waited with breaking heart for the letter that would never come; how she turned away with a look of hopeless despair in her beautiful eyes; and how, at last, a letter came, and proved fatal in its cruel mission; a night of sorrow, and the cloudless morning dawned upon a beautiful newborn babe, and the lifeless form of the young mother; how she and the old nurse, Mrs. Butterworth, had watched with pride and wonder over baby Claire until Manville came, telling her that Richard was in Europe, and advising the sale of Rose Cottage, and her removal to the eastern part of the State.

Richard grew more astonished and indignant as each successive revelation served to disclose more fully the duplicity of Manville. When Juno concluded her narrative, he related all that had taken place after he bade them farewell at the door of Rose Cottage, until he stood with gentle Addie Villiers by his young wife's grave. When he had finished, Juno said, "I never believed the wrong was in you, Master Richard. I always thought and said you would come. I never told Claire who her father was, because I wanted her to respect you; but, thank God, it will all be made right."

Julia C. Collins

A long time they remained talking over the past. Martin returned from the field and was met at the door by the triumphant Juno, who exclaimed:

"Martin, Martin, he has come! Master Richard is here!"

Martin could only gaze upon his wife as one in a dream. He listened incredulously as she excitedly repeated, "Master Richard has come!" and seriously began to think his better half was not quite right. But his doubts were dispelled by the pleasant voice of Miss Elwood:

"Come in, Martin, and see Mr. Tracy."

Martin received an introduction awkwardly enough, and regarded Richard as an object of great interest and worthy of his undivided attention.

After doing justice to Juno's spring-pullets, the company took their leave in order to secure a good night's rest ere they started on their long journey South. They bid Juno and Martin goodbye with much regret, and proceeded on their way with hopeful hearts; and, for once in his life, perhaps, Mons. Sayvord was silent. The travelers left L— by an early train on the following morning. But, leaving them to pursue their journey alone, we will precede them to New Orleans.

CHAPTER XXIX.

September 9, 1865

Convalescent.

Claire was convalescent, and an air of cheerfulness reigned throughout the household of the Tracys. Mrs. Tracy spent the most of her time by the couch upon which the invalid reclined—she whose cheeks and short raven locks formed a beautiful contrast with the crimson pillows. Everyone, from the stern old Colonel down to the youngest urchin about the establishment, seemed desirous of doing something to show their love for the young creature, who received their smallest attention with heartfelt gratitude. The Colonel was always thinking of something that would add to her comfort. It was either a new easy chair, a rare painting, or a choice engraving—always something new and diverting. Lloyd would drop in and while away an hour in pleasant chat. The Count brought her favorite authors, and read to her for hours, sometimes stealing a stealthy glance at the rose which deepened upon the white cheek for one short moment, and then faded. Laura and Nellie robbed the gardens and conservatories of their choicest treasures, which were laid as an offering of love before Claire, who repaid each with a sweet kiss. Jim and the cook did their part also. Never were choicer delicacies prepared to tempt the palate of an invalid than those which found their way to Claire's room. And Isabelle, who seldom visited the sickroom, now asked, in a cold, formal manner, each morning, after Claire's health. Drs. Singleton and Thorne called each day, more from force of habit than that Claire required their professional services.

Count Sayvord watched Dr. Singleton with interest. Reason as he would, he could not divest himself of the thought that the Doctor knew something of Claire's parents. Times without number he had determined to seek the old gentleman's confidence, and as many times gave it up, from the fear that his intentions might be misconstrued.

Dr. Singleton regarded young Sayvord with a friendly eye, and thought he should like to know more of him.

Who knows, thought the Doctor, *but he may have met Richard Tracy somewhere during his years of travel, or may know someone that has seen him! And I may be enabled to get trace of him; for at this rate, the confession of Manville is likely to lie in my private drawer for a century to come.*

An opportunity soon presented itself, which was improved by the Doctor. During a pause in the conversation, he asked the Count if he had ever met an American gentleman by the name of Tracy during his lengthy travels.

"Years ago," replied the young man, "I met a gentleman of that name at my Uncle Sayvord's country-seat. Richard Tracy was the name; I remember well. He was a thoughtful, sad-browed man, over whose life a shadow seemed to have fallen."

"The same! the same!" exclaimed the Doctor, excitedly. "Have you heard any thing of him since—or do you know where he is now?"

"I received a letter from him about six weeks ago, and am expecting another by every mail. He is at present at my Uncle Clayburn Sayvord's, in the southern part of France."

"Can it be possible!" ejaculated the Doctor. "Will you allow me to see the letter you received from Richard?"

"Certainly," replied the Count, passing him the letter.

"The same clear, manly hand," said the Doctor, glancing at the superscription, as he proceeded to read the contents of the letter. When finished, he again turned to the young man, saying:

"So you too had a suspicion of the truth; for Claire Neville is indeed the daughter of Richard Tracy, and granddaughter of the Colonel."

"Let there be full confidence between us, Doctor," said the Count. "Tell me of her mother; for there is a secret somewhere which I have failed to ferret out."

Dr. Singleton looked very thoughtful for a moment, and then replied, very gravely:

"Count Sayvord, if you will first answer truthfully two questions which I shall ask, I will cheerfully tell you all I know." The Count readily assured him that he would answer to the best of his ability any question he might ask.

The Doctor hesitated a moment, and then abruptly asked:

"Do you love Claire Neville? Do you wish to make her your wife? Or—"

"Enough, sir!" angrily interrupted Sayvord. "I did not expect this. Such questions are intrusive."

"I beg your pardon, if I have offended you," replied the Doctor, courteously, "but, believe me, I was actuated by no idle curiosity." The Count, somewhat mollified, felt a little ashamed of his hasty temper. The truth was, he had never analyzed his feelings toward Claire. But the Doctor's question told him that he did love her with the whole depths of his ardent nature.

"I do love Claire—and if she will accept me, I will make her my wife, beloved and honored above woman."

The Doctor grasped the young man's hand and shook it warmly.

"That is the right kind of talk. None of your sentimental nonsense for me. I am a plain man, and always express my thoughts in the plainest phrases. I have foreseen all this for some time, and have thus seemingly interfered with your private business to prevent trouble hereafter, and, perhaps, a great deal of unhappiness to both parties. Caste has proved the bane of Richard Tracy's life. It may prove the bane of yours."

Sayvord was somewhat mystified by the Doctor's language.

The old man continued:

"Richard Tracy's wife, the mother of Claire Neville, was a quadroon and once a slave, owned by her own father, and sold by him to Colonel Tracy."

Sayvord was greatly excited at this revelation, and exclaimed:

"Impossible, Doctor! You are laboring under some mistake!"

"Not a bit of it!" was the emphatic reply, and he related the entire history of Richard's life. When concluded, he remarked, "I have told you these facts, that you may accustom yourself to thinking of them—and if you marry Claire Neville, you do so with a full knowledge of her origin; and, knowing these facts, if you give her up, you alone are the sufferer, and she is spared the bitter knowledge that caste is the bane of her life's happiness."

The Count had been swayed by various emotions during the Doctor's narrative. He now sat thoughtful and silent. He at last said slowly:

"I must think of this, Doctor. It is best to accustom one's self to look unpleasant facts steadily in the face, and I thank you for your forethought."

"And now," said Dr. Singleton, "let us talk of Richard Tracy. He is, or was, when last heard from, with your uncle, in France."

"Yes," replied the Count; "but if he is not already, he soon will be, on his way to America, for I have written him to come without delay."

"All the better. I hope he will come—"

The sentence remained unfinished, for at this moment Jim entered the room, and said, with an overwhelming bow:

"A letter for de Count Sayvord."

The Count hastily broke the seal, and read the almost unintelligible scrawl, exclaiming, as he roughly shook the Doctor's arm:

"My uncle and Richard Tracy are in New Orleans at this moment."

CHAPTER XXX

September 16, 1865

MISSING—This chapter appeared in an issue of the *Christian Recorder* that has yet to be located.

CHAPTER XXXI.

September 23, 1865

Strange Events.

The meeting between Dr. Singleton and Richard was an affecting one. The first greeting over, the doctor held Richard at arm's length, and surveyed him scrutinizingly. He could not realize that the beardless boy he had bade adieu eighteen years before had returned to him after these years, a prematurely old man. He could hardly realize that this bearded, sad-browed man, with form slightly bent, was the young Richard, over whose couch of suffering he had watched for days and weeks.

Richard read the doctor's thoughts, and asked, with a sad smile:

"Am I, then, changed so much?"

"Time and sorrow has indeed dealt hardly with you, my boy," and the old man's voice was low and trembled with sadness.

Monsieur Sayvord presented the Count to Richard, and Monsieur, in turn, was presented to Dr. Singleton.

Claire's advent in the Tracy family, her late illness, Manville's death, Col. Tracy's pride and prejudices, were the subjects under discussion. All except Richard thought that the Colonel's pride was pretty well subdued. A sigh of relief escaped Richard as Dr. Singleton related the closing scenes of Manville's life.

"It is well," he repeated, softly. And the trio knew well of what he was thinking.

Richard was impatient to see his daughter, but it was thought best that in her present weak state, she should be somewhat prepared to meet her father.

"I will undertake that task," said the doctor. "Her life is too precious to be periled by a sudden and indiscreet disclosure!" and he glanced significantly at the Count, who flushed slightly. Richard's eyes followed that glance, and he read its possible meaning, while his tried heart uttered the prayer—

"God spare my child the ordeal through which I have passed!"

It was decided that the doctor should inform Claire of the arrival of her father. There was a more difficult task to be performed. Who was to convey the intelligence to the irascible father? The Count and Monsieur Sayvord undertook that mission, and felt hopeful of the result.

313

"I will write a few lines which I wish you to bear to my mother," said Richard, addressing the Count, who promised to deliver it to Mrs. Tracy.

"But that confession of Manville's, doctor, when will you bring it?"

"Early tomorrow morning, or, on his return, Monsieur Sayvord will bring it this evening."

The three gentlemen took their departure, leaving Richard to the company of his own thoughts, but first bidding him be of good cheer, and hope that all would yet be well.

Claire had awaked from her long, refreshing sleep, and was wondering what kept Mrs. Tracy from her side so long. Then she thought of Col. Tracy's manner towards her, so full of remorseful tenderness, and wondered if she was indeed his grandchild. And if she were, where could her father be? Was it not strange he never made inquiry concerning her? But perhaps he did not care to find her. And ere she knew it, Claire was weeping piteously.

In a little while she became composed, and for the first time since her illness, thought over the exciting scenes of that short interval preceding her loss of reason. She recalled her conversation with the dying Manville, and she murmured softly,

"My poor father was cruelly wronged, and my delicate young mother hastened to a premature grave. How he must have loved her and mourned her early death. No one ever loved me. It must be happiness to know that someone is always thinking of one's comfort. I do wish father would come. I think Col. Tracy would forgive him."

It was the hour the Count usually came in to read, but this afternoon he came not. Even little Nellie failed to make her accustomed visit. What did it mean? Had everyone deserted her? Her quick ear caught the sound of wheels and the steps of several persons entering the hall. She heard steps ascending the stairs and pass to the library. Next she heard someone approaching her door, and the genial face of Dr. Singleton peered into the apartment. Seeing Claire awake, he entered. Taking a seat by her side, he took the white and almost transparent hand in his, saying,

"How do you feel this afternoon, dear?"

"I am feeling quite well, doctor, only a little weak, you know," replied Claire, with a cheerful smile.

"I am glad to hear it," replied the doctor. "Now tell me what you have been thinking of this long afternoon?"

"Oh, a great many things, doctor! I have been thinking of my father and my mother, and also of Manville's death, and how kind everyone is to me. And I was wondering if Colonel Tracy would forgive my father if he should return."

"I trust he would," was the doctor's fervent reply.

"You knew my father very well, did you not?" asked Claire, eagerly.

"Yes, dear," was the quiet reply.

"Is it very long since you saw him?"

"Not long," returned the doctor, evasively, while a queer smile played upon his lips.

Claire was looking straight into the old gentleman's eyes, when she said,

"But tell me how long. Just exactly how long ago it was?"

"Why, how exacting you have grown, little one," he said, smiling. "But tell me, would you like to see your father very much?"

"Would I," repeated Claire, "how can you ask me?"

"Well, Claire, if you will promise me not to become excited, nor make yourself sick with asking questions, I will tell you a secret."

"I promise," replied Claire, eagerly, a thousand thoughts thronging her mind in an instant.

"Well, Claire, your father *has come*, and you shall see him soon." Claire remembered her promise, and, with a desperate effort, controlled her feelings, and asked, quietly:

"When can I see him, doctor?"

"As early tomorrow morning as you wish."

She was forced to be satisfied, and asked:

"Who knows of his arrival besides yourself?"

"Count Sayvord, whose uncle arrived this morning with Richard."

"Did Count Sayvord know my father?" she asked.

"He saw your father some years ago at his uncle's, in France. But it is owing to the Count that he has returned to New Orleans. Your resemblance to Richard Tracy first attracted his attention, and he wrote to his uncle concerning you, and asking about Richard. Your father saw the letter. Others followed, and the result is that Richard Tracy is now in New Orleans, seeking his daughter."

Dr. Singleton soon took leave of his young friend, promising to call early, with her father, the following morning. Claire sank back upon the crimson cushions, her pale cheeks flushed with excitement. An hour passed, and no one came, until Rose brought in the tea tray.

"Rose, where is Mrs. Tracy?"

"Don't know, Miss Claire, I'm sure. There's great times 'bout this house today. The missus fainted away in old Mattie's arms this afternoon. I was going through the hall, and heard a scream for help. I thought the sound came from the east room. I went in. There sat Mattie, on the floor, crying over missus, who looked as white and lifeless as a piece of linen. We worked hard with her a long time. She had just revived so as to be able to sit up and talk a little, when a knock was heard at the door. I opened it, and there stood Count—what's his name?"

"Sayvord," interposed Claire.

"Oh, never mind the name," said Rose. "He had a note for Mrs. Tracy. I handed it to her. When she looked at the writing, I thought she was going to faint again. But she didn't. Old Mattie asked: 'Missus, is it from him?' 'Yes,' she said, 'it is. I am going to him. Tell Jim to get the carriage ready. I wish to go out.' And away she went, and hasn't come back yet. That young Count and a funny little old man are up in the library with massa now. Mattie's crying, in the east room, fit to break her heart. Jim looks awful wise, and Dinah's as cross as fury. I don't see what the house is coming to," repeated Rose, as she passed out.

"And I am happy," murmured Claire.

ABOUT THE AUTHOR.

JULIA C. COLLINS (1842–1865) lived in Williamsport, Pennsylvania where she worked as a schoolteacher and essayist for *The Christian Recorder*.

Collins passed away from tuberculosis while writing and releasing *The Curse of Caste*, leaving the story unfinished.

"Studio portrait of woman wearing glasses and cross-shaped earrings."
George Daniels Morse. 1880-1889 (Approx.). From The New York Public Library.

THE HAZELEY
FAMILY

A. E. JOHNSON

First edition published in 1894.

I.
THE HAZELEY HOME.

Sixteen-year-old Flora Hazeley stood by the table in the dingy little dining room, looking down earnestly and thoughtfully at a shapely, yellow sweet potato.

It was only a potato, but the sight of it brought to its owner, not only a crowd of pleasant memories, but a number of unpleasant anticipations. Hence, the earnest, thoughtful expression on her young face.

Flora was the only daughter. She had two brothers, one older and one younger than herself, Harry and Alec, aged respectively, eighteen and thirteen. The mother was of an easy-going, careless disposition, and seemed indifferent to the management of her household. Especially did she dislike responsibility of any kind. She was well pleased, therefore, to receive one day a letter from her sister, Mrs. Graham, a childless widow, offering to take Flora, who was then just five years old, promising to rear her as if she had been her own daughter.

Mrs. Graham was well off. In her case this meant that she lived in a pretty home of her own, with a nice income, not only supporting herself in comfort, but permitting her to provide a home for her elder sister for many years, who had entire charge of the housekeeping. This sister, Mrs. Sarah Martin, was also a widow and childless. The resemblance went no further, for they differed, not only in manner, but opinions, thoughts, and character.

Mrs. Graham, after a great deal of careful thought, had come to the conclusion to adopt her little niece. In fact she had often thought it over ever since the child first began to walk, and call her by name. She was a sensible woman, and it always annoyed her when she would visit her sister to see the careless way in which the children were being trained. Seeing this, she had long wished to take and train Flora according to her own idea of what constituted the education of a girl.

"It will be so much worse for her than for the boys," she had said one day to Mrs. Martin. "I do dislike to see such a bright little child brought up to be good for nothing; and that is just the way in which it will be, if I do not take charge of her myself."

The latter clause was intended to draw indirectly from her sister an opinion of such a proceeding, for Mrs. Martin was by no means partial to children. However, it was received with the indifferent observation:

"Esther never did have any interest in children anyhow. She never had any idea how to take care of herself, much less anybody else," to which was added a remark to the effect that if her sister Bertha chose to burden herself with a troublesome child, she was sure she had nothing to do with the matter, and did not intend to have.

Mrs. Graham was rather surprised to have her suggestion received so coolly. She had expected a great deal of trouble in getting Sarah to consent, even provisionally. She was very glad to meet no more serious opposition, for, although she had fully decided in her own mind regarding the matter, yet her peace-loving nature dreaded unpleasant scenes. She purposely and entirely overlooked the expression of stern determination in the sharp-featured countenance of her sister, and forthwith resolved to send for Flora without further loss of time.

Thus it was that Flora Hazeley changed homes. She was not legally adopted by her aunt, but was simply taken with the understanding she would be returned to her parents in case Mrs. Graham should in any way change her mind, or weary of her charge. This provision was inserted by Mrs. Martin, who determined, in spite of her seeming indifference, not to be ignored by her sister, upon whose bounty she considered she had a primary claim.

For eleven years Flora lived in the pretty home of her Aunt Bertha. Her time was filled by various occupations, school, caring for the flowers in the garden, and dreaming under the old peach tree, which never bore any peaches, but grew on contentedly in the farthest corner of the yard.

However, these were by no means the only ways in which Flora spent her time, for Mrs. Martin, notwithstanding her stern resolve not to have anything to do with her, had suddenly taken an equally stern determination to do her share toward "bringing sister Esther's child up properly."

This was fortunate for Flora. Aunt Sarah instructed her thoroughly and carefully in the details of housekeeping, cooking, serving, washing, in fact, everything she knew herself. How fortunate it was that she learned how to do these things, Flora realized some time afterward, as Mrs. Martin had intended she should. While she was learning them, Flora's progress was due rather more to the awe she felt of her stern aunt than to the desire to excel.

Mrs. Martin was ever ready to scold and find fault. Mrs. Graham never criticized, but always had a bright smile and something pleasant to say. As a natural consequence, she was dearly loved by her niece.

Mrs. Hazeley, Flora's mother, delighted to be relieved of her troublesome little girl, settled down more contentedly than ever, to enjoy the quiet of her daughter's absence, and became daily more and more indisposed to exert herself in order to make her home attractive.

It was usually pretty quiet now, because neither of the boys stayed in the house a moment longer than necessity demanded. Mr. Hazeley was employed on the railroad, and consequently was away from home a great deal. Mrs. Hazeley did little but turn aimlessly about, making herself believe that she was a very hard-working woman and then imagining herself much fatigued, found it necessary to rest often and long. She was at heart a good woman, when that organ could be reached, but possessed a weak, vacillating disposition, entirely lacking the gentle firmness of her sister, Mrs. Graham, or the uncompromising energy of Mrs. Martin.

Mr. Hazeley had long ceased to complain of his home and its management, for his words had no further effect than to bring upon himself a storm of tearful scolding, which drove him out of the house to seek more genial quarters. He was by nature a peaceable man, and when he found that neither ease nor peace could be had at home, remained there as little as possible. In fact, as Mrs. Hazeley's sisters had often said, "if the whole family did not go to ruin, it would not be Esther's fault."

Flora's life at her aunt's pleasant home had been a very happy one, and the time passed rapidly away. She was nearly through school, and looked eagerly forward into the future, that to her was so full of brightest hopes. It was her ambition to be of some use in the world. Just what she wanted to do, she did not know—she had not yet determined; but that it was to be something great and good, she was confident, for small things did not enter into her conception of usefulness.

Aunt Bertha was her confidante for all her plans, or rather, dreams; she could do nothing without Aunt Bertha, for had not she the means? Flora felt sure nothing great could be done without money, that is, nothing she would care to do.

But, alas! Her summer sky, so promising and brilliant with hopes and indefinite plans, was suddenly overcast. Aunt Bertha was taken ill one day; the doctor said it was prostration, and he feared she might not rally. Flora was told. Her Aunt Bertha, whom she loved so dearly, and who loved her so much! Must she die? "I love her far more than my mother," she whispered to herself. This seemed very disloyal in Flora. But in truth, she had little cause to love the mother who had been so eager to relinquish her claim, and who, in all these years, had never expressed a wish to have her daughter at home.

During her sister's illness, Aunt Sarah spent her time in constant attendance upon her. She was cold, stern, and unapproachable as ever, giving the child little information in regard to the sick one who had been so kind to her. She was not allowed to enter the sick room during the first of her aunt's illness, although Mrs. Graham had often asked to see her niece.

One day, just before the spirit passed away, the sick woman called her sister, and said in a weak, trembling voice:

"Sister, I suppose you know I cannot live long, and that my will is made."

Mrs. Martin silently nodded.

"Well," continued Mrs. Graham, "I have left everything to you—I thought it would be best."

Again a silent nod.

"But, Sarah, I want you to promise one thing; that you will see Flora has what she needs to carry out her plans. The dear child has so longed to carry out some of her plans. I want her to have means to make whatever she may decide upon a success. And one more thing," she continued, pausing for breath, and looking pleadingly into the face above her, "I do hope, Sarah, that you will keep Flora here with you. Do not send her back to her home. I have left all I own in your hands, and I trust to you, sister, to do what I wish."

This long expression of her wishes had so taxed the fast-failing strength of the invalid, that she sank back, exhausted. No answer was expected, and Mrs. Martin was silent; and silent too, because she had not the slightest intention of doing as her sister wished. It was truly heartless; but Mrs. Martin was one of those people who do not present the harsh side of their nature in all its intensity until the reins of power are placed in their hands. So long as Mrs. Graham held the purse-strings, she acquiesced with as much grace as possible in her sister's plans. Was not the money Mrs. Graham's to do with as she pleased? It was quite a different thing, however, to feel that now everything would be in her hands to use as she chose. No matter if the donor was still looking into her face, her mind was made up that things should be ordered in the future according to her good pleasure. It was not at all her wish to burden herself with Esther's child, and forthwith she decided that back to her home Flora should go. However, she did not allow these unworthy thoughts to disturb the last moments of her tender-hearted sister, by giving expression to them. So good Mrs. Graham passed peacefully away.

Flora was allowed to see her shortly before she died. The kind voice whispered words of comfort, telling her that Aunt Sarah would take care of her. These words fell unnoticed at the time upon the ear of the sobbing girl, who had been so accustomed to have Aunt Bertha think and plan for her.

II.
FLORA AT HOME.

Mrs. Graham's life had been a quiet, unobtrusive, but truly Christian one. She had neglected no opportunity to implant in her young niece a love and reverence for holy things; and now that she was about to die, she felt that she had nothing to regret, that she had left no duty unfulfilled, so far as Flora's training was concerned. It was with a heart full of peace that she commended her charge to the "One above all others" and took her leave of earth.

Flora was almost inconsolable. She had no one to comfort her, for Aunt Sarah was as distant as ever, being entirely too much occupied with plans for the future to care about Flora. Her mother came to the funeral, but neither was overjoyed to see the other after their long separation. It could scarcely be otherwise. Natural affection had never been conspicuous in the Hazeley home, and the influence of these years apart had not helped matters at all. Indeed, they were little more to each other than strangers.

After they returned from the cemetery, however, Aunt Sarah informed Flora she was to return with her mother to her former, and as she deemed it, rightful home. The feelings with which the girl received this intelligence were by no means pleasant ones. But there was no use in crying or fretting about it, for when Aunt Sarah said a thing, she meant it, and could not be induced to alter her decision, even if Flora had felt inclined to ask her to do so. This she had no thought of doing, for she was not at all anxious to make her home with her cold, distant aunt.

"It is too bad!" she exclaimed, as she thought of all the bright helpful plans she and Aunt Bertha had made together, and which they had hoped to be able to carry out. "It is too bad!" she sobbed, as she bent over her trunk in her pretty little bedroom, the tears falling on the tasteful dresses, and the many loving tokens that had been given her by the dear hands now at rest beneath the unfeeling earth in the churchyard.

Mrs. Martin was surprised that Flora's mother made no objection to taking her daughter home. The truth was Mrs. Hazeley had been wanting this very thing for some time. It was not, however, because of any particularly affectionate or motherly feeling toward her child; but she had been thinking that Flora, of whose ability she had heard much, would be a very great help to her in caring for the house. Thus it was that Flora returned to the home she had left eleven years before.

Just as the train was preparing to leave the station, Lottie Piper, one of Flora's friends and admirers, came running to the car, and tossed something through the open window into Flora's lap, saying hurriedly and pantingly, as she pressed the hand held out to her:

"There, Flora, take that. Don't laugh. I raised it all myself, and I want you to have it; but don't eat it! Keep it to remember me by. Goodbye," she called, as the train moved off.

Flora waved her handkerchief out of the window to Lottie, until her arm was tired. As she looked about the cars her attention was attracted by a titter from the opposite side. At first she could not understand why the girl who sat there should look at her and smile. As her neighbor gazed at her lap, Flora's eyes followed, and there she saw the cause of the merriment in Lottie's parting gift—a yellow sweet potato.

At first she felt inclined to be provoked with Lottie for bringing such a thing and causing her to be laughed at. However, the remembrance of her parting words, "I raised it all myself; but don't eat it!" made her smile in spite of herself. This encouraged the girl opposite to slip over to the seat beside Flora, as Mrs. Hazeley was occupying the one in front, and the two girls, although entire strangers to each other, chatted away busily, until the train stopped at one of the stations, where the girl and her father, who sat farther back, left the car. Soon after, Flora found herself at home, Bartonville and Brinton being but a short distance apart.

This brings us to the opening of our story.

It was Lottie's potato that lay upon the table, and Flora had been wondering what to do with it. The memories it awakened were of Brinton and the many pleasant strolls and romps she had enjoyed with Lottie in her father's fields, which joined Mrs. Graham's, of Aunt Bertha herself, and much more.

"But what am I to do with the potato?" she questioned. "I am not to eat it. I don't care to, either. Oh! I know, I will plant it in a jar of water and let it grow. That would please Lottie, I guess."

She soon found a jar such as she wanted, and after washing it clean and bright, filled it full of clear water, and carefully placed the potato, end up, in it, and then looked about for a suitable place for it.

"That window has a good broad seat," she said to herself; "and it is sunny, but the glass is so grimy! However, it will do. Better yet, I will open the window."

This was more easily said than done, for, although the weather was still warm—it being September—the window did not appear to have been opened for some time.

Flora struggled and pushed, and at length succeeded in opening it, making noise enough as she did so, to attract the attention of a young girl who was passing. She stopped, looking up, inquiringly.

Flora was heated with her exertions and the thought of having attracted attention, so that before she realized what she was doing, she was smiling and saying:

"This old window was very hard to raise, but I was determined to do it."

"No," said the girl, looking as if she was not quite sure that it was the right thing to say.

"What is that in the jar?" she asked, as she came closer, and looked at the potato curiously, and then at Flora in a friendly way that pleased her.

"This," said Flora, patting the vegetable; "it is a potato."

"But what have you put it in there for?" persisted the girl.

"To grow, to be sure."

"Will it grow?"

"Of course it will," replied Flora, with an important air. "See! water is in this jar, and soon this potato will sprout, send roots down and leaves up, and then—and then—it will just keep on growing, you know." And Flora felt sure that she had put quite an artistic finish to her description of potato culture.

"Oh, yes," cried her new acquaintance, with an intelligent light in her eyes; "I know very well what will happen then."

"What?" asked Flora, rather dubiously.

"Why, little sweet potatoes will grow on the roots, of course."

"I—I don't think they will," said Flora, hesitatingly, not being well versed on the subject.

"Yes; but they must—they always do," returned the girl, positively.

"Well, but there would be no room in the jar for potatoes to grow," said Flora.

"That's so." And the girl looked puzzled; then they both laughed, not knowing what else to do.

"What is your name?" asked Flora, by way of changing the subject, for she was a little fearful she might be asked to explain why little sweet potatoes would not grow in her jar.

"My name is Ruth Rudd," was the answer. "What is yours?"

"Flora Hazeley."

"Is it? Well, I live just back of your house, on the next street. Goodbye. I guess I will see you some other time." And she hurried away.

She is a real nice girl, Flora thought, as she turned away from the window; *I hope I can see her again.*

She stood for an instant looking about the room. It was nicely furnished, but it looked neglected and untidy, and Flora, having been so long accustomed to the attractiveness and order of her aunt's house, felt homesick. Her loneliness came over her in a great wave of feeling, and running through the kitchen, out of the door, went into the yard, which was a good-sized one, but so filled with rubbish and piles of boards, scarcely noticed through her tears, that she met with many a stumble before she reached the farther end. She wanted some quiet place in which to sit and think, as she used to do under the old peach tree at Brinton. She was sure she "could think of nothing in that house," and the best she could do was to seat herself on an old block at the very back of the yard. She felt she could think better out in the open air, under the sky, for she was a great lover of nature, and loved to look at the blue sky. The sun was under a cloud, but the air was warm and pleasant.

How different were her thoughts now from what they had been under the old peach tree! Then she had reveled in rose-colored dreams; now she was confronted by gray realities. Her thoughts went rapidly over her life since Aunt Bertha's death.

She had been here not quite a week, and she found it such a different place from the home she had so lately left, that she was almost unwilling to call it "home." But while she considered her present home not very desirable, she had given no thought to the inmates, whether or not they had found in her a very desirable addition to the circle.

She was young, and she soon wearied of her sombre thoughts, which could avail her nothing, and she glanced at the houses on each side of her own. There was a marked difference. It was not in the style of the building, for hers was the most attractive. It was, however, in the general appearance, and Flora felt she would like to begin at the topmost shingle and pull her home down to the ground. But the thought came to her that then she would have no home. She knew there was no room for her with Aunt Sarah, who was, no doubt, at this very moment enjoying her absence.

No, indeed, I do not want to live with Aunt Sarah, she thought; and then began to wonder vaguely if she had not better go to work and try to make her present home a more congenial one.

The more she thought about it, the better the idea pleased her. Just as she was endeavoring to decide upon something definite to do, she was startled by seeing a board in the fence, just behind her, pushed aside. Before she could move, a round, fat, little face was thrust through the opening, and a pair of inquisitive brown eyes were fastened upon her. For a moment they looked, and then the owner squeezed through, and stood still, eyeing Flora complacently.

"Well, and who are you? And what do you mean by coming in here that way?" asked Flora, amused at the odd-looking little creature.

"I'm Jem," answered the midget, coolly; "and I didn't mean nuffing."

"Jem? I thought you were a girl," said Flora, looking at the quaint, short-waisted dress, that reached almost down to the copper toed shoes, and the funny, little, short white apron, tied just under the fat arms, which were squeezed into sleeves much too tight for them.

"So I am a girl," answered Jem, indignantly; "don't you see I've gut a napron on wif pockets in?" And she thrust her chubby little fingers into one of them.

"But you said your name was 'Jem,' and that's a boy's name," persisted Flora, enjoying her odd companion.

"'Tain't none," was the sententious reply; "it's short for 'Jemima'; that's what my really name is."

"Well, Jemima, what do you want in here?"

"Nuffing."

"Nothing? Well, that isn't in here."

"There ain't anythin' else's I can see," retorted Jem, turning down the corners of her mouth very far, and looking about disdainfully.

Flora laughed outright at this, but her visitor's countenance lost none of its solemnity.

"You do not seem to admire my yard, Jem."

"Don't see anythin' to remire," retorted Jem. "You'd just ought to peep in ours," and she moved over to the fence, and pulling away the board with a triumphant air, motioned Flora to look. Flora looked, but the first thing she saw was not the yard, but the young girl with whom she had been talking not an hour since.

III.
RUTH RUDD.

Ruth, standing by a long wooden bench, in the neat, brick-paved yard, was engaged in watering some plants that were her especial pride.

Hearing a noise at the fence, she turned, and recognizing Flora, smiled and asked:

"Won't you come in?"

"Thank you," replied Flora, smiling in return. "I think I will."

Jem looked on wonderingly as her sister and the visitor, whom she considered her especial property, chatted.

She could not understand how they knew each other. At length, as they took no notice of her, she determined to assert herself; so, going up to Flora, she demanded:

"What do you think of my yard?"

"Oh," said Flora, recollecting for what purpose they had come, "I like it very much indeed, Jem."

"It's a pretty good yard, I think," said Jem, with much emphasis on the pronoun. "Come and look at the flowers, and I'll tell you the names of them." And she drew Flora nearer the bench.

"This is a gibonia," she continued, pointing with her fat finger to the flower named.

"You mean a 'begonia,' don't you, Jem?" said Flora.

"Yes," answered Jem, without changing countenance in the least, or seeming in any way abashed; "and this is a gerangum."

"A geranium," corrected Flora. "Yes, I see."

"And this is a chipoonia," pointing to a petunia, "and—Oh, there's Pokey!" and breaking away in the midst of her explanations, she gave chase to a fat little gray kitten that just then scampered across the yard, and into the house.

"What a cute little girl Jem is," said Flora to Ruth; "is she your sister?"

"Yes, that is, she is my half-sister; her mother was not my own mother, you know."

"Oh, she is your step-mother," said Flora.

"She was," corrected Ruth; "but she has been dead ever since Jem was a little baby. My own mother died when I was quite small," she added, with an elderly air.

"Who keeps house for you?" asked Flora, in surprise.

"I do," replied Ruth. "I keep house for father, and take care of Jem. She is all the company I have."

"What a smart girl you are. How old are you, Ruth?"

"I'm sixteen, but I feel ever so much older. You see, it is a great responsibility to have everything at home resting upon one," and Ruth looked very wise.

"I should think so," said Flora, thoughtfully. "I am sixteen too."

"Are you? That's nice. We ought to be good friends," returned Ruth, smiling.

"Yes, I am sure we shall be," replied Flora, earnestly. "I like you ever so much, Ruth. I am very lonely here. I know nobody in this place except my home folks."

"How strange," said Ruth, in a puzzled way. "Tell me about it."

Flora was glad to tell her story.

"You poor child!" exclaimed matronly Ruth, taking her hand between both her own, and pressing it. "How sorry I am for you."

"Are you?" said Flora, laughing nervously, for she felt more like crying. "I was just feeling sorry for you."

"Sorry for me? Why?"

"Because you have to live here all alone, or almost alone, and have so many responsibilities. You must get very lonely."

"Oh, but my responsibilities keep me so busy I have no time to be lonely. Besides, I like responsibilities."

"You do? Perhaps if I had a few I wouldn't be so lonely either; but then you see I have none."

"I think you have," returned Ruth, soberly, and added, after a moment's thought, "I think you have a great many."

"What are they?"

"Your mother, and father, and brothers, and your home. You are responsible for your conduct toward your parents. It is your duty to be a good daughter. There's your home, it is your duty to make it pleasant and comfortable. And there are your brothers—"

"Oh, do stop, Ruth!" cried Flora. "You have told me enough. You talk as if you were thirty years old instead of sixteen. No, no! I will not hear any more today about responsibilities; I have had enough for one day," and she playfully placed her hand over Ruth's lips.

"I wasn't going to say any more about them," said Ruth. "I was only going to ask you to come into the house, for I must begin to prepare our supper."

"No, thank you!" replied Flora; "I must go now; but I should like to come again soon."

"Indeed, come as often as you please; the oftener you come the better I shall like it. Come right through the fence whenever you want to; you will almost always find me here."

"Thank you," said Flora. She bade Ruth goodbye, and returned home the same way she had come, entirely unconscious of the look of disapproval with which little Jem was regarding her from the window of an upper room, whither she had retreated with her precious Pokey.

Jem felt quite slighted. Flora and Ruth had been so much occupied with each other as to forget entirely her important little self, and she determined to severely punish "Sister Ruth" for her conduct. She immediately proceeded to put her determination into execution by stowing herself and Pokey away in the darkest corner under the bed, and there she remained in spite of Ruth's coaxing calls.

Ruth found her there fast asleep, when she went to look for her at teatime. Ruth was well acquainted with Jem's various modes of punishing her, and she readily guessed the cause of her little sister's present displeasure; and likewise knowing her well, she decided to let her alone until she was ready to come down. At last Jem came down while Ruth was washing the dishes. She was in perfectly good spirits, for she felt satisfied that her sister had been sufficiently punished in having been deprived of her company for so long a time. She sat down quietly and ate her supper, which had been set aside for her. She did not say anything about the events of the afternoon and neither did Ruth, who was busy thinking about Flora. Strangely enough, influenced by some unseen power, Flora was at the same moment thinking of Ruth. When our young friend entered her home, she found her father had returned in her absence. Her mother was hurrying about in an aimless, impatient way, trying to get supper and at the same time set the table. These two occupations were not progressing very rapidly in her nervous hands.

Harry and Alec were both in the dining room; the former sitting by the window reading, and the latter whittling a bit of wood with his pocketknife, and letting the chips fly and settle where they would. It was not a very inviting picture, but with Ruth's gentle face before her, and her words "It is your duty to be a good daughter" in her mind, Flora stoutly determined she would begin immediately and undertake her responsibilities in the very best way she could. With these thoughts she quietly said to her mother she would finish setting the table. It was not much to do, but she felt a great deal better in making this first effort to be of use in her home.

"What have I been thinking about not to have been doing this before? It is an actual treat to be busy," she continued to herself, as she placed the plates, cups, and saucers on the table. She did not know it, but both Harry and Alec were watching her whenever they were sure she was not looking.

The boys had not paid any attention to their sister since her return home; in fact, they both thought it a bother to have a girl about the place. Moreover, Flora had made no effort to prove herself a very valuable addition to the little family. But this evening, as she moved back and forth, the neat and tasteful way in which she arranged the table, was so different from the usual careless manner, that both boys were favorably impressed. Mrs. Hazeley too, when she hurried in with the supper, gave a sigh of relief, as she noted that everything was ready. And the father, although preoccupied with his own thoughts, glanced about with a pleased look in his eyes.

Although Flora was not aware of all this, she did not fail to notice there was a difference from the ordinary meal. The boys refrained from their usual snappish behavior, the mother was less peevish, and her father's face wore a look of quiet approval. On the whole, there was change enough to cause Flora to determine she would follow out the suggestion of her friend Ruth, and endeavor to make her home what she desired it to be.

When supper was over, Harry and Alec took their hats and went out, no one asking where they were going, or when they would return.

How queer, thought Flora, who had volunteered to clear the table and wash the dishes, how queer, that neither mother nor father seems to care where the boys go, or what they do. And realizing the indifference of her parents, Flora began to feel an interest in the pursuits of her brothers.

When Flora retired to rest that night, she felt quite pleased with her experience of the afternoon and evening, and she intended that this should be the beginning of a new departure in her life; and she felt glad that she had found such a friend as Ruth. She arose early the next morning, and was downstairs before her mother was stirring. It was Sunday, and the entire family were in the habit of rising later than usual on that day.

"What a dingy old place this is, to be sure," said Flora. "I'll make the fire and straighten things up a little."

When she had finished she looked about, and shook her head.

"It doesn't look a bit comfortable, or homelike. No wonder the boys go out every evening. I do wish I knew where to begin to improve things, but I don't, and I have no one to ask about it, except Ruth; yes, I will talk to her about things. Perhaps she can help me."

When Mrs. Hazeley came downstairs, to her surprise and unbounded delight she found the fire burning, the kettle boiling, and the table daintily laid, ready for breakfast.

"Why, Flora! I did not know you were up," she said, looking around, well-pleased with the generally improved condition of the room.

"I do believe your aunt has made quite a housekeeper of you," she continued, a moment later, as she inwardly congratulated herself upon the circumstance which had sent her daughter home.

Flora flushed at this unexpected, and for her mother, somewhat unusual word of commendation, but made no reply, for the simple reason that she did not know what to say. In spite of this feeling of pleasure that her effort was appreciated, she could not help wishing herself back in her aunt's home, —not as it now stood, with Aunt Sarah at its head, but as it had been under Aunt Bertha's gentle control. The more she thought of it, the more intense became the longing to be there in the old, happy, carefree life at Brinton. But there was nothing to be gained by wishing: Aunt Bertha was dead; Aunt

Sarah was there, and there to stay; and she was at home, and here to stay; so there was nothing to do but to make the best of things, and get as much comfort out of life as she could. Then she thought of Ruth's life, and her brave effort to make a home for her father and Jem, and inwardly Flora determined to emulate her example. How well she succeeded the future will show.

IV.
FLORA'S FIRST SUNDAY.

Breakfast over, and the dishes cleared away, Flora looked about, wondering what else there was for her to do. Her father was reading a paper, and the boys had gone away. She went to the window where Lottie's potato stood in its jar. The sight of it carried her thoughts back so vividly to the old days, that she half resolved to look at it no more.

She felt dull and spiritless today; it was no wonder, for there was little to make her feel otherwise. At Aunt Bertha's, everyone had been accustomed to attend church, and Flora remained to Sunday school. She had been converted and received into the church about a year before her aunt's death. Her sudden sorrow, her hasty trip from Brinton, and her unfamiliar surroundings in her new home, caused her to feel as if she had been removed to a heathen land.

None of the Hazeley household attended church, and Flora knew of no place to which she could go, for all was so new and strange to her, and being somewhat timid, she would not go alone.

Still standing at the window, and looking drearily out on the quiet street, she saw Ruth and little Jem passing, on their way to church. When they saw Flora they stopped, and she, glad to see a friendly face, hastened to open the door.

"Would you not like to come with us to church, this morning?" asked Ruth.

"Indeed I should," replied Flora. "I was just wondering what I was going to do with myself to day. Wait a minute; I will be ready in a very short time."

As good as her word, she was soon ready. "I am so glad that you stopped for me, Ruth," said she, as they walked along. "I know nothing about the churches here, and no one goes from our house."

"That is too bad," returned Ruth, sympathizingly.

Flora was indeed glad that she had come when, as they ascended the church steps, she heard the deep tones of the organ pealing out a welcome to all who entered. As they walked up the aisle, it seemed as if the sweet notes of the music twined around them, as though enfolding them in a loving embrace. A feeling of quiet content filled the heart of the young girl, and for a time the realities were forgotten in the soothing sense of rest that stole over her. Nor did she attempt to arouse herself until the opening services were ended, and the minister arose to announce his text.

In clear, distinct tones he read: "Whatsoever thy hand findeth to do, do it with thy might." Twice he slowly read the words, until Flora thought he surely must have pressed them right into her brain, for she felt that they were indelibly imprinted on her memory. Whether the sermon was intended especially for young people, or not, she did not know, but she felt that it was peculiarly adapted to herself. I have no doubt that the older folks felt the same with regard to themselves. It was one of those texts and sermons that suit everybody.

"I wonder how many of my hearers can say truthfully that they have done with their might 'whatsoever' their hands found to do," said the minister, looking, as Flora thought, directly at her.

She dropped her eyes uneasily to the floor, and mentally admitted, I, for one, have not, unless it was to grumble and fret with all my might. I have done that, but nothing else, at least since I came home.

"I am sure you cannot say that your hand has found nothing to do. You can perhaps say that your hand has not found what you wished it to do; but that is not what the words of the text teach. It says, 'whatsoever thy hand finds to do.' Then too, it is to be done 'with thy might'; not half-heartedly."

"Oh," commented Flora to herself, "why should he talk so straight at me? If he is not describing Flora Hazeley, I am mistaken."

"Did you ever notice," the minister continued, "that when you did a thing heartily, even though it was not the most agreeable occupation to you, it became more easy and pleasant to you?"

Flora thought of the little help she had voluntarily given her mother the previous evening, and again inwardly agreed with the speaker. The minister said a great many things that morning, some of which had never entered Flora's mind, and they made her very thoughtful; so thoughtful that she paid but little attention to the strains of the organ that accompanied her out of the church. She remembered he had spoken of many kinds of work the hands might find to do, and which were to be done faithfully and heartily. Perhaps it would be church work; perhaps professional work; perhaps mechanical work; and perhaps housework and homework. The last two, he thought, ought to go together, as neither could do very well without the other, although each differed in character. "Housework," he said, "as all knew, was sweeping, dusting, cooking, and the other duties connected with caring for the house; but homework was the making and keeping a home; helping those in it to be contented and happy; brightening and making it cheery by both word and deed; shedding a healthful and inspiring influence, so that those around us may be the better for our presence."

"According to that, we all have a 'whatsoever,'" said Flora, emphatically to herself; "and the sooner I decide to start on my own part, the better it will be for me."

With her mind busy with many things, Flora was very quiet on her way home. The sermon to which they had listened was plain and practical. It was not brilliant, but it was helpful. The ideas were not necessarily new, but the words fell upon at least one heart already prepared and softened by circumstances to receive and profit by them. To Flora they were seed, falling upon the prepared ground of her heart, and in due time the fruit came forth. Most of the suggestions were new to her, for never before had she viewed them in this particular light.

Ruth respected her friend's silence, for she saw that she was busy with her thoughts, and guessing something of what they were, she was also quiet. Jem was unaffected by the silence of her elders. She walked along at Ruth's side, with her hand closely holding her sister's. Her happy life caused her every now and then to lapse from her dignified walk, and give a little jump and a skip. A continual volley of questions was thrown at Ruth, whose replies were not always as obvious as occasion demanded.

Jem's quick retort, "No, it isn't, Ruth," brought her to a realization of her abstractedness, and she resolved to be more attentive.

They left Flora at her door, Ruth asking if she had enjoyed the service, and added:

"Will you not come to Sunday school with us this afternoon?"

"I did enjoy the sermon very much," Flora replied, "and I shall be pleased to go to Sunday school. If you will call for me, Ruth, I will be ready when you come."

A number of things grew out of Flora's experience on this Sunday. Its influence stayed with her, and had no small part in shaping her future life. She soon became an earnest worker to make the world better for her living in it; striving patiently and faithfully to render her daily life a power for good to those around her. How she succeeded our story will tell. Last, but not least, a strong affection sprang up between Ruth and herself, which proved a blessing to both.

Ruth taught a class in the Sunday school, and persuaded Flora to consent to take one also, if the necessity arose. She introduced her to the superintendent, who welcomed her cordially to the little band of Christian toilers.

"One class is in need of a teacher," he said; "will you not take it? It is composed of girls from ten to twelve years of age."

"Oh, I should not dare to undertake a class of girls so old!" exclaimed Flora. "I am too young myself. Give me little girls, such as Ruth has."

"But," said Mr. Gardiner, "there is no such class in need of a teacher. Besides, it is not the age that has to do with your success as a teacher; it is the earnestness, perseverance, patience, and true piety which you bring to the work that will bring forth the results you desire."

"I am so inexperienced," murmured Flora.

"Neither has that anything to do with the matter," contended the gentleman, smiling. "Experience will come, all in good time," he added.

"Well," said Flora, "I will do my best."

"That is right," answered Mr. Gardiner, heartily. He felt sure that the young girl before him would succeed, for energy, conscientiousness, and determination could be read plainly in her bearing, and these, he knew, were characteristics of a successful teacher. He was glad, therefore, he had persuaded her.

Ruth, also, was pleased, for now her friend would be also a co-worker.

Flora felt sad when she thought that her family were the only ones of those who knew her who were entirely indifferent as to what she did or where she went.

"Only think, Ruth," she said to her friend, "it doesn't matter to them, whether I go wrong or right. What encouragement is there for a girl in my place to try to do right?"

"It does seem hard, dear," the gentle friend replied; "but then you will shine out all the brighter in the end for doing right in the face of discouragements; and God cares, you know."

They were at the gate, and bidding Ruth goodbye, Flora slowly went up the path to the house, her brain very active with new thoughts and purposes.

"Yes, God will help me, if I ask him," said Flora, softly, as she went to her room, and after doffing her hat and jacket, she knelt beside her bed, and asked the dear Lord to bless and strengthen her in her new surroundings, and let her life tell for him.

V.
THE BEGINNING.

Monday morning was cloudy. Flora felt gloomy and dispirited, and notwithstanding her good resolutions, not in a mood to make any extra exertion.

Mr. Hazeley had gone to his work, Harry and Alec to school, and the mother was in bed with a sick headache. Flora was lonely. There was much to be done, she realized, but just where to begin she did not know. There was no one to tell her what to do, and everything looked very dark to her on this Monday morning.

The dishes were nicely washed, and carefully put away. The little dining room had been swept and dusted, and looked somewhat more inviting. The window where the sweet potato, the last link binding her with the past at Brinton, stood, had been washed until the glass fairly shone, and now she stood gazing listlessly out into the street.

Presently she saw Ruth, on her way home from market. When in front of the house, Ruth looked up, and saw Flora's woebegone face at the window. She stopped, and gave her a smiling little nod. Flora's countenance brightened immediately, and she hastened to meet her.

"You look lonely, this morning," was Ruth's greeting.

"Indeed, I feel so," admitted Flora.

"If you are not busy come home with me for a while."

"I should like nothing better," cried Flora. "Just wait until I tell mother."

In a moment she was back, and the two walked on, Flora insisting on helping Ruth with her market-basket.

Jem met them at the door of the tiny house, and conducted them in with great dignity. Flora was delighted with everything.

"What a dear little house," she exclaimed, glancing about her admiringly.

"I am glad you like it," said Ruth, looking pleased.

"And what a dear, little, old-fashioned housekeeper you make!"

"Do you really think so?"

"Of course I do," said Flora, heartily. "Ruth, dear," she continued, abruptly changing the subject, "I want a talk with you."

343

"I shall be so glad to have you," said Ruth, seating herself, with a pan of apples in her lap. "Sit down beside me, and you can talk while I pare these apples."

"I will help," replied Flora. "Run, Jem dear, and get another knife for me, like a good girl."

Jem obeyed, and soon returning, brought with her a box filled with bits of calicoes, and various odds and ends, seated herself also, and proceeded to fashion what she was pleased to call "doll's clothes."

"Ruth," began Flora, after they were all settled and busy, "I like you ever so much, and I hope we always will be friends. You seem to know so much, and you have had so much experience, that I am sure you can help me a great deal, if you will."

"Of course, dear," was her gentle reply, "I would be glad to help you all I can, and I shall be as pleased as possible for us to be friends. As to my knowing much, you are mistaken; I know but very little of anything; and experience,—well, I have had some, I suppose; but then, it isn't the sort that would help you, I am afraid. However, I shall be glad to do anything I can for you."

"I am sure you can help me, Ruth. You have helped me already," said Flora, decidedly. "And I mean to do as you suggested, and try to make my home just what I would like to have it. I don't know how to begin exactly; and then, mother never seems to care how things go, and that makes me feel as if I did not care either."

"I don't like to hear you talk about your mother so, Flora dear," said Roth, in a troubled tone.

"How are you to help me, if I don't tell you just what I think and feel?"

"Perhaps, if you were to let your mother see and know that you wanted to help her, and make things bright, and talk with her—"

"Talk!" interrupted Flora; "I don't believe she would do it, even if I were to try."

"Oh, but have you tried yet?" asked Ruth, looking up archly. "You cannot tell until you do."

"Very well," said Flora, laughing, "I guess I shall try. But there is another thing," and the troubled look returned to her face. "It is about the boys, my brothers. They stay at home scarcely ever. I don't know where they go so often, and I am sure mother does not, and I don't believe she cares—you need not look grave again, Ruth—I don't. Harry and Alec seem to be good boys, and it is a pity they are not restrained. They may get into bad company —if they are not in it already—and do something dreadful, and bring disgrace on us all. What can I do about that?"

"It would take a wiser head than mine to tell you that," Ruth answered; "but you might try and see if you could not make it so pleasant at home they would not care to be away so much."

"It seems pretty plain to me that that is easier to say than to do," retorted Flora, just a little impatiently.

"Yes, I know," assented Ruth, meekly; "I don't pretend to be a Solomon; I only said you might try."

"I don't believe they would stay for me," contended Flora, stubbornly.

"That is another thing you have never tried yet," said Ruth, smiling mischievously.

"That is so," laughed Flora, as she took two or three curly parings, and put them on Ruth's hair, to show penitence for her contrariety. "I guess I had better not talk any more, until I have tried to do something. I don't know how to begin my reformatory measures, but I suppose all will be well if I start with 'whatsoever.'"

By this time the apples were finished, and she rose to go.

"You haven't remired my doll's things," said Jem, reproachfully.

"So I have not," said Flora, and she sat down beside the little seamstress, and began to "remire" the various articles held up for inspection. She was compelled to see through Jem's eyes, however, for the shapes of the garments were not so striking or familiar as to suggest their names.

When at length she reluctantly took her leave, Ruth invited her to come soon again, to which she laughingly replied she certainly should. After this, matters went on more pleasantly at Flora's home. She busied herself with making the house look as cosy and as attractive as the shabby furniture and worn carpet would admit. She succeeded beyond her own expectations. She was gratified also that her brothers seemed to enjoy the improved condition of affairs, and so did her father when he was at home. Lottie's potato was now adding its mite to the general reform, and was sprouting nicely, sending its delicate white roots downward into the clear water, and its closely folded leaflets upward, to grow green in the warm sunlight. It seemed to be quite at home in the bright window. Flora had ceased to dream when she looked at her quaint friend. The days now, were too full to build air-castles. Mrs. Hazeley was pleased to shift her responsibility to Flora, who enjoyed nothing better than to have all her time occupied. Often, when tangles would come, Flora would run over to the ever-sympathetic Ruth, and receive advice from her. Thus, in being busy, Flora became more content, and often, as she thought of Aunt Sarah, she knew she would not be found fretting.

She had not yet attempted to influence the boys by word, but they soon noticed the new air of homeliness pervading the rooms, and consequently did not go out so much as had been their custom. Alec, the younger boy, was very mercurial and mischievous, while Harry, the elder, was quiet, and fond of reading.

One evening Harry seemed to be more than usually inclined to be sociable, and gave his mother and sister an animated account of something that had happened "down town," that day. When he finished he took up his book, and was just preparing to read, when Flora, eyeing the volume distrustfully, asked:

"What are you reading, Harry?"

Harry looked up at her quizzically, and answered her question by another.

"Why? What is it to you, anyway?"

"Nothing," said Flora, rather disconcerted. She was unaccustomed to boys, and had but little tact in dealing with them.

"I thought so," replied Harry, coolly, returning to his book.

"Will you not tell me what you are reading?" again asked Flora, not willing to be so easily vanquished.

"Why do you want to know?" demanded Harry, looking at her suspiciously.

Flora's lips again framed "nothing," but no sound came, for like a flash she thought, "If I say that, he will say, 'I thought so,' as he did before. No, I will give a reason," so she said:

"You seemed to be so interested in it, I thought it must be very entertaining."

"So it is," replied Harry, throwing a mischievous glance over to the corner at Alec, where he sat thoroughly engrossed in his favorite pastime of whittling, and in serene thoughtlessness allowing the clippings to fall according to their own sweet will.

Harry was confident that Flora intended to "read him a lecture upon trashy literature," as he afterward privately told Alec. He replied:

"It is interesting, Flo, about murders, and bears, cutthroats and burglars, and other horrors that would make you nervous to read about."

"I am not made nervous so easily as you may think, my dear boy," retorted Flora, condescendingly, and at the same time glancing cautiously at Harry, to see what effect this would have.

She had determined to try and gain an influence over her brothers, and felt that to show an interest in their occupations would be a good beginning. She realized the task she thus imposed on herself, but she meant to do her best, for this was another "whatsoever."

Harry was for a moment too much surprised to speak. Then he said, saucily:

"Ah, indeed! Well, let me read some to you."

"I shall be glad for you to read to me, if you will read a story I have just started. I feel sure you will enjoy it. If yours is a book for boys only, I fear I could not appreciate it."

"Oh, you couldn't?" said Harry. "Why not, may I ask?"

But Flora was up and away ere the sentence was completed. Harry congratulated himself on having put her to flight, and returned to his book with a self-satisfied smile. Flora, however, had only gone to her room for a paper. Hurrying back, she spread it before astonished Harry, and, pointing to its columns, said, in a peculiarly persuasive manner:

"Now, Hal, I would be ever so glad if you would read that story aloud to us, while I crochet, and Alec whittles on the floor."

Alec looked confused, and began to pick up some of the litter he had made.

"Never mind, Alec," said Flora, laughing, "I will clear it up this time. Could you not put a newspaper under you to catch the cuttings, another time?"

"All right," said Alec, looking relieved.

"We are all ready, Harry," said Flora, sitting down and taking up her work.

"Humph!" said Harry, glancing carelessly down the page. "There's nothing in such a story. I don't want to read it. It is too flat."

"You are mistaken," replied Flora, spiritedly. "It's not a bit flat, and there is something in it. It is about a brave boy who saved a train."

"Oh, yes, I know," said Harry, skeptically, "and was not hurt."

"Yes, but he did get hurt. Why not read it, and see?" suggested Flora.

"Yes, read it, Hal," said Alec; "let's see what it is, anyway."

"All right," and Harry began to read with a comical nasal twang, very rasping to Flora's feelings, but she had the wisdom to say nothing. She was very glad, later, because Harry gradually dropped the false tone, and she could see by his manner that he had become interested, in spite of himself. Alec too, had ceased whittling, and was listening intently.

Forgetting to criticize, Harry read the entire story, which, in truth, was a pathetic little incident, very gracefully and entertainingly told. He was silent, as he laid the paper on the table, but his thoughts were busy.

"I was right, was I not, Harry?" asked Flora.

"Yes," drawled Harry, smilingly, "you were. I did enjoy it, and I am glad you asked me to read it. But, let me see," he added, turning to the clock, "what time is it? Well," and he laughed, "I was good. It is nearly ten. Guess I will retire; I was going out, but it is too late."

Flora was secretly rejoiced to hear this, but she simply said, "Good night." She felt a glow of satisfaction as she realized a beginning had been made toward gaining the hold upon her brothers she so much desired.

"Flora, will you lend me that paper?" asked Alec, as she was preparing to go to her room. Flora willingly placed the paper in his hand, remarking, as she did so,

"I am glad you like the story. I have others, if you want them. Aunt Bertha kept me well supplied."

"Good night," returned Alec, and he was gone.

Flora was more nearly content than she had been for some time, as she sank into peaceful slumber that night.

VI.
SOME RESULTS.

"I believe I am going to realize some of the dreams I used to have, after all," Flora said to herself, as she laid her head upon her pillow that night.

She was right. The first step had been taken by her in the path of becoming an earnest worker, and to influence those about her as she had planned she would like to do, although not in such a way as this, nor in such surroundings. Her cherished dream of being instrumental in leading others into a higher and better life was now, she began to realize, leading her into the lines of duty in her own home, and among her own people. She could not wish for more.

She would not be like so many others, who in their desire to do great things, neglect the opportunities near at hand, and who, in longing to lead the heathen to a higher plane of life, forget those at home, who possibly for want of a word or act, have slipped, stumbled, and fallen on life's pathway.

Flora was growing, and with an earnest prayer to the Christ for guidance, strength, and tact, she cheerfully assumed more duties in the home, and greater responsibility. Her bright, sunny disposition, her pleasant face, her extreme willingness to respond to requests, gradually won a place for her in the hearts of those in her home.

The class in Sunday school was assumed with a feeling of great apprehension. It was composed of five girls between the ages of ten and twelve. At first sight of their youthful teacher, these girls had been inclined to be displeased, but when they grew to know the sunny, sweet good-nature, born of the great desire to do them good, and which shone out of the earnest eyes, they loved her dearly. The teaching of this class was fraught with great good, both to the teacher and scholars, and this meeting with the eager, bright girls was soon eagerly looked forward to by Flora from week to week.

"How things have improved at Mr. Hazeley's!" soon grew to be a common remark among the neighbors.

"Yes, since Flora came home, it has become very different from what it formerly was," would be the spirit, if not the words of the reply.

Flora overheard a similar remark one day, and it gave her a feeling of great joy to know the change was becoming apparent. Her resolution was strengthened to sustain this newly made reputation.

It must not be supposed that she always had an easy time. This was not so, for as she often said to Ruth, "When mother and Harry are not in a good humor, things do become tangled."

However, to do the family justice, they were beginning to see and to more fully appreciate the changes made in their home since Flora, who had left them a small maiden, had returned with her thoughtful ways and mature manner. They forgot sometimes that she was but sixteen, and would fancy she was older than she really was. In fact, almost imperceptibly, she assumed all responsibility, and they deferred to her judgment in many things. Best of all, however, they began to love her.

Her younger brother Alec seemed to have entirely surrendered to her gentle, loving rule, and was ever willing to listen to her advice. He was always ready to help her by running errands, chopping wood, drawing water, and performing a dozen other little tasks quite new to him, for he had never aided his mother in any way. In fact she had never asked her boys to assist her, or to save her extra steps or work, forgetting it ought to be required from them.

Mrs. Hazeley also had changed under the magic wand of Flora's sunny influence and determination to win the love of all. She had become at least a willing agent to the general change taking place in her home, and which recommended itself to her because her responsibilities were lightened and carried by other shoulders.

The house itself was transformed. Even cynical little Jem was becoming satisfied with it. It still contained the same furniture, but there was an air of comfort and home life about it never there before, but introduced by the magic of Flora's presence.

Lottie's sweet potato added its share to the general improvement which was going on. The long thread-like roots looked very white in the jar of water in which they were growing, and the graceful tendrils and light-green leaves were quite refreshing to the eyes. Flora had trained the vine about the window on small cords, and already it had nearly covered the lower part with its delicate branches. Flora would have felt lonely without it to care for; especially after being accustomed to have plants in profusion around her at her old home. Then too, it carried her back to the happy days at Aunt Bertha's, bringing a feeling of joy that she had been permitted to live there so long, and to be trained in such a gentle, firm, loving manner. Frequently she mentally contrasted her carefree life there, and her life of responsibility now, and she determined, with the help that is from above, she would not sink to her surroundings, but would elevate them to her level. Bravely, patiently, hopefully did she go forward with this end in view.

She was really surprised to find how fond she had grown of her brothers, and they of her. She could think of her mother very differently now, and she in turn began to show signs of an awakening affection for her daughter.

As to Ruth, she was ever the same, a quiet little home body, whose hands were always too full to allow her to come to Flora, but whose demure little face never failed to smile a welcome to her friend, and whose wise brain could turn over Flora's tangles and straighten them.

The two girls loved each other dearly; and no safer, truer friend and guide could Flora have found than Ruth Rudd, who, although no older than she herself, was very mature in thought, manner, and speech. Her face however, was childlike and innocent, reflecting the pure soul within. Flora was fortunate indeed in having her for a friend and confidante.

Harry Hazeley was a manly fellow with fine qualities. He had been allowed to do as he pleased, and had not been greatly benefited by this freedom. No restraining hand or guiding voice had been held out to him, or to cheer him on his way. Not being evil minded, he had taken but few wrong steps, and now his attention had been attracted to higher and better things.

As I have said, Harry had good qualities; one of which was a kind disposition, and although it was not always apparent to his everyday associates, was brought into play whenever he met any one who seemed in need of assistance.

One morning, as he was walking through the market on his way to school, his attention was attracted by an old man. One of his feet was swathed in bandages, and he was hobbling painfully back and forth, from his wagon to the stall, where he was trying to arrange a quantity of vegetables and some flowering plants which formed his stock in trade.

Harry had a quarter of an hour to spare, and he immediately offered to help the old man, who was only too glad to accept the proffered assistance, and who introduced himself, between the journeys from stall to wagon, as "Major Joe Benson, a gardener on a small scale."

Major Joe was an old ex-soldier, who had been wounded, and later imprisoned. The title "Major" was only a nominal one, and not indicative of any rank. His name, as he informed Harry, was Joseph Major Benson, Major being his mother's maiden name. He preferred to transpose this and call himself Major Joseph Benson, shortened for convenience to "Major Joe."

"It sounded sort of big, you know," he said, drawing himself up and looking dignified, until reminded by a sharp twinge in his foot that "rheumatiz" and dignity did not agree.

Major Joe was very talkative, and would not cease his persuasions until Harry had promised to drive out to his home with him someday, and see his nice little farm and Mrs. Benson, and he added:

"She will be delighted to see you, because you possess such a kind heart, and because you helped me. You must come."

"Yes, I will," returned Harry, "but I must be off to school now. Goodbye." And away he went, mentally pronouncing the major a jolly old chap.

The visit was made, and strange though it seemed, a fast friendship sprang up between the two, and the visits became quite frequent. Harry had taken Alec with him several times, and he too had greatly enjoyed the trip. Major Joe could tell any number of quaint tales and reminiscences of interest to the brothers. Mrs. Benson, who was more active than her husband, was always desirous for Harry and Alec to remain to tea. Her heart had been reached by the kindness of Harry to her "Major," as she lovingly called him, and she could not do enough for them.

Harry had passed his old friend's stall a number of times since Flora's return, and had of course told him about his sister. The major had a strong desire to see this wonderful girl, as he deemed her to be, from the glowing descriptions that came to him. Finally he insisted, and Mrs. Benson sent in a kind invitation that the three, Harry, Flora, and Alec must come home with him to spend the afternoon and take tea.

He chose a beautiful day in early summer for the visit, and Flora was anticipating it with no small degree of pleasure, for it would be the first real holiday she had had since coming home. The thought that the boys cared enough about her to plan a trip for her was a very pleasant one. Her mother seemed as much pleased with the idea as the rest, and had insisted upon her going, so Flora felt warranted in thoroughly enjoying her new experience. Mrs. Hazeley was daily becoming more energetic, and seemed really arousing to the fact that she had a place to fill in her home.

Major Joe was to call for his three young friends on his way home from market. He had promised to be on hand by noon, and as punctuality was an economizer of time, in the old gentleman's opinion, it was barely twelve o'clock when he drew up with a great attempt at flourishing before the Hazeleys' door.

VII.
A VISIT TO MAJOR JOE.

Quite an effort was necessary in order to arrange the board for an extra seat for Flora and Alec. At length it was made ready, and Flora was helped in, and Alec followed, while Harry took his place beside the major, who commented as follows:

"So this is your sister, Harry? Well, well, she's a sister to be proud of; and I haven't a doubt but you are proud of her. Here, you Jacob, git up, will you?" and he shook the reins vigorously over his horse's back. "You never do come to a standstill but what you think it's meant for you to go to sleep."

Jacob, roused from his intended doze, lazily shook his fat sides, and slowly moved along. It was a lovely June day, and the little party had a very pleasant ride of about an hour and a half, Jacob not being inclined to hurry.

Major Joe was conversationally inclined, and nothing pleased him more than to hear the sound of his own voice. He chatted continually: now about the orchards they passed, and their probable yield of fruit; now about the styles of the houses, as they came into view, and interspersed these remarks with reminiscences of the time when he was in the army.

The ride seemed quite a short one to Flora, who had enjoyed it thoroughly.

Mrs. Benson stood at the gate, watching for them; and in her white kerchief and neat cap, looked good-natured and comfortable. A saucy little spaniel sat in the middle of the road, watching too; and he was the first to catch sight of the wagon. He gave notice of the same by a sharp bark, and springing to his feet, doubled himself together, and bounded away, raising a cloud of dust in his haste to reach and greet his master. How happy he was when he reached the carriage! He sprang up at old Jacob, who paid no attention to such a small animal, but merely turned away his head with an air of supreme indifference.

"Jump, Dolby, jump!" said Major Joe. After several ineffectual trials, and two or three hard falls into the dusty road, Dolby landed beside his owner, who had made room for him, and gave himself a vigorous shake, which sent the dust he had gathered in his long hair, over Flora's clothes and into her face, causing her to choke, and a moment later to laugh. Dolby concluded this was in recognition of himself, and turning around, eyed Flora quizzically, and gave a satisfied little friendly bark.

The garden and nursery belonging to Major Joe were not large, but they were very fruitful, enabling him to realize considerable from the sale of his flowers and vegetables. He did not carry on his trade in a scientific manner, but merely for his love of the beautiful and useful things of the vegetable kingdom, and because to be inactive was for him to be unhappy. His receipts from the sale of the products of his land, together with his pension, enabled himself and Mrs. Benson to live very comfortably in their own snug little cottage, and, in addition, to lay aside something for a rainy day.

"Well, mother, here we are," said Major Joe, throwing the reins over Jacob's back.

"So I see," answered Mrs. Benson, nodding smilingly to the entire party. "Just come right in," she added, as Alec sprang out on one side of the wagon, and Harry helped Flora from the other.

The young people followed their hostess through the gate, and up the box-bordered walk into the cosy little cottage. Flora was soon seated in a low rocking-chair by the window, whose broad sill was filled with potted plants.

There Harry and Alec left her in good Mrs. Benson's care, while they went for a walk over the place.

Flora soon discovered that her hostess was as sociable as the major, and but a short time passed before they were chatting like old friends.

By-and-by, Alec thrust his merry face in at the door, and said:

"Come out here, Flora; the major wants you to see his garden."

"Yes, dear, go, if you are perfectly rested," said Mrs. Benson. "I will stay here, and see about preparing our early tea."

Flora joined her brother out of doors, and found Major Joe and Harry waiting.

"Come and see my little greenhouse," said the old man, waving his hand, and looking at them from over his spectacles with an important air. Flora complied quite willingly, for she was very fond of flowers, and immediately won the major's good opinion with her enthusiasm over his pet plants, and the interest with which she listened while he enlarged upon his management of them. The care of his garden was a tax upon his time, and really constituted quite a little labor. Then, outside, it was so pleasant to walk up and down among the neat flowerbeds, in the small, but nicely kept orchard; and in the kitchen garden, for the major prided himself on his choice vegetables, some of which frequently took prizes at the county fair.

The major himself was in his glory, for he had someone to whom he could talk. Talking was an occupation of which he never wearied, and now he chatted about the various departments of his labors, and how pleasant it was to watch the growth and development of the plants.

His tongue was still going very fast, when Mrs. Benson appeared in the doorway, and called to them that tea was ready. Reluctantly the old gardener relinquished his young listeners, who were, however, quite willing to vary the program, for they were hungry. The sight of the pleasant room, neat tea table, and their genial, motherly hostess, was a very inviting one. In a lull of the conversation, during the progress of the meal, Mrs. Benson remarked, with a sad little smile, that Flora reminded her of her Ruth.

"So she does," exclaimed her husband. "I knew she made me think of somebody, but couldn't make it clear who it was."

"Is Ruth your daughter?" asked Flora.

"She is, or leastways she was," said Mrs. Benson, heaving a sigh, and adding, in a low voice, "She's dead now."

"I am very sorry," said Flora, with ready sympathy.

"Yes, our Ruth was a fine girl, but a little headstrong. We did all we could to make her happy and contented at home, but it seemed as if we did not succeed, and so, one day she ran off to marry a man we couldn't care for, because we were sure he wouldn't treat our girl kind—not that there was anything against him, but he was so cold and unfeeling. But she wouldn't listen to us, and went off, and we never saw her again."

"How sad!" said Flora; "but couldn't you go to see her?"

Mrs. Benson shook her head. "No; he said we were not to have anything to do with Ruthie, after he married her, and they moved away somewhere, we never knew where, until we heard in a roundabout way that she was dead." Here Mrs. Benson paused to wipe away a tear. "I had hoped she would at least have stayed near home, and been a comfort to us in our old age; but, I suppose it's all right, and for the best. But excuse me for telling you so soon of our great sorrow. I should not have done it. Have you ever heard," she continued—and soon all were laughing heartily at her quaint sayings.

Flora, however, could not send from her thoughts this sad story. When the pleasant visit was drawing to an end, and they all were bidding Mrs. Benson goodbye, promising to come again, it still lingered with her. As old Jacob was soberly and deliberately trotting homeward, she revolved it over and over in her mind. Somehow it fastened itself upon her in a way she did not understand, and not until she was home, and had retired to her room for the night, did she arrive at even a partial solution of the perplexing problem. Then it dawned upon her with surprising clearness, that it certainly was because of the similarity of names in Mrs. Benson's daughter and her friend and adviser, Ruth Rudd.

This was very slight ground on which even to build an air-castle, but Flora did not stop to consider that, but in the midst of her dreaming resolved to go the next day, and rehearse to Ruth the story she had heard from Mrs. Benson.

Accordingly, next morning, after the work was done, and her mother was seated with her sewing, Flora donned her hat, and went to see her friend, expecting to find her busy as usual. She was, therefore, very much surprised to be met at the door, even before she had knocked, by Ruth herself, whose gentle face wore a troubled, anxious look, and she spoke in a low tone, as she responded to Flora's query:

"What is it, Ruthie?"

"Father is very sick."

"Oh, I am so sorry! What is the matter? When was he taken ill? Was it suddenly?"

"Yes, and no," said Ruth, answering simply the last question put by Flora. "He was compelled to stop work yesterday, and come home. He has been in poor health for a long time. I have been afraid, for quite a while, that he would break down."

"The doctor does not think he will die, does he?" whispered Flora, in an awed tone.

"Yes, he does," said Ruth, as she wiped her eyes with the corner of her apron.

The two girls, with their arms entwined, and a deep tenderness in their voices, then went into the little kitchen, where Jem sat, holding her beloved kitten close to her for comfort.

"Yes, the doctor says that he cannot last long. But what bothers me is, there seems to be something on his mind, and I can see he is worried."

"What about? Do you know?" asked Flora, sympathizingly.

"Well, I can guess," Ruth answered, taking from a work-basket a stocking of Jem's, and beginning to darn it in an abstracted, mechanical way.

"You see," she continued, "father married my mother—my own mother, I mean—against her parents' wishes—she was young—and he never would be reconciled to them, because they had objected to him. Neither would he allow them to have anything to do with each other afterward. He was very stern, and it all made mother so unhappy it just broke her heart, I am sure. She died when I was very small. He has told me, since Jem's mamma died, he wished he had tried to pacify my grandparents. But he had moved far away from them, and now, if he should die, he has nobody with whom to leave Jem and me. But he was always so proud; and now we shall be all alone," and she gave a sorrowful little sigh.

"See here, Ruth," exclaimed Flora, a sudden thought flashing across her mind. "What was your mother's name?"

"Ruth, it was the same as mine," was the reply.

"Yes, but what was her last name?"

"Benson, I think."

"Well, then, I think I know your grandparents," cried Flora.

"You do? How? Where?" returned Ruth, in a puzzled, disjointed way.

"Wasn't, or isn't, your grandfather named Joseph Benson?" asked Flora.

"Yes, Joseph Major Benson; but how did you know?"

"Oh, I found out," was the answer. "And they live just a little way out in the country."

"But, how do you know all that?" persisted Ruth, incredulously.

"Because I was there yesterday."

"Oh, Flora, are you sure? Don't raise my hopes and then disappoint me."

"My dear, you will not be disappointed; I should not like to do that," said Flora, gravely; "but let me tell you, and you can see for yourself." And then she told the story Mrs. Benson had told her, ending with, "So, you see, there can be no mistake."

356

Ruth was delighted, and thanked her friend again and again.

"Just see how God works," she said. "Who can tell what he will bring about. How glad I am! I must not tell father anything about it just yet. We must manage to send word to grandfather, and have him here before we tell. It would not do to excite father unnecessarily; he is so very weak."

"That is so, Ruthie," said Flora; "you are wise, as usual, in thinking of that. I should have done quite differently. I should have rushed right in at once and told him."

"Not if you had been in my place," was the gentle answer. "You see, I have been accustomed to think about such things ever since Jem's mother died, as father never took much interest in the management of our household affairs."

After some more talk, it was arranged that Flora should go and bring Major Joe to see his son-in-law in the morning, and then the friends parted, Flora to hurry home and enlist her brothers' aid in her new project; and Ruth to return to the bedside of her father, with the pleasant hope of not only easing his mind, but the feeling that should he die, she would not be left entirely alone in the world; a possibility which she had dreaded more because of her little sister, than on her own account.

VIII.
MORE RESULTS.

When Flora entered the house she found her brothers there before her, and both very quiet. It had grown to be such a pleasant thing to find their cheery sister at home when they came in, that they had almost unconsciously commenced to look forward to seeing her, and hearing her merry voice. They hastened home from school, and felt, but never expressed, disappointment when she was not there.

Flora, while not yet so wise and thoughtful as her friend Ruth, was daily learning lessons of usefulness, and continually using and developing new powers heretofore latent, and with her natural tact refrained from commenting upon many changes easily observed, going on in the habits of her brothers. And now she simply smiled at Harry, and pinched Alec's ear playfully, as she passed him.

Then she went to her room to remove her hat, and hastened back to help her mother with the dinner. While putting the dishes on the table she imparted her news to Harry and Alec, between her trips from table to pantry. They were both well pleased to have the prospect of being able to brighten the lives of Major Joe and Mrs. Benson. They considered Flora very bright to come to the conclusion she did.

"I forgot all about that story soon after I heard it," said Alec, conscious stricken. "Didn't you, Hal?"

"I am afraid I did," laughed his brother. "But what else was there for me to do? I knew no way in which I might help, as Flora did."

"That's so," rejoined Alec, in a relieved tone, willing to share in his brother's self-absolution.

"Of course neither of you could have done anything, for you did not know Ruth. But tell me, what will be best to do?" asked Flora, pausing with a dish she was carrying to the table.

"I know," said Harry. "Tomorrow is Saturday and market day also, and we all can go and see Major Joe in his stall, and tell him what we have heard, and what we think. If he is interested, one of us can stay at his stall while he goes and sees Ruth."

"How glad he will be; and how glad I am," said Flora. "It would be dreadful for Ruth and poor little Jem to be left with no one to take care of them."

Thus the question was decided.

The next morning Major Joe was surprised by a visit from all three of his young friends, and nonetheless delighted to see them, however, because they came unexpectedly, and he gave them a hearty welcome. It was understood beforehand that Flora was to be the one to open the subject, and explain matters. She did not tell everything at once, as Alec thought she ought to do, but approached the object of their visit in a delicate way.

"Major Joe; guess what brought us here today."

"I'm sure I can't say," answered the old man, rubbing his rough hands together, with a beaming smile. "Maybe to see your old friend?"

"To be sure; we're always glad to do that," replied Flora, as she placed the little bunches of parsley and thyme in more perfect order. "We have come for something else. Something very important," she added, seeing that Major Joe had no curiosity as to the nature of their errand with him.

"What would you say if I told you we had found somebody who belongs to you?"

"To me?" queried the puzzled man. "I don't see how you could do that."

"Yes, but I have," said Flora. "I am sure of it."

The old major shook his head doubtingly.

"And I want you to come with me and see if what I said is not true," persisted Flora, coaxingly.

"But how can I?" questioned Major Joe in reply. "I cannot leave my stall—who would wait on my customers?"

"Why not let me take charge until you return," asked Harry, speaking for the first time.

"And I can help," added Alec.

"Now you see it's all fixed," said Flora.

"Surely you're not afraid to trust us, are you?" asked Harry, as he saw his old friend still undecided.

"No, no; it's not that, my boy; only—"

"Only nothing," interrupted Flora, laughingly. "You must come, so say no more about it." And she caught his arm and led him away, an unwilling and unbelieving captive.

Ruth opened the door in answer to Flora's gentle tap. The latter could no longer restrain her impatience.

"Now, Major Joe," she exclaimed, softly, for fear of disturbing the sick man, "whom does this little sobersides remind you of?"

At first the old man looked from one to the other in a bewildered manner. Then his eyes rested on Ruth's face long and attentively. The tears gathered, and he involuntarily held out his hand, and said, softly, "Ruthie."

Scarcely realizing what she was doing, Ruth, probably drawn by the tender, loving tone that touched her heart, put her own in it.

"Who is she? What does it all mean?" asked the major, looking helplessly at Flora.

"It means," answered Flora, softly, "that this is truly Ruthie. Not your own Ruth, but her daughter and namesake—your granddaughter Ruth."

"Is that so? Are you sure? Don't say so if you ain't," pleaded the old man. And then the thought flashed across Flora's mind that perhaps after all she was mistaken, and had only brought her old friend there to be disappointed.

"Ruth dear," she said, dropping into a chair, weakened by the very thought, "tell him—tell him all about yourself; your mother's name, and everything. Do, please, quick!"

Ruth told the history of her dead mother's life, as she had heard it from her own lips.

Eagerly Major Joe listened, and when she was through, he held out his arms to her, saying:

"You are my poor Ruth's daughter," and the tears prevented him from adding more. Ruth and Flora wiped their eyes in sympathy: Ruth rejoicing in the possession of a grandfather; Flora, that provision was thus made for Ruth.

This tearful trio was interrupted a moment later by the entrance of Jem, carrying her doll under one arm, and her beloved Pokey under the other.

"Why, Ruth Rudd, I'm astonished at you, hugging a old market man!" and Jem looked at her sister with unbounded disapproval.

"Hush Jem, you must not talk so," said Ruth. "This is our grandfather."

"Not mine," returned matter-of-fact Jem, standing still in the middle of the room, and looking suspiciously at the visitor. "Not mine. I never had any, and don't want one."

"Who is this?" asked Major Joe, looking at the defiant little figure dubiously.

"She is my half-sister," answered Ruth.

"Well, well," said her grandfather, "she ain't Ruth's child, so I've no call to take her when I take you, Ruth. Her father can send her to his own people."

"Then, grandfather, I cannot go with you," said Ruth, sadly, but firmly. "I will never leave Jem."

"Ruth, you're not going to leave me, are you?" cried the little girl.

"No, indeed, dear, I shall not leave you. It was not very nice for you to speak of grandpa as you did just now. You should always be polite to an old person. Remember this, Jem."

"I don't care," said Jem, defiantly. "He's horrid. He wants to take you away, and you're all I've got 'cept father, and—and he's going to die," she sobbed, hiding her face in Ruth's arms.

"Don't cry, Jem. I will not leave my little sister. What could I do without you?"

"No, no, little one, Ruth's grandfather won't part you, if you're so fond of each other." And the major came over and patted the sobbing child's head, soothingly. His was too tender a heart to withstand the sight of a child in distress, so it was soon settled that he was to be Jem's grandfather also, which arrangement was accepted by the little girl as readily as she had rejected the idea a moment before.

Then the major, his heart made very tender by memories of the past, was ready to visit the invalid.

John Rudd had always been a quiet man, but willful and determined to succeed in whatever he undertook. He was not bad at heart, and when a wrong act was committed it was invariably caused by obstinacy. He usually quickly repented of his course, and made all reparation in his power.

Knowing that Mr. and Mrs. Benson did not like him as well as he had hoped, he determined to marry Ruth, and to prohibit all intercourse with her family. In everything else he was thoroughly honorable, but he tenaciously held to this point. Ruth Benson, loving him devotedly, and believing all he said or did was infallible, implicitly obeyed this strange request without a question, and neither did she hear of or from her parents.

That the unnecessary sacrifice did not add to her happiness, was proven by the fact that she lost her free, light-hearted ways, and became quiet and melancholy, after a year or two of married life. Her husband was proud—too proud to admit that he had made a mistake, until it was too late for such an admission to do any good, and so after a few years she died, leaving behind her little namesake, Ruth. She seemed to have transmitted to the child in a large measure her own disposition, for Ruth was always a grave, silent, little thing, entirely unlike other children, and quite old for her years.

It was nice too, she possessed such a sweet disposition and even temper, for when her father brought home a new mother for the little Ruth, many changes were made in the home, and great would have been the discord but for Ruth's peaceful characteristics. Shortly after his second marriage, John Rudd moved to Bartonville, whether for business openings, or to be near the early home of Ruth's mother, no one ever knew.

Ruth knew the story of her mother's married life, of the home of her girlhood, and of the kind parents, but she did not know where the home was.

Whatever the reason for his coming, it was well for Ruth and Jem, for as I have said, provision was now made for them both at Major Joe's farm.

Ruth's life thus far, since the cares of the home were put upon her at the death of Jem's mother, had been an uneventful one. She had no companion but her little sister, who so filled her brain, and heart, and time, that she had no opportunity to grow lonesome. Personally, Ruth would have felt happier if her father had allowed the love, she doubted not he held for her, to find expression in a word of praise, a tender kiss, or appreciation of her efforts. But her father never thought of this longing of his daughter: he was so self-contained himself, and unemotionally inclined, that he could not have understood this craving, even had he known of its existence, which it is needless to say, he did not.

It was rather hard for so young a girl to persevere in her homemaking with such a singleness of purpose as Ruth displayed, to give up her beloved studies without a sigh of regret, and to strive to train her younger sister, knowing she would receive no word of approbation from her father.

IX.
RUTH'S NEW HOME.

Flora was very glad to know that at last her tender-hearted, patient Ruth had found someone to love her as well as to require of her duties. Love is a lightener of labor, and Flora felt that, in this respect at least, she was more fortunate than her friend. She felt sure, moreover, she was fast gaining the affection of her brothers and of her mother, who was gradually awaking to love for Flora and the desire to make the home attractive. She had something to work for. But Ruth—she had no one to whom to look for love, except Jem, as it was impossible to think of their quiet, undemonstrative father ever expressing any of his love for his daughters. One could only judge from his manner, for he never said much, and that was the same as when she first knew them.

John Rudd apparently took it as a matter of course that Major Benson came to see him as he lay ill, and expressed neither pleasure nor displeasure when he stated that should he not recover Ruth and Jem would be well cared for. He accepted, without feeling, the heartily expressed forgiveness from the major, thinking that perhaps it was due in some degree to the presence of two faces standing near by with earnest, pleading looks at the newly found grandfather, who, deprived of his daughter, would fill the vacancy in his heart with Ruth and Jem.

It was very difficult for Major Joe, with his tender heart, to leave his grandchildren. At last, however, he did, promising to return in the afternoon with Mrs. Benson, who would be overjoyed to see them, especially Ruth, who was so like her mother at her age.

As they returned to the market, Major Joe was prolific in his expressions of gratitude to Flora for her part in bringing about this delightful reunion, for had this not been done, Ruth and Jem would have suffered, and would have been left without parents or home.

Harry and Alec were well pleased with their new position, and because trade had been very flourishing during their period of power. Major Joe heartily thanked them all for their kind help to him this morning. Flora then returned home, but Harry and Alec remained to do anything else possible for Major Joe, as he wished to go home at once, and must pack his wares.

It is neither necessary to recount in detail all that pertained to the last hours of John Rudd, nor how attentive Grandfather Joe was to his newly found grandchildren; nor how overjoyed Mrs. Benson was when she first saw them. It will be enough to say that all that could be done toward rendering the dying man's last moments peaceful was done. Toward the last he roused, and in a simple, but earnest way, expressed himself content to die. He said that, although he had not spoken of the matter for fear of distressing the children, he had known for some time that it was to be so, and that long ago he had made his peace with God. He regretted his past careless life, both as to his duty to his Maker and to the children entrusted to him; "but," he continued, "God is good, and ever willing to forgive, and to accept a truly contrite spirit, and my trust is stayed on him." He expressed himself as very grateful to him for his goodness in providing for his children. He blessed them all with his last breath and passed peacefully away.

When the last sad rites had been performed, Ruth's grandparents immediately began preparations to take her and Jem home.

The modest furniture of her home was entirely removed, although it somewhat crowded the cottage, but Ruth could not now part with these mementos of her former life, which had been her mother's.

At last, everything was ready, the little house was given up, and Ruth was spending a few moments with Flora, who, although instrumental in finding a new home for Ruth and Jem, was full of sorrow at the prospect of her loss in the parting with her friend.

"Don't look so sad, Flora dear," said Ruth. "Think what a blessing it is that poor little Jem and I have not been left altogether alone in the world. Had God not led you to find our dear grandparents, how very wretched we should be now. Besides, you know, we are not to be so far away; we can see each other often."

"That is true," returned Flora, brightening up; "I am glad of that; but it will be so lonely not to have you near me. Besides, I don't know any other girl as intimately as I do you."

"Oh, you will," said Ruth. "I am sure you will meet and become acquainted with someone as you did me. I hope, if you do, you may be permitted to do them as much good as you have done me."

"And me, too, Ruth," said an unexpected voice behind them.

Both turned, and saw Mrs. Hazeley standing in the doorway with a smile upon her lips and tears in her eyes.

"I used to be very unhappy, as you both know, and it was because I expected life to form itself for me—either for pleasure or unhappiness. Then Flora came," and she went over to her daughter and placed an arm about her, and looked lovingly in her eyes; "I watched her closely, and I soon discovered that she had determined to make this house a home, and a delightful one. No untoward circumstances seemed to discourage, but she was ever cheery and sprightly. We have gained by her homecoming—how much I cannot tell. She seems to have the mere power of will to mold circumstances as she chooses—"

"Not my will, mother," softly interrupted Flora, her face suffused with happy smiles; "it is God's will."

"Yes, yes, my dear," said Mrs. Hazeley, "I believe it. I want his will to mold my life too. A godless life is a wretched life, my children."

Harry and Alec had entered during the conversation, and were standing listening in amazement to what they heard from their mother.

"And the boys too," continued Mrs. Hazeley; "I am sure they have been helped by their sister's example."

"I know I have!" exclaimed Alec. Harry's only reply was to remark that the major was at the door waiting for Ruth. Then he turned and went out.

Flora felt a strange mixture of feelings at that moment. She was glad to know she had helped Ruth; unutterably grateful for her mother's words; and hurt at the seeming indifference of her brother. It was not her way, however, to dwell on what she could not prevent, so she only determined to strive harder than before to penetrate the armor of cold indifference worn by Harry of late.

As Harry left, they all went to the gate to wave a goodbye to Ruth. In the wagon was Jem, perched on a seat beside her grandfather, to whom she had clung with all the strength of her loving little heart. Immediately after the funeral she had gone home with him, taking "Pokey," and leaving Ruth in peace to pack. This was really a comfort to Ruth, as Jem's presence would not have been of any great assistance.

Soon everything was settled, and with many injunctions to come soon, the party drove off, little Jem holding the reins with a steady hand, and a determination to drive all the way home.

A new life thus opened for the orphans, Ruth and Jem—a life of freedom from care, of joyous liberty to run at will in the garden of their grandfather, who delighted in the company of Jem, and who returned his affection in full measure. The life at the cottage was blessed by the loving guardianship of the grandmother, who saw in Ruth her own daughter of long ago.

Under this beneficent influence Ruth lost some of her seriousness, becoming more like other girls, and grew rosy and stout.

The life at the farm had so absorbed Jem's mind and time that, for the time being, "Pokey" was forgotten, much to the latter's satisfaction, for now she could lie in the sun and sleep in peace without fear of being unceremoniously awakened by her erratic little mistress.

Flora watched the wagon containing Ruth and Jem until it was out of sight, and then went into the house.

Alec and Harry had gone away. Mrs. Hazeley was sewing, and Flora, having no especial duty, and caring for none, went over and stood at the window, listlessly gazing into space. Her eyes soon dropped, and her attention was attracted by the yellow leaves on the sweet potato vine. Flora felt as if all to which she had clung was leaving her in her loneliness. She looked closer. The potato was still firm and hard, and the jar was quite packed with roots, but the leaves on the vine were dying

X.
LOTTIE PIPER.

Flora had stood for some little time, mechanically caressing the vine, when she was surprised to hear near at hand, in a voice strangely familiar, the words:

"Well, I declare!"

Looking up quickly, but scarcely crediting her own eyes, she exclaimed:

"Lottie Piper!"

"Flora Hazeley!" returned the voice, and in a moment the friends were locked in each other's arms.

"Where did you come from? What are you doing here?" asked Flora, eagerly, in her desire to account for Lottie's presence in the village.

"Only one question at a time, if you please," laughingly returned Lottie. "Can you not guess?" she added, glancing at her gown, and for the first time Flora noticed it was black.

The quick tears sprang to Flora's eyes.

"Oh, Lottie, who is it? Not your mother?" she said sympathetically, her arm tightening in its grasp, and her thoughts running back to her sorrow when Aunt Bertha passed away.

"Yes," returned Lottie, sadly, "mother is dead. Father felt that he could not be happy at home, and so he went away out West, and left me with my aunt, Mrs. Emmeline Durand. And Flora, if you want to know what misery is, just you come and take my place for a while." And she looked at Flora with such a mingled expression of regret at her lot, and assumed resignation, that Flora was tempted to laugh, in spite of her sorrow in learning of the death of Mrs. Piper.

"If you want to laugh, you may," said Lottie, seeing her difficulty, and appreciating it, as was shown by the merry twinkle in her bright black eyes.

"No, no, I must not laugh," said Flora, squeezing her friend's arm affectionately. "I'm so sorry that your mother is dead. Where does your aunt live? I will come and see you."

"No, you—I mean you—can't—that is, she won't let you," stammered Lottie, blushing hotly.

"Yes, I understand. It is all right. It is not your fault," said Flora, hastily, appreciating the situation; and wishing to relieve the embarrassment of the other, she added, "You can come and see me."

"I don't know," answered Lottie, glad to find that Flora understood. "I hardly think she would let me come. I have not asked her to go anywhere, as yet. I have been with her about five weeks, and this is the first time I have been out, except on an errand. She says she doesn't approve of girls 'gadding the streets.' I must go now. I have stayed longer than I ought to already, for I had a long walk before I saw you. Flora," she added, an instant later, as she glanced at the window, "isn't that a potato in that jar?"

"Yes," answered Flora, "it is the same one you gave me when I was leaving Brinton."

"Really? The very same?"

"Yes. You know you told me not to eat it, and I didn't know what to do with it at first. Then I thought it would look very nice if I put it in the window; I did, and it has grown splendidly and has kept green all winter."

"I am so glad you thought of that, Flora, because that was what I first noticed as I passed. And I thought it looked like a sweet potato vine. And then, you know," Lottie continued, "if you hadn't I should not have stopped or seen you ever, because I did not know where you were going when you came away. But what will my aunt say? I guess I'll not get anything for supper but a bit of tongue, and I don't fancy that, I can tell you. Goodbye." And with a hurried kiss, and a warm embrace, Lottie hurried down the street.

She was sorry to go, as it was so good to meet somebody she knew—somebody connected with the old, happy home life, for while Lottie's mother lived, she had been very happy. But now she was so lonely.

She hurried along the streets until she came to one near the suburbs of the town. This street had trees on either side, and was very quiet. The houses were small and nearly all set back from the street.

Lottie walked along briskly, turning deftly in and out, and at length arrived safe and sound at the little gate leading into her aunt's yard. This gate opened upon a small space, which doubtless had been intended by the builder of the house to he beautified with flowers; but Mrs. Durand's front yard was closely paved with red brick. Not a flower, or a vine, or a bush broke the monotony, which, however, was not wearisome, as the yard was small.

A high board fence enclosed the little yard on each side. Close to the gate stood a large, old poplar, strangely drawn toward the quiet narrow street, as if weary of the unattractiveness of the house.

Lottie was nervous; she dreaded the reception she felt sure awaited her. The only thing that occurred to her to do was to knock, and she did so.

Receiving no response, she knocked again and waited. There was still no response, and thinking she had not been heard, she knocked again and again.

At length, just as she had decided that her aunt must be out, a calm voice from behind the door said in deliberate tones:

"If you will take the trouble to turn the knob, the door might open."

A. E. Johnson

This idea had not occurred to Lottie, and the knowledge that the door was not locked somewhat confused her. However, she opened the door, and went in.

"There is a mat in front of the door," suggested the voice in the same slow, measured tones.

After wiping off the infinitesimal amount of dust from her shoes, Lottie timidly ventured into the room.

"Go to your room, if you will, and lay aside your wraps," came the voice, in an authoritative way.

Without speaking, Lottie obeyed. She felt as she slowly climbed the stairs that she had become a veritable automaton, without volition or energy, and compelled to do certain things. This grated on the sensitive nature of the girl, to whom, in the happy days that had passed, freedom to live in and enjoy the open air was everything. And now—and Lottie inwardly groaned at the thought—her actions were directed by one who seemed to forget her own girlhood, or that she had ever enjoyed the bright blue sky, the green fields, the merry, twittering birds, or the companionship of those who were of her own age.

Lottie had often wondered in her own mind if her aunt had ever been young, and if she had enjoyed her youth. There was no one to whom she could go for an answer. Had there been, Lottie would have been surprised to learn that she had been full of bright, merry fun, and had enjoyed life as she had at home.

At home, Lottie thought, and paused, thinking of her mother, of the comforts and freedom of home, and then she looked in the glass to see if she was not old, for those happy days did seem so far away.

Mrs. Durand had met with many disappointments and a great deal of trouble in her life, of which Lottie knew nothing, and which had embittered her disposition, making her crabbed and disagreeable. As she now was, Lottie supposed she had ever been.

For some moments Lottie had looked in the glass, musingly. Now, as her thoughts returned to herself and her surroundings, she saw a dreary, woe-begone face looking at her from the quaint, cracked, old-fashioned mirror on her bureau. It was so doleful and forlorn, that Lottie nearly cried in sympathy with the miseries of the face before her. In a moment, realizing that it was her own reflection she saw, and enjoying her mistake, she laughed heartily, whereat the face in the mirror smiled pleasantly in return.

"Humph!" said the voice downstairs.

"Oh dear!" exclaimed Lottie softly; "I have made her think that I don't care about staying out so long." And she slowly turned from the bureau and her mirth-provoking vis à vis, and leaving her room, slowly descended the stairs to her aunt.

The room in which her aunt sat was furnished very plainly. Some cane-bottomed chairs, a black horse-hair sofa, a small wooden stand, adorned with a red cloth on which was the family Bible; two or three pictures upon the dingy walls, a pair of tall lamps with a bit of red flannel in the bottom, graced the mantelpiece. A dull ingrain carpet, and some homemade mats covered the floor. These, with a cloth-covered brick used to keep the door open, completed the furnishing of Mrs. Durand's parlor.

Mrs. Durand herself was a small, thin, wiry woman. Her features could hardly be called attractive; her lips were thin and tightly shut; her eyes were colorless, and she wore three stiff, little curls on each side of her face. She wore a dark gown, over which was a black apron, and on her head was a black lace cap. She was busily engaged in making another mat to adorn the floor, from long, bright-colored strips of cloth.

For some time she continued her work in silence. Lottie would have spoken had she had anything to say.

Presently, to Lottie's great surprise and relief, her aunt remarked:

"You may as well set the table, as you are here."

Lottie was glad to have something to do, as she was so much happier when employed.

"She hasn't scolded me yet, but it will come, that's certain," she said to herself, as she placed the dishes on the little round table in the back room which answered for both kitchen and dining room.

While at supper, Mrs. Durand questioned her niece about her walk, and Lottie told her, not forgetting the chance meeting with her friend, Flora Hazeley.

After supper, as was her duty, Lottie washed and put away the dishes, without further conversation with her aunt. That done, she took up a book and began to read.

XI.
CHANGES.

Time passed on, and with it as usual came changes. The summer was gone and it was November, and the weather was cold and dreary.

Lottie's life was much the same from day to day; there was little variety to make the life of the young girl pleasant. True, she did not have a hard time, nor was she overworked, nor did she ever go hungry; but the atmosphere of the house was always chill and drear, and Mrs. Durand was as unsociable and unsympathetic as ever.

It was perhaps true, that Lottie was somewhat prone to slightly exaggerate her unhappiness, and to dwell upon it until it seemed almost unendurable.

One morning, as she was dressing, she heard her aunt call, and upon going to her room, discovered that she was suffering from an attack of acute rheumatism. Then, indeed, Lottie was sure her misery was at such a height, that it could go no further.

As may be supposed, the sharp pain she endured did not render Mrs. Durand a more pleasant companion, and Lottie found that while it had been difficult to please her before it seemed utterly impossible to do so now.

Lottie did her best, with a determination pleasant to witness, and with the knowledge that it was her duty to care for her aunt under such painful conditions.

Lottie was lonely; she seemed to be entirely cut off from everybody she knew and cared for. She seldom heard from her father, and never from her brother, who had left his home when she was quite a little girl. She sometimes wondered if he was dead. She was industrious, and soon learned to keep house for her aunt very acceptably. She was not hard to please and was of a loving, sociable disposition. If her aunt had only made an effort to be agreeable and interested in her, Lottie would have been perfectly content.

If the months had brought but little change to Lottie, they had wrought a number of very important ones in the life of our friend Flora.

First, the news had reached them one day that the husband and father was killed in a railroad accident. This, of itself, completely revolutionized affairs at the Hazeleys'. And then, just as they were trying to become a little accustomed to the sad change in the household, Harry disappointed them.

This was indeed a great blow, for Harry was, in a large measure, their main dependence. He was now about twenty years old and had been steadily at work for some time, and seemed on a good road to a successful business career. At first, he gave his earnings to his mother, only reserving enough to clothe himself neatly and comfortably, for he felt anxious to supply, as far as he could, her loss in the death of his father. This money, added to what Mrs. Hazeley and Flora made by doing plain sewing, and what Alec could earn out of school hours by keeping his eyes open, and his willingness to be of assistance to any one, was a great help toward keeping things going. For, although the little home was their own, of course there were the extra incidental expenses.

Mrs. Hazeley and Flora soon grew to depend on Harry, far more than they realized, until taught by his increasing fondness for remaining from home in the evening, and not infrequently, all night. Great, indeed, was their sorrow when they learned how these evenings were spent—in the gambling house and the saloon. Had it not been for their hope in the Christ and his saving power, they would not have seen the faintest brightness in this cloud, which was a great burden to each, a sorrow about which they hardly dared speak.

Flora spoke earnestly and lovingly to her brother several times about the way he was conducting himself, but, as we have seen, he was not one to take this kindly, and knowing this, Flora felt she could do nothing but pray for her erring brother, who was so young, and yet so willful.

She never lost hope, nor did her firm belief that his better, nobler nature would prevail, weaken through those long, dark, hard days.

Mrs. Hazeley and Flora were compelled to devote all their attention to their work, as Harry could no longer be trusted to aid them financially; and, despite their brave, uncomplaining efforts, it was ofttimes difficult to make both ends meet.

Aunt Sarah had not visited them for some time, in fact, not since Flora came home, nor did they hear from her; and though knowing she might help them in their need, they could not bring themselves to inform her of their condition.

At length, one night they watched and waited for Harry to come home.

He did not come that night, nor the next, nor the one following; nor could they hear anything of him, except that he had not been around for days.

Where had he gone and what would he do? These were questions that Flora asked herself with a sick heart.

Mrs. Hazeley, with her naturally weak disposition, would have given way to despair under this new trouble and drifted back into the same condition in which we first found her, had it not been for her newly found trust and hope in her Heavenly Father, and the inspiring example of her courageous, self-reliant daughter. Flora seemed to grow stronger and more dignified under the added trials, and her mother, now a true Christian, was to her a great help and comfort; in fact, the two were all in all to each other, and the home that had at one time appeared to Flora most miserable, was now a haven of rest; and the mother from whom she had once turned away coldly, was now warmly loved and loving. Truly, there was sweetness mixed with her cup of bitterness.

Major Joe Benson, who had kept up his acquaintance with his young friends whom he greatly admired, and who by this time was considered quite a friend of the family, offered to take Alec to live with him. There was a very good school, he said, at no great distance from his home, and he would be glad to have the boy's help on his little place, especially now that Zeke was getting on in years, and had gotten above doing the many odd jobs he had performed when a boy, which state, while it was not many years distant, sufficed to make Zeke act, as Major Joe said, "very mannish."

No sooner was the proposition mentioned in Alec's hearing, than he was all enthusiasm, for nothing did he desire more than to live in the country. His mind was fully made up to become a farmer, and no recital of the hardships connected therewith, could divest such a life of its charms for him.

So it was settled, and it was really a great comfort to have at least one of the family well provided for, with the prospects of seeing him an upright and industrious man.

Now that provision was thus made for Alec, and he was but little expense to them, Flora and Mrs. Hazeley could manage very well by practicing strict economy.

Life progressed very evenly and uneventfully, we might almost add happily, except for the sorrow caused by their ignorance of Harry's whereabouts.

One day, into their quiet and peaceful lives, very unexpectedly came Mrs. Sarah Martin, who was surprised at their comfortable surroundings.

She was greeted pleasantly by Flora and Mrs. Hazeley, who were determined to forgive and forget her treatment of them, but the warmth, which affection gives, was lacking. This did not fail to make itself manifest to Mrs. Martin, and, strange to say, instead of displeasing her, it seemed to have quite a softening effect upon her callous heart. The memory of this visit, and the picture of her niece's heroic efforts to keep her mother and herself from want, proved a veritable ever-present and sharp thorn in the side.

Here I am, alone in the world, with plenty to supply all my wishes and some to spare, she thought one evening. We must do her justice; she was not miserly, but she was selfish—she wished to insure for her lifetime comfort for herself, and the gratification of her desires. "Here am I with plenty and to spare, while those of my own flesh and blood are struggling to keep the wolf from the door," she mused.

Having commenced to reproach herself she did not hesitate, for at every step seeing herself as others saw her, she discovered more cause to regret her attitude toward her sister.

"Have I been false to my trust?" she soliloquized, questioningly. "No—not exactly—because I gave no promise. And yet—Bertha supposed I would follow her request. However, I am not bound to do as she wished.

"Bertha would not have left me in charge had she supposed I would not carry out her wishes," she continued. "Probably she would not have given her property to Esther. She is so careless and extravagant that such a course would have been equal to her throwing the money away. Suppose the money had been left in trust to Flora? Would Esther have done more than I have done? No, she would have wasted it. What is the difference? Nothing; I am doing as Esther would have done. Anyway, I will leave all to Flora, who will enjoy it after I am dead, and that will make it all right."

Another thing Mrs. Martin tried to argue in support of the idea that she had done all for the best, was that Flora had developed such astonishing qualities of self-government and ability. "She has almost made another woman of that mother of hers," she said to herself. "One can easily see that the material for a real, sound, sensible, practical woman is not in Esther, and if Flora were not there with her she would be the same as before, only worse."

There was a good deal of truth in what Mrs. Martin said. Some people cannot do or be anything without a definite motive, or an active example. But what did all this arguing amount to? Nothing at all, save to keep her mind in a constant state of turmoil, by her efforts to ease her conscience.

At last, with the constant strain she became mentally exhausted, and in spite of her efforts to the contrary for a long time lay upon the bed, a sufferer from nervous prostration. Her brain was unnaturally active, and she gained but little benefit from her enforced quiet. A neighboring physician was called, but found it impossible to benefit her in her present condition. He might prescribe medicines to meet certain symptoms in her case, but he could not reach the seat of the trouble. She did not consider that it was her business to add a description of her mental condition to that of her physical one. She grew no better, and finally she decided to take a course of heroic treatment.

First, she proceeded to pay her physician and to inform him that she had no further need of his services, much to that gentleman's disgust, who left muttering that it was queer that the patient should be the one to decide whether or not the doctor had been of service to her.

Next, she wrote in a feeble, trembling, and unintelligible way, the following short, blunt note:

> NIECE FLORA:
> I am sick. I want to see you.
> S. MARTIN.

Flora and her mother were sitting sewing very busily that afternoon when the postman rapped on the door.

The sun was streaming in at the window, no longer adorned by the sweet potato, which was long since dead, but touching brightly the green leaves and scarlet blossoms of some geraniums—some of Ruth's "gerangums," according to Jem, that held the place of honor.

"From Aunt Sarah, mother," said Flora, carelessly, handing it to Mrs. Hazeley, who in turn read the short note.

"Well, Flora dear; what will you do about it?" she questioned, resuming her work.

"Oh, I guess I had better go and see her; hadn't I?" asked Flora, as she cut her thread.

"You may do as you please about the matter," returned Mrs. Hazeley, and there the matter dropped.

They continued their work in silence, their thoughts as busy as their fingers.

XII.
LED AWAY.

And what had become of Harry Hazeley in all this time? Let us go back a little.

Probably all would have gone well with the lad, who was beginning to see a new life stretching out before him under the sunny influence of his sister, had his father lived.

While Mr. Hazeley exercised but little restraining power over his son during his life, the fact that he had a father had considerable influence over Harry. When Mr. Hazeley was killed, Harry realized that he was thrown on his own resources, and the fact that he was subject to no higher authority, took a firm hold upon him. At first, the idea aroused in him an innate, but undeveloped manliness, and he determined to stand by his mother and sister, and be a comfort to them as well as a support.

But the inherent weakness in his character soon gained the supremacy, and for the time overruled all his resolutions, which had been made in his own strength.

It was inevitable that he should mingle with his companions in work, and soon they gained an influence over him that was not for his highest good. Being somewhat older than he himself was, they instilled into him a false idea of their superiority, and it was by this means they retained him in their "set"—a set of wild, dissipated young men.

Where was his judgment? Alas, he had inherited sufficient of his mother's weak disposition to overrule it, and consequently, he was one of the kind most easily deceived and led.

One of the youths, whose name was Edward Hopkins, gained considerable influence over Harry. He it was who persuaded him to leave his mother and sister, and seek employment in another town, where, he said, work could easily be secured, with shorter hours and greater pay. This seemed very inviting to Harry, who, at that time, never thought of deserting his home, but was anxious to earn more money, and thus become better able to care for the family and have more for what he called pleasure—cards and gaming and wine, for he had now become addicted to the use of the latter, through whose insidious influence he was fast losing his manly bearing.

Poor boy! How many noble men has Satan conquered and then cast off? How many homes has he ruined, and hearts broken, and hopes destroyed?

But I am glad to say that I shall not be obliged to trace Harry Hazeley to the bottom of the pit into which he had fallen, for God had most graciously heard the prayers of his loving, trusting sister, who had first set the example of prayer to the mother, who now frequently joined her, and he was not permitted to reach its utmost depths.

True, he went down pretty far, and his rescue was effected by rather severe means; but what mattered that, so he was saved?

After leaving home, Harry plunged into his new, reckless life, with a strength that not only surprised, but very soon disgusted Hopkins, who wished to preserve the appearance, at least, of a gentleman.

Harry had been able to secure a first-class, remunerative position very readily, but so much went to satisfy his craving for excitement, that none was left to send home to make life a little easier for Mrs. Hazeley and Flora.

After a while, however, his increasing unsteadiness secured for him dismissal from the shop where he had been employed. He was fortunate in securing place after place, but unfortunate in being unable to retain them, until at length he did but little work and a good deal of gambling. The work he then did was around and about the saloons where he had chances to game and drink.

One bitter cold night in December, a group of men stopped in front of one of these places, and after some discussion, entered. It proved to be Harry's stopping place, and he was sitting by the fire, for the time being idle.

To look at the sunken cheeks, restless eyes, and uncared-for appearance, one would never suppose this was the once straight, tall, active Harry Hazeley, so greatly was he changed.

The leader of the group of young men who entered the barroom appeared to be attracted by the forlorn figure near the stove, as soon as he came in. He seemed to know him, for presently he walked over to him and tapping him familiarly on the shoulder, cried:

"Why, hello, old chap! How are you?"

Harry immediately recognized his old acquaintance, Edward Hopkins. He did not appear particularly glad to see him, however.

"Say, old fellow, you don't seem ready to shed tears of joy at seeing your old chum," remarked Ed, in a jovial tone, sitting down beside him.

Harry said nothing, but sat looking into the fire.

"Look here, now, Hal; you do look a little hard up. Haven't been getting along so well lately, I guess?"

"No, I haven't," said Harry, without turning around.

"Well, listen to me," resumed Ed. "The old proverb, 'a friend in need is a friend indeed,' is true, isn't it?"

"What of it?" questioned Harry, still apathetic.

"Just this," replied Ed, bringing his hand heavily down on his knee, "that I'm going to be a friend to you now."

Harry smiled incredulously. His confidence in the friendship of such a flashily dressed fellow as Ed was, had been shaken.

"Come, don't be so glum, Hal. I've something to say to you," Ed continued, glancing around the room.

His comrades were all occupied in another part of the room.

"Now," went on Hopkins, lowering his voice, "we fellows," nodding toward the group, "are planning a little business. And if you want to, you can help us."

"What is it?" asked Harry, indifferently.

Edward took no notice of his manner, but went on:

"Well, we're going to—er—ah—walk into a small establishment, you know," and he winked slyly at Harry.

"Steal?" asked Harry, in a cold tone.

"If you like to put it that way, yes."

"Look here, Ed Hopkins," and Harry turned in scorn upon this hypocritical friend, who seemed so desirous of ruining him entirely. "Look here," he repeated, "let me tell you I don't want to share any of your 'little plans.' I've fallen low, I know, but I'm not a thief yet," and Harry straightened himself up and looked with a flashing eye into the crafty face beside him.

Hopkins was angry, as much because he had partially let Harry into his secret, as because he had refused to join him. However, he congratulated himself that he had not gone very far, and he left him abruptly, in a high temper, going over to the group at the other end of the room.

A heated discussion was progressing there about something in connection with the game of cards they were playing. They appealed to Hopkins as he joined the group. This did not seem to add peace to the scene, for the quarrel waxed hotter, and the voices grew louder.

Presently there was the sound of a scuffle, during which was heard the report of a pistol. Immediately there was a stampede, and when the officer, who had been attracted to the spot by the noise, rushed in, followed by a small crowd of men and boys, no one was to be seen but Harry Hazeley. He was lying on the floor by the stove, and gave no sign of life as the officer rolled him over. Whether the pistol had been fired accidentally or intentionally, nobody knew. The shot, however, was certainly not intended for the one who received it. It was found on examination that Harry was wounded in the side. He had also, in falling struck his head against the edge of the stove, and cut it.

"Well," said the officer, "I guess we'll have to take this young fellow to the hospital. From his looks he'll not be likely to have a better place to go to, even if he could tell where he belonged."

XIII.
IN THE HOSPITAL AND OUT AGAIN.

When Harry Hazeley returned to consciousness, he found himself in bed in one of the wards of a hospital, with his head bound up, and a dull aching in his side. He was in too much pain to wonder how he came there, so he closed his eyes and tried to go to sleep, but he could not. It seemed as if his mind had never been so active as it was now that he longed to forget everything, in the hope that this might ease his throbbing head. But that troublesome thing, memory, would assert itself, and his thoughts would travel back to the home he had left, and the sorrowing ones in it, and,—perhaps it was owing to the weak state of his system,—the tears forced themselves from underneath his eyelids, and rolled down his cheeks.

But what is the good of thinking about these things? he mentally asked, and so he impatiently brushed the tears away.

Poor Harry had a hard time of it. He did not improve very rapidly, although he had the best of attention and nursing. His system was so poisoned by the use of alcohol, and he was so weak from having been so long without nourishing food that, while his wound was not a very serious one, it nearly cost him his life.

The pain from his wound, together with a low fever, racked his system until it was almost unbearable. His brain, however, was unusually active, and over and over again did he recall his life since he left home, and each time his repugnance grew; and when he began to convalesce, and he realized there was hope for him, he determined to lead a different life as soon as he was able to be around again. He sincerely and deeply repented of the past, and he felt the need of a Saviour, as he had never done before. He longed for someone to come and tell him of the Christ and of his saving power. He fully realized that he must have a helper, stronger than his will or his resolutions.

One morning, when Harry was getting a little more strength, there hobbled over to his bedside a crippled young man, who supported himself upon crutches. His body was distorted, and his legs were drawn up and twisted in a sad manner; but his face was bright and cheerful and intelligent, and his shoulders, arms, and hands had a look of manliness and strength about them that was greatly at variance with the feebleness of the rest of his frame.

"Well, friend," said this odd mixture of strength and weakness, as he seated himself slowly and cautiously by the bed. "Well, friend, how goes the world with you?"

"I'm sure I don't know," replied Harry, drearily. "I haven't been caring much about the world lately. I ain't in much of a hurry to care either. There'll be time enough when I get out in it again."

"Time enough! Time enough! Yes, that's the cry," said the young man. "That's what has caused more misery in the world than anything else; it's a rope that has lost many a soul forever."

Harry turned away impatiently. He did not want to hear.

"Of course you don't want to hear me talk that way," said the lame man bluntly, divining his thought. "I didn't suppose you did. But, let me tell you, young fellow, there's enough of that rotten rope left for you to lose your soul with. Will you turn your head away when you feel it snap, and find yourself dying, with nothing to hold on to, I wonder?" Without more ado he grasped his crutches, and painfully hobbled away.

Harry tried to be glad he was gone. He did not succeed as easily, however, in dismissing from his mind the words he had heard. Perhaps it was the odd, abrupt way in which they were spoken, that made them fasten themselves so tenaciously on his memory. Certainly he would have been angry had any one else spoken so plainly and unceremoniously to him. The sight of his body, telling such an eloquent tale of suffering, made it almost impossible for any one to be angry with Joel Piper. Harry presently found himself wondering about him, and wishing he would come back and talk to him again.

He did not come, and one day Harry found courage to ask the nurse, who was busied near him, to tell him the name of the lame young man who talked to him one day.

"Oh, do you mean Joel Piper?" she asked in return.

"I didn't know that was his name," replied Harry, looking amused.

"Yes, it is," replied the nurse. "It's an odd name, I know, but he is just as nice as he can be. He's had a world of trouble and pain; but he's come out pure gold."

"Wasn't he always that?" asked Harry, curiously.

"No, indeed, he wasn't. He was one of the wildest young men, and it was that which brought on the sickness—rheumatic fever—which twisted him up so. It was this illness too, that brought about his conversion; and now he likes to visit the hospitals and talk to all the young men he can find, and try to get them to turn about. He says he's trying to make up for lost time. Some think he's crazy, but he isn't—only eccentric."

"Does he come here often?" asked Harry.

"Well, sometimes he does," was the answer. "Would you like to see him again?"

"I wouldn't mind having a little talk with him," admitted Harry.

"I'll tell him," said the kind woman.

Joel came; but Harry could not tell from his manner whether he was pleased or not at his having expressed a desire to see him.

Now that he was there, what should he say? Harry asked this question, but no answer came.

But Joel seemed to understand all about the matter, and began right away:

"You've had a rough time, eh? Didn't expect it, now, did you, when you started out? Going to have a good time, enjoy yourself, and all that? Well, it's all right. You've had about enough of that sort of thing, I guess. You'd like to turn right about face now, and go back to your mother, perhaps?"

"Who told you I had a mother?" asked Harry, sharply.

"Nobody," was the calm rejoinder.

"How did you know?"

"I didn't know; I only guessed. Somehow or other, you look as if you had. Have you?"

"Yes, I have," groaned Harry, "and a sister too; but I came away and left them, and now I'm ashamed to go back."

"Well, if you're made of the right kind of stuff you'll go to work as soon as you're out of this, and fix things so you'll not be ashamed to go back," said Joel. "Between us," he went on, bending over and looking at Harry with one eye shut up tightly, "I've got a mother and sister too. I did pretty much as you did, only worse, I guess. I've been working hard to make a man of myself before I go back to them. I'm going soon too."

"To work!" exclaimed Harry, looking at the crooked figure pityingly. "What can *you* do?"

"Do?" repeated Joel, raising his brows, and opening wide his eyes. "Look," and he held up his long slim fingers. "I can write beautifully," he continued, with the simplicity of a child. "And I'm a clerk in a large clock and jewelry establishment. A good kind friend who came to see me at the hospital when I was so ill, secured the situation for me. And if you mean to turn about sure enough, and no going back about it, I will try and get you taken on as a salesman."

Harry was completely won by Joel's plain, straightforward manner and hearty kindness, and gave his promise to turn over a new leaf. Of more importance, he kept the promise faithfully.

When Harry was discharged from the hospital, he looked quite different from what he did when he first entered it, or rather when he was carried there. He was worn almost to a shadow, it is true; but his sickness had taken from him the look of the outcast, and his intercourse with his new friend, and the hopes he had for the future restored to him once more the ability to look the "whole world in the face."

He was clad in a suit that had been worn by Joel ere his body was so distorted by rheumatism. It was not a perfect fit, but it was clean and neat, and gave to Harry a very presentable air.

True to his promise, Joel tried and succeeded in getting the situation he spoke of for his young friend toward whom he had been strongly attracted.

Harry was also naturally smart and intelligent, and now that he had put off the shackles of the false friends with whom Satan had provided him, promised to do well in his new position. Joel was determined that through no fault of his should Harry fail. He never lost sight of him for any length of time. The two boarded at the same place, and Joel insisted on his accompanying him to church. They read, talked, and walked together, and as a natural consequence became much attached to each other.

XIV.
A CHAPTER OF WONDERS.

It was a dull, gray, rainy morning when our friend Flora found herself standing in front of the house that had been her home for so many years.

What a flood of memories the sight of the familiar scene brought to her! She paused a moment or two to revel in the pleasure she thus felt. She did not feel at all excited, or even curious as to the cause for, or the probable result of her trip. Turning to the house, she stepped to the door, and lifted the knocker.

The door was opened by the neat, but uncommunicative maid, who was in charge of affairs during Mrs. Martin's illness; and who silently, and apparently acting on previous arrangement, led the way direct to the sick room.

Although the day was dark and cloudy, the window shades were down, and heavy curtains lent their aid to darken the room still more.

Mrs. Martin's greeting was somewhat of a surprise to Flora as she stood on the threshold, scarcely knowing whether to enter the darkened chamber or not.

"Why don't you come in and shut the door?" came in fretful tones from the bed.

"I should like to do it, indeed, Aunt Sarah, if I could only see my way," returned Flora, mischievously. She wondered at her own temerity. At one time she would not have dared use such liberty of speech with this punctilious aunt. But she had grown to be very independent since she had been thrown so entirely upon her own resources, and had become accustomed to think and act both for herself and others. She felt that she had grown, in that she no longer stood in awe of Aunt Sarah's cold tones. Why should she? She had come to ask no favor.

"Well," came in questioning tones from the invalid.

"May I draw up the shades, Aunt Sarah?" asked Flora, advancing slowly into the room and closing the door softly.

"I suppose so. You can draw up anything you like, it makes no difference to me," was the somewhat ungracious reply.

Flora paid no attention to the tone, but drew up the shades, making it possible to see what was in the room.

"Aunt Sarah, how thin you are!" she cried, incautiously. "Why, you have been sick."

"Of course I have. You didn't suppose I was pretending, did you?" retorted Mrs. Martin.

"No," said Flora, "I did not, nor did I know you were so ill. And now tell me, can I do anything to render you more comfortable?"

"No, I think not," she replied. "Yes, you might bring me some toast and a cup of tea," she added a moment later.

As she turned at once to leave the room, Flora wondered in her own mind, whether Mrs. Martin really wished for something to eat. The truth was, Mrs. Martin, now that Flora was here in the house, even in her very room, wished to decide how she could broach the subject which had lain on her heart so long. She was thinking deeply, and did not notice Flora's entrance until she heard:

"Here they are, Aunt Sarah, nice and hot."

"What?" the invalid returned, in a surprised way.

"The toast and tea," replied Flora.

"Oh yes, put them on the table."

Flora did so, daintily arranging them so as to be inviting to the eye as well as the palate, and inwardly wondering what new caprice her aunt would develop next. However, she had decided to yield to all her peculiarities, and to bear with her whims, and so with unruffled face, she turned to arrange the room, as only a woman's hand can. The grace and care were not lost upon her aunt, whose eyes closely followed every motion as she moved silently about the room.

"Sit down," said Mrs. Martin, after a few moments' silence.

Flora did so; and after a slight hesitation, Mrs. Martin began, having concluded to open the subject at once, for nothing was to be gained by delay.

"Niece Flora," she said, looking in the young girl's face, "I sent for you to tell you I feel that I have done what I had no business to do."

"What have you done, Aunt Sarah?" asked Flora, half suspecting what she wished to say to her.

"I mean in sending you away from here as I did," was the blunt reply.

"You had a right to do whatever you wanted to," stammered Flora. She could stand unmoved before the cold, hard Aunt Sarah; Aunt Sarah repentant, she did not know how to meet.

"No, I had no right to do it," continued Mrs. Martin. It was plain she did not intend to spare herself in the least. "I had no right to do it. Sister Bertha wanted you to stay, and I know she did. I had no right to take her money, and live in her home, and use her things when I knew she only left them to me because she trusted me to do what she wanted."

"Never mind, Aunt Sarah; I knew nothing about it, so do not worry. It is all right." And Flora moved nearer the bed, and took her hand in her own and tenderly held it.

Instead of complying, Mrs. Martin seemed to gain strength, and she went on:

"No; you knew nothing about her wishes, but I did. And, Flora, I have not been happy in this house. In fact, I did not deserve to be."

"You can talk about that when you get well."

"I will never be well unless I make right what I have made wrong," returned Mrs. Martin. "I want to know, Flora, if you can forgive your selfish old aunt for driving—yes, driving is the word," as Flora started to speak—"you from the home which was intended for you? Will you not come back to it?" And the tears began to gather in the eyes that had long been strangers to such an expression of emotion.

Flora felt very helpless now in the face of all these different moods. She could think of nothing else to do but stroke the sick woman's forehead gently and soothingly. After a moment or two of silence, she said: "I forgive you, Aunt Sarah, if you think there's anything to forgive. Everything has turned out for the best, at least so far as I am concerned. As to coming back, I think I don't care to—that is, I couldn't leave mother, you know."

"I don't want you to leave your mother, child. Why can't she come too?"

"Do you mean to come here to live?"

"Yes,; here to live."

"She would like that, I know," said Flora, adding mentally, *providing you were different*.

She soon discovered that her unspoken thought had been realized before it had been expressed.

"Now," said the sick woman, drawing a breath of relief, "I can be at peace. It is not too late for me to make amends and carry out sister Bertha's wishes. Ah, child, you do not know what I have suffered of late; but it's all right now."

"Try to go to sleep now, won't you?" asked Flora, coaxingly, fearing the effect of the conversation upon the invalid.

"No; I don't want to go to sleep," said Mrs. Martin, with a shade of her old firmness; "I just want to lie here and think."

She did go to sleep, however, very soon, and awoke greatly refreshed, for her mind was at ease, and she was surprised to find how much more pleasant the prospect of recovery was since she had something to look forward to.

And Flora? She was delighted, for to her the old home had never lost its charm.

Faithfully she nursed the sick woman, who, in spite of her efforts to the contrary, now and then yielded to her old-time habit of fault-finding, when nothing pleased her. Mrs. Martin was very regretful for these outbursts, and after each, more carefully watched her own tongue, and the movements and manner of her young nurse and daily became more attached to her; and the more necessary it seemed to her to retain her sunshiny presence.

Flora was as happy in her present position, and at her future prospects, as it was possible for her to be with the ever-present feeling of uncertainty and sorrow at the absence of her dearly loved brother, from whom she had expected such great things. She was a very sensible girl, and had learned long before this that to waste her time in worriment over what she could not help in any way, would not enable her to discharge her present duties as she would wish. Knowing this, as I say, so well, she put Harry into the charge of the One "who never slumbers nor sleeps," and went about her daily duties with a light step and merry smile. For days she planned her mother's coming, and how she would enjoy the life here. Her own pleasant little room was hers again, and many were the happy hours she passed there. Every few moments throughout the day she would be in her aunt's room reading to her, or perhaps giving her a daintily arranged meal, or placing the pillows more comfortably.

One of her greatest pleasures was in arranging her Aunt Bertha's old room, preparatory to the coming of her mother, to whom she had assigned it. Very lovingly and carefully did she do this, for her heart was filled with tender memories of the past.

Mrs. Martin had told her to fix everything to suit herself, and refused to have a word to say further than to heartily approve of all her arrangements.

"I have been at the head of affairs a long time," she had said; "it is time now for us to change places."

"I think you are trying to spoil me, Aunt Sarah," remarked Flora, one day, when she had been told a number of times to do just as she liked.

"I think there is no danger of that, my dear," said Mrs. Martin.

She was right, for the experience Flora had gained in the years since she had been home had so strengthened and developed her that it would have been well-nigh impossible to "spoil her," as she had termed it.

As soon as her aunt was able to sit up, Flora was to return home to get her mother, and in fact the whole family, if she could find them, and bring them to Aunt Sarah's, to live there.

Mrs. Martin insisted that she wanted a house full; adding, smilingly:

"The more, the merrier, my dear."

Flora wished this could be possible—she longed to be able to bring Harry back with them; and, safe in that peaceful home, win him from his evil ways. She sighed, even as she thought, *That is quite impossible*. She had forgotten for the moment that "With God, all things are possible."

XV.
GOING HOME.

During all these weary months, Harry Hazeley had not once written home; and neither his mother nor sister knew where he was.

His friend, Joel Piper, had written to his mother, but to his regret, had as yet received no reply. This saddened him, as in his letter he had told of the changes in him, not only in his body, but in his heart and life, for he wished his mother, who had done so much for him, to know.

Harry as yet had no news to write home. Joel was working slowly, it is true, to induce Harry to attend some meetings which were being held successively in different churches. Harry became interested, and later he had the happiness of knowing that he had accepted Christ, and been received by him.

In the meantime he had applied himself steadily and faithfully to his business, and not only earned the respect of his employers, but saved a good share of his money.

And now, he thought, triumphantly, *there is nothing to prevent me from going home.*

This thought took complete possession of him, and in his leisure moments he did little else than picture to himself his homecoming, and the sight of mother, sister, and brother. They would rejoice, he was sure, in his new life. He wondered if Flora had changed much, and in what way Alec passed away the days.

These thoughts of home and home-folks, together with the great desire to see them again, gradually wore away the feeling of shame with which he had been assailed whenever his thoughts had turned that way before.

"Joel!" he exclaimed, as they were sitting together, one pleasant evening, "I see no other way but to do it!"

"What is it you mean, my boy?" asked Joel, as he looked at Harry for a moment, and then returned to his book.

"To go home, and see them all," returned Harry.

"Believe I will too," said Joel, slapping his book by way of emphasis. "By the way, Harry," he continued, "my home isn't so very far from yours; only a couple of hours' ride. You live at Bartonville and I live at Brinton, or rather, I did."

"Is that so? Well, then, let us go together."

"What do you intend to do? Give up your situation here for good, or just ask for leave of absence?" asked Joel.

"Oh, I shall give it up entirely," was the answer. "I prefer to get something to do nearer home. What will you do?"

"I shall come back," said Joel, decidedly. "My people are farmers. I could be of no service now on a farm, you know, even if I cared for it, which I don't."

Thus the matter was decided, and arrangements were made accordingly.

One evening, as Mrs. Hazeley sat in her home, all alone, stitching away busily, she was startled to hear a loud rap on the door.

Who can it be? she thought, rising to answer the knock. She found herself confronted by a tall, rather slight young man, with a grave face, which, however, was now illuminated by a smile of expectancy.

"Harry! Harry! My boy Harry!" she cried, holding open her arms. The mother's quick instinct and penetrating love could not be deceived by appearances, no matter how altered. The form might be changed, and the features matured, but there was something that brought to her the memory of her child, the baby of long ago.

After the first greetings were over, Harry settled down, and prepared to unburden his mind. His mother noticed that he glanced about him wistfully and inquiringly.

"No," said Mrs. Hazeley, answering the query in his eyes, "Flora is not here. She went to stay with your Aunt Sarah, who is very ill. I am expecting to go myself, whenever I hear from her to that effect. Alec too, is away. He is living with that good old man, 'Major Benson,' you used to call him, you remember. Alec enjoys a country life. He intends to be a farmer, he says. It was very kind of him to give the boy such an opening. The poor child was so afraid of being a burden to us. I have every reason to be grateful for my children."

"Except me, mother," said Harry.

"No, my boy," returned his mother, looking keenly at him. "I am sure I have reason to be grateful for you too. But tell me, Harry, where have you been, and why did you not write to us, and keep us posted?"

The entire absence of reproach or fault finding, and the warm affection with which he was received by his mother, touched the young man very deeply, and with his heart made tender with these thoughts, he determined to confide fully all his past to his mother, from whom he felt sure he would receive ready sympathy.

When the story was told, Mrs. Hazeley could but exclaim, "Bless the Lord, oh my soul!"

"And forget not all his benefits," added Harry reverently.

They were interrupted at that moment by a knock upon the door—a quick, business-like, energetic knock.

"I know who that is," said Mrs. Hazeley, smilingly, as she arose to admit the newcomer. It was Flora.

"Did ever returned prodigal receive a more hearty welcome than I?" exclaimed Harry, laughingly, but gratefully.

His old habit of reserve was being gradually overcome, and he was becoming accustomed to express his feelings quite freely, much to the present and subsequent delight of his family.

This evening, a memorable one in the history of the little family, was by no means over. Just as the happy trio were seated, with heads bowed reverently in thankfulness to the Giver of all good, the knocker was raised another time.

As the heads were lifted, and Flora arose to open the door, she remarked, merrily:

"That must be Alec. I suppose the magnetism of our presence is drawing him to us."

It was not Alec It was our good friend Joel Piper.

"I was told Mrs. Hazeley lived here," said he.

"So she does," answered Flora, trying to recall where she had seen the familiar face before her. Joel was doing the same. He was the first to ask, however, "Haven't I met you before?"

"I was just thinking I had seen you somewhere," said Flora, looking puzzled.

"In Brinton, perhaps?" suggested Joel.

"That is just it—you know—Lottie Piper," exclaimed Flora disconnectedly.

"Yes, yes," said Joel, eagerly; "I'm her brother. I remember now. You are Flora Hazeley. Well, well," he cried, accepting Flora's invitation to enter the room, where he saw his friend Harry, for whom he was hunting. "I was just looking for you, Hal," said he, having first been presented to Mrs. Hazeley, who was delighted to welcome the young man who had done so much for her Harry. "I was looking for you, Hal, but I had no idea I should meet an old acquaintance, in the shape of your sister. But that reminds me," he added, sadly, "I have been to the old home. No wonder I didn't hear from them. Sickness, death, and desolation! I found the home, but no one in it."

"How could that be?" asked Harry.

"I know," said Flora, gently. "I saw Lottie for a few moments the other day, and she told me all about it. I am so sorry."

"Is my sister here?" Joel asked, eagerly.

"Yes, she is here—in Bartonville; she is living with her aunt."

"I know," said Joel, "my father's sister. I shall be glad to see Lottie; but mother is gone, and now it is too late."

"No, no, Joel, don't talk that way," said Harry, soothingly. "You have no need to say that. You haven't come home as you left it. And suppose your mother is not here, don't you think she knows all about it? And then, there is your sister, you know."

"That is all true, Harry. It would have been hard to have come back as I went away, and found her gone. I could not have helped the little girl then. But one thing more," he said, turning to Flora, who was wiping her eyes in sympathy. "Where is my father?"

"Lottie says he went away somewhere, to work."

"Then I shall hope to see him, someday, and that will be one consolation." Joel was comforted by his friends, and his own kind, helpful deeds were bearing fruit for him.

It was arranged that Joel should board—he would hear of no other arrangement—with Mrs. Hazeley until he should find his sister, and see how she was situated, before returning to his employment.

Flora's news was almost forgotten in the general rejoicing over Harry's unexpected return and the equally unexpected addition to the little household in Joel. But when things were somewhat quieted down, she had something wonderful to relate also.

"Well, well, well," said Mrs. Hazeley. "To think of sister Sarah softening, at her age. When will wonders cease!"

Harry did not approve of this proposed breaking up of their own little home. He feared it might be but a passing whim of Aunt Sarah's.

"Oh, no," maintained Flora, stoutly. "Whatever else Aunt Sarah is, she is not fickle. When she says she means to do a thing, that thing is as good as done."

"That's very true," said her mother. So it was settled that, after due preparation, the family should move to Brinton.

The only regret that Flora felt at leaving her home in Bartonville was that she would be obliged to part with her class of girls, whom she loved and who loved her. She comforted herself with the thought that she would have another, if possible, in Brinton. The girls she left behind always cherished the memory of their young teacher, and strove to imitate her gentle, earnest ways, and noble traits. Surely, the seed she had sown in their hearts would spring up, blossom, and bear fruit for the Master's kingdom.

XVI.
LOTTIE'S TRIALS.

"Well, things have come to a pretty pass! Here I've been running up and down, here and there and everywhere, like a chicken with its head cut off, trying to please Aunt Emmeline, and I'm just about as near doing it now as I was when I commenced. It's grumble, grumble, grumble, every minute in the day; and I will not stand it—not a day longer, now!" and Lottie gave the fire a vigorous shake that sent the sparks darting hither and thither, in every direction.

It was hard for her. Lottie conscientiously did all she could for the fretful invalid upstairs. But her efforts were not appreciated. Instead, Mrs. Durand seemed to grow more irritable daily. Nothing Lottie did pleased her; the tea was either too weak or too strong; the toast either too hot or too cold; the beef-tea was too highly seasoned, or not enough. Thus the fault-finding continued, day in and day out.

Heretofore Lottie had succeeded in bearing with her captious patient fairly well, her natural patience and sweetness of disposition being a great help to her. But this day her task seemed a little harder to bear than usual, and a short time before the outburst at the opening of the chapter the climax was reached, when her aunt struck her with the cane she used to aid her in getting about the room, for she was able to go about a very little during the day.

Lottie had been sent for some water, and in her zeal to please her aunt by being quick about it, had spilled a few drops in that good woman's lap, and she, without stopping to think, had given her niece a rap with her stick.

"No, I shall not stand it another minute," muttered Lottie, as she angrily paced the floor of the little room, whither she had rushed from her aunt's presence.

Apparently she had determined to do something, for she went to work energetically to put everything to rights. She put more coal on the fire, and, in fact, did everything she deemed necessary. Then she stole quietly up to her room, packed some things in a bundle, and noiselessly left the house.

Where was she going? She did not know. What was she going to do? She only knew that she was going far away from her Aunt Emmeline's, where she had been insulted. The old poplar solemnly waved its long, bare arms over her head, as if wishing her "goodbye." She had a vague idea she would go and find her friend Flora; she would at least advise her what to do, for, after once fairly in the street, the fact that she had no home but the one she was leaving behind, made itself felt very plainly.

She had not seen Flora since that first day when they had met accidentally, and she had almost forgotten the way she had come, for she had been in such a hurry she gave little heed to anything. She would go as best she could remember. It seemed to her that she was walking a great distance, and when at length she came to a small public square, she sat down upon one of the cold, damp seats, almost discouraged, and utterly unhappy. No mother, no home—nothing but misery. The tears were very near the surface, when she heard her name called at no great distance.

That was strange, though the voice sounded familiar. Stranger still, however, was the sight of a young man making his way rapidly toward her with a shuffling gait, and leaning upon two canes. Although the face seemed familiar, Lottie was frightened, and was preparing to run away when her steps were arrested by the strange young man saying, in half-laughing, half-vexed tones:

"Why, Lottie, girl, don't you know your brother Joel?"

"What? Not my brother Joel?" exclaimed Lottie, joyously, yet distrustfully.

"The very same, and yet not the same," replied Joel, sadly, as he remembered how great was the physical change in him, and which was so apparent.

"I was straight and strong when you last saw me, Lottie," he said, looking down at his twisted limbs. "I was straight and strong when I left the old home, and now you see what I am." And he seated himself beside Lottie, who had remained on the bench.

"Oh, Joel, what made you so?" she cried, in a distressed voice.

"Never mind about that now, little sister. I will tell you all about it some time. But mother—"

"Didn't you know? She is dead." And Lottie burst into tears, while the half-repressed sobs of the utterly miserable girl, shook her slender frame.

"Yes, I know," answered her brother, softly.

"How did you know?" asked Lottie, as she raised her tear-stained face in surprise at his knowledge, when she knew he had been away so long.

"Never mind that, either," returned Joel; "but tell me everything."

Lottie told about the death of their mother, then added:

"Oh, Joel, she so wanted to see you before she died, and now it's too late."

"Yes, too late." The words found an echo in the young man's own breast. He had put it off too long, this homecoming. Hoping and wanting to come back to his home and parents well able to take care of himself and to help them too, he had waited, and worked, and saved, and now she for whom he so longed was not here to bid him welcome. The thought also came to him that it was well this "too late" came only in the disappointment of earthly hopes. Suppose it meant the loss of his soul as well? Then another thought came, this time full of comfort and peace:

"She will know I am changed, and I shall meet her in heaven."

Then he turned to his sister, feeling that here was a work for him—a legacy left him by his mother.

"Where is father, Lottie?" he asked a moment later, inwardly wondering at her presence here.

"Father? Oh, after mother's death he couldn't stay there any more, he said, and so he went away to work. Out West, I believe," she added, rather glad than otherwise to break the silence that had followed her last words. "I haven't seen him since he brought me to live here."

"Live here? With whom?" inquired her brother.

"With Aunt Emmeline." And then she poured forth into sympathetic ears a recital of her woes, inflicted largely by her aunt.

"What are you going to do?" asked Joel, when she finished. "Are you going back?"

"No, I am not. That settles it!"

"Never?"

"No, never!"

Joel was amused. He well knew that the angry girl would be obliged, sooner or later, to modify her emphatic and hasty assertions. However, he thought it best to make no criticism, at least until she should see her folly and mistake herself; so he only said:

"Well, I guess you had better come with me just now. Both of us will catch cold if we stay here much longer."

Unquestioningly, Lottie arose. She did not care where she went, so long as she was with Joel, who now was all she had to cling to.

The sight of poor, deformed Joel, hobbling painfully along, touched Lottie's heart as nothing else could have done, as she contrasted his shrunken body with her own strong, robust self. She felt almost glad her mother could not see him now—she had been so proud of Joel's strength.

At length they halted before a small house that appeared strangely familiar to Lottie, and Joel rapped on the door. What was her surprise and delight to see the door opened by Flora Hazeley.

"Lottie!" the latter exclaimed.

"Flora!"

Joel stood by, smilingly, while Lottie was introduced to the rest of the family.

"It seems so strange that both your brother and mine should be returned runaways, doesn't it, Flora?" remarked Lottie, when all were seated.

"How about Lottie?" slyly whispered Joel, as he sat by her side.

Lottie deigned no reply, but tossed her head willfully, while she thought: *No, I will never go back to Aunt Emmeline's.*

It was a very pleasant little home party that sat and chatted in the old dining room that evening, but it was not until Lottie and Flora were alone in the room which they were to share for the night, that Lottie opened her heart, and poured out her woes into Flora's sympathetic ear.

"Oh, Lottie, how could you?" asked Flora, when the recital was over.

"Oh, Flora, of course I could do it, and so would you have done, in my place," returned Lottie, in an injured tone.

"Is it possible that you have left your poor, sick aunt all alone?"

"She isn't very sick; she only thinks she is," said Lottie, sulkily. "She can get about her room well enough. It won't hurt her to go a bit farther, and go downstairs."

Flora, after a few more ineffectual words, saw Lottie was feeling too bitter and hurt to be ashamed of her desertion of her poor, sick aunt, and, with her customary tact, dropped the subject entirely. For a few moments there was silence, each busy with her own thoughts.

As Flora was brushing her hair, of which she was justly proud, she said:

"Lottie, let us sit here in front of the fire. I often do, and watch the sparks as they flit here and there. I feel like talking tonight. I have listened to your story. Now, you come here with me; I want to tell you mine."

Nothing loth, Lottie seated herself, and listened attentively while her friend told of her own life, with all of its disappointments, hardships, and trials.

"What has all this to do with me?" asked Lottie, suspiciously, for she had a vague idea that Flora had an object in view.

"It has this to do with you, Lottie dear," answered Flora, as she put her own shapely hand, gently but firmly, over the rebellious one in Lottie's lap. "It will show you that none of us can have things exactly as we want them, and we are cowards if we run away from our duties. Had I been left to choose what I wished, I should not have chosen a single thing that came to me, and yet I am sure everything turned out for the very best. In the first place, Aunt Sarah's sending me home made me think and act for myself and others, and in doing so I became far stronger than I would have been had I stayed with, and depended on Aunt Bertha, if she had lived. In doing the second, I found pleasure, and now that after all our worrying Harry has come back so changed, I am just as happy as I can be. But suppose I had run away, when things were dark and discouraging, would I now have anything to be happy over?"

"But nobody ever struck you, Flora. That is different," said Lottie, looking less stubborn.

"No," replied Flora; "that is very true, dear; nobody ever struck me. But I have had other things quite as hard. Indeed, things that I thought I could not possibly endure. But, you know who helped me bear them, don't you, Lottie dear?"

"Yes," was the subdued reply. "You mean God helped you."

"Yes, and he will help you too, Lottie, if you will let him. But you must take up your duties again, you know."

"What? gGoo back to Aunt Emmeline?"

"Yes, I mean just that. I am sure she did not intend to treat you badly. She will tell you so, I have no doubt, someday."

"I don't know about that," said Lottie; "but, I guess I ought to go. But, suppose she will not have me back again; what then?"

"Oh, don't borrow trouble. It will be time enough to think about that when it happens," replied Flora. "But come, it's time we were asleep."

Sleep, however, did not come to Lottie as soon as it did to her friend. Her mind was too busy, turning over the events of the day, and anticipating the possible ones of the morrow. Nevertheless, Lottie was not really a coward, and when she had decided on a certain course, she kept to it, as we have already seen.

XVII.
MORE SURPRISES.

Next day, Lottie informed her brother of her decision to return to her aunt, and apologize for her unceremonious departure.

Joel was very glad that she had come to this conclusion of her own free will, for he had feared he might have trouble in bringing her to it. He more than half-suspected that Flora had a good deal to do with his sister's present submissive state, and was accordingly grateful.

Lottie bade her friends goodbye, and with Joel to keep her courage up, turned her face determinedly toward her aunt's home, only making a comical grimace, as Flora whispered to her some words of encouragement, adding the assurance that all would come out right.

The brother and sister walked on together in silence, for some time; and then it was Joel who talked, for Lottie was too busy thinking to care for conversation. She acted as guide until they stood under the old poplar in front of the quiet little house, and then she took refuge behind her brother, who marched undauntedly up to the door, and gave a knock, which said plainly: "Here are some people who mean business."

The knock evidently surprised Mrs. Durand, for she opened the door herself, instead of telling them to "Come in," as was her usual custom.

At first she saw no one but Joel, and seemed strongly inclined to close the door upon him; but when she caught sight of Lottie, standing demurely behind him, she steadied herself firmly upon her canes, and inquired, "What do you want?"

"In the first place, Aunt Emmeline," said Joel, calmly, "I suppose you know me?"

"No, I can't say I do," was the reply.

"I am not much surprised. It has been some time since we met. I am Joel Piper, your nephew, and Lottie's brother."

Mrs. Durand said nothing, but only stood and looked.

"Lottie, come here; Aunt Emmeline, Lottie has something to say to you."

Lottie came from behind her brother, and speaking rapidly, as if she were afraid she would lose courage if she did not talk fast, said: "I've come to say that I am sorry I acted so badly, Aunt Emmeline, and if you will let me, I'll come back again."

"Come in," was the brusque command. Joel and Lottie entered, and Mrs. Durand closed the door. Then she turned to them, and said, simply:

"If you want to come back, I guess you may."

Lottie shrugged her shoulders. She wanted so much to say that she did not come back because she wanted to, but because she thought she ought, and she bit her tongue, by way of admonishing that unruly member to keep still.

Joel guessed something of what was passing in his sister's mind, and hastened to engage Mrs. Durand in conversation.

She seemed really touched as the young man recounted the history of his sickness and sufferings in a strange city; and Lottie, sitting silently listening, was more than half convinced that she had judged her aunt too severely. By the time Joel was ready to go, she was quite satisfied that she *did* want to come back. Then the old house really looked homelike, especially after the feeling of loneliness and homesickness she had experienced the day before as she walked the streets not knowing which way to look for shelter.

That evening, after everything was done, as Mrs. Durand was seated by the fire in her easy chair, and Lottie was hemming a tablecloth, Mrs. Durand asked abruptly:

"Why did you come back?"

Lottie looked up in astonishment, scarcely knowing what to say. But deeming it best to tell her exact reason, she said: "Because I thought it was my duty to do it."

For a while there was silence, during which Lottie glanced up timidly to see the effect of her words upon her aunt, but she could discover nothing.

"I suppose you were pretty angry with me, when you went?" was the next remark.

"Awful!" said Lottie, catching her breath at her own temerity.

Again there was silence.

"Well," returned Mrs. Durand, "if you hadn't been in such a hurry, I should have told you I didn't mean to strike you; but, I suppose I can tell you so now, can't I?"

"Oh dear, Aunt Emmeline, you needn't say anything at all about it," said Lottie, eagerly. "I acted just horrid; I know I did."

"I can't blame you much, child. Old people like me, with the rheumatism, are apt to be snappish. But I guess we both have had a lesson we will not be likely to forget. Come, now, I think it is time you were in bed, so put away your sewing, and go."

"Can I get you anything, aunt?" asked Lottie, as she prepared to obey.

"Nothing at all, my dear," was the soft reply, that sent Lottie upstairs in a state of pleasurable surprise at the turn things had taken. Never had she felt more glad of anything than she was to find herself in the little chamber again, because it was home.

Joel, in the meantime, after he had seen his sister fairly reinstated in her old place, returned to Mrs. Hazeley's, where he duly reported the success of his visit.

Flora was very glad things were straightening out for her young friend, Lottie, for she was really fond of her, because of her open, truthful nature.

A few days more Joel spent with his friends, and then, after arranging with his aunt for his sister's future, insisting on supplying her needs outside of her board, for which Mrs. Durand would accept nothing, he left, to return to his work, feeling at least contented, if not carrying back with him the memory of a happy home welcome and reunion. It was good to have somebody to work for and care for, and Joel was accustomed to placing full value upon present blessings or privileges, and his example had not been lost upon Lottie, whose lot, while greatly changed and improved, was by no means entirely freed from thorns, for Aunt Emmeline was still Aunt Emmeline, and was likely to continue to be so. However, since Lottie's return, she had treated the girl with a fair amount of consideration, much to her satisfaction and enjoyment. Lottie was beginning to feel at home. In fact, as the months rolled by, and she grew in age and experience, Lottie gradually became the household manager, and her aunt was content to oversee.

After a time, Mr. Piper grew tired of "rolling around," as he informed his sister and daughter, and determined to marry a second time. He moreover informed Lottie that it would be more agreeable to all concerned if she would conclude to remain with her aunt.

"Humph!" said that good woman. "It's well that it is agreeable to all; but suppose it wasn't? As it is, child," she added, "you know you are welcome to a home with me just as long as you want it. I have no wish to part with you. But I must say, your father is pretty cool."

At one time Lottie's heart would have beaten tumultuously at the prospect of a permanent home with Aunt Emmeline, but it was not so now, and she felt very grateful, when she lay down that night, that God had so cared for her, when she could not care for herself.

To return to our friends, the Hazeleys. They had all removed to Brinton, all but Alec, who seemed so well-contented with his quarters at Major Joe's, that he did not wish to change. There was really no necessity for him to do so. He was doing well at school, although he was by no means what might be considered a brilliant pupil. In fact, his own prediction that he would be no scholar, but a practical farmer, seemed likely to come true.

Major Joe had other help now, and Alec gave his time out of school and during holidays, to the owner of a large farm in the immediate neighborhood, where he was learning many things that were needful to know in his chosen calling. He always came home at night, and was known all around as a "fine lad." Major Joe had grown too feeble to attend market any longer, and so he had turned that part of his business over to the young man, who now had charge of his garden, and who, it seemed more than likely would have charge of Ruth some time in the future, when he had grown able to do so. The major remained at home, alternately nursing his rheumatic limbs, and helping "mother" and Ruth with the poultry, of which they raised a quantity, and, as Jem said, were "getting awful rich off the eggs and things." Ruth was a thrifty, thoroughgoing little housekeeper, one after her grandmother's own heart, while Jem was just a lively little girl, who insisted on bestowing her help, which, however, usually proved more of a hindrance. She was, however, the pet of the old people, and made things merry in the little cottage.

Alec Hazeley had gone to see his brother as soon as he had heard of his return, and had spent somedays at home prior to the removal of the family. And he was the last object they saw as they steamed out of the station. Mrs. Martin was no longer the active, stirring woman she had been before her illness, but was now a confirmed invalid. She was much altered, in every way, and was very glad to have her sister and family with her; and they were altogether a peaceful, happy, little household.

It was not Harry's intention to remain at home long after he had seen his mother and sister settled. But, somehow—perhaps it was because everyone seemed glad to have him there—he stayed longer than he had intended; and, surprising to himself, and altogether delightful to Flora and his mother, he one day informed them that he felt he had received a decided call to the ministry.

"Oh, Harry!" cried his sister. "How sudden! I wasn't dreaming of such a thing; but I am *so* glad."

"Yes," answered Harry, seriously, "I feel as if I must prepare myself to preach. Something tells me, and I feel sure it is the voice of God, that I shall prosper at nothing else but winning souls for Christ. As I was snatched from the toils of the Evil One, so must I help save others. I believe that God rescued me for that very purpose."

Aunt Sarah was delighted, and would hear of nothing but that he should immediately begin to fit himself for his new work. The family circle was again broken, but this time, how different the circumstances, and how hopeful the future appeared, with all united in the bond of love for Christ and a hope for his reappearing.

XVIII.
A Christmas Invitation.

Years have passed, and long since the grass was green over Mrs. Martin's grave. Side by side she lay with her gentle sister, and over the two graves the graceful branches of the willow drooped, and in summer the sod was starred with daisies.

It was December. The trees were bare of leaves, and the grass was withered. The weather was cold. The folks in Brinton predicted a hard winter. In the cosy home where Mrs. Hazeley now presided with a calm demeanor, and Flora flitted about happy and contented, there seemed no need to fear the searching winds of winter. Flora was no longer a girl, but a well-grown young woman—changed, and yet not changed. She had matured with years; but it was easy to discern the same merry, thoughtful Flora of the old days.

Shortly after his conversion, Harry had heard and followed the voice of his Master to "preach the gospel," and now he was the pastor of the church where Aunt Bertha had sat and listened to the gospel, eagerly taking in the blessed words of life—the same church where Aunt Sarah had listened, stern and cold, with her hard features turned upward to the minister; and the same church where two happy faces—one of a quiet and attractive-looking matron: the other of a fair, bright-eyed younger woman—were seen every Lord's Day.

Very proud was Flora of her manly, earnest brother who had won so completely the hearts of the people; and equally proud was Harry of his sister, who was loved and respected by all. They saw but little of Alec, who had never outgrown his love for the country, and who still lived in Brinton. He was industrious and economical, and his friends were sure he would someday be a wealthy man.

It wanted but a few days to Christmas, when, one afternoon, during a few idle moments, Flora stood by the window lightly drumming against the pane, and smiling, as if her thoughts were very pleasant.

She had not been standing there long when the front gate opened, and Harry came toward the house.

Flora hurried to open the door for him, and pausing to remove his overcoat, he said:

"Here is a letter for you, Flo."

"A letter for me?" she repeated. "I wonder from whom it can be." She returned to the room with the letter in her hand.

"A letter, Flora?" inquired her mother. "Who is writing to you, dear?"

"It is from Alec, mother," was the answer, a moment later.

"What does the dear boy say—anything of importance?" asked Mrs. Hazeley.

"It is a very short letter. Shall I read it?"

"Never mind, Flora; just tell us what he wants."

"It is simply a very short, but very urgent, invitation for us all to spend Christmas with him. You, especially, Harry."

"Me? I wonder why?"

"Shall we go, mother?"

"Of course. I would not disappoint the boy for anything; besides, we have not seen him for so long."

All were satisfied with this arrangement.

Christmas morning dawned bright and clear, but very cold.

Harry held service in the morning in his church, and of course Mrs. Hazeley and Flora were present. Everything was in readiness to start away immediately at its close.

"It will not really matter; and we cannot miss seeing our Harry conduct his first Christmas service," said Flora, positively.

The exercises were simple but impressive; the singing sweet and solemn—the sermon earnest and tender. It seemed to Flora as if she were shut in from everything, and that she really moved among the circumstances connected with the Savior's birth. It seemed to her that she was with the wise men who brought gifts, and came to worship the infant Jesus; and the words of the anthem, "Glory to God in the highest, peace on earth, good will to men," echoed and re-echoed through her whole being.

Truly, she thought, *that peace has entered my soul, and how can I have aught but 'good will to men'?*

Mrs. Hazeley's feelings found expression by the tears rolling down her cheeks under her veil. Flora saw them, but knew they were for joy.

Never had Harry spoken as he spoke that morning. He scarcely recognized himself in the preacher whose impassioned words were holding spellbound the people who filled the church, drawing from them alternately tears of sympathy and smiles of joy.

When the service was at an end, and the usual interchange of Christmas wishes over, the young minister joined his mother and sister, who were waiting for him, and, with one upon each arm, directed his steps to the depot, where they boarded the cars for Alec's home.

Flora felt too peaceful and happy to talk, and, in fact, they were all disinclined for conversation, and so the short journey was made in silence. True to his word, Alec was at the station to welcome them, and delighted that they had all come.

He conducted them to a carriage he had in waiting, and helped them in.

"What do you want to ride to Major Joe's for?" asked Harry. "It is such a short distance."

"Oh, I want you to ride today, so ask no more questions," was the saucy reply.

"Alec has some new project in his head," whispered Flora to her mother, who nodded and smiled, as if anything and everything were in order, so far as she was concerned.

Harry asked no more questions, but was busy looking about him, and trying to decide where they were going; if to Major Joe's, why take such a roundabout course? All to no avail, however, and he abandoned the matter to the driver.

There was no snow, to cover with its white, glittering blanket, the rough spots, but the brightness of the sun made amends for this lack by gilding the bare places. It was a green Christmas, but there was a lurking promise of snows and storms yet to come, in the brisk, sharp wind, that drove the withered leaves—reminders of the summer's beauty—along, as Flora remarked, "like little, old women dressed in brown, and caught in a windstorm." Alec noticed, as they drove along, that his brother still glanced about inquiringly, evidently not yet satisfied as to the road to Major Joe's from the station. Alec was amused. It was so long since Harry had been there, he felt sure he could not remember. It was with a view to drawing his attention from this, and thus prevent his asking more questions, that Alec began to talk diligently. He pointed out the different objects of interest along the way, and then would branch off into a series of remarks or conjectures concerning them.

"This now," he said, pointing to a pretty house they were passing, "is Mrs. Brown's new residence. Isn't it tasteful? Contains all the latest modern improvements—at least, so they say. And here is the homestead of a well-to-do widow. Very benevolent. Quite a good thing for widows." He was interrupted by Flora's inquiry:

"Why widows especially?"

"Oh, because, you see, all they need is to have just enough to keep them comfortably while they live. They don't care about making improvements, and buying or speculating as a general thing, like—"

"Like what?" asked Harry, drily, as his brother paused.

"Well, like me, for instance," returned Alec.

"So, I suppose you think there is no necessity for you to be benevolent."

"It's not but that I should, so much as I cannot afford to be. You see, I am a young man, and I need to be very prudent about the way I invest what money I have, in order to accumulate a little more."

"Oh, Alec," laughed Flora, "you certainly have accumulated a pretty good stock of self-complacency, and have cultivated a fine opinion of yourself."

"Yes," returned Alec, good-humoredly, touching up his horse with the end of his whip. "One must blow his own trumpet, if no one else will for him."

"Bad policy, my boy," interposed Harry, who seemed for the time being, to feel himself a boy again. "Bad policy. It is better not to have a trumpet blown at all, than to do it yourself. True worth will always receive its proper recognition."

"Not always; you are wrong there," said Alec, his eyes twinkling mischievously at the success of his plan for diverting his brother's attention.

"Yes, always," persisted Harry. "Probably not from the direction you desire, or are looking toward; but, if one looks in the right direction, he will find that if he is worthy of esteem, honor, and respect, he will get it from those upon whom his course has made an impression. The trouble is, that people often look too far away. Either they do not think to look among those immediately about them, and among whom they live, or they do not place the proper value upon their opinions and respect."

"Well, well," said Alec, coolly, as he drew up before the gate of a new and very pretty cottage. "I am very much obliged to you for your valuable homily. I hope I shall profit by it. But, my dear brother, 'all is well that ends well'; and as my chief object in engaging you in conversation was to give you something to think about besides which way we were going, I am delighted that I was successful." And with a polite bow, the saucy fellow jumped down and proceeded to help his passengers to alight.

XIX.
A HOMELY WEDDING.

No sooner had the little party alighted, than the cottage door flew open, and a crowd of familiar faces met their astonished gaze.

There was the old major, wrinkled and lame, leaning on his cane, but smiling as if he had forgotten that there was any "rheumatiz" in the world.

There was the bright-faced little Jem of long ago, now grown into a stout maiden, and looking as sober and matter-of-fact as ever.

And motherly little Ruth was there, with her face wreathed in smiles.

There was good Mrs. Benson, busy and bustling with the weight of some unusual responsibility.

Such a royal welcome as our friends received. Tongues were kept busy with stories of the generosity of the dear old Saint Nicholas, and wishes for the new year.

"What a pretty house!" exclaimed Flora, as the hum of voices was lessening.

"I am glad you like it, sister mine," returned Alec who was at her side, "because, you know, it belongs to me."

"To you? Then you have been industrious in all these years. Are you going to live here all alone?"

"Yes, you are right there, Flora," Alec answered, totally ignoring her question. "I have worked hard, and saved too. But, there! I am blowing my own trumpet again, in spite of Hal's lecture!" And he glanced roguishly at his brother.

But Harry only smiled.

"What on earth do you want with a whole house?" asked Flora, curiously. "Are the major and Mrs. Benson going to live with you?" she added, wishing to understand it all.

"No," said Alec, "they are going back home."

Flora and Harry were thoroughly puzzled, and from time to time glanced at their brother questioningly, as if they feared he was joking them. Flora noticed, however, what the others were all too busy to see, that Alec was constantly glancing out of the front window, as if expecting someone.

At last her curiosity and his evident uneasiness were both satisfied; for a buggy drove up to the door, and from it alighted a young girl and an elderly woman, and—Joel Piper, who after dismissing the conveyance came toward the house, where they were met by Alec, who presented them triumphantly to the rest.

"Lottie Piper, is this you?" cried Flora.

The young girl was really Lottie, and the elderly woman was Mrs. Emmeline Durand, her aunt.

"Yes, it's me," answered Lottie, serenely and ungrammatically.

"This is a delightful surprise. What next?" exclaimed Flora.

"Shall I tell you?" asked Alec, coming forward and offering Lottie his arm, who evidently understood the whole situation; "it is simply this,"—and the two fine-looking young people walked toward the window where Harry was standing, and paused before him,—"I love Lottie, and I think she loves me." Lottie's bright eyes dropped to the floor, her face suffused with blushes, with a bright little smile trembling around her mouth. "I love Lottie; and, Harry, I want you to pronounce us husband and wife."

Mrs. Hazeley and Flora looked somewhat dazed, and then, turning to each other, locked arms and walked toward the bridal pair, each face showing surprise, but also betraying real joy at the event.

The others were happy. All knew what the day would bring forth, and each had united with the others in mystifying Mrs. Hazeley, Flora, and Harry.

The last named, while much surprised, as was but natural, understood the situation and the part he was expected to take, as Alec and Lottie stepped toward him.

"Very well, Alec. I am glad you have made such a happy choice. Are you both ready? Please stand here. That is it. So."

Then, amid the hush that fell upon the little company, Harry's voice was clearly heard, saying:

"'What God hath joined together, let no man put asunder.'"

At the close of the short, but very impressive service, Harry offered a short prayer that the "great All-Father would watch over, guard, and guide these two lives that had linked themselves together for all time."

Then came congratulations, and everybody tried to talk at once. Then came dinner. This was in charge of Mrs. Benson, and it is only necessary to say that it was one long to be remembered; for she was an excellent cook.

In the course of the dinner, Alec was pressed by Flora to tell how he had become acquainted with Lottie. He quite willingly complied.

"I first met her on the day I came down to see you off on the cars when you all left for Brinton; and just as the train was disappearing around a curve, and I was turning about to go home, a girl came running up all out of breath.

"'Oh,' said she, 'has the train gone?' I said, 'Yes; did you want to get on?'

"'No,' said she; 'but my friend is on it, and I wanted to say goodbye.' 'I'm sorry,' said I, 'but who is your friend?' Not that it was any of my business to know, but somehow or other I felt interested, and she didn't seem to mind, but said: 'Flora Hazeley.' 'That's my sister,' said I; 'do you know her?' 'I guess I do,' was the answer. 'It is too bad; but it can't be helped, I suppose. I'm always late when I should be early, and early when I should be late.'

"This sounded so odd that we both laughed, and then she turned and was out of sight in a very few seconds. I didn't see her again until one day several years afterward, when I was doing business for myself—taking my vegetables and things to town to sell, you know. It happened on this morning I had some fine, fresh vegetables left over from market, and I wanted to sell them before going home. I went through several streets, knocking at the doors and asking if the folks would like to buy what I had. At one of the houses I met Lottie again. She did not recognize me at first, but amused me very much by the close bargains she drove. 'Well,' said I, 'you are a case.' She looked up at me suddenly, as if she would like to give me a bit of her mind, and she saw who I was. Then, of course, she began to ask after you all; and that is the way we became acquainted. I always went there afterward when I had anything left over, and, when I saw what a close bargain she could drive, and what a good housekeeper she made for her aunt, I thought: 'Lottie is the girl to help a fellow get on in the world.' So, after a while, with the consent of the good aunt and no objections from our brother Joel here, to whom we wrote about the matter, and who came on to see us and give us his blessing, we made the arrangements that you see have been carried out today."

"How about Lottie's father?" said Flora, slyly.

"We wrote to him too, and he didn't object, either—that that is, he didn't answer—and silence is consent, you know."

"Alec," said Harry, gravely, "I am glad, of course, to see you doing well; but it hurts me to hear you talk so much about getting rich and saying nothing about higher and better things. What is to become of you when you are called to lay aside the possessions you are striving so hard to get?"

"Now, never you mind Alec, my good preacher brother," interposed Lottie, looking at him with a complacent smile. "Alec is fond of mystifying people. He is just as good a Christian as ever a young man was. He and I both—to set your mind at rest—were converted over a year ago, at a revival in Bartonville. We mean to try and live right—don't we, Alec?" And she beamed on everybody, in no way abashed by her frank confession. It was plain that Lottie would be matter-of-fact and practical to the end of her days.

"My dear Alec, give me your hand!" cried Harry. And the two brothers clasped hands warmly, while Joel nodded approvingly. Flora, who sat next to Lottie, slipped her arm around her waist and gave her a sisterly embrace; and Mrs. Hazeley exclaimed, wiping the tears away: "If ever a woman was blessed in her children, I am that one. Truly, God is good."

"That he is," rejoined Mrs. Benson. "My husband and I can testify to that." And her eyes rested lovingly upon Ruth and little Jem.

"Well," put in Mrs. Durand, Lottie's aunt. "You are all rejoicing; but I am not so sure that I can join you. I lose my housekeeper and the only companion I have when I lose Lottie. One doesn't mind living alone so much when one is used to it; but when you have had company for so long, it comes awkward to go back to the old habits."

"Remember the old proverb, Aunt Emmeline, 'Never cross the bridge until you come to it,'" laughed Lottie. Then, turning to Alec, who sat quietly smiling, she said: "Tell her, Alec, do."

"Aunt Emmeline, come with me a moment; I have something to show you," and offering her his arm they left the room. Crossing the wide hall, they ascended the stairs, and stopping at a closed door, Alec said, as he pushed it open:

"This room is for Aunt Emmeline, as long as she will occupy it. We could not do without her."

Mrs. Durand's fears were thrown to the wind when she heard this, and saw the dainty room. Turning to Alec, with her eyes bright with tears, she said, as she threw her arms around his neck:

"Oh, Alec, I do not deserve this. But it makes me very happy to know you think enough of me to do this for me."

As they entered the room, where all was gayety, her face wreathed in smiles, Mrs. Durand said:

"Now I can join in the general rejoicing. I have a new home—this one—with Lottie and Alec."

Everybody was pleased, and Lottie looked her happiness; for her face was ever very expressive of her feelings.

For a long time Jem, who was as quiet and quaint in her ways as ever, had been occupied in the effort to make peace between Dolby and Pokey, who were now old and feeble, but very dear to the heart of their mistress, who had insisted that they must come to the wedding.

During Alec's story, Flora had caught a look of decided disapproval on Jem's face, and determining to ascertain the cause, she asked:

"Jem, dear, does anything trouble you? What do you think of this?"

"Do you mean the wedding?" Jem questioned.

"Yes."

"Well, then,"—and the words came slowly, distinctly, and decisively,—"I think it was a very disinteresting one."

"How would you have had things, if you could have had your way?" asked Flora, much amused at Jem's positive tone.

"Oh, I'd have had white satin, and orange blossoms, and lots of presents, and a great big wedding cake, with a beautiful ornament on top, and all such, you know." In her earnestness she had forgotten that Pokey was on her lap, hidden under the tablecloth, for fear her indulgent grandma would see her and be disgusted, and banish her from the room. Pokey, feeling that the little hands were no longer pressing her down and reminding her that she must lie still, quietly dropped to the floor, and began cautiously to explore.

"Now, Jem," went on Flora, argumentatively, "suppose we did have all the fine things you named, how much happier would that make us all?"

"Oh, I don't know anything about that. I only know it would have been prettier, and more to my taste as a guest, you see," returned Jem with dignity, much to the amusement of her listeners.

"Ah, Jem," said Harry, shaking his head at her, and pretending to be very serious: "Ah, Jem, you little know how much unhappiness often follows the orange blossoms and satin."

"I don't know anything about that, either," was the cool rejoinder. "I only know they are prettier to look at."

"Everybody to his taste, say I, Jem," remarked Alec, solemnly; which bit of philosophy was promptly put into practice by Dolby, who evidently found it to his taste just then to spring upon Pokey while her young mistress was busy talking, and who received a sharp box on the ear for his pains. Of course such behavior necessitated the removal of poor Pokey in disgrace by Jem.

Before anybody was ready for it, the hour of separation had come. After a great deal of talking and a good many "goodbyes," the Hazeleys were on the cars, being carried back to Brinton, and the unique reunion was over.

"What a queer Christmas party we have been to!" laughed Flora, when they were again at home. "But I enjoyed it."

"Yes," answered Harry. "So did I."

"And I," added his mother, "more than all. Just to think, what wonderful things God does bring about!"

"Yes," said Harry, reverently, "how well the words of Isaiah apply to us: 'I will lead them in paths that they have not known. I will make darkness light before them, and crooked things straight.'"

THE END.

ABOUT THE AUTHOR.

AMELIA ETTA HALL JOHNSON (1858–1922) was born in Toronto, Ontario, Canada. After an education in Montreal, she moved to Boston, Massachusetts, in 1874, marrying Reverend Harvey Johnson three years later, forming a family that would grow to include two sons and a daughter.

In her lifetime, Johnson wrote poems, children's literature, articles, Sunday school fiction, and three novels: *Clarence and Corrinne, or God's Way* (1890), *The Hazeley Family* (1894), and *Martina Meriden, or What Is My Motive?* (1901). She founded and edited the magazines *Joy* and *The Ivy*, which focused on stories for young Black girls and Black American history, respectively.

Notably, Johnson is the English translator of Charles Perrault's fairy tale *La Belle au bois Dormant*, or *The Sleeping Beauty*, which was the basis of Disney's 1959 adaptation.

ABOUT THE EDITOR.

CHANCE SION-RAIZE CALLOWAY (b. 1986) is the author of several novels and book series including *The Charismatic Chronicles*, *The Never Novellas*, and *The Gay Man's Guide to Heterosexual Weddings*. Calloway founded CSRC Storytelling for printed media in 2012 with a passion for creating and promoting stories that change how people see themselves and the world around them.

In 2015, Calloway created the digital series *Pretty Dudes*, serving as showrunner and director for the LGBTQIA+ dramedy. Calloway and the series have picked up numerous awards, including Show of the Year at the 2017 National Youth Pride Services Awards. *Pretty Dudes* is currently available through Stoopid Ambitious, a streaming service and banner Calloway created as a hub for innovative and inclusive works by independent filmmakers with voices overdue for amplification.

All of Calloway's most recent projects—including this very anthology—have been produced during the onset of the COVID-19 pandemic, in spite of his ongoing struggles with chronic homelessness. In the face of personal, global and systemic challenges, Calloway continues to focus his efforts on advocacy and change through art.

CONNECT WITH C.S.R. EVERYWHERE.
OFFICIAL SITE: chancecalloway.com
TWITTER: @ChanceCalloway
MEDIUM: @csrcalloway

MORE FROM CSRC STORYTELLING

Promoting and providing positivity, power and presence in print.

Natty Girl Saves the World
C.S.R. Calloway

The New Negro: An Interpretation, Revised Edition (Magna Releases)
Alain Locke

Passing (Magna Releases)
Nella Larsen

Peculiar, INC
C.S.R. Calloway

Pretty Dudes: The Novel
C.S.R. Calloway

The Princess and the Goblin (Magna Releases)
George MacDonald

She (Magna Releases)
H. Rider Haggard

DOUBLE BOOKED™

Two titles bound together with one spine (tête-bêche binding).

Desiderio
The Veil and the Shade

The Turn of the Screw
Shadows Against the Dark: Collected Horror Classics

Cane
The Conjure Woman: Uncle Julius and His Stories

Marie and the Nutcracker
A Christmas Carol

Man Cub: The Complete Mowgli Stories
Rikki-Tikki-Tavi and Other Tales from The Jungle Book

Peter Pan
The Never Boy

Alice's Adventures in Wonderland
Through the Looking Glass